'*The Tutor* plunges fearlessly into the uncharted years of history's greatest bard to give us a sumptuous, page-turning account of 1590s England in the brutal throes of the Tudor dynasty. Katharine de L'Isle, the book's riveting heroine, isn't just young Will Shakespeare's muse, but his teacher in every sense, challenging and elevating his verse even as she unwisely loses her head and heart to him. I was completely captivated. Andrea Chapin is a writer to watch' Paula McLain, *New York Times* bestselling author of *The Paris Wife*

'Sexy and cerebral, Andrea Chapin's romp through one of Shakespeare's lost years will beguile lovers of poetry and romance alike. A literary delight' Elizabeth Gaffney, author of *When the World Was Young* and *Metropolis*

'In her captivating debut novel, Andrea Chapin offers an unusual love affair . . . *The Tutor* is a terrific achievement, one that in recounting the story of Katharine and Will allows us a glimpse into the workings of Shakespeare's mind and heart' James Shapiro, author of *Contested Will: Who Wrote Shakespeare?* and *A Year in the Life of William Shakespeare: 1599*

'History springs to vivid life in this beautifully written novel about a young William Shakespeare and the passionate, intelligent woman who changed the course of his life – not to mention literature – forever' Christina Baker Kline, *New York Times* bestselling author of *The Orphan Train*

'A delightful literary fantasy. Imagine being Shakespeare's muse, the lively smart beautiful being who has the good fortune not only to be loved by the young Bard, but to critique his poetry almost as he writes it. In Andrea Chapin's absorbing *The Tutor* we have a woman to thank for the shape of western literature' Martha McPhee, author of *Gorgeous Lies*

'An elegant entertainment and an impressive debut' *Kirkus Reviews*

'With all the fire and spark of the best romance novels but the detail and weight of finely rendered historical fiction, debut novelist Chapin has crafted a fascinating and masterly background to Shakespeare's first published work . . . Fans of historical-fiction writers such as Philippa Gregory, Rosalind Miles and Anne Easter Smith won't want to miss this one' *Library Journal*

ABOUT THE AUTHOR

Andrea Chapin has acted professionally, touring Germany in Edward Albee's *Seascape*. She has been an editor at art, film, theatre and literary magazines including the *Paris Review*, *Conjunctions* and the *Lincoln Center Theater Review*, and has written for *More*, *Redbook*, *Town & Country*, *Self*, *Martha Stewart Living*, *Marie Claire* and other publications. Chapin is also a writing teacher and private book editor. She lives in New York City with her husband and two children.

THE
Tutor

ANDREA CHAPIN

PENGUIN BOOKS

PENGUIN BOOKS

UK | USA | Canada | Ireland | Australia
India | New Zealand | South Africa

Penguin Books is part of the Penguin Random House group of companies
whose addresses can be found at global.penguinrandomhouse.com.

First published in the United States of America by Riverhead Books,
a member of Penguin Group (USA) LLC 2014
Published in Penguin Books 2015

001

Set in 10.46/14.14 pt Fournier MT Std
Typeset by Jouve (UK), Milton Keynes
Printed in Great Britain by Clays Ltd, St Ives plc

A CIP catalogue record for this book is available from the British Library

ISBN: 978-0-241-96816-1

www.greenpenguin.co.uk

MIX
Paper from
responsible sources
FSC® C018179

Penguin Random House is committed to a
sustainable future for our business, our readers
and our planet. This book is made from Forest
Stewardship Council® certified paper.

Saint Cathern favours learned men, and gives them wisedome hye:
And teacheth to resolve the doubtes, and always giveth ayde,
Unto the scolding Sophister, to make his reason stayde.

—Thomas Naogeorgus, *The Popish Kingdome*,
translated from the Latin by Barnabe Googe, 1570

. . . for there is an upstart Crow, beautified with our feathers, that with his Tygers hart wrapt in a Players hyde, supposes he is as well able to bombast out a blanke verse as the best of you: and being an absolute Johannes fac totum, is in his owne conceit the onely Shake-scene in a countrey.

—Robert Greene, *Greene's Groats-worth of Witte,*
Bought with a Million of Repentance, 1592

For

David, Brandon and Carden

THE

Tutor

I

lies were at him, but the larger animals hadn't gotten there yet. Richard and his men were out hawking when they found the poor priest next to a clump of gorse. If he'd fallen victim to robbers, they were scared off, for the blood-smeared purse he clutched was swollen with gold. Field and vale, even the bosky banks of the river, were parched and rattling from weeks without rain. And now, word of the deed spread through the estate as quickly and willfully as a torch to dry scrub.

Mercy came running, eyes wide, fresh milk spilling from her pails. She tried to curtsy.

"Speak," said Katharine. She held a basket of herbs and had just cut a sprig of thyme with her thumbnail.

"His throat is slit, my lady," the dairymaid said, looking down at her milk-wet wooden shoes.

"Whose?"

"The sad fellow . . ." Mercy's raspy voice sounded older than her years. Her russet hair was plastered to her sunburnt forehead. "Who learnt the lads yonder," she said, cocking her head in the direction of what used to be the family chapel but was now the schoolhouse.

"Master Daulton?"

Mercy nodded. "He's on a plank behind the kitchens," she said, then added, "Stabbed in the heart, too."

If Mercy knew that Father Daulton was a priest, she was not letting on. That was the protocol at Lufanwal Hall. He was Master Daulton to the outside world and Father Daulton to the family.

By the time Katharine reached the courtyard, the men had covered his corpse with a cloth. She knelt, made the sign of the cross and placed the herbs she had gathered on the body. It was the fifteenth of August, Assumption Day. In the past, these sweet bundles of nature would have been blessed by a priest and then used as remedies and to ward off harm. But the blessing of the herbs and the feast to celebrate the Virgin's ascension had been banned.

Richard approached on horseback. In spite of the heat, he wore a black cloak flecked with dirt. When he saw his cousin he frowned. "Nothing you need to see," he said, dismounting.

"I came to pay my respects," Katharine countered, still kneeling.

"Don't worry, we'll give him a proper funeral," he said, stalking into the house through the kitchens and knocking into one of the scullery maids. A pot crashed to the floor.

Father Daulton had left that morning dressed as a schoolmaster in a white cambric shirt, black linen jerkin and large black-rimmed hat. He had said he would be gone less than a fortnight. He did not say where he was going, and Katharine had not asked, thinking perhaps he was on a mission for the Jesuits. While she'd watched him set out on his journey, she had prayed for his safety. Now she wished that weeks ago the young man with the chiseled chin had burned the forbidden chasuble and fled—that he'd gone to France, Italy, Spain or the Low Countries on the North Sea. He often said he wanted to live where he could hear the waves, breathe the salt air, and she'd taken to imagining him in his life after Lufanwal, alone, reading, in a whitewashed cottage by the sea.

Katharine was tempted to pull the cloth back and place her lips on his forehead, but she'd seen too much death over the years, and she wanted to remember Father Daulton alive, not as he was now: a reliquary of bones and rotting flesh. She pushed herself up, wiped the tears from her eyes and brushed the dust from her skirt. On his last evening, the young priest had given her a copy of the New Testament in English, translated by a group of exiled priests. The inscription was in Latin . . . *date et dabitur vobis* . . . give and it shall be given unto you . . . *Dei gratia* . . . by the grace of God . . . *amicus usque ad aras* . . . a friend until the altars, until death; and below those words he had signed his name. Then as a postscript he had added, *Deus nobiscum, quis contra?* God is with us, who can be against us?

Who indeed? Katharine thought as she walked toward the house.

The priest sent by the Molyneux family had skin so pale that Katharine wondered if he was a visitation from the great beyond. In the dim light of the secret chapel his face was translucent, a stain of blue beneath the white. He was tall but frail—the space between skin and bone hid no fat—and he seemed no wider than the flickering taper next to which he stooped. His chasuble dripped from his arms like wax. *"Domine, Jesu Christe, Rex gloriae . . ."*

Katharine recalled how Father Daulton believed the hidden chapel was a triumph, a symbol of their resistance. The entrance looked like a grand fireplace and was constructed between the great hall and a stairway to the second floor. The cross, the altar cloth, the altarpiece, the missal and the chalice had been brought from the old chapel. A large painting of the Virgin Mary with John the Baptist, Michael the Archangel and the Saints Anthony and Paul hung on the sidewall. In truth,

Katharine had never liked this inner chamber, for the narrow walls and want of windows made it feel cramped and confining.

Only the De L'Isle family, their steward Quib, the chief usher, Sir Edward's valet, Lady de L'Isle's gentlewoman and a boy from the kitchens were present at the requiem. Father Daulton's head faced the altar; the tapers' yellow flames outlined his bier. The shroud had been tied at the head and the feet by the women who had bathed the body. The scullery boy with knuckles red and raw had been hastily pressed into service. Fear filled his eyes as he swung the incense pot: the heady smell of spice cloaked the scent of white roses strewn upon the wood floor.

Lord Molyneux's priest had arrived disguised as a groom. No servant had walked through the estate that morning ringing a bell to call the mourners to mass, nor had the bell tower in the old chapel tolled before the service—both rituals were stamped out when the reformers took hold. The preparations for the mass had been furtive. The family had filed into the chamber in silence.

The borrowed priest's solemn prayers hovered with the haze of incense above Father Daulton's shroud. Katharine watched the purple clouds lift into the air and evaporate.

When Katharine was ten and her daub-and-timber house burned to the ground, she tumbled awake to black smoke forcing its way through the walls and wild flames darting through the floorboards like knives. She didn't try to find her little sister, her brother or her parents. She tried to find a window. She tried to find a door. After stepping off the stairs, she turned to see the whole staircase collapse behind her—it was then she heard her mother call. She didn't stop. Outside, before rolling down the frozen hillside, she smelled her own flesh burning.

The fire was in 1569—the eleventh year of Elizabeth's reign—a few weeks after the Northern Rebellion when the earls of Northumberland and Westmorland tried in vain to rescue their faith. The times for Catholics turned sharply for the worse after the uprising. No mass was held for Katharine's family. Trust was thin, fear thick and worry constant that at any moment servants might betray their masters. Now, one and twenty years later, their church was still condemned, and the torture and slayings continued.

Father Daulton had described the horrors fellow seminarians—charged with high treason for refusing to take the Oath of Supremacy or for allegedly plotting the queen's death—endured at the hands of Her Majesty's interrogators: rackings, whippings and mutilations, being shackled to the wall for hours on end. The tortured were lucky if they could ever walk again. Father Daulton had recounted a friend's plight, where after the rack the priest's hands and feet were numb—he could not rise. When he could finally hold bread, he looked akin to an ape, for he had to use both hands to eat. And those were the poor priests who lived to tell their tales. Others were burned at the stake or hanged, drawn and quartered, with their dismembered remains fixed atop poles on the major roads for all the world to see.

Since the discovery of Father Daulton's body, Sir Edward had held meetings behind closed doors with his older sons, Richard and Harold, other relatives and various Lancastrian lords. Edward's wife, Matilda, looked hard at everyone; Lady de L'Isle had never been a woman of warmth, Katharine could count on one hand the number of times her aunt had smiled, but now her large blue eyes were edged with worry. Was it the young priest's murder? Or the scorched wheat, barley and rye? Or was it that their son Ned, dear, sweet Ned, was somewhere in Italy, drinking too much wine and spending every coin he wrapped his beautiful, slender fingers around?

"*Dies irae, dies illa,*" the priest pleaded, day of wrath, day of mourning, "*solvet saeclum in favilla*" . . . day the world will dissolve in ashes. What sorrow was this, what sadness, what sins? In the Bible, in Zephaniah, *dies irae* was a day of whirlwinds, calamity, darkness, distress and misery. What would this deadly battle between the churches bring? Day of wrath or day of judgment? Or would it beget the end of the world? This sickness, this canker King Henry had passed on to his heirs, was now eating the flesh of his people.

Sir Edward, Matilda, their daughter Isabel and Matilda's mother, Priscilla, were closest to the bier—their married daughter, Grace, lived too far north to journey for this day. Behind Edward were Richard and Harold, his sons by his first wife. Richard stared ahead, his brows knit, his jaw hard. At one point he turned and spat on the floor. His blond wife, Ursula, waved her fan while staring up at the ceiling, then occupied her time by changing the many rings around on her fingers. Her eldest daughter, Joan, tried to keep the three younger children quiet.

Harold, whose mother died giving birth to him, had red hair and freckles that spoke of Scottish blood. His left arm was smaller than his right, and he often hid his hand by resting it on a dagger in his belt. Harold's wife Mary's dark hair was neatly coiffed and her somber attire without satin or lace. She was no beauty, but she was perhaps the most pious member of the household after Sir Edward. Katharine sat next to their two sons. The trusted household servants stood in the back.

When Katharine first came to Lufanwal, Matilda barely spoke to her, and Sir Edward's two oldest sons completely ignored her. As time progressed, Katharine never penetrated those particular fortresses, but she made loving inroads with Edward's younger children, Grace, Ned and Isabel. Her cousin Ned was the special one. As children they had created imaginary worlds with long and ever-changing stories of adventure; they would play knights and ladies, whose bravery and cunning helped them survive tempests and plagues, cruel kings and dragons. With Katharine's own family gone, Ned had seemed a gift from heaven, and she cherished him. But Ned had been away from Lufanwal for seven long years.

"*De profundis clamavi ad te, Domine,*" the mourners recited. Out of the depths I have cried unto Thee, O Lord. *"Domine, exaudi vocem meam."* Lord, hear my voice . . .

A black bird swooped down, darting above the heads of the mourners. Katharine soon realized it was not a bird but a bat with winged limbs opening for height, then closing as it dove. As the priest groaned on with the mass, Katharine watched the flying creature. Its movements were sharp and erratic. At one point it dropped quickly and she could see its bared teeth. Finally, it disappeared into a crevice in the rafters.

"Non intres in judicium cum servo tuo," chanted the priest. Enter not into judgment of thy servant . . .

Katharine could not concentrate on the rest of the mass. She shut her eyes and tried to focus on the *Pater noster*, but saw the grinning bat instead, with wings spread and claws sharp and ready.

Katharine did not go down to supper that evening. Wishing solitude for her sorrow rather than company, she slipped out the door and strolled through the rose garden and past the ivy wall to the orchard. The lack of rain had dwarfed the apples, turned their skins a mottled brown. Many had fallen to the ground. As she stood under an apple tree, breathing in the savory scent, she remembered a moment with her father on a warm autumn day. She was a girl dancing, twirling round, and he said, "Kate, I fear for the man who marries you, for you are a horse that will never be tamed."

Her father could have said *filly*, but he had chosen the word *horse*, a grown animal, solid and not necessarily feminine. Had she now—at one and thirty years—been tamed? Not by a husband, surely, for he had died too soon. By what, then? Time? Loss? Loneliness? The books she read? The plodding of the days? She ate well and slept comfortably most nights, and her tiffs and annoyances with the women at the hall were petty, not painful; she never let them ruffle her for long. People visited and reports arrived from contacts at court and abroad, but most days were little affected by the queen and her constant wars—though the grisly discovery of Father Daulton could prove that was changing.

For the five years Mary Tudor had ruled, with much torture and bloodshed, she'd brought back priests, inquisitors and the Church of Rome. When her half-sister Elizabeth became queen, she returned the country to Protestantism. Elizabeth had reigned for more than thirty years since, and at every instance pressed on with her father's battle against the foreign Pope.

Katharine walked through the orchard to a path that wound behind the house to the old chapel. The old chapel had two doors: one that opened to the path she was on and another that led internally to the great hall. When open worship became impossible, her grandfather had built the hidden chapel and converted the old chapel to a schoolhouse. The wall paintings of Saint George, the dragon, the princess, the king and queen, two images of the Virgin Mary, and several saints were white-washed, and the old papistical books, the chest full of vestments, damask copes and tapestries, and all the other relics of the family's long bond with the Roman Catholic Church, were removed. Even stripped of its finery, the old chapel still felt holy, and Katharine was comforted every time she entered.

She already missed Father Daulton. He was quiet, but they had taken long walks and sat peacefully reading in front of the fire. When he did speak, he'd chosen his words carefully. As Katharine stood on the threshold of the old chapel now, she thought of how the young priest had been a good man and a brave man, and he deserved to be remembered as such. These were not times for the tame or the meek. Her father's words from long ago rushed back to her again, and she said them out loud as she pushed the door open.

The chancel and the stained glass from the old chapel still remained, and in the early evening the windows caught the light in a maze of ruby, sapphire, emerald and topaz. Katharine had the urge to genuflect and started to walk down the aisle, but stopped. A man was laid out on the long wooden table in the center of the room. The colors shining through the windows glittered across his body like scattered gems. She moved closer. Another corpse? She leaned over the man and peered into his face—at the same moment his eyes opened wide. She gasped and pulled away.

"A horse that will never be tamed," he said. "Did you speak those words just now?"

The young man rose up, swung his feet over the side of the table and sat staring at her. His green eyes gleamed with an unnatural light.

"I pray I didn't frighten you," he said, pushing himself off the table. He did not move toward her.

"I expected no one here," she said.

There was silence—save the chorus of crickets outside in the dry brush.

"I was startled," she continued, focusing on the table now empty behind him. "I thought you might be . . ." she began.

"Asleep?"

"Dead," she said. "Were you . . ."

"Dead?" he asked.

"No, asleep?"

"No. I was thinking."

"I see," she said, standing, not looking him in the eyes. "Good. Sorry to disturb—"

"Was that you, then? Shouting about the horse?" he asked.

Katharine tried to place his station by the cut of his cloth: his doublet traced the line of his broad shoulders, but the fabric was coarse and the stitching not particularly fine. Her eyes traveled from his boots, which were rather worn, up the hose and shape of his legs, and from his breeches back to his doublet.

"I was not shouting," she said.

"I was lying here in the quiet when those words came galloping at me from somewhere. I do think it was your voice."

"I . . ."

"So tell me about this fine horse. This *Equus caballus*. Was it a courser? A stallion? A charger? A scudding steed?"

"My good sir, I . . ."

"A stud."

"No," she said.

His gaze was fastened upon her.

"Me," she said.

"You."

"My father said it of me ages past." She regretted this confession the minute the words flew from her mouth.

"You frown," he said. "But come, 'tis a compliment. Cannot be tamed. No iron bit 'tween your teeth."

"Pray, sir, do you know me?"

"Aye. You leap, you neigh, you bound, you care not for curb nor pricking spur." He paused. "Round-hoofed, sure-jointed, broad breast . . ." He began to walk round her, his hand on his chin, gathering her, appraising. "Legs—I imagine—are passing strong, round buttocks, tender hide, thick chestnut mane, crest rising, slender head . . ." He was standing in front of her. "Wondrous eyes, aquiline nose, dimples . . ."

"I crave your pardon . . ."

"Ruby lips."

"Who *are* you?" she asked.

"A horse trader," he said.

"From?"

"Warwickshire."

In a flash, equal to a few breaths in and out, she felt the contest, but she had lost the round, turned soft when she should have stayed strong. An odd feeling swept over her swiftly and without warning, like the onset of a fever. She glared at the stranger, then sucked in her courage, walked past the danger, and, indeed, as a horse breaking free from a stable, she burst out of the old chapel into what was now night.

2

ir Edward sat in the library. He was holding a book, but his focus was elsewhere; he was staring at a moth circling the flame of an oil lamp on the table before him.

"May I come in?" Katharine asked from the door.

"Dear Kate, I would treasure it."

Her uncle was not a man to boast, except when it came to his books. The walls of his favorite room were lined with many volumes, and as far as the family knew he had the largest library in the north. New books arrived weekly from the bookstalls at St. Paul's churchyard in London, and new shelves were added every year. What would happen when the shelves reached the ceiling? Katharine wondered. Where would Edward put his books then? It was in this room, when she was a child fresh from the loss of her own family, that her uncle taught her to read and to write English, then Latin and Greek. He had found her one morning surrounded by his beautiful leather-bound books. She had pulled the books off the shelves and was looking through them—before she could even read a word on their pages.

Edward did not scold her, nor did he make her put the books back, but he sat down on the floor with her, picked up his prized volume of Chaucer and started to read "The Knight's Tale" to her. Katharine remembered listening to the story and the powerful authority with which the strange words issued from her uncle's mouth. Her own father had never read to her, so this listening was new.

Lufanwal Hall had been altered several times over the centuries. When Katharine's grandfather expanded the old Norman manor, he built the library that her uncle Edward turned into a magnificent book-filled sanctuary. The white plaster ceiling was festooned with patterns of honeysuckle and vines that echoed the frieze around the oak-paneled walls. Two tapestries framed the carved alabaster chimneypiece: one depicted the suicide of Lucrece, and the other, smuggled from a doomed monastery by old Father de La Bruyère—who had tended to the family before Father Daulton—showed the winged and feathered Saint Michael, his sword raised, weighing a departed soul, while the Virgin Mary, in crown and golden halo, placed her rosary on the soul's side of the scales in an attempt to save it.

Katharine sat across from her uncle, put her elbows on the table, cupped her face in her hands, and watched him gaze at the moth.

"It will burn its wings," he said finally, "and our sport will come to an end." He looked over at her. "You look five years of age."

"The light does not serve you, Uncle. The lamp needs a new wick. And you scarce knew me when I was five."

"You still hold the curiosity of a child. You keep the rest of us young, my sweet Kate, or at least from remembering we are ancient."

Edward's straight blond hair had gone white in the last years, and his once-fair cheeks were stained red, but his azure eyes were still spirited and bright.

"You are kind," Katharine said. She didn't confess she felt her youth had gone stale. "I met a curious fellow last night in the old chapel. He claimed he dealt in horses."

"I've exchanged no gold for horses this fortnight," said Edward.

"He was lying on the table and did comport himself in an odd and familiar manner."

"I'll speak to Quib. Let us pray he knows of this stranger's business. We are not safe, Kate, we may never be." Edward was quiet for a moment and then said, "Did you know Father Daulton well? I saw you sitting in the gardens with him, at other times walking."

"He found solace, I believe, in my company," she said.

"I never warmed to Father Daulton. He rarely broke bread with us. I suppose my allegiance stuck with De La Bruyère. Thank the Lord it was nature that took De La Bruyère from us."

Old Father de La Bruyère had been caught in another time. He had come from the abbey at Furness when King Henry dispatched the monasteries. Katharine remembered the old priest sitting with his wine, shaking his white head and sighing over the dashed dreams of Queen Mary's reign. "All too brief," he'd mumble wearily. "All too brief."

"Father Daulton was not a man of flattery or false words," Katharine offered. "It was a struggle for him to say his thoughts. He found it easier to speak the word of God."

"Indeed, he seemed a solemn fellow."

"One time he tried to make a joke, but the words hung together all wrong—like an ill-fitting doublet. I tried to make him laugh. It was a task."

"If any person could bring a stone to life, it would be you."

Katharine was caught by Edward's wistful tone and looked closely at him. He seemed to talk of one thing while his mind pursued another path.

"A shame to think laughter such a rare commodity," he said. "Let us hope, before the hardness took hold, this man of the cloth knew how to make merry." He paused, then added, "Methinks, my dear Kate, our young priest was in love with you."

"No," she said.

"Yes," he said simply.

She'd never thought of that before.

"One would have to be blind to miss the way his dark eyes fixed on you."

"I assumed his intensity was religious, not amorous."

"He would never have said anything."

Katharine thought of the Bible Father Daulton had given to her.

"Whatever the direction of his heart," Edward continued, "he was a noble soul."

They were silent.

"Kate, why have you never married again?"

Katharine was not expecting this. Sir Edward was her father's older brother, and when she came to the hall as a child after the fire, her grandfather was still alive and lived at Lufanwal as well. At eighteen she had married Thomas Hightower, who died two years after they wed. He was thrice her age, the second son of the Earl of Danby and a widower, and his wealth and property went to his sons, who were older than Katharine. After Thomas's death, she had returned to Lufanwal and lived there ever since. Why had she never married again? Edward's question seemed a labyrinth with each path blocked and no apparent exit.

"I have a million reasons but no good answer," she tried.

"Lend me one," he said.

"I am set in my ways."

"Another."

"I am a widow with a meager dowry."

"I promised I would augment it."

"No man I've met is cunning enough or . . ."

Sir Edward waited for her to continue.

"Has adequate wit."

"True cunning takes time to measure, and wit is dangerous when it masks the soul."

"I haven't met a man who reads . . . as much as you do."

"I've spoiled you rotten with the honey'd words of others."

"'Tis true. I live too much in the tales by men who write of war, fairies and romance. You've ruined me."

"Reading, my sweet Kate, is no replacement for living."

She narrowed her eyes and pretended to frown, then said, "I have your answer, dear uncle!"

"Speak."

"There is no man equal to you, my lord, no man even close, and I'd rather stay sans husband than to have to leave you."

He chuckled, then reached over and patted her hand. "Did Father Daulton talk of his family, Kate?"

"I learned not to ask him too many questions. Much was locked inside. He seemed to take comfort in knowing I was an orphan, and I came to believe he was an orphan, too. Perhaps the plague took his family. He mentioned study abroad at the Catholic colleges in Douai and then Rheims. I gathered he was one of the students who helped the priests with the translation of the English Bible. He moved on to Rome and became a Jesuit. He was clearly English, but he mentioned a Spanish grandmother, never a mother. He spoke of his desire to live in a cottage by the sea, but I don't believe he had ever lived by the sea. He knew his profession put his life in danger. He accepted that possibility."

"There was pain in the young priest. I regret I did not take the time nor make the effort to open him up a bit," Edward said, "help him with that which he kept hidden."

Edward was usually precise with language—his mind one step ahead of his words. But tonight Katharine noticed he was circling something but couldn't quite get at it. She was distracted by this tension but mesmerized by the moth, for now she, too, couldn't pull her eyes from the flutter of its gray velvet wings.

"The Tudors have opened a Pandora's box that will never be shut," Edward said, rising from his chair and walking to the open window. He was wearing his favorite robe, gold and red brocade, fraying at the hem, and a simple white linen shirt and black breeches. Age had not diminished his presence. He still had an athletic build and sat a horse well.

"I was served with the Oath of Supremacy. I refused to sign, and now this blood on my doorstep." He gazed out the window. A bullfrog's gloomy horn heralded from the brittle reeds below.

"But you are no priest," Katharine said, looking up from the flame.

Edward turned to her. "No, but my coffers are full. In spite of what the queen has stripped from me, in spite of the land I've had to sell to pay preposterous fines for my religion, I still have quarries, forests crowded with timber, fields of plantings and hills rich in minerals. I still have my turf, and I still have my faith. She needs what I have. She imprisoned me for a year and could not keep me, and when the Mary business was on, I am sure the queen was convinced our northern geography meant we had a hand in that poor Scottish queen's conspiracies. If Her Majesty or her spymaster Walsingham could have pinned any of that on me, they would have seized the chance."

"Sir Edward, I must caution . . ." Katharine rose quickly, shut the door, and sat down again.

"My own servants? Spies? Oh, Kate, I am too old for this. Our queen wishes me as barren in land as she is in babes. And now rumors of another Spanish-led armada against our shores feed the queen's flame anew and bring trouble to our door. I've never cared for life at court. I have no ambition for it. I'd rather open a book than bow to a queen. I have stayed out of her way. The old virgin must need new targets now, so she threatens me."

"You are certain Father Daulton's death was by her orders?"

"Why else the gift of his corpse on our land?" Edward returned to the table and sat down. "The official report is that our schoolmaster was attacked by robbers. The village doctor said his wounds were so fresh that he met his fate where he lay."

The moth took this cue to fly into the flame, where its wings caught fire. Katharine wondered if this fiery show was a sign from the dead priest—his soul finally released to heaven. The moth struggled, fell into the oil, slowed its movements and then sank to the bottom.

"We are all Icarus," Edward said wearily, staring at the oil-entombed creature.

"I shudder to think the ill-mannered stranger I met last night was connected to this gruesome deed."

"The murderer lodging here? This tale tears further at our house. I'll send my men to search the grounds."

"He's gone by now, I imagine," Katharine said. "Perchance he was a traveler, a wanderer, seeking shelter for the night, whose nimble words did mollify the men at the gates."

"Let us hope," said Edward. He picked up a gilt-tooled leather-bound book and showed it to her. "You speak of nimble words, my dear. Well, here is the new work by Edmund Spenser."

"It arrived!" Katharine exclaimed.

"I could not resist," Edward continued, "though I don't relish the thought of lining that scoundrel's pockets. Spenser would brand us papal-lovers and slit our throats if he had the chance."

Katharine had heard at one of Sir Edward's lively banquets how Spenser, the king of English poets, had traded on his lyric title to take advantage of land stolen from Irish Catholics by the British Crown. He became one of the new English settlers, making his home on thousands of acres on the Munster Plantation, next to the tens of thousands of acres appropriated by the newly emigrated, Catholic-hating Sir Walter Raleigh.

She reached for the gleaming book, which Edward playfully held from her.

"This volume commences with a letter from Raleigh. 'And all for love, and nothing for reward,' he says. 'All for love.' I would like to think that is true," said Edward.

"Oh, Uncle Edward. You miser."

"Let me tonight, while the earth is opening beneath my feet, let me sit here awhile and read his *Faerie Queene*. I am tired of mortals."

"Will you read to me?" she asked.

"A changing of the guard," he said, smiling, for several days a week Katharine read to her cousins' children. She was neither nurse nor governess, but reading was what she could offer.

"Lege, domine," she said. Read, master.

She crossed her arms on the table and laid her head down. And Edward began to read.

3

atharine sat on a stone bench in the orchard, mopped her brow with a kerchief and swatted at flies. "But, for the Sunnbeame so sore doth us beate," complained the sunburnt shepherd in Spenser's *Calendar*, "Were not better, to shunne the scorching heate?" Scorching, indeed, thought Katharine. Ned had sent her an *ombrello* from Italy, but the midday hour was sultry, and the pigskin no shield for the pounding heat. Was this unnatural summer an augury? More death? More destruction? Would the drought be followed by forty days and forty nights of rain? She plucked a gnarled apple from a low branch and pitched it at a pear tree. The day before, she'd taken the children down for a dip in the water that wound through the three-thousand-acre estate, only to discover the river had shrunk to a trickle.

As she lifted her skirts above her ankles to let in air, she heard the strumming of a lute and singing.

> *"When I was a bachelor*
> *I led a merry life,*

But now I am a married man
And troubled with a wife . . ."

She rose and walked toward the music's source. High-pitched laughter rang through the air, and cries for "another, master, another!" The old chapel door was open. Katharine paused at the threshold and peered in. None of the boys were seated at the table: their hornbooks were dormant, their quills likely dry. A stack of books lay unopened on the old pulpit. The boys had gathered round the balladeer, who was standing with one foot on a bench and a lute in his arms. Six-year-old Robert, Ursula and Richard's youngest son, had climbed onto the table and was dancing to the hoots and hollers of his kin.

The rude fellow she'd found lying on the wooden table now tipped his head at her and smiled, but did not put down his instrument. He shoved his foot from the bench and started walking around the room, embarking on another tune.

> *"If ever I marry, I'll marry a maid:*
> *To marry a widow I'm sore afraid;*
> *For maids they are simple, and never will grutch,*
> *But widows full oft, as they say, know too much."*

He stepped this way and that in what looked like a jig.

> *"A maid ne're complaineth, do what so you will;*
> *But what you mean well, a widow takes ill;*
> *A widow will make you a drudge and a slave,*
> *And cost ne' so much, she will ever go brave."*

Katharine snapped her umbrella shut and marched through the door. He bowed so low his knee almost touched the floor.

"What is this?" she demanded.

"Why, 'tis school, madam."

"You are . . . ?"

"The new tutor." He bowed again.

"I meant, what may I call you?"

"A rogue, a rascal. I pray not knave or a cur."

The boys tittered.

"Your name!"

"Will Shakespeare." He bowed once more. "We met. You tutored me on a breed of horse that can never be mounted."

"I did nothing of the sort," Katharine said, wondering if the steward Quib was responsible for hiring this jester, who seemed to mock her with every bow.

"Forgive me, a breed of horse that can never be broken."

"Master Shakespeare, you dissemble. Not of the equestrian trade as you led me to believe, but a lesson-monger." She shook her head, looking directly into his moss-colored eyes, and continued in a voice not quite her own. "Is this what the lessons are now? Pipers and fiddlers and filthies?"

"No piper here, my lady, and filthies . . . well . . ."

"These hours are for you to teach these precious young minds Latin, Greek and mathematics, not to regale them with your musical cunning."

"The orders issued me were that these *precious* young gentlemen must sing their part sure and at first sight and be able to play the same on a viol or lute."

"And these ditties will suffice?"

"Madam, next you'll catalogue dancing a plague and piping a pox. Singing is a knowledge easily taught and quickly learned where there is a good master and an apt scholar. The exercise is delightful to nature and good to preserve the health of man. The better the voice, the better 'tis to honor and service God therewith. Whom God loves not, that man loves not music."

"I see no music sheets here," Katharine said, sounding much the sheriff, even to herself.

"'Tis here, my good Minerva." Shakespeare tapped his temple. "When I was a child I lived music—I did not have to learn it. The barber in our town drew teeth, bound wounds, let blood, cut hair, trimmed, washed and shaved, but a lute and a cittern hung on his walls and virginals stood in the corner of his shop. Every day I went and played, while the other poor sots sat in their chairs and brayed."

Katharine glared at him.

He seemed to be awaiting a response to his little speech and, not getting one, he paraded on. "I crave your pardon, my lady, time passes and we must launch into Latin, for if we do not, then you'll have to sit through several rounds of 'Hey, nonny, nonny, nonny, noes,' and perchance even a 'Sing willow, willow, willow.'" Shakespeare hung the lute on a peg on the whitewashed wall. "Back to the benches, you louts!"

Little Robert hopped down from the table, and Master Shakespeare picked up the leather-bound books from his pulpit-turned-lectern.

"Come, my gentle jade. Now that you have charged into my school, why not graze in the pasture of the ancients and regale us with your learning?"

Her cheeks flushed. His eyes were fixed on her: they had changed color, seemed a lighter green now, like fresh grass.

"Art thou cunning in Latin?" he asked.

Katharine nodded. The children were staring at her. She was trapped in this man's volubility. "My good Minerva" was one thing, but "my gentle jade" was an utter insult.

Shakespeare held up a dark brown leather book, with gold tooling on the cover and down the spine.

"William Lily's lovely *short* introduction to Latin grammar, which always seemed to me too long. *Amo, amas, amat.*" He put the book down on the pulpit without opening it, then held up another book. "*Sen-*

tentiae Pueriles. I pray, madam, you approve of this volume. No ditties here, I assure you." He placed *Sententiae Pueriles* on top of Lily's grammar book.

Katharine had studied both books.

"Ah, but my heart is tender for this." He held up a book. "Ovid. Pray, my patroness of heavenly harmony, be seated."

My patroness of heavenly harmony? From where did he pluck these words? He had a calling, surely: not as a schoolmaster but as a court fool. He riffled through the pages of a worn copy of Ovid, muttering, "We might read this. Or this. Or this. Aha, this, yes, this. 'Pygmalion.'" He addressed his pupils: "I will read the Latin, repeat after me, then try to pen its equivalent in English. Those who are not as proficient, try a word or two you recognize." Then he turned to Katharine: "Will you join us, my lady?"

"No, gramercy. My duties at the hall await me."

He bowed and began: *"Quas quia Pygmalion aevum per crimen agentis . . ."*

Katharine started to leave. When he finished the fourth line, she stopped, turned and translated out loud what he'd read: "Pygmalion had witnessed the wicked ways of the women, and, disgusted by their sinful and deceitful nature . . . offended by their shameful conduct . . . their life of vice, he had forsworn all women." She glowered at the tutor. "Ah, a lesson in the wantonness of womankind. Was this an order issued you as well, Master Shakespeare?" she asked, and, not waiting for his response, she trotted out the door.

After supper she hunted down Ovid's *Metamorphoses* in the library. She hadn't read "Pygmalion" in years. With two candles lit, she read the original Latin. Pygmalion takes no wife. To pass the time, he carves a maid out of ivory. His skill is so great, when he kisses the statue it seems to kiss him back. He fears that if he holds her hard, there will be bruises where his hands have been. He caresses her, whispers words of love and lavishes her with gifts. He drapes her with rich robes and gives her rings with fine gems. He hangs pearls from her ears and sets her on his couch, her head on feather cushions.

At the feast of Venus, Pygmalion prays at the goddess's altar, and Venus hears and understands him. He has wished for a wife of flesh like his maid of ivory. A flame leaps forth from Venus's altar three times, darting high into the air. He races home and kisses his ivory lover. Under his lips, there's warmth. He puts his mouth to hers again and touches her breast. The ivory becomes soft, like wax beneath the sun. With his hand, he satisfies his wishes, again and again. Her pulse throbs under his thumb. He presses his mouth to the maid's: lips on lips, she blushes, then raises her timid eyes to him.

The words warmed Katharine right down to her very loins, and she worried the tale was too lewd a conceit for young boys, with the kissing, the touching *again and again*, the hard ivory turning into pliant flesh. "Pygmalion" was surely a lesson of Eros, with all its tantalizing passion. The new tutor seemed determined to shock and to make his mark at every occasion.

By the time Katharine replaced the book on the shelf and made her way to her chamber, the grand house was dark and mostly quiet—though she could hear singing and laughter coming from down in the buttery or maybe from out in the barns.

4

he hour was hot, the house hushed. Even the servants hid from the sun, staying within the cool confines of wood and stone. No pots clanged in the scullery, no dogs barked in the courtyard, even the stables were silent.

Katharine had written to Ned. She'd been careful in her letter—for it could fall into the wrong hands—saying only there had been trouble and that it had passed. After Katharine returned to Lufanwal a widow, she and Ned were—as they had been as children—inseparable, walking, reading, laughing, lying on her bed for hours telling each other tales. When Ned left, she inured herself to his absence. The first year was the most difficult, for they were accustomed to sharing every shred of their lives, and to be unable to seek him out was indeed a bitter draught. She tried to keep a steady correspondence with him, but as time went on their letters grew farther apart. Several years earlier he had sent a sketch an Italian friend had drawn of him. She kept it framed by her bed. There was no taming Ned's beauty: it burst through the lines. Whenever she gazed at his portrait, she painted in the violet color of his eyes and the sable sheen of his thick black hair.

Katharine's room had originally been part of the keep built by her Norman ancestors: the turret used as quarters for sentries, who slept on hay. Her oak bed with four carved columns and canopy overpowered the scant space. A few centuries back, the circular walls had been paneled in wood as gloomy as the rest of the dark oak furniture—the cupboard, small table and a chair—that crowded the room. When Katharine returned to Lufanwal after her husband died, she'd tossed out the faded red and green curtains and bedcover and replaced them with muslin, canvas and bleached linen, hoping the blond cloth would brighten the room, for there was only one small window.

The ink dry, she was dripping wax when shouting, sharp and sudden, made her spill the red liquid across the paper. Quickly pressing the seal, she went to the door—left open with the hope of a breeze. She would have expected Ursula and Richard to be the players of these harsh chords, but it was not their voices that rang through the halls. The unlikely duet was Sir Edward and Lady Matilda.

Katharine stepped from her room. She had never heard her aunt and uncle raise their voices, yet she recalled all too clearly how her own parents had battled hard into the night: sometimes the walls and floors of their timber house seemed as thin as parchment. As a child, she would climb out of bed, venture to the stairs, sit on a step and listen; often her brother and sister, awakened by the clamor, came to her side. She had, those nights, put her arms around them and vowed to let no harm come to them.

As she crept toward Edward and Matilda's lodgings, she heard fragments of what they were saying: *Informers . . . a plot to kill . . . the enemy within . . . Sir Edward, Sir William and Sir Rowland Stanley, Thomas Langton charged with harboring seminary priests . . . imprisoned in the Tower . . . Oh, Edward, you mustn't, you mustn't . . . What will we do? . . . What will I do?*

Katharine was at the door of their antechamber when Edward burst out.

"Sir Edward, I . . ."

He put his hands on her shoulders, his eyes brimming with grief. "Kate, Lord Molyneux's priest is dead, murdered with his men on their way back from our estate. His head was piked on Preston Road."

"Dearest uncle," Katharine began.

Edward sighed and added wearily, "'Tis a wretched world we live in."

Katharine was searching for something of comfort to say when he turned abruptly, went back into his rooms and shut the door.

Three nights later, Katharine awoke to the sounds of horses neighing and to her uncle's grave and commanding voice. She rose from her bed and went to the window. A group of men were on horseback, Sir Edward's hair lucent in the moonlight. She could see his noble profile. There was urgency in the way the horses moved, nervously clattering on the stones, then thudding away on the hard earth. She watched the band of riders drop below the rise. One second they seemed a small army, and then they were gone.

There was no bloodshed, yet Katharine felt the night oddly pillaged. She stayed at the window. Before the first cock crowed, when the moon was down, the stars fading into the hoary blue, she heard the raucous sound of rooks cawing. The noise grew, becoming loud and fierce, and then the rebellious birds burst forth from the rookery, swooping and plunging, steering wide, then rising into the sky. She waited for them to settle down and come back round again, but they did not. Instead, they shot out into the distance, in the same direction as Sir Edward, and then they, too, vanished. Had the rooks deserted the rookery? Never before, to Katharine's knowledge, in the history of the De L'Isle family, had they lost their rooks. It was a disturbing sign.

The first beams of light were now climbing the rough-hewn façade, creeping into her room and warming her skin. She untied the ribbons of her smock and watched the crimson streaks kindle the sky. A thrush started singing. She was about to pull her head in, when she saw the tutor walking swiftly. When he got to the gatehouse he turned, retraced his steps, then turned again and embarked on the path anew. His mouth was moving, as if he were talking to himself. She watched him walk back and forth, again and again. At one point he tore off his doublet and threw it onto a bush. Then, after another round, he unbuttoned his blouse. His skin glistening in the morning heat, he looked more a chanting druid than a schoolmaster. When he finished whatever ritual he was enacting, he grabbed his doublet and blouse and disappeared from view. Katharine pulled the window shut and knelt down to pray.

5

er cousin Richard called a meeting in the great hall. The darkness blinded Katharine when she came in from the sun-baked gardens, but once the lamps were lit and she was sitting, her eyes adjusted to the dimness. The cool gritstone provided some relief from the heat, but the linen hanging in the windows did nothing to keep the flies out. Richard, his short legs dangling, looked like a child perched on his chair. The large Flemish tapestry of a boar and bear hunt that hung behind Richard only dwarfed him further: the hunters woven into the piece were twice his size. The family was sitting on chairs and stools, fans aflutter, with the younger children scattered on the stone floor. The rest of the household stood in back.

If only Ned were here, Katharine thought, to stand by his mother during this troubled time. But he had never taken any real interest in family matters. He loved his painters and his poets, and the way the light in Italy made "everyone and everything look as if they had been kissed by gold." Barred from attending Oxford and Cambridge because of his

Catholic faith, he had pursued his studies on the Continent. After touring Paris, Venice and Vienna, he had circled back to Italy, where he took up residence in Florence and then in Rome.

A servant rang a bell and the room hushed. Richard started to speak. "Our great family . . ." He coughed and cleared his throat before continuing. "Our great family has resided in Lancashire for centuries upon centuries. Our esteemed ancestor, the courageous Walter Grancourt, was a great companion to William the Conqueror, and our lineage on the maternal line is descended from the great Lady Wenlock, wife of Prufroc, Earl of Bucknall. The good Lord has smiled upon our deeds and our lands have grown and we have as a great family prospered. We are now and always have been the most loyal of subjects to great England, our motherland. Thus it is with great sadness that I relate to you that certain recent events have caused us great concern and that because of these events, my esteemed father, Sir Edward, has found it necessary to leave this country for France. He has safely made passage . . ."

It was true, then, the rumor Katharine had heard from her maid Molly, who had heard it from Ursula's maid Audrey, who had heard it from Harold's manservant. That was how news traveled at Lufanwal: as if the dairy barns, hawk houses, chicken coops, stables, kitchens, nursery, schoolroom and maids' chambers were all inns along a post road, where tales of indiscretion, sickness and death stopped for a brief rest.

Richard droned on. How many times could he use the word *great* in one address? The word should have been hoarded and used only once, to describe Sir Edward, for he was a great man and certainly more eloquent than his eldest son. And "certain recent events" seemed a tame way to describe the gruesome tales that arrived daily: the beheading of Lord Maltby on Shrove Tuesday for his supposed ties to the Irish rebels; the jailing in the Tower of the Jesuit Christopher Bagshaw, upon his return from France—Bagshaw would probably never make it out of his cell alive.

On the way back to her chamber, Katharine heard Harold's youngest son, Thomas, say to his older brother, Henry, "I think it shows a weakness, the running away. I would have stayed. Even if they locked me in the Tower. Even if they chopped my head off."

Henry, who was now fifteen, tapped the side of his little brother's head and said, "'Tis complicated, Thomas. You are still a child and know nothing of this world."

I know nothing of this world, Katharine thought as she climbed the stairs. She had felt Sir Edward's exile the night she watched him leave under the moonlight but had not wanted to admit it to herself. He was gone. He was across the sea.

Ursula rarely played with children, hers or anyone else's, but today she was gamboling across the tilt field with her little spaniel Guinny, and the younger children were running after her.

Lufanwal Hall was on a hill. When it was first built in the eleventh century, the steep incline made it a natural fortress. The surrounding valley was rich with rectangular fields, apple orchards, plots of woad and weld and madder. Even with the dearth of rain, the land below seemed the stuff of a weaver's loom, with warp and weft of orange, red, purple and green.

"Put that book down and join us!" Ursula squealed as she scampered past Katharine, who was reading *The Faerie Queene*.

After Sir Edward left, a servant had brought Spenser's leather-bound volume with a note tucked in its pages: *Though we started this together, you may take the virgin read. I will resume when I return.*

Ursula wore no cap, and her blond hair was spilling out of its pins. She looked more a girl than a mother of four. She had tiny hands and tiny feet, and her waist was the size of a man's neck. Katharine reckoned she could put her hands around that waist and her fingers would touch. Ursula's eyes were light blue and her skin naturally white. She began to twirl, and the children watched her with glee.

"The world is turning," she cried, her skirts and her petticoats swirling around her. "Round and round and round." Ursula kept on so long Katharine began to worry. She finally came to a giggling stop, walked unevenly toward Katharine, fell to her knees beside her, then dropped all the way onto the grass, her chest heaving. "'Tis still spinning!"

The children were twirling now, with Guinny nipping at their heels.

"I might vomit," little Lucy said.

"Perhaps you all should play another game," Katharine called.

One by one the children dropped to the grass, then they started rolling down the hill.

"See what you've started?" Katharine said, smiling.

"'Tis better than wine!" said Ursula.

Katharine chuckled. They were quiet for a time. Ursula turned on her side facing Katharine, who was sitting on a stool.

"I want your life," Ursula said solemnly. The blue of her bodice and the white of her skirts and skin made her look like a piece of china.

"My life?"

"You are free."

"How so?"

"You have no husband and no children and you can lose yourself in all those books you so love."

"All true. But my life is nothing to covet."

Ursula rolled onto her back and gazed up. "'Tis endless."

Katharine wondered if Ursula was talking about the sky or her marriage to Richard or her life.

"I married young because I was with child," Ursula continued. "I should have become a nun."

When Richard had traveled to Antwerp to meet Ursula for the first time and to marry her a week later, she was fifteen and pregnant with someone else's child. She gave birth to Joan only four months after the wedding; Ursula's parents, no longer able to invest in her virtue, had offered Richard a dowry he could not refuse.

"A nunnery seems not the life for you," Katharine said.

Ursula laughed at Katharine's joke, for the word *nunnery* meant a brothel as well.

"In truth, marriage to God must be better than marriage to a mortal," said Ursula, still staring at the blue sky.

Ursula usually seemed far younger than her years, childlike, even silly, but today her current had changed.

She sighed. "Come down off your stool," she beseeched Katharine, "and feel the ground beneath your back."

"My farthingale will surely pinch."

"I don't have one on!"

"Ursula!"

"I hate them. As if our lives are not prisons enough, why do we have to wear such . . . such cages?"

Katharine shielded her eyes from the sun and watched a goshawk stooping and soaring. The hawk whooshed up into the sky, circling. What? Looking directly below, she saw Ursula's little dog running across the rolling land. The children were no longer with Guinny. The flat-headed spaniel was the size of a hare. The goshawk marked its prey and stooped, closing its wings and diving, its talons ready to hack.

"Guinny!" Katharine yelled. "The hawk!"

Ursula was on her feet and running. Katharine jumped up, threw down her book and followed. The hawk paid no heed to the women, but having missed its mark rose into the air and then hurtled down again at Guinny, who now realized she had gone from pet to prey and was in a panic, darting this way and that. By the time Katharine was two hundred paces from the little dog, she could hear not only the hawk screeching and the beating of its wings, but also the bells attached to the bird's feet, which meant the hawk was not wild but most likely from Richard's mews.

When the hunted dog charged for the nearby brambles, the bird soared into the air again, then fell with talons ready, cutting the pup off. A tall workman in an apron strode toward the dog, and in one graceful movement scooped her into his arms. The goshawk swept up into the air, shrieking in anger.

Ursula and Katharine were out of breath by the time they reached the man, who had slipped the frightened dog under his apron. Guinny's little brown and white face peered out at them, panting.

"Gramercy, Mr. Smythson," Ursula said tearfully, then introduced Katharine. "Mr. Robert Smythson is a master mason who's come to look at the house."

The man bowed and Katharine nodded.

"I had a dog killed by a hawk, a wild hawk, though," he said, patting Guinny's furry head.

"I would like to know why one of Richard's hawks is out, hoodless and unattended!" demanded Ursula.

Guinny's savior had a strong nose and a head full of brown curls thick-twined as ivy tods. He was outside the fashion of the times, had no beard, not even a mustache, and his skin was dark from the sun. He handed Guinny over to Ursula, who started cooing, petting and kissing her dog's face. Katharine thanked the mason and bade them farewell. Then she started walking toward the hall but turned and glanced back. Mr. Smythson was still patiently listening to Ursula, who was going on about Richard and his hawks. Katharine wondered if she should try to rescue the poor mason just as he had rescued poor Guinny—for there was no stopping Ursula once she'd launched into a rant. One of his men arrived, and as they were bowing and taking their leave, Mr. Smythson looked up at Katharine. Katharine, not quite sure what to do, smiled and then hastened to the house.

6

he clamor of insects, metered and rhythmic, rose up from the dry brush. Katharine was standing at an open window in the library, thinking of how the trip across the sea could not have been easy for her uncle at his age. By now the queen would know Sir Edward was gone, and she would, Katharine hoped, fix her focus elsewhere.

And here was Henry, breathless, grinning, fresh from his flight up three score steps, asking for help with his Greek.

"Plutarch?" she asked, turning to him.

"Yes. 'Julius Caesar,'" he responded.

Henry went to the leaded window on the other side of the room and pushed it open. He leaned out over the courtyard. "Martin," he bellowed to the boy below, "get ye off your sleeping arse and get to work." He hid behind the casement, then stuck his head out again. "Get ye off your—"

A stone came whizzing through the open window and Henry ducked. Katharine stepped back and the stone hit a chair.

"Henry, such a vulgar tongue. What would your mother say?"

As another stone shot through the window, Henry picked up a green leather-bound book and used it as a shield. Katharine swept past him and, standing with her hands on her hips, shouted, "Enough!" down at Martin, the steward's son, who was gazing up with his hand over his eyes to block the sunlight. He hung his head when he saw her and scurried in through the scullery door. She pulled the window shut.

Henry put the dark green book back on the marble table. Then he picked it up again and opened it. "*Il Decamerone*," he said, poking through the pages. "Italian?"

"*Sì.* You were talking of Plutarch?"

"We read a translation of 'Caesar' last year, so I don't see why we need bother . . ."

"Perhaps your new schoolmaster wants to see if you can learn from the original text. Henry, try your best. And then you are welcome to ask me. But do not reach for me first."

"How did you come by Greek, coz?" Henry asked, dropping into a chair and swinging his legs over the wooden arms in one athletic motion. He was good on a horse and skilled with a lance, and she thought, if not for the changing times, with chivalry on the wane, he would have become an excellent knight, perhaps even made the Order of the Garter.

"Your grandfather Sir Edward taught me. It started as a game when I was your brother Thomas's age, and then it turned out I had a head for it."

"And Latin."

"I had a head for that also. With the Latin, I taught myself Italian. You could, too, and then in time you could read this instead of using it as a shield." She picked up the copy of Boccaccio's green-leathered book and tapped him lightly on the head with it.

"My mother doesn't have a clue about the ancients." Henry was sitting but couldn't keep still. He picked up a crystal globe the size of an orange from Seville and tossed it from his left hand to his right. The translucent orb belonged to Katharine. Sir Edward had given it to her when she turned sixteen. It had the aspect of a sorcerer's shewstone used for peering into the future.

"Your mother, Mary, knows many things of which I know nothing. It all balances," Katharine said, her eyes following the crystal ball as Henry threw it in the air. "Henry, put that down," she said finally. "It might shatter."

Henry placed the crystal back in its leather box.

"In truth, cousin, who needs Greek?"

"You do, and Latin, too."

"Well, *he* doesn't."

"Who?"

"Master Shakespeare."

"Why?"

"Because he confessed to us that he doesn't really know Greek . . . but for a bit. And Latin he says he learned but not well, for in his school it was rare that a boy went on to anything that needed it, except maybe the Church, but even that has all changed now. And, he says, everything is being translated."

"Henry, our language is built on Latin and Greek. And French and Saxon and . . . but so many of our words come from Latin and Greek and you need, must, study them. And much history is still in Latin. Only parts of the Bible are in English—our fellow Englishmen are working hard in France translating the rest. So you still need to know Latin to know the Bible, for a few more years at least. And you need to know the Bible." Katharine was walking back and forth in front of Henry, her little leather heels trilling across the wooden floor.

"Why?" said Henry.

She turned and faced him. "Don't ask that, Henry. I pray you were speaking in jest." She paused at the map of England, stretched out and pinned under glass like one of Thomas Moffett's butterflies. Then, placing her hands on the rosewood frame, she straightened her back as if she herself were a schoolmaster at a lectern or a priest preaching the gospel from a pulpit. "Is this Shakespeare unsound? 'Tis not his place to fill your head with such foolish thoughts."

"He isn't a good tutor," Henry whispered. "He doesn't seem . . ."

"What?"

"Learned. He makes us laugh, though. He also confessed to us that he never attended university and—"

"He likes to confess."

"They could have found someone who had gone, maybe not to Oxford or to Cambridge on account of our faith, but to university abroad like Ned."

"Or at least someone who kept quiet about his lack of the academe," said Katharine.

"Exactly," said Henry, then added, "He does sing rather well."

"Go." She pointed to the door. "'Caesar' awaits."

Henry got up from the chair, walked past her and pulled a brown leather book down from the shelf as he was leaving.

"Henry . . ."

"What?" His back was to her.

"Sir Thomas North's translation." She held out her hand.

"Aw . . ." Henry turned around. He was smiling. Katharine saw he was taller than she was now. And his hair, though it still gleamed, was no longer white-blond but more the golden color of harvest rye. Henry put the book in her hand.

"Is that what you came up here for?" She replaced it on the shelf.

"I came to find you," said Henry with mock sincerity.

"Of course. Go."

When Henry left, Katharine drew a high-backed chair close to the window to get the full slant of sunlight. Long hours of candlelight often hurt her eyes. She had been waiting for this moment all day, and now, tucked in a corner, hidden almost entirely by a screen of staghorn filigree and mother-of-pearl inlay, she sat in the cool shadows above the garden with the unbound pages of "Astrophil and Stella" by Sir Philip Sidney on her lap.

Sidney had come to a banquet at Lufanwal while staying with Lord and Lady Strange. Katharine was married then and lived an hour's ride away. Less than a fortnight earlier she had suffered the loss of an unborn child, but she had forced herself to get out of bed and go to the hall that evening—not because she knew anything about Sidney, but because she had stared at the ceiling for too many days. At the time of his visit, Sidney was five and twenty, five years older than Katharine. He had left Christ Church, Oxford, without taking his degree and traveled the Continent. Young men like Sidney, like Ned, journeyed to foreign cities, while young women stayed at home.

Sir Philip Sidney had regaled the dinner guests, not with his poetry, but with his views on the purpose of poetry. He drank enough wine to launch a loud attack on a book just published called *Schoole of Abuse* by one Stephen Gosson, who thought all poets immoral and faulted them for creating unnatural desires. Gosson had, according to Sidney, in "the spirit of malice" dedicated his book to Sir Philip. "Who is this knave," Sidney fumed, "who claims to be a scholar but is nothing more than a squire—no, a page, better a fool—in the employ of unsound ideas? *Schoole of Abuse* . . . *he* should go back to school!" There was laughter. "I would not, I daresay, want to be a maid or page in his household, or a cow in his barn or a poor sheep in his meadow, for a man who rails against unnatural desires is most often the keeper of such fare . . ."

Katharine remembered thinking how the handsome young nobleman with dark brown curls was at one end of the spectrum and her aging husband at the other: except for a few long gray strands, her husband had lost most of his hair. He was kind, but with his days of hunting and hawking behind him he had very little to occupy him. He did not read. He loved his three sons, who were older than Katharine, and who, like their father, were avid sportsmen. He spent most of his afternoons in their company.

She had come to Lufanwal that night still grieving for her lost child and praying she would not weep before the first meats were placed on the table, but by the time dinner had ended and she was returning home, her cloak wrapped around her shoulders and the rugs in the cart swathing her feet, she had resolved to read as much as she could. Reading was something besides stitching she could do: she would make it her vocation.

Sir Edward was so taken with Sidney, he had encouraged his charming guest to write a book that defended poetry, and now Katharine wondered if he ever had. She'd never encountered Sidney again, but she'd followed the stories of him. He'd been a darling at Elizabeth's court for a while—the fate of all handsome smart nobles—and lingering there, he had become an unabashed anti-papist; so many poets were, all playing into the queen's silky hands—a prioress with her coterie of favorites. How could any young man at court refuse such adoration from a queen? Until, of course, her blood thinned to him, and she found something upon which to unleash her fury—that he was betrothed to a woman of whom she didn't approve; or perhaps the young lord or earl was too passionate about her Protestant Church or not passionate enough; or maybe he'd cooled on Her Majesty's endless battles with Ireland and the money and lives spent there—reports continually came from Ireland that yet another soldier or settler's throat had been cut; or he voiced a political point which she thought either futile or dangerous, or he had too much hubris or he had too little. It seemed all too often the queen's displeasure with these young men was a whim. Whatever the reason, one by one she tossed each one of them out—sometimes wooing them back again, other times chopping off their heads.

Sidney was two and thirty when, in a battle in the Netherlands, a musket ball in his thigh took his life. All of England mourned. He was given a funeral fit for a king. As far as Katharine knew, now four years since the gravediggers lowered him to rest, no printer had yet issued a volume of Sidney's words. His sister Mary Sidney Hubert, the Countess of Pembroke, tirelessly copied his poetry in beautiful curling black script—the busywork of a woman's hands, like needlework or lace-making—and passed it around to family and friends. A cousin had sent a copy of his sonnet cycle to Katharine.

Katharine had read sonnets in Italian: Dante and Petrarch. Henry Howard, the Earl of Surrey, and Thomas Wyatt had both tried their hands at the form in English, but the sonnet—with its prescribed syllables, meters and lines—was still relatively new to England. She held the paper up to the light and read Sidney's first sonnet once, twice, three times. Here was a whole story in fourteen lines! Sidney's language was graceful, marked with emotion, yet muscular and utterly masculine; he was able to get at the truth of the moment. "Great with child to speak . . . Biting my truant pen . . ." His images were thrilling, and at the same time simple and direct. "Beating myself for spite . . ." The tension grew between the meter and the speech, and then the last line rode the crest of a wave and trumped the rest of the poem. "'Fool,' said my Muse to me, 'look in thy heart and write.'"

She read it again. His words affected her bodily. They seemed to leap from the paper directly into her veins. This intense, and only the first of many poems in Sidney's cycle—she was not sure she could live through the rest of it. She tried to calm herself, tried to breathe evenly. She sat very still. It was silly, but that was the way she was, the way she always had been. Words did this to her.

Someone entered the library. She peeked through the tiny holes between the carved ivy leaves in the screen.

She saw the broad shoulders first. As he examined the volumes, he did not round his back but kept it surprisingly even, bending from the waist.

He wore no doublet, no jerkin, but a simple white tunic, the sleeves blooming round his wrists. He pulled out books, glanced through them, put them back on the shelves. She did not move but watched him. He was searching for something. The air was warm, but she shivered, and just as the straight-backed visitor pulled out a dark red volume with gilt tooling, she sneezed.

He spun around, book in hand. "God bless you."

Katharine was silent.

"A favorable sign from the gods, say the Greeks," he continued.

She sneezed again.

"God bless you. Twice blessed by the gods. And twice blessed by me . . ." He walked up to the screen and leaned in close—a priest awaiting her confession? She felt his breath, and from his skin was a hint of herbs, of lavender or rosemary. How unusual for a man not to smell like a horse.

"You think it a blessing? More would have it that my sneeze augurs death," she said.

"Then twice blessed by me . . . to protect you from such an end."

He walked around the screen and stood in front of Katharine. Again she was struck by his insolence. He was no lord, yet his carriage spoke otherwise. He had practiced, perhaps, for years in front of a looking glass. She heard from Ursula he had come to Lancashire from mucking about in theaters in London and that his father was a glover in Warwickshire: no noble lineage this—making skins for the hands from other skins.

He stood as if waiting for something. She stared at him, not knowing what to say next.

"Twice blessed by me," he repeated.

"So, a giver of blessings. Art thou God?" She rose from her seat. She wanted to walk out of the room, but this man, this Shakespeare, stood in her way.

"A plain gramercy would do."

"I'll thank God," she said.

"A lady I once knew, not my wife," he continued, "told me a sneeze is akin to what a woman feels when she is . . ." He paused, leaned in close to her and lowered his voice. "When she is in the throes of Eros."

Katharine slapped him. He did not step back but put his hand on his cheek, his eyes steady on her. When she saw a grin appear on his face, she raised her hand to hit him on the other cheek, but he caught her wrist and held it. Yanking her wrist from his grasp, she calculated her exit. In the throes of Eros, indeed! She had heretofore only been in the grasping arms of a juddering old man.

"How fares my lady?" Shakespeare asked, his voice now supple.

She glared at him. Any other swain of his station would have, after such a cuffing, bowed so low his nose touched the ground, begged a thousand pardons, and scurried out the door.

"I'll with the Greeks align," he said, no longer closing in on her but with a timbre now light and open and sunny, "that good will come, not death. Odysseus's son, when his father returned home dressed as a beggar . . ."

"Sneezed?"

"Yes. And Penelope laughed, was hopeful again."

Katharine wondered if the quick manner in which he jumped from one subject to another—Mercury's swift flight from place to place—was a sign that he was mad. Had anyone at the hall checked his previous employ? "So you read Greek?" she asked.

He bowed. "I am a schoolmaster. And a poet." He bowed again.

"And you read Latin."

"Of course."

"How learned you are."

"More than many, less than some."

"And what Greek are you teaching your pupils now? Aristotle?"

"No. The man in the marble chair."

"His seat culled from the quarries of Paros," she said, "Mestrius Plutarchus."

"You know of him?"

"A master of history and a priest at the temple of Apollo in Delphi."

"You know *of* him," he said. "For I cannot assume you've read Plutarch—he's far too rigorous a regimen for your fair sex. There are no knights, no maidens, no love songs. Though, fairly, there is much from him that women can learn, for he is not as much a chronicler of history—though war, death, valor, all walk upon his stage—as he is an examiner of character, a physic to mankind, in search of the pieces of the puzzle of men."

"The puzzle of men. You are a poet."

"A poet of mankind."

"Ah. A poet of mankind. What a princely title. And do you fancy that men puzzle women?"

"Women puzzle men in that we know not what you are or how you work."

"But in the last grain of sand, you spoke of the puzzle of men. I am puzzled. Are you now changing it to the puzzle of women? Do you include women in this riddle? As the puzzled or the puzzlers?"

"I—"

"Or is it that we women have our hands full of womanly things, of babies and stitching? And thus our minds are too weak to worry about how to put all the pieces of the great manly puzzle back together again. How lucky Master Plutarch was, with his powerful puzzling head, to have time to sit upon his marble chair. No babies crying to suckle at his breast, no children to wash or to put to bed or to cool their feverish brows." Katharine sat down again and straightened Sidney's pages on her lap; then turned them over so the ink was hidden from his sight.

"I would not—" he began.

"I suppose to complete the puzzle of man is an impossible task. Since the Garden, when poor Adam lost a rib, brought an end to any manly order. Was Eve up at night wide-eyed with worry that by gaining a rib—or is your history that she stole it?—she forever rendered the puzzle of men incomplete?" A newly sharpened blade would have been duller than her tone.

He backed away, leaned against the windowsill, the open air behind him. "I dare not presume that a woman—"

"My good sir, you have already presumed too much. But I've forgotten, you are the self-anointed poet of mankind and are used to such presumptions." Katharine jumped up and pushed past him, Sidney's sonnets now rolled in her hand like a club. "Which life are your young men studying?" she asked.

"'Julius Caesar,'" he answered.

He was following her across the room. She was heading for the door.

"And they can read it?" she asked.

"They are at different levels. And they translate," he said to her back. "From the Greek to English."

"Yes."

"And when they make mistakes, you correct them?" She finally turned to look at him.

"I read Greek," he said.

The dark red leather book with shafts of wheat engraved in gold at its edges was now behind his back. He obviously did not read Greek well, for he had pulled a translation of Plutarch from the shelf.

"I'd venture to say you speak Greek," she said, spitting out the words.

"I speak Greek and—" He stopped mid-sentence when she waved her hand to cut him off.

She meant he spoke nonsense, but he had taken her literally. She rolled her eyes toward the heavens. "And you also read our fair language . . ."

"English? Yes, fairly. Our Saxons may have been fair of hair, but their tongue was dark and brutish. When William conquered our lands, he brought a fairer, lighter lilt."

"So when your students exchange Greek for English, do they use other texts to aid them or are they on their own?"

"The beauty of Plutarch is that he writes of character, of qualities, of the person first, the event second. Lessons we can all learn from . . ."

"So you said. But you have not answered my question. Are your students allowed to use another text to help them in their translation?"

"No."

"So you must be truly a master, then, to sit with their ink scratches barely dry and read their creations."

"Their translations. I am a schoolmaster."

"Yes, a master, but of what I cannot tell." Katharine stopped at the door and, facing him, pointed to the book he was holding with both hands behind his back. "That is Amyot's Plutarch in French—you, I assume, want Sir Thomas North's Englished version," she said, pulling the brown leather binding from the shelf and handing the book to him.

Without waiting for a reply, she charged through the door. She felt like laughing but was afraid the sound would come out of her mouth in gales. At the end of the next room, when she was out of his sight, she picked up her skirts and ran.

7

ad they fallen to the floor? She pushed her skirts and bone farthingale to the side, got down on her hands and knees and looked under her bed. They were not there. Nor were they on the table, in the oak cupboard or under her pillows. She hoped to dear God that her maid Molly hadn't thought they were rubbish and thrown them in the fire.

Sir Edward's library was on the second floor, with two doors at opposite ends of the long room, one opening to a staircase and the other to a withdrawing chamber and several guest quarters. There was no central corridor in this part of the house, so Katharine retraced her steps with candle in hand, through one guest chamber and then another. The rooms boasted broad beds with fringed canopies trunked by oak pillars of carved thistles, ivy and doves. She passed windows framed in teal, emerald, gold and damask. The chambers of the grandest suite were elegant enough for a king, and indeed Henry VI had slept there.

She scanned the edges, the rugs and the planked floors for her lost pages. She had hungered for Sidney's sonnets all day, and then, at the moment she started to feast, the tutor had interrupted her, and now all the glorious morsels—the words and their rhymes, the rhythm and the form Sidney had worked so hard to create—had vanished into air.

Katharine pushed open the library door. Her candle cast shadows along the rows of bindings. She hunted the floor, then the chair by the window. She searched the seat creases with her fingers—nothing hiding there. She'd held the sonnets high as she ran from the room. Why hadn't she struck the silly man over the head with them? When she returned to her chamber without the sonnets, she climbed into her bed, feeling empty and out of sorts.

"*You told* the cook what?" Matilda asked.

Matilda was sitting by the window in her antechamber, alternately fanning herself and wiping her face with a white cambric cloth. Her skin glistened from the heat; dark circles of sweat stained the light blue silk under her arms.

When Katharine's grandfather reconfigured the house more than twenty years before, he had added a great chamber for entertaining—smaller and more intimate than the ancient great hall—several parlors and withdrawing chambers, the gallery, the library, the secret chapel and the three priest holes for hiding their priests in case of a raid. Edward and Matilda's lodgings were part of that new wing. The women often gathered in Matilda's antechamber to sew, and though the windows were neither large nor plentiful, the colors and the fabrics made their own kind of light, for the room was dressed with a rich confection of heavy red velvets and golden brocades, tapestries of several sizes, exotic carpets from the east and a large carved stone fireplace. Usually a fire was lit, even in midsummer, but the recent relentless hot spell had vanquished any chill in the air.

"I told the cook that's what I desired," said Ursula, feeding her yapping dog a piece of kidney pie.

Katharine did not look up from her lace: she was making a collar for the christening of her cousin Grace's new baby.

"What our family and our guests eat, Ursula, is my duty," Matilda said slowly, enunciating each syllable with a thrust, as if it were a knife.

Matilda often had to scold and to reprimand Ursula as a mother does a spoiled child. But Matilda's tone today was different, sharper, less tolerant.

"She asked me," Ursula said, kissing her dog on its mouth.

"Next time find me," said Matilda.

Ursula popped a piece of pie into her mouth and gave a giggle. "I've heard you do it a million times. Why shouldn't I have a try?"

"'Tis not your place."

Ursula uttered a little cry, as if she had been poked in the ribs, and plopped in a pout on the same chair as her daughter Joan. Joan looked nothing like her mother. Where Ursula was tiny at the waist, Joan was thick. Where Ursula was blond, Joan was black-haired. Where Ursula had skin as smooth as white marble, Joan's skin was dark and pitted. Joan was a solid girl, a somewhat sad girl, who tended to her younger siblings as though she were their mother.

Katharine sat on an oak stool, and as she pushed and pulled the lace hook, she wondered what Matilda had heard from Sir Edward. She hoped, with Matilda's permission, she could write a letter to Edward soon. In all the years she'd lived with Matilda their relationship had never been intimate. She often pondered if anyone, even Edward, could penetrate that wall, for Matilda remained aloof even with her own children. Katharine couldn't imagine that; she dove into moments when Matilda would have held back. Katharine sometimes thought that was why Sir Edward sought her out, that Matilda made him feel lonely.

Katharine's currency with Edward was books and writers, for his admiration for poets was second only to his veneration of the Pope and certain prominent priests. He saw no problem with his love of God and his penchant for poetry; for him the beauty and grace of words was no different from the beauty and grace of nature. Katharine wasn't sure Matilda could even read. She'd never seen her with a book and never dared ask, afraid of offending her.

Isabel came running, and they all looked up from their stitching.

"There's a letter, a letter," she cried.

Isabel, who was not yet sixteen, had large chestnut eyes and barley-colored hair. Katharine gave her lessons, and the girl already showed talent in Latin and Greek. She was playful, full of laughter, loved to dance and to sing and was the anchor of her father's heart. Katharine prayed her glow would never dim.

Matilda rose. "From your father," she said.

"No, no, Mother, from Ned. He's coming home! He wrote to me."

"Read to us, then," said Matilda.

Isabel sat on the windowsill and, leaning into the light, read: "'My dearest sister, Father's haste has caused me much grief, but I find solace in his safety and assure you he will be home before the summer crops are sown. I will depart from these burnished hills forthwith and promise to be by your side by the first day of Advent. Kiss mother for me and pray read her this letter . . .'"

Isabel leapt up, kissed her mother on the cheek and continued, "'Prithee, tell the family I am eager to return. Your servant and brother, Edmund.' He signs it Edmund, not Ned, he's all grown-up now," she said. "I knew he would come. How I've missed him. I've grown! He will never recognize me."

"He will recognize you, treasure. Your spirit remains the same. Even a blind man would recognize you." Matilda kissed Isabel on the top of her head.

Katharine had rarely seen Matilda display such warmth and assumed the news of Ned answered one of her prayers; indeed, she made the sign of the cross as she walked toward Priscilla, who, frail and almost blind, was dozing in a chair by the window.

"Mother," she said loudly.

Priscilla awoke. "Yes, yes, yes."

"Mother." Matilda bent down and spoke to Priscilla as if she were a child. "Ned is coming home."

Priscilla smiled and promptly went back to sleep. Matilda left the room, Katharine imagined, to kneel in front of the altar in the hidden chapel.

Isabel threw her arms around Katharine. "What gifts will he bring? I know you asked him for books, but I begged him for a prince."

"If he forgets, we'll find one for you," Katharine said.

"For you, Kate, I begged him to bring home a prince for you."

"Your kindness overwhelms, but I've no need for princes."

"I need princes!" Ursula declared, plucking the letter from Isabel's hand.

"You have a prince," said Isabel, snatching it back again.

"Who?"

"Richard," said Isabel, speaking of her half-brother.

"Richard is no prince. If my parents had not been so eager, if they had been patient—"

"Let us not talk of gifts or princes," Mary, Harold's wife, said quickly, cutting Ursula off. "Let us pray to God for Ned's safety and health, for he has a long journey home."

Mary favored dark colors to light, and coarse fabrics to smooth. She wore no ornamentation around her neck, and her hair was always pulled tightly into a plain cap. A simple gold band was all that adorned her fingers. Mary had wanted to become a nun, but her parents had considered the match with Harold too advantageous and refused her the veil.

"Isabel," Mary continued, "rather than imagining the Venetian trinkets Ned will bring you, why don't you sit down and put that beautiful handwriting to good use? Write a letter to your sister telling her of your brother's plans. She will rejoice in the good tidings."

"Cousin Kate, come with me. You will write to Grace. You always sound so natural, where I sound silly and stiff."

"You flatter me to make your work shorter," said Katharine. "I am weak and will do as I am bade. My fingers cramp with this stitching, though I doubt they will fare much better wrapped around a quill. Come, dear Isabel, come."

Isabel sprang from her chair and grabbed Katharine's hands in a dance. "Ned, dear, gentle Ned, is coming home!"

She would not go down. He was sitting under a tree in the rose garden. She was in the library, at the window. The last time she had seen him, she had run from him, run out of the very room she was standing in now. It had been three days, and she had still not found Sidney's sonnets. With Sir Edward gone, no one else at the hall would know what the pages were, or even care.

She would not go down. He was working with his hands, with a penknife. Carving a piece of wood, perhaps. He was careful, precise, swift in his movements. She thought of his father, the glover in Warwickshire, a man in a leather smock with hides and skins as neighbors, a man who clocked the hours of the day with tanning, dying, snipping, trimming and sewing the lines of a hand. Why had this young man not gone into glove-making with his father?

Smoke was in the air. A black coil twisted into the blue sky. More brush fires. It was Michaelmas, Saint Michael the Archangel's feast day and one of the few celebrations the queen allowed. There seemed a sordid vengeance from above, for the crops that had been salvaged from the drought were now in danger of being consumed by flames. In the last fortnight, three leas of wheat, ready for reaping, had been swallowed by fires. The farm laborers, the stable hands and the kitchen help from Lufanwal and the neighboring estates had battled the smoldering stalks through the night. They had worked in a long chain, passing leather buckets from the well—the barrels were empty of rainwater and the ponds and river had dried up. Everyone lived in fear that timber or thatch would catch fire and the barns and huts, like the uncut hay, would burn. But they had managed to contain the embers. The men and women had returned from the fields at dawn, coughing, their faces, arms and hands dark with soot.

Katharine pulled the window shut against the acrid smell. There had been hope of rain a few days past, the sky growing dim with clouds, and then after a tease of a shower the sun had come out and left the land gasping for more. Would the ancient roots of Lancashire shrivel and die and the soil become sand? She had read of deserts in faraway lands—in an account by Raleigh or Drake or Hawkins, she couldn't recall—where waves of sand stretched as far as the eye could see and shot up as high as mountains.

She sat down with Spenser's *Faerie Queene* on her lap. Her fingers drummed the amber-and-gold-leathered cover. She had wanted to read but now had no inclination for it. In a whirl, she tossed the book on the table, descended the stairs two at a time, picked up her skirts and jumped over the last three steps—flew, really. She pushed the door, the hinges groaning in complaint; as soon as the sluggish oak was behind her, she hurried over the cobblestones and through the archway to the back garden. Her journey, she tried to convince herself, was for the sole purpose of discovery. She wanted to find out if he had picked up Sidney's poems, and she wanted to see what he was making.

Once she rounded the corner, she bridled herself, forcing a walk, and she took her breathing down, so her bodice rose and fell gently instead of heaving from the passion of exercise. She strolled, as if she'd been intent on that: strolling, not discovering. He was focused, but she knew he knew she was nearing; there was a certain tilt to his head, a self-conscious way in which he held himself, always an actor on a stage: his hands his soliloquy. He had cut the feathers off a goose quill. Now he was sharpening the end. The hairs on the back of his hand were fine, his fingers surprisingly long and graceful, not thick or rough, and his fingernails were clean.

She stood over him, but he did not look up until he stuck the nib in his mouth. With the fashioned feather between his lips, he raised his eyes to hers and smiled. He had a strong chin. He pulled the quill from his mouth and examined the nib. It would take a master like Nicholas Hilliard to draw lips so perfectly shaped: they were full but not feminine.

"Ever make your own pen?" he asked.

She shook her head.

"Thought not."

She didn't want to be drawn into his game of words. Every time they met, it was riposte after parry, and she said things she never usually said, in ways she didn't usually say them. He compromised her tongue.

"My father taught me how to make a quill before I knew how to write," he continued. "Always plenty of geese. Ink harder to find. Had to make that, too. Ever make ink?"

"No."

"You missed one of the joys of youth. We were wizards or witches making a potion: eye of newt, tongue of dog . . . burnt wool or lamp-black crushed into powder, gum of Arabic or galls of oak, and wine or vinegar, maybe a drop of rainwater, let it stand, stir, then . . ."

"Then?"

"Dip the quill, of course, then think, then write. Or write before you think. Lampblack is best for darker paper."

"Darker paper?"

"Not everyone in this land has linen the color of clotted cream. Perhaps if you are Sir Philip Sidney's scribe you do, but we common folk are used to making our marks on murky sheets of brown or gray, the color of the Thames."

There again was the swift current: his mind traveled from the nib of a quill to the color of the Thames.

"You found them!" she exclaimed.

"Ahhhhh!" He handed her the finished black quill, picked up another feather and started whittling. "To be rich and to be a writer is a blessing, never a curse, to make riches on words is a chest of gold few stumble upon."

"You have the Sidney!" she said.

He jumped to his feet. "Sounds like an ague when you word it thus. The pox, the plague, the gout, the Sidney." He held out his arm. "Doctor, I am ailing, leech me, call for the cupping glasses . . ."

"May I have them back? I had but only started when you interrupted—"

Then he interrupted her again:

> "Queen Virtue's court, which some call Stella's face,
> Prepar'd by Nature's choicest furniture,
> Hath his front built of alabaster pure;
> Gold in the covering of that stately place . . ."

He grimaced. "Furniture? To write words in rhyme is an art, madam; to rend them, beat them into submission, is a sin."

Katharine crossed her arms, a nurse scolding a child. "He's done no violence. His words are beauty. His feeling pure. What right have you to mock him?"

"'In truth, oh Love, with what a boyish kind . . .'" he recited. "'Yet of that best thou leav'st the best behind.'" He grinned. "Is he musing on his fair Stella's behind? I should hope, after he compared her features to nature's furniture, he has at least the grace to praise her buttocks."

She could have sworn, with a movement as quick as a cut to a quill, he peeked at her backside. This fellow's rudeness had no bounds.

"I'll not listen to you dismantle one of the world's most gifted poets," she lectured, "who if he had not died so young—"

"Aye, the mantle of such greatness hangs heavy upon his poor soul. What he hath writ, my dear, stands separate from pity. Another poet down. A playwright dies every week, it seems, yet one Sir Poet takes lead in his leg and the whole world stands still. I cannot weep because I cannot follow where this poet leads. A maze of language, with trees scarce cut to fit, stops me at every turn."

"'Loving in truth, and fain in verse my love to show . . .'" She recited the first sonnet in the cycle. "His path is easy. You cannot follow it?"

"You are more nimble than I. Perhaps you've not read far enough to get lost in his woods. I read all. The songs, too. A woman, it seems, by your fair example, is not the weaker sex with Sidney." He waved his hand in mock surrender. "Yet a man must have stamina, perseverance and strength to couch with him."

"And you are not such a man?"

"With him? I have tried and I have failed."

"You are jousting with a dead man because you cannot come close to his wit, nor his rhyme, nor his meter, and that angers you. I don't pity Sidney. I pity you!"

He smiled, keeping her eyes in check with his, and declaimed, "'But with your rhubarb words you must contend,'" and then in a melodramatic voice, "'To grieve me worse, in saying that desire / Doth plunge my well-form'd soul even in the mire / Of sinful thoughts, which do in ruin end'? Many a sugar'd sentence doth your fair Sidney pen. The sweetness, I suppose, counteracts the rhubarb, or perhaps counterattacks it.

'Tis not his 'sinful thoughts' that 'do in ruin end,' but 'tis his insufferable rhymes." He took the roll of Sidney's sonnets from his belt and handed them to Katharine. "I have no more use for these."

"The envy you wear upon your sleeve does not become you," she said. "Find a glass and gaze at the image there."

"'Oh no, her heart is such a citadel, / So fortified with wit, stored with disdain, / That to win it, is all the skill and pain . . .' Dear lady, to write that is all the pain and no skill."

He seemed to have read all one hundred and eight sonnets and memorized a good portion of them, though he'd only had them for less than three days. She'd heard of people who read something once and held pictures of every single word in their mind, so they could recall not only lines but whole poems without ever having to study them again. Perhaps he was one of those.

He chuckled. "Sidney vexes me. A few stanzas inspire envy, yes, but sonnet after sonnet of eyes beaming and gleaming. Oh, and the dreary repetition of 'Stella's rays' and the dull 'two stars in Stella's face.'" He paused and looked into Katharine's eyes. "Could he not think of a better image for beautiful eyes? Something to do with heaven, perhaps? His pen too often marks with 'dribbed shot,' to steal a phrase from the master himself. 'Desire, mire, sake, slake, same, shame' . . . come, now, even I could do better than that. Love and virtue, love and virtue . . . up and down, a seesaw, again and again, how tedious."

"Then do it." She glared at him.

"What?"

"Have you ever tried to write a sonnet? Have you one hundred and eight tucked under your bed? Or perhaps they are the stuffing of which your bed is made!"

"I certainly have written . . ." He put his blade in his belt. He stared at her, his eyes steady. "I—"

"Oh, I mustn't forget," she continued. "You are the self-anointed poet of mankind. Do you actually put those quills to paper, or do you just spend your hours carving up feathers and poets alike, poets who have created whole books, whole worlds?" All of a sudden she felt faint and leaned against the tree. "The smoke . . ." she began but did not finish.

He moved to her, but she put her hands up to stop him from coming closer.

"'Tis nothing," she said, straightening herself and walking to a stone bench. She was mortified that she and this glove-maker's son were in plain sight, for the windows of the household above were prime seats for viewing. She wished she'd never ventured down from the library.

"Where did you come by your learning?" he said when she was seated. He remained on foot.

It was the first time she'd heard the tutor utter a word that did not sound choreographed, and she was as much taken aback by what he said, that he had asked about her, as by his tone, which had lost its edge and was gentle.

"Sir Edward," she said, her eyes filling with tears. If her uncle were at the hall, she would have leaned on his warmth to shield her from the man who stood before her.

Shakespeare nodded. "Sir Edward was a scholar. The walls lined with books, which I have started to plunder. I thought a father, or a brother, or a husband had sat you down with a hornbook."

"Sir Edward *is* a scholar. He *is* still with us, though for a time abroad."

One black crow landed in the garden, and then another and another. It wasn't the rooks, for they hadn't returned, but carrion crows, their beaks black and stout. Shakespeare waved his arms at the cackling tribe and shooed them away.

"And no one sat me down with anything," Katharine said.

"How came you to live at Lufanwal?" he asked, sitting on the bench next to her.

"I was brought as a child, when my parents and my brother and sister perished. I married and moved five leagues from here. My husband died and I returned. 'Tis not a complicated history."

"A child robbed of parents is always complicated—a hollow in the heart that endures. The plague?" he asked.

"A fire," she replied, her tone sharp, scorning his softness.

She looked away and felt a touch on the scar on the back of her neck. The movement was so swift, so light, such a feather of unfathomable liberty, that in an instant she convinced herself she'd imagined it, that indeed it was the breeze that had skimmed her skin, not his finger. Yet in a flash the contact wreaked havoc on her flesh, moving down into the depths of her body. She was relieved to hear voices—though at this moment Ursula's high-pitched giggle was unwanted music. Katharine rose from the bench.

Ursula swept across the brown grasses, gathering dry leaves in the hem of her full red skirt as she walked. She was with her brother-in-law Harold and the master mason who had saved her little dog. Harold began to introduce Katharine, gesturing with his right arm, the hand of his shorter arm hidden in the fold of his doublet.

"Katharine met Mr. Smythson when he rescued Guinny from Richard's horrid hawk," interrupted Ursula.

Mr. Smythson bowed his head but not his body. He ran his fingers through his hair in an effort to keep his dark curls out of his face. His mop was as unruly as the hair on the sculpture of Laocoön Ned had sketched and sent from Italy.

Harold presented the tutor last. "Walter Shakespeare, our new schoolmaster up from Stratford."

"William Shakespeare," Ursula corrected.

Shakespeare bowed deeply.

"We are considering some changes to the hall," continued Harold, his cropped light red hair and neatly trimmed beard making a sharp contrast to the rough-hewn appearance of Mr. Smythson, whose leather jerkin was stained and who wore no proper doublet underneath.

"Richard and I are to have our own set of chambers," said Ursula. "With Sir Edward away, we think it's time to make additions. We are to have our own wing. We've been crowded in the back for too long."

Katharine wondered if the departure of Sir Edward had given birth to Ursula's interest in the shape of the house. The black crows in the garden masked nothing of their greedy nature when they attacked the berry trees and busied themselves in thieving. Was Ursula perhaps a bird of a similar feather?

"I met a Smythson in London," said Shakespeare. "He creates scenery for theaters. He is a magician."

"My brother," said Mr. Smythson, nodding.

"Ah," said William. "A family of magicians."

Katharine could not gauge whether Shakespeare's comment was a compliment or an insult.

"I'm no magician," said Mr. Smythson. "Merely an artificer. A stonemason by trade. Not skilled at sleight, never have been."

"Your houses are splendid," Ursula said with a sigh. "This marvelous man is largely responsible for Sir John Thynne's beautiful home at Longleat. And he did the renovation of Sir Matthew Arundell's castle in Wiltshire. Wollaton Hall in Nottinghamshire is one of his masterpieces, and recently he's been quite taken up with the Earl of Shrewsbury—"

Harold cut Ursula off. "We are flattered that the talented Mr. Smythson has taken time away from his many projects and duties to look over our humble cottage here," he said.

Mr. Smythson nodded and squinted his brown eyes at Harold in what seemed a smile but might have been a grimace. Perhaps, Katharine thought, it was hard for the builder to be in this circle of strangers; maybe stones were easier for him than people. Shakespeare whispered something to Ursula. He was as nimble with his attention as he was with his words.

"Pray pardon, I must leave," Katharine said. Her voice was higher than usual, and sounded artificial even to herself.

Katharine tipped her head but did not bid a proper farewell. In truth, the tutor-poet addled her, and she needed to escape. She left by way of the orchard and the chapel and continued walking. As she passed the barns, she saw the milkmaid Mercy. When Mercy curtsied low, Katharine noticed something dangling between her ample breasts.

"Ho, there, lass, what have you round your neck?" she asked, pointing to the small discs.

"I . . . I . . ." the girl stuttered.

"What?"

"I found 'em on the floor 'neath the birds, my lady, yonder," she said, nodding in the direction of the mews.

Katharine couldn't help but notice how Mercy had grown from a girl to a young woman. She had curves now, her broad hips filling her skirt.

"Give them to me," said Katharine.

Mercy hurriedly pulled off the cord with the wax discs. "I didna mean no harm, my lady. They were in the hay."

"Do you know what these are?"

"No'm."

"They are what priests wear. They have been blessed by the Pope. What were you doing there?" She did not question her further. She could imagine what Mercy might be doing in the hay in the hawk house. No doubt some lad had taken her in there for a doddle.

"Get along, now," Katharine said to the girl, who curtsied low again before she fled.

Father Daulton had said the priests from Rome rarely carried Agnus Deis anymore, for they broke any disguise the instant they were discovered. The wax discs impressed with the Paschal Lamb had been outlawed by the Parliament close to twenty years before as "popish trumperies," and the punishment for wearing them was death.

Katharine had heard tales of the miracles worked by Agnus Deis. Once, during Lent, an elderly lady was at death's door. An Agnus Dei was hung around her neck, and that instant she recovered her voice and memory, and the following day she was perfectly cured—to the great confusion of her heirs, who, having prematurely taken away her possessions, were forced to bring them back.

Whose Agnus Deis were these, and why were they on the floor of the hawk house? They had to belong to a priest. Were they Father Daulton's? Perhaps one of the birds had found them and brought them in its beak. Or Richard had taken the wax discs from Father Daulton's neck when he found him dead? If so, why leave them in the hawk house? Katharine would have taken the blessed medallions directly to Sir Edward, but his chair was still empty. On her way up the stairs, she met Mary going down.

"I met one of the milkmaids outside, and she was wearing these around her neck." Katharine held the Agnus Deis up to Mary. "She found them in the hay."

Mary's eyes widened. "I wonder why Richard would hide these in the hay."

"I don't know that they were hidden," Katharine said, thinking it odd that Mary had assumed Richard had hidden the Agnus Deis.

"Next thing, someone will find a bloody dagger in there, and then the tongues will surely wag! Get rid of them with haste. Throw them in the river."

Katharine continued to her chamber, resolved to lock the discs in a chest under her bed.

8

Ursula was dancing. There was no music.

The other women sewed in front of the fire, while Ursula pranced across the wooden planks, her little dog nipping at her heels. What song was Ursula listening to in her head while she dipped, turned and curtsied? A flush on her cheeks made Katharine wonder if she might be with child again, but her girth was no thicker.

"I must perfect this," Ursula said.

Katharine waited for someone to give Ursula what she wanted: *What dance is this you're worrying over, Ursula?* But no one looked up.

"'Tis new, from the Continent, called the courante," said Ursula, answering the unasked question.

Ursula had never completed a tapestry or even one small piece of embroidery—no threaded stories of her handiwork seated a chair or covered a bed or hung on a wall. Sad piles of her half-finished cloths sat dejected and dusty in baskets throughout the house.

"Monsieur LeBlanc, my new dancing master, taught me. I will dance with the duke, and he will surely know the steps. Oh, I do hope Ned returns in time to welcome the duke and his men. Ned is so skilled at dancing," Ursula said.

"We do not know when Ned will arrive," said Matilda, biting a red thread with her teeth. "But surely we will provide a warm welcome for our guests."

Ursula stopped dancing. "*My* guests. *Mine*. Richard and I invited them. The duke is my cousin. The new cook and I have gone over the menus. Monsieur Delaney is from the duke's province, and Monsieur Delaney is an expert in the dishes of that country. I have been fitted for my new gown: the lace is from Belgium, the silk from France, the velvet from Italy. I will look like a queen."

"Queen of what?" Katharine asked, sticking a needle into the spiraled horn of a unicorn and drawing gold silk through the linen. She was stitching a linen coverlet for a bed.

The question gave Ursula pause and she was silent for a moment. "The queen," she replied flatly. "Our queen. Her Majesty."

"What alchemy is this, dear Ursula?" Mary said, her head still bent over her stitching. "Your tailor must be a sorcerer, verily, if he is able to transform you into our queen right before our eyes. Better pay your dressmaking wizard well, for all of England will be knocking at his door."

Isabel giggled, Katharine smiled, and Joan suppressed a grin.

"Cease!" said Ursula, her tone shrill. No one looked up. She sighed loudly and then stalked out of the room.

"What next? The Virgin Mary?" Katharine said.

There was laughter.

"Ursula is a child," Matilda said.

Ursula was past thirty. Katharine recalled their conversation on the grass that day. She'd seemed no child then. And now she appeared to possess a newly found hunger. She could stomp her feet one minute, yet she also seemed quite capable of dropping poison into Matilda's wine the next.

Katharine stood to give her legs a stretch and went to the window. Mr. Smythson was below with several workmen. Two men were rolling something that looked like a large skein with a ribbon round it. They staked one end of the ribbon to the ground and continued walking. Mr. Smythson called out numbers while a man next to him hurriedly wrote them down. The mason cut a striking figure with his height and his long black coat. Katharine assumed they were measuring the dimensions of the new addition. At one point Mr. Smythson looked up at the window, held an instrument to his eye and peered through it. Then he removed the instrument but continued to gaze at the window where Katharine stood. She did not know if he had seen her and was intentionally looking up, or whether he was blind to her and merely intent on gauging the height of the house. She had just raised her hand to wave, when he turned away to talk to one of his men.

The children were gathering leaves and jumping feetfirst into the piles. Henry brought a three-legged stool for Katharine to sit on, and she held her umbrella to shield the sun. Henry no longer ran with the younger children, and his voice had deepened. He stretched his long legs on the linen spread on the grass and read not a leather-bound book but pages sewn together with thread.

"Whose pages?" Katharine asked, glad Henry was near and that his head was buried in words.

He held up the slim volume, a cheap penny pamphlet, the type sold on the streets in London. "Robert Greene," he said.

"Don't know him," she said. "A new curriculum from Master Shakespeare?"

Henry grinned. She remembered when he was born and the first time she was allowed to hold him. He had a shock of black hair at birth that fell out before he was a month old. And then the blond hair grew in, and even at this age it was soft and bright. Katharine had to stop herself from reaching down and running her fingers through it as she used to when he was a child.

Two girls from the kitchens brought baskets filled with bread, cheese, quince, nuts, cider, ale and a few stunted apples and pears from the orchard. When the food appeared, the children leapt from the leaves and dove for the offerings. They ate and then played again in the leaves. Henry helped himself to food and ale and fell asleep, Greene's pages slipping from his fingers.

Katharine loved these children. She relished how they grew and changed, how they became by turns angry, sad, happy, thrilled and curious. When she read to them, they often talked and played among themselves; other times they were quiet and settled down, their heads dropping back on pillows or their little bodies curling up like puppies on rugs. Today, fed and worn from their frolics, the children wandered back to the hall as the slate-colored clouds above them moved in from the west.

Henry woke and stood.

"You are a tall Lancastrian elm," Katharine said, still perched on her stool.

Henry smiled, then brushed the leaves from his hose and picked up the baskets. She watched him make his way back to the hall—he was not in any hurry, his head filled with his reading. She was on the verge of rolling the linen, when a voice called.

The tutor was coming toward her in a flame-colored doublet and white ruff. Full doublet, slashed, gray silk peeking through. Narrow waist, flaring hips, broad shoulders. Dove-gray hose. She waited. He looked quite handsome in his fiery hue, surely not the attire of a glover's son. She doubted such a rich doublet was in accordance with the queen's Sumptuary Laws. He held a sheaf of paper and knelt, a knight before a queen, and placed seven sheets in a row, a card dealer now.

"Seven sonnets," he said, still kneeling.

She wanted him to rise; his countenance was off—the supplicant had replaced the challenger.

"Seven sonnets," he repeated, his head down, his eyes still lowered.

"Seven sonnets," she said finally, in an effort to come to his aid.

"That I beg you . . ."

She nodded.

"Beseech you . . ."

She nodded again.

"To read."

"Of course," she said quickly, worried that he would keel over or start to weep. How strange he seemed, how fragile, how humble. "I will read them," she said. Was he feigning or in sooth frightened?

"You forced my hand," he said.

So he was a gambler. She knelt across from him, picked up the first sheet and read it, and then the second and then the third, until she had read all seven. She was shocked. She hadn't expected this. She and Shakespeare faced each other; if they hadn't been in the orchard, she would have thought they were in a chapel, kneeling in prayer.

"It has vexed me," he said, "what you might think. Do my little songs . . . have merit?"

"I am no judge."

"Thou art mine."

"Your sonnets are very good indeed."

"But not perfect," he said. "I am an apprentice yet. I have studied the form . . ."

"Perhaps in these two," she said, pointing, "o'erstudied it."

"When Petrarch's octave is followed by his sestet, therein—"

Katharine put up her hand. "Master Shakespeare, I beg you keep your equations to yourself. I tire quickly of mathematics."

He pointed at the sheets laid on the linen. "What think you of the subject?" he asked.

She was silent.

"Love," he said.

"'Tis the subject of sonnets," she replied.

"Some say the path to poetry is to write it first as prose," he said.

"How did you start these?"

"With rhyme and meter. I let my quill race across the page."

"No need to follow the rules of others," she said. "Your engine is your own."

"Your master Sidney has pushed the iambic pentameter ajar. And when he steps into the hexameter . . . he . . ."

"I know not the details of the form, but I can see how his sonnets vary."

"And my sonnets?"

"The beat is unexpected in those." She pointed.

"Petrarch's kin."

"The two that follow Sidney's form are even, perhaps too even."

"Sidney was your anointed . . ."

"The evenness did not occur to me when I read his verse. I was overcome by . . . his sentiment," she said.

"Yes, he is sentimental. And I agree with you, he is monotonous as well."

She gazed at him but said nothing.

"Teach me," he said.

She was, with these two words, distracted by his lips. Again she noticed their shape.

"I do not presume to teach," she said, "but I can relate to you what I read and how it makes me feel." She studied each sonnet anew. "These are the weakest." She held two sheets in her hand.

He frowned. "Why?"

"They follow convention, lack emotion. The words plod across the page."

"Plod across the page? My words may be donkeys, but yours are daggers." He placed his hand on his heart and toppled from his knees to the ground as if stabbed.

She smiled. "If you cannot shield yourself, then we should end."

Shakespeare sat up, cross-legged, took one of the papers from her hand. "I was guided by the Greeks in form. Yet I invoke the Roman deities," he said, "Cupid and the goddess Diana."

"I know the story. Love put his torch in care of Diana's nymphs while he slept. Perhaps 'tis those ties to antiquity that make your words weary."

Lines formed above Shakespeare's brows, and his eyes married hurt with humor. Katharine watched his mouth curve from a pout to a grin. Then he laughed: the sound was glorious and warm.

"'Seething bath' and 'sovereign cure' are well chosen," she said.

"You flatter me," he said.

Katharine turned to the second of the two poems and said, "This sonnet lacks grace. Perhaps use *brand* instead of *wand*, and then change *frond* to *hand*. A plant has a frond, but does a maiden? Even in poetry that seems most stretched." She continued, "The bitter end does resonate. A nod to the Song of Solomon, yes? 'Love is as strong as death: jealousy as cruel as the grave . . .'" She glanced at him. "So love is a disease that hath no cure?" she asked, eyebrows raised.

She did not wait for his response but sat back on her skirts. "Both poems fret and fume about distemper and disease. There is much 'cure' business. I see Petrarch in the complaint. Yet the shrill fury of the speaker is *after* the physical union, not before—unusual. If Sidney has pushed the form ajar, perhaps 'tis time for you to split it wide." She paused. "Think you that women are the givers of disease, not the receivers? We steal ribs and health and lead men to debt and to death. How vile we are."

"Some more vile than others," he said with a chuckle. He was on his knees again. He snatched another page from the linen and held it to her. "The verdict?"

"This has much mirth."

"Ah. You are my advocate."

"How well you love yourself, your name. *Will* makes its entrance in your poem—once, twice, thrice, four times, five, six, seven, eight, nine, ten, eleven, twelve, thirteen times in fourteen lines, but—"

"This sonnet may be too common for your chaste ears."

"I am no nun. But with all the planting you have done with your *will*, I am still not sure what is the *thrust* of this sonnet. Are we to care about this man, this Will? With these puns you dance well, your feet are swift."

"A jig at the end of a play," he said forlornly.

"Aye, a touch of the jig-maker. Use those same feet to tread deeper."

Katharine started to stand. He rose to help her. She tightened at his touch, which was delicate. Perhaps reading his verse was not a good idea.

"This wearies you?" he asked.

"No."

"Which is the best?" he asked.

"The third sheet in," she said.

"Why?"

"The first line, 'They that have the power to hurt,' hails from the heart, not the head," she said.

"It has history," he said, his eyes filling with tears.

His tears surprised her. He had dropped his shield. For the first time, she felt no need to parry.

"I feel that history when I read it," she said.

He nodded. "'Tis good, then?"

"Aye."

He smiled now, the tears of a moment ago gone. "Since meeting you, dear lady, I have put quill to page every day. I write and write and write. I have been in London, at the playhouses, writing verse but never finishing it. I count poets and playwrights among my friends—Kit Marlowe, Thomas Watson, Robert Greene."

"I know not these men. Your wife . . . is she among the living?" Katharine asked. He had mentioned his wife the day he said a woman *other* than his wife had told him what felt akin to a sneeze, but he had not uttered the word *wife* since. Perhaps, Katharine thought, his wife was dead.

"Aye, I have been in Stratford, too. My wife, Anne, is very much among the living. She is eight years older than I. Or perhaps I am eight years younger."

"What is your age?" Katharine asked.

"Six and twenty." He was quiet for a moment, then added, "I'd rather my wife not be currency between us."

What did he mean? There was no "between" between them. "I was not bartering with my question," she said, "I was curious."

"And I have three children," he offered.

"How fortunate you are. What are their names?" she asked.

"Susannah, Hamnet and Judith."

"How lovely."

They were silent for a moment.

"How came you to Lufanwal?" she said finally.

"I traveled on horseback from London," he said.

"I meant, by what reference?"

"The De Hoghtons'. I was with them when I was scarcely out of grammar school. My old schoolmaster brought me north when my father's affairs took a tumble."

"Are your parents still living?" she asked.

"My father has been on his deathbed twenty times. 'Will, my son, Will, my end is nigh.' He said this to me when he was still a young man. He has been dying since I was born. 'Will, get me the priest . . .' Ah! You did not hear that . . ."

"Surely you know this household is not afraid of priests."

He winked. "'Get me the Archbishop of Canterbury, my end is nigh.'" When he spoke in his father's voice he spoke from the back of his throat in a thick Warwickshire accent.

Katharine laughed. "Is he still a glover, then?"

"He has been everything and nothing. He's never been a king, but he's been a trader of corn, wool, malt, meat, skins and leather, a glover, yes, a husbandman, a butcher, a plaintiff and a defendant in suits, a creditor, a debtor, a debtee, an ale-taster, a bread-taster, a burgess, a petty constable, an affeeror, a borough chamberlain, an alderman, a bailiff, a chief alderman, an overseer, a litigator, ah, and yes, a father."

"Your father is an ambitious man, and you are your father's son, for you are as ambitious as he."

"You have that wrong: he is as ambitious as I. My father tried to buy a coat of arms and failed. I will have one."

"I never knew a coat of arms was a thing bought and sold."

"In your world, no. In mine, yes. Mark you, I will sell my work as my father sold his gloves."

"'Tis a good plan," she said.

"I will make more pounds of silver in one week than my eternally dying father has earned in one month, a year, perhaps in his whole life. I will buy the largest house in town, a house with glass windows, not air, with tapestries, not cloth."

"Your words will bring you riches?" She'd never heard of such a thing.

"To stay solely a player would mean a life of wanting. 'Tis not by mouthing the words of others my coffers will be filled. Yet 'tis not from writing a play that fills the purse, either, my lady—for many a poor wretch watches his words strut across a stage but has neither bread nor sack at home. There are other ways: poets have patrons, players can share in a company and make a tuppence cut from every penny made.

Mark you, my work shall be published and my work shall be performed before the queen."

"Well then, the riches await you."

"Are you mocking me?"

She did not answer.

"Will you be my patron?" he asked.

"Now you are mocking me," she said.

He bowed. She nodded. They stared at each other.

"Can you keep a secret?" he asked.

"I am skilled at that."

"The company of players I was with in Shoreditch disbanded. I slipped out of London. My peers think me in Stratford."

She wondered if his family in Stratford thought him in London.

"I don't confide in many," he continued, "but I feel I can confide in you. I trust you. I am so searingly envious of all the young poets who are producing pages that are in print or performed—I cannot stand myself anymore. Until these last nights, I had never even written to the end of a sonnet. You have cast a spell."

"I am no witch. It is you who dipped the quill into the inkhorn."

"'Then do it,' you said. I heard your words in my head long after I left you. These may not be perfect, but I have finished seven sonnets because of you."

Even though the sun was hidden and the sky overcast, Shakespeare's eyes glinted. The leaves started to swirl. A drop of water fell from the sky, and then another and another.

He moved his shoulders close to her, brought his hand to her face, and in one swift movement wiped a raindrop off her lower lip. She was so startled it took all of her control not to jump.

"Your kindness today encourages me," he said. "I thank you most humbly. I do not know you yet, but I will know you." He bowed. "Will you read my verse again?"

"Yes," she said. The rain was coming down faster. "How many months we have waited for this!"

"Blissful dew from heaven," Shakespeare said.

He gathered up his pages and stuck them in his doublet. She rolled up the linen, and they walked toward the house.

"No one need know our business," he said, "for I am a novice. Others knowing would only bring me shame. 'Tis our secret, one of our secrets."

"No one will know," she said. One of their secrets?

"You may call me Will," he said.

"And you may call me Katharine. Will, you are dressed very . . ." she began.

"Taffety?" he said.

"Yes, a taffety gentleman. Why the boisterous apparel?"

"Do you think scarlet suits me?" he asked. "I was sitting for a portrait."

It was pouring now. The smell and the feel of the rain seemed foreign after so many months—it was a cleansing, a baptism of sorts. The ground was drinking the water in, and the perfume from the plants and the soil started to rise from the earth. Will held the leather umbrella over her head.

"Who is painting you?" she asked.

"Ursula," he said.

"Ah, she's a portraitist now. Your finery is getting wet."

"Play clothes from my trunk. When on tour . . . I borrowed them."

"And what character were you in these borrowed flaunts?"

"A duke from Italy."

"Well, Duke, your doublet is bleeding."

The downpour was making the red dye run down Will's dove-gray legs. The rain had attacked his ruff, too—the starch was dissolving and the ruff looked like a limp rag around his neck.

"You've descended from a duke to a clown, I'm afraid. Poor Ursula. I do hope she was finished," Katharine said. "You may keep my umbrella for now. It'll need stretching after this rain, and who knows, it, too, may be ruined."

At the door, she ducked in front of him. "Continue on," she said.

Will bowed slightly, then turned and left her standing at the door. His lodgings were on the way to the stables. She watched him walk. With head held high, even with the rain-stained pigskin above him and the dripping clothes, he carried himself well—more duke, truthfully, than clown. She went into the house. She'd meant "continue on" with the sonnets but was worried he might think she was dismissing him. She brushed the wet off her sleeves and skirt and went to find Molly.

9

he first thing Katharine noticed when she rushed to the table was Ursula's dainty white hand on the Duc de Malois's plush thigh—her fingers strummed his puce velvet hose as though she were playing a lute. The duke was Ursula's cousin on her mother's side. Though Sophie, the duke's flame-haired mistress, was sitting farther down the table, the duke was gazing at Ursula—not into her light blue eyes, but lower. She had rubbed something between her breasts, rose oil perhaps, and her skin glistened in the candlelight.

"How honored we are you have decided to join us, Katharine," Ursula announced, forcing an edge into her voice.

Katharine reached for a goblet. As she brought the cold metal to her lips, she noticed the person sitting next to Sophie. Will. Katharine had learned that along with Will's duties as the schoolmaster, he had agreed to take part in theatricals at the hall. Wasn't he supposed to entertain guests, then, not laugh and dine with them? With whom had he curried favor for a seat at this fine table? Matilda? Richard? Harold? Most likely Ursula.

Will had sent more sonnets, and they'd met. Katharine lent him books, even *The Faerie Queene*. Then thrice he sent word for her to meet him, and thrice he sent word he could not come. Finally, he had come to her in the orchard with the beginnings of longer poems. She marveled at Will's skill. He had not gone to university, yet his mind was strong and quick, perhaps the strongest and quickest she had ever encountered. From where did his hunger for words issue?

The sound of Ursula rang out through the great hall. Recently, Katharine noticed her laugh had become loud and high, and tonight she sounded like the parrot she kept in a large gilded cage at the foot of her bed. She claimed the parrot came from one of Drake's or Raleigh's voyages. Now when Katharine passed the doors to her chamber it was not clear who was laughing—the poor parrot trained by Ursula or Ursula herself.

Ever since Sir Edward's departure, a dimming had begun, even during the day when sunlight streamed in the windows or at night when candles lit the tables and torches ringed the walls. Katharine could feel the shift, as if throughout the great house brightness of spirit and honesty of heart were systematically being snuffed out. Matilda sat next to Edward's empty chair at the head of the table. How could Matilda bear Ursula's brazen attempts at becoming mistress of the manor? Every time Ursula laughed, Matilda—with her broad shoulders and towering height—seemed to shrink.

Edward's empty chair presided over the feast—a show of constancy, a sign to all he would return. Katharine remembered Edward holding forth at banquets: the sovereign of his castle. Matilda refused to allow the chair's removal and yet forbade either of Edward's sons, Richard or Harold, to sit there. The chair, more a throne, was made of walnut; a dragon was carved at the center of the back with a crown hovering over its head. Urns and face masks flanked the dragon, and a carving of acanthus leaves ran down the arms and legs. The seat and back were covered in orange-red silk that glowed in the candlelight like a harvest moon.

The Duc de Malois's entourage numbered more than two score, but no one would go thirsty at this banquet. Flagons of cider and ale and bottles of wine crowded the side tables. When the servants finished bringing ewers, basins and cloths to each of the guests, the parade of fine meats from the kitchen began: a quarter of a stag, a whole boar, choice cuts of a doe, a loin of veal dripping with pomegranate sauce, stuffed capons laced with sugarplums, and herbed and roasted hare. Next came a procession of steaming pies with pigeon, gosling, minced lamb and rabbit enclosed in crusts.

The chief usher, whose chins spilled out of his white ruff like bread dough, swept past Ursula and Richard. With theatrical flair, he motioned for the platters and dishes to be set in front of Matilda. Ursula, who had not yet learned the art of concealing, gasped, for apparently she thought the food would be set in front of her. Richard's scowl deepened. Matilda, a gracious smile on her lips, bowed her head and proceeded with a lengthy prayer thanking God for their meal. Katharine wondered what largesse Matilda had bestowed upon the usher to secure his fawning performance. Matilda was no fool, but her privilege within the house had always been easy, and now, with her husband far away and her stepsons too close, the waters were suddenly rough.

A tall man, hat in his hands and dust covering his jerkin, came running to the table, bowed and then whispered into the Duc de Malois's ear. A smile spread across the duke's mustached face. "*Grâce à Dieu,*" he said, making the sign of the cross on his chest. He stood, glass goblet in hand.

"I have just received word of the birth of my son," he bellowed in thick-accented English, then drank the wine in one gulp and called for more from the servant standing by his side.

The group erupted with cheers and whistles and the pounding of pewter tankards on the long wood table.

"To the duchess," the duke continued. "My beautiful Emilie, who has brought our fourth child and our second boy, Henri Emanuel, into this world. Mother and child, *grâce à Dieu*, are robust."

Richard rose, also with goblet in hand. "What a great honor, sir. What a blessing to have the esteemed duke at our table, at this great and blessed moment. We thank our lord God . . . *à votre santé* . . . to the health of son and mother."

Richard walked over to the beaming duke and stiffly embraced him, while Ursula squealed and waved to a servant to refill her goblet. In the flickering light, the new dress Ursula had bragged of was indeed impressive—elaborate both in fabric and in style. She wore no partlet, no ruff or collar, but a cross with emeralds rested just above her breasts. Her low, square white bodice was trimmed with lace and embroidered with tiny colorful butterflies that matched the silk that peeked through the split in her gown. Her silk sleeves were woven with gold and silver thread, the shoulders and cuffs lined with pearls.

De Malois swallowed more wine and then amidst greetings and congratulations made his way down the table. Katharine watched him with interest, wholly unprepared for where his stroll would end—at Sophie. He promptly pulled his woman up by her tiny waist and kissed her on the mouth. Sophie was stunning. With red hair, green eyes, green gown and pinkish skin, she looked like some exotic bird.

The past spring the Duc de Malois's army had suffered a horrible defeat at Ivry when he had joined forces with the Duc de Mayenne's Catholic League. The losses were in the thousands. After the Protestant King Henri's successful slaughter at that battle, his Huguenots had moved on to Paris and starved half the doomed city to death. It was amazing that De Malois was still alive, much less heralding the birth of a son while his lips grazed the skin of his mistress. Katharine wondered how one could ever fully excise the stench of blood and burned flesh on the battlefield from one's memory. And the human bleating? The chorus of the dying? Was that so easily blocked out?

The world outside Lufanwal seemed almost impossible for Katharine to fathom. Tapestries and paintings depicted battle scenes, but she relied more on the pictures conjured by what she read. What was De Malois doing here? Was he en route to Spain? How had the queen even allowed him passage? Surely there were spies attending to him. If Sir Edward were in residence, it would have been risky but not unusual for such a prominent Catholic and powerful leader to be dining at their table. But Edward was in exile in a house gated by vineyards in De Malois's own country. Katharine hoped the duke had brought word of Sir Edward and that he had carried letters from him.

With more wine poured and the meats begun, the duke was still kissing his mistress. When Katharine turned to speak to the young French nobleman next to her, she felt Will watching her. She lifted her eyes. Indeed Will's eyes were fixed on her. She felt her heart quicken, and when she nodded her head in his direction, she caught sight of his attire. His doublet boasted a sheen so bright it seemed to reflect the candlelight on the tables and the torches on the walls. Will's fine weave was the color of herbs, while the hue of a spring garden—damask rose—peeked through the slashes on his arms. He was overdressed for someone of his station, as though he were at court in London rather than dinner in the country. His velvet hose were the color of goldenrod, a weed that in the sunlight ignited fallow fields. She would not have placed those colors together, but they were beautiful, and there was genius in their pairing. Was this outfit from a masque or play? What had his role been—a prince? The duke had gone back to his seat next to Ursula, and Will was now talking to Sophie. His arm was on the back of her chair. In this great house, Master Shakespeare with his striking plumage had assimilated well.

The eel, pike, brill and turbot arrived from the kitchens, followed by pigeons, larks and quail. Then came the marrow on toast. Will was no longer gazing at Katharine. He was eating. He had no doubt grown up shoveling food with stale bread from a wooden trencher, but he used a spoon well, as though he had been using one his whole life. He was a player, after all, trained to mimic. He said something to the duke, who now sat next to him with Sophie on his lap, and the duke threw his head back and laughed. Was it Will's wit or his impudence that tickled the duke so?

As the guests ate their way through Ursula's carefully planned menu, the carcasses from the meal were tossed on the rush-strewn floor for the hounds. Katharine leaned toward the young man from the duke's party and asked him in French how he had passed his time in England.

"I try," he said, placing a hand on her blue and black brocade sleeve. "I try to English speak."

He had no beard. His face was smooth and he had a cleft chin. Katharine had the urge to put her finger in the indent—or her tongue. He was maybe twenty.

She laughed. "You try to speak English."

He nodded happily. "Yes, yes. You teach me?"

"Oh, I'm not a good teacher, but Joan is." She pointed across the table to Ursula's daughter.

"But I like your noses," he said.

"My noses?"

He gently touched the side of her eye.

"My eyes." She smiled and pointed to her eyes. "Eyes."

"Eyes . . . *de couleur* . . ." He touched the blue of the brocade on her bodice.

"Blue." She laughed again and removed his hand. "Coventry blue."

"And that I like."

"What?"

"The ha-ha."

"My laugh?"

"Yes, laugh. You is a tutor good."

"You are a good tutor."

"You are a good tutor." He smiled.

"But Joan is better." Katharine called across the table, "Joan, this young man needs *assistance*," she said in a French accent, "with his English words. Help him. You go to her," she said to the young Frenchman, and then pointed at Joan. "Your tutor."

The wine had made the blush on Joan's cheeks deepen. Her dark curly hair was pulled up with several silver satin ribbons that fell to her shoulders. The young Frenchman rose, walked around the long table and sat next to Joan.

As the natural light slipped from the windows, wafers and currant, plum and apple jellies were brought out. Then came quince, cheeses and more wine, followed by cheesecakes and custards. With the delivery of each new delicacy, Katharine's eyes kept wandering back to Will, who was laughing and talking with those next to him.

Ursula stood and, once upright, made a show of pulling the pearls from her hair and throwing them at the guests, who *oh-la-la*'ed and dove for them. Ursula's blond locks fell to her shoulders. But she did not stop. She dragged her hands through her hair several times so that the strands, once smooth and obedient, became chaotic and unruly. Then she started to clap her hands. "We are so honored," she shouted, trying to tame the noisy crowd. "We are so honored," she repeated shrilly. Then she walked unsteadily over to Edward's chair and climbed up on it.

"Friends," she shouted. "Friends!"

The room quieted.

Katharine glanced at Matilda to see what her reaction was to the doeskin soles of Ursula's velvet pantofles stepping and stumbling upon Edward's newly upholstered chair. But Matilda's profile was pointing away from Ursula.

"Our poor Edward gone." Ursula sighed. "Not dead yet, but gone."

Richard rose. "Ursula."

"He never liked me," she continued. "Never, ever . . ."

"Ursula, my dear . . ." Richard gazed up at her. He was shorter than Ursula. His neck disappeared into his shoulders—a mushroom without a stem. The ruff he wore seemed to cut into his skin.

"I never liked him," said Ursula, who, standing unsteadily on the chair, almost fell off while trying to sit on it. She landed sideways, with her skirts over the chair arm, as though she were sitting on someone's lap. "Oh, Edward, how you glare at me." She poked the air with her finger. "Never one pleasant word from de pleasant man. How he loathe me." With the drink, Ursula's Dutch accent had returned.

Few hid their sniggering. Master Shakespeare may have had the night free, but there was theater for the guests nonetheless.

"Ursula, my dear, come outside. The breeze might heal your mood." Richard was standing by the chair now. "Ursula, come."

"No," she said simply.

"Ursula, come with me," Richard pleaded.

"No, no, no, no." She held her head high, pointing at her husband. "Thou art a ghost like your father—flesh but no blood. Who flees conflict? Who banishes himself? I thought banishing was the business of a queen. Men whose spirits are like feathers, I sssssssuppose—not those made of ssssssssteel and ssssssssstone. Men whose bones have no marrow. We have learned tonight, with the birth of his son, that our brave duke is of different mettle than this family. His sword is strong and valiant."

There was hooting and hollering. Men held their goblets and tankards in the air, as if to toast; several made obscene gestures. Ursula swung her legs to the front of the chair and with difficulty landed her two feet on the floor. Then she grabbed a goblet off the table.

Katharine couldn't help but be impressed by Ursula's warbling oratory; at least she seemed honest. Perhaps she was not the anointed family fool after all.

"To the De Malois offfffffsssssspring, may they fffffflourish and proudly carry their mighty father's mantle upon their shoulders." Ursula downed her drink, then vomited all over the table.

Richard winced. His passion was falconry; they often trained the hawks by sealing their eyes with a needle and thread, a temporary blinding. As the servants rushed to Ursula's side, Katharine wondered if at this moment Richard would have preferred to have his eyes sewn shut.

Laughter turned to whooping. Several Frenchmen stood, bowed, cheered and clapped, as though Ursula had just recited a beautiful piece of poetry. For a moment she looked startled, but she waved a servant away, calling instead for more wine.

The feast was finishing, and it was Matilda who gave the sign to the musicians in the balcony to start the song. Katharine caught Matilda's eye. With Edward gone, there seemed to be a warmth growing between them.

While the women withdrew to the gallery adjacent to the balcony to listen to the music through the grillwork, Katharine planned her escape from their chatter. Ursula would not be joining the women. Her heavings had been cleared, and now her head was on the table, her eyes shut, her cheek resting upon a piece of yellow cheese.

When Katharine had last looked at Will, he was in conversation with a Frenchman. She was almost out the door when she heard his voice.

"And how fares my lady?" he said.

She turned. "You are looking very . . . full of color," she said.

Will bowed.

"A peacock would pale next to you," she added.

"Pray, madam, do not mock me." He stared at her. "Your eyes are the color of your gown, two blue windows."

"Yes, my eyes, my gown, seem a subject of fools' flattery tonight."

"We are but subjects to them," he said, bowing again.

"Subjects to fools or to my eyes? It is the eyes of fools that weave false flattery. Must I be subjected to such foolishness? 'Two blue windows'? Come, now. You can do better than that." Katharine smiled.

There was something brazen about how he looked into her eyes, something prying and challenging and delightful. They had never been together at supper and certainly not at a banquet as glittering as this one. The music had begun, and the air was filled with the pleasant sounds of a violin, flute, lute and viol.

"What thought you of my last sonnet?"

"It spoke of torment. I could feel the wound in the heart. A lover crossed by his lover and his friend," Katharine said.

"If a man sees his mistress with another man, even his best friend, he assumes his mistress has forsaken him."

"All men assume this?"

"All men."

"You are an education," she said.

"I have started the new poem we spoke of in the orchard. Might you read it?" He leaned his broad frame close to Katharine, his voice low. "It is untried. The ink not yet dried," he said. "I pray you like it." He took her hand and kissed it.

It was the first time she'd felt his lips on her skin. His lips were warm.

Katharine took the pages he held out to her. She wished she weren't leaving the great hall when he came to her, for if she turned now and went back in, it would seem she was doing so to be with him.

"I thank you in advance," he said, bowing.

She nodded, not knowing exactly what to do. "Adieu," she said finally.

Will bowed again and left her at the door, returning to the hall, where music and laughter filled the air. The guests were drunk and loud, and the gentle notes could not do serious battle with the harsh sounds of revelry.

She climbed the steps to the old turret, then put Will's folded paper on the table next to her bed and stood at the window, staring into the last glow of light. There was something deliciously expectant about this time of night, in the gloaming, before darkness finally descended—a waiting. She sighed, unfastening the gold chain girdle at her waist that held a tiny Bible and then unpinning the lace coif that covered her hair. Molly came in and helped her out of her blue satin stomacher and blue and black brocade gown.

"You've come up early, my lady," said Molly as she unlaced Katharine's bodice. Molly had a face full of freckles, and orange ringlets that refused to stay captive beneath her cap.

"I am tired, Molly, bone-tired."

"And a bit sad that Sir Edward is not here to enjoy the revels?" asked Molly.

"I suppose that's why I left."

"Feels off the center of things without him presiding at the table."

"'Tis very true, Molly. The other day I heard horses and was convinced he'd returned. When I rushed to the window, it was Richard and some of his men. That was all."

By the time Katharine's black petticoat had fallen to the floor and the farthingale was undone, she had decided against reading Will's words. She would snuff her candle and go to sleep. When Molly let down her hair, Katharine told her she could go.

As Katharine ran the brush through her hair, she watched herself in the oval looking glass perched on the table. Many women her age dyed their hair blond like Saxon girls. Though she had strands of gray, she preferred her own chestnut color. If she could change her appearance, she would wish away the lines on her forehead and around her eyes and even the laugh lines from the dimples on her cheeks. She would wish for smooth where there were now furrows. When she was young, she'd wanted to erase the burn marks on her back and her neck. Even in the summer heat she used to wear high-necked, long-sleeved stomachers, but now she accepted those scars as who she was, as much a part of her as her eyes, her hair and her heart.

In her white cambric smock, she pulled up the linens and blankets in her bed and listened to the revelers below. They would all gather in a few hours for a light meal, if they were not too drunk. Katharine wouldn't go back down. The candle flame was unsteady. She would read Will's work in the morning, when the natural light would lift the quill marks off the page. She heard laughter and song. Then she leaned toward the candle with the snuffer but stopped. Snatching the paper off the table, she unfolded the pages and squinted into the candlelight.

In the orchard, two days before, Will had presented her with something new. They were not sonnets, but the beginnings of longer pieces— poems with stories. She had read each one, then spread them on the ground before her, and, like a mystic with tarot cards, pointed at a page and said, "This one." She liked the tension between Venus and Adonis. It drew her in.

And now he'd worked on that poem and written much. Three pages. Nine stanzas. She read and reread the verse, then she climbed down from her bed and went to her table; pushing aside combs, ivory hairpins, necklaces and clay pots filled with skin potions, she dipped a quill in ink and started to write on Will's pages, circling words, querying meaning and placement and feeling. Her lines stretched out at strange angles from his neat and careful handwriting, connecting her words to his. By the time she finished, the pages looked like maps, his words countries whose boundaries and allegiances had been called into question.

She opened the heavy door and listened. The musicians had stopped playing, but the house was not quiet. Footsteps, singing, the sound of iron pots in the scullery, a horse whinnying. The night was far from over. She grabbed her cloak. The way Will described his recent nights of writing it was unlikely he was carousing below. Candle in one hand,

Will's pages in another, she pulled the hood over her head and started out her door. Molly and several other chambermaids slept in a window-less room not far from Katharine's in the old Norman side of the house, partway down the circular stone steps. Katharine peeked in: Molly's cot was empty. Who was the freckle-cheeked, redheaded lass lying with to-night? One of the foreigners?

Katharine had to pass Ursula's rooms. Shrill squeals of delight stabbed the air. Had the parrot roused? Katharine knew it wasn't Ursula's hus-band in there. She hoped Richard—that dreary, dull-worded soul—was with someone: perhaps that was whose bed her maid was spreading her thighs in tonight. Katharine traveled down another back staircase, through the kitchens and the scullery. Praying she would pass unnoticed by those whose red hands still worked, she snuck outside. She had never done anything like this before. The moon was full: no wonder the great house stirred like an animal unable to sleep.

She would go to Will's lodgings, give him his marked-up verse and tell him: *There is vigor in thy words*. His launch into the Venus and Adonis tale wasn't perfect, yet his nimble mind seemed to stretch and to flex with each line. Will was working in a field where Ovid had plowed and Spenser had planted. Katharine had always loved Venus's passion, her undeterred fixation on the beautiful mortal Adonis. Katharine imagined Will on a stool, bent over a table, the candle burning until the sun crept up. *There is vigor in thy words* . . . she'd say, after she'd knocked on the door and he'd let her in.

With the night folding round her, she felt cold. She wore only her woolen cloak over her smock. When a gust of wind snuffed her candle out, she paid no heed; the glow from the moon was so strong and white it lit up everything it touched: stone and bark, flowers and grasses. The shadows on the ground outlined even the tiniest branches with magical precision and made a carpet under her feet.

While she gazed at the moon, a movement on the highest roof of the house caught her eye. She saw one dark figure, then another. They were passing a tankard back and forth. Were they squires from the Duc de Malois's party? Or were they Richard's or Harold's men? They were drunk, alternately swaying and clinging to each other. One man was narrow in limb, while the other was taller, broader. The small one held the tankard for the larger man, and then, when he pulled the pewter away, he leaned in close and kissed him.

Perhaps she was wrong. Perhaps it wasn't a kiss. Perhaps she'd woven one moment out of quite another. The man who had held the tankard to the other man's lips, the man whom she thought had then kissed the other man, climbed up on the old parapet and stood barely balancing, then he sat on the edge, his legs dangling over the side. The other man followed him. And there they both sat, high up on the ledge, the tankard still traveling back and forth until the last drop was drunk, and the vessel was hurled out into the night. The clanging sound of metal hitting stone echoed below.

They now had their arms around each other, and they started to kiss. The kiss was long and endless, and Katharine couldn't pull her eyes from them. One shift, one error, one twitch, would fling them both to the unyielding earth below. But they didn't stop. She couldn't move. She was afraid if she went forward to Will's room or retreated to her bed they would lose their fragile balance and tumble to their deaths. She didn't want to shout at them to come down, to be careful, not to test fate, for she worried the sound of her voice might throw off their risky embrace and cause them to slip. It was as if her watching ensured their safety, their survival. While she stood beneath them, a chill seeped under her cloak, and she started to tremble.

The one who seemed to lead, who was wiry, and even while drunk seemed nimble, got to his feet on the narrow bridge of stone and jumped back to the roof. Katharine sighed, waiting for the other to follow. But he didn't. And much to her dismay, the leader returned with yet another tankard, climbed back up and dangled his feet over the side as before, and they started the drinking again, the back-and-forth, the dance.

And then, as if they were thoroughly enjoying their reckless behavior, their taunting and tempting, they threw the second tankard to the cobblestones below and started kissing again. She could see in the moonlight that the one who had followed and not led now held the other's head in his hands and was kissing him on the eyes, the cheeks and the neck; then he moved his lips to the other man's lips, and though she couldn't actually see this she knew that his tongue had gone in deep. The spry one's arms were now around the other's waist. Was this some chivalric code of honor? Were they testing their loyalty to each other? If one made the wrong move, both would fall. Did the tension of their stance add to their need, their excitement? Or were they boys and not men yet, pushing each other to an extreme, a jousting of sorts, a competition, a game, daring, thoughtless, silly?

The kissing went on and on. She could not stand there under the milky moon any longer. She finally pulled herself away, her eyes tracking them as she withdrew. While she returned to the house, she was sure any minute she would hear the terrible sound of bodies hitting stone.

Upstairs in her bed, swaddled in wool and with skins layered on her feet, she realized she'd not glanced at Will's quarters, not even checked for light in the window, a candle flame at the desk. She still had his pages. But the poetry on them was different from what she'd witnessed on the parapet. Will had backed down, shied away from the risk and the drunken balancing. While there was indeed vigor in much of what he had writ, he was still too conscious of what he was trying to do. It was as if he held a looking glass to his face and admired his own reflection instead of losing himself and forgetting about his features altogether. The pressure in his passages fell off. She now saw this was not the stuff of shepherds and maidens. From the start, Venus had to wax wild and raw instead of controlled and contained.

Katharine would press Will to make what he penned feel as real as the passion and the danger she saw tonight.

She would find him in the morning.

In the darkness of her room, through her window, the same full moon cast its web on her. She felt caught, as she tossed and turned and worried about sleep.

IO

n Saint Crispin's Day, Katharine heard the men below dragging dead trees to the great lawn. There would be feasting, sport, bonfires and dancing. Will was to perform with a company of traveling players, tragedians he knew from London. According to legend, Saint Crispin was a Roman cordwainer, and in many villages the shoemakers still celebrated the holiday by choosing a king and, after crowning their patron saint, parading down the streets with music, torches and banners. Katharine wondered what sort of play the family and their guests would see tonight.

The lovely aroma of spiced wine and butter-crusted meat pies crept under the doors of the house. It was to be an earthy affair, with pigs, goats and deer roasted on spits. Tables were brought outside, while the children ran from the forest and threw branches, twigs and brush onto the growing woodpile. After the damage from the drought and an early frost, the weather had righted itself and warmed the fields enough for the wheat to be sown, so the day was in part to celebrate the October planting, and most of the servants were well into the cider and the ale—the kitchen maids having put pitchers out soon after the sun came up.

Grace and Isabel caught up with Katharine at the door and they walked out into the flood of sunshine together. There was not a cloud in the sky.

Lady Planchet, Matilda's eldest daughter, Grace, had arrived from Yorkshire in the night with her family. She had a twinkle in her eye like her father and was tall like her mother, indeed taller than her husband Sir Hugh Planchet, whose short stature was made up for by his noble lineage—his ancestor was Ilbert de Lacy of the famous Pontefract Castle, where Richard II perished. Grace was thirty years old and had given birth to five children, but only three remained, and those three were all under the age of seven and very spirited.

"My dear Kate, you look radiant," said Grace as she kissed Katharine. "I have faded and gotten fat and you have not!"

"You have not faded!" said Katharine. "And you are always radiant!"

"But I have gotten fat!" countered Grace.

"Kate, you've done something different," Isabel said. She stopped and examined Katharine. "Your hair."

"The same," said Katharine.

"Did you powder your face? Paint your cheeks?" pushed Isabel.

"No. My cheeks are still stained from the summer sun. 'More white and red than doves and roses are.'"

"'Doves and roses'?" asked Grace.

"'Tis verse," said Katharine. It was a line from Will's new poem describing Adonis.

"A new gown!" Isabel exclaimed.

"My first in years. Your brother sent the fabric from Italy to your mother, and she never used it. Your mother was very generous, and I am most grateful."

"The embroidery . . . in gold," said Isabel.

"Ned does not buy on the cheap," Katharine said. The gown had a saffron bodice, burnished gold silk peeking through the slashes, and marigold trim.

"It matches the luster of your hair," said Isabel. "Look how the sun lights you up."

"'Her garments all were wrought of beaten gold . . . and all her steed with tinsell trappings shone,'" Katharine recited from *The Faerie Queene* the description of the lady pursued by a brute in the forest. "I seem to have mislaid my milk-white palfrey, alas," she added.

"What tongues are you speaking in?" said Grace.

"Edmund Spenser," said Katharine.

"I've heard of this Spenser," said Isabel.

"You should read him."

"Aye, after I read the twenty books you and Father assigned me this year." Isabel put her hand to Katharine's cheek. "There is a glow to you this afternoon, Cousin Kate. You positively shimmer and look no older than I."

Katharine laughed. "And you, my dear Isabel, positively shine and are much wiser than I."

"And what will you wear tonight? For the dancing? If you are teasing us with the new frock now?"

"Tonight? This again, I suppose. For I already wore my blue. And my green is old and out of fashion."

Sir Hugh joined the ladies and tried to bow, making a spirited attempt to put his right leg forward, though his gout made him wince. He still managed to bend at the hips, but he could only sweep one arm open, as the other was pressing on his ivory-handled cane.

"You are a vision, my sweet Katharine. You are our harvest queen," said Sir Hugh gallantly, and offered his hand. Katharine placed hers lightly on top of his, and he kissed her fingers. Hugh had always thought himself quite dashing; Katharine imagined his present aches and pains did not blend well with his mannered ways. He had, poor soul, after all these years, lost his gloss.

Lord and Lady Strange were attending the revels today. They flanked Matilda and the Duc de Malois at the head of the table. Ferdinando Stanley, Lord Strange, who was in direct line to the crown of England, would inherit his father's title when the time came and become the Fifth Earl of Derby. The lord and lady had three young daughters, and the family was in London at court part of every year. The queen, who was not known for finding warmth in her heart for the mistresses or wives of her favored, was known to like Alice as much as she liked Ferdinando—and that was no small feat.

Alice, Lady Strange, was a year younger than Katharine, and her beauty was much remarked upon in Lancashire and throughout the whole of England. Ferdinando was also beautiful, and both were patrons of poets and playwrights. Lord Strange supported what had been a troupe of acrobats and tumblers but had since turned into a company of players, as was the fashion now. Several times a year, Sir Edward's family was invited to the Stanley seats at Ormskirk or Merseyside, and several times a year, the family invited the Stanley clan to Lufanwal Hall.

Katharine hadn't seen Will since the banquet two days before. She'd sent Molly with the marked-up pages of his poetry. As the family and guests settled into their chairs and benches, Katharine scanned the crowd all the way to the maids' and servants' tables for the tutor, but he wasn't there.

The drinking had started early, and the air was thick with merriment. Ursula did not vomit on the table this time, but she sat in the duke's lap at the end of the meal. The duke's large hand held his cousin Ursula's tiny waist, yet his eyes were locked on Sophie. Katharine realized how much she relied on Sir Edward, that even at grand feasts and entertainments he always included her, sitting her next to him or walking her to each new guest. For the first time in ages, Katharine did not know her place. She thought she had outgrown these worries, but with Edward gone, and the festivities long, she felt a gloom descending.

She stood and smiled at the elderly Frenchman to her left and the young Nicholas Barlow to her right. She was not sure either of them noticed; the old man was dozing, and the young man was speaking French to one of the duke's men across the table. The mulled wine had made Katharine's limbs weak. She made her way to the library to read *The Faerie Queene*, which Will had returned to her. Still dressed in her golden gown, Katharine picked up her skirts and sat back in her favorite chair. She could hear the cheers and the clapping from the tilt field. The sun was dropping behind the trees, long shadows stretching across the lawn. The branches for the bonfire were almost as high as the library window.

Katharine turned the pages to "Chastity," the legend of the female knight Britomart, which she'd been reading before she lent the book to Will. She loved that Spenser put such a strong and valiant woman in disguise. When Katharine reached the stanzas where Britomart and the Redcrosse Knight enter Malecasta's Castle Ioyeous, she found writing on the pages of Sir Edward's new book. Words like *lust* and *unrequited* adorned the margins now, and *Kit's Adonis rose-cheeked* and *desire* and *death*. Katharine saw that Spenser's canto possibly influenced Will's new direction, for in a chamber in Malecasta's castle hangs a tapestry with the tale of Venus and Adonis woven into it. Spenser's Venus entices and woos the stunning Adonis, each line brimming with sensual desires. And as in Ovid's story, Adonis pays no heed to Venus's warning, and it is with the boar that he finally fulfills his fate, "for who can shun the chaunce that dest'ny doth ordaine?"

After the sun dropped to the west, the sky gleamed opal, and the crackling of the kindling and the first slender spirals of smoke announced the bonfire had been lit. The fire would be bright tonight, the flames high. Katharine closed her eyes and let her head fall back on the chair. She thought of Will and how his bright eyes seemed to shift shades of green.

The bells were ringing. On her way down to dinner, Katharine stopped and ran her fingers over the rectangular lid of the virginals in the gallery. She still carried the key next to the small Bible on her girdle chain but had not used it in years. Wiping the dust from the fine wood, she unlocked the case. Sir Edward had given her this set as a wedding present; they were newly crafted and brought over on a boat from Flanders. The master instrument-maker Hans Ruckers had adorned his beautiful box with ivory, mother-of-pearl and marble inlay, and the soundboard was painted with flowers, fruits, birds and caterpillars. The scene painted on the inside of the lid was of a hunt with two manor houses in the distance and a crowd of dogs, and men on horses and on foot in the foreground. The box had been closed for so many years that the colors still gleamed; indeed, the painted sky looked as if it were lit from behind and glowed with a rose-gold hue.

There was another pair of virginals in the balcony in the great hall where the musical instruments were kept, but they were not nearly as fine as these. As a child, Katharine had spent hours learning the notes and playing the bone keys; those moments had soothed her soul, helped heal her heart perhaps more than prayer.

A servant rounded the corner, bobbed his head in her direction, touched his fire stick to the torch on the wall and scurried away.

The swell of noise—voices, dogs barking, laughter and the notes of a lute—rose from the garden and the great hall, but when Katharine placed her hands on the keys, she felt an ancient tranquillity within. Her fingers used to roam the keys, nimble tumblers at a fair, the jacks plucking the strings, but at this moment she did not dare strike a key; she stood in the dim gallery with her fingers resting on the keys, and then without warning her eyes filled with tears.

Katharine slowly and carefully put the lid down. She had lost two children: one months before birth but the other she'd carried full term, and two days after birth the little girl had died. Katharine remembered the weight of the wood as she shut the tiny coffin. Was that the last time she had played music? She had brought the virginals with her when she returned to the hall after her husband died, but she had never played again; she had left the pair in the gallery, figuring someone would surely play them, but no one ever had. Over the years, she had taken to averting her eyes from the instrument when she passed.

She heard voices.

"I crave your pardon, my lady." It was Mr. Smythson, the master mason.

Wiping her eyes, she tried to gather her senses. Mr. Smythson re-introduced himself and then turned and introduced the tall young man next to him.

"My son, John," he said.

John bowed. Mr. Smythson and his son were images of each other—not mirror images but reflections. John was almost as tall as his father, yet his features were finer and his hair was clipped and neat. He was a smooth-faced youth no older than Joan or Isabel.

"Are you here for the revels, Mr. Smythson?" Katharine asked.

"Revels? Oh, no, madam, we are here to map the additions to the house."

"On such a holiday as this?"

"We take few holidays," Mr. Smythson said.

"You'll not stay for a meal, at least?"

"No, many thanks, most gracious lady, but no. We'll be on our way."

Mr. Smythson did not move, and Katharine waited. He seemed to be on the verge of saying something else, but no words issued forth. Finally, his son came to his aid.

"Good even, my lady," John said, and bowed.

Mr. Smythson hastily said good-bye and bowed, and they took their leave. How fortunate Mr. Smythson was, Katharine thought, to have such a well-mannered and attentive son to work with him.

The orange flames of the bonfire leapt and charged at the black sky. Saint Crispin's Day was in full glory. Katharine was tired of hatching conversations with the French and tired of the overabundant tables of steaming meats, cheeses, bread, ale, sack and wine, and if Will had not been set to perform, she would have fled to her chamber before the dancing began. As a child she had seen moralities performed at the fine house of their neighbors the Heskeths. She remembered the players with beards freshly trimmed, wearing their master's livery. Last year she had seen a wonderful performance by Lord Strange's own company of players. But Sir Edward had never had the inclination to employ permanent players at Lufanwal. Will's double role, of schoolmaster and player, was new. She wished her uncle were standing next to her in the great hall so he could also watch tonight's interlude.

The servants snuffed the torches, one by one, along the walls. One torch at the end of the great hall remained lit. Will entered through the door from the west parlor. The servants stood in allegiance, sentries, their long snuffers held at their sides like spears.

"I come before you this eventide not as Saint Crispin," he said.

Indeed, Will looked not the role of a shoemaker—no leather smock tied round his neck. Instead he wore a simple tunic and breeches with a mantle of mail plucked from the family's cabinets.

"But as Henry the Fifth," he continued, "on this very day in 1415, when our heroic king found victory in the fields of Agincourt."

While Master Shakespeare rattled on about how the brave King Henry and his men overpowered the French so many years ago, Katharine felt the room shift—but not settle. Richard scowled, Harold's jaw hardened and Matilda stared straight ahead. Instead of celebrating the martyred Saint Crispin's defense of Christianity, instead of commemorating the duke's valiant battle against the anti-Catholic Huguenots at Ivry, Will had seized this moment to memorialize France's dreadful loss to the English.

He likes to gamble, Katharine thought.

"O for a Muse of fire, that would ascend." Will began his performance. "The brightest heaven of invention . . ."

A dog started barking and Harold reached down and smacked it with the back of his hand. The poor hound staggered from the blow into silence.

Will directed their imagination to the battle at Agincourt. With fine words, he painted the muddy field, the French with fresh horses and full bellies, the beleaguered English foot soldiers, the French outnumbering the English.

Where were Will's fellow players? Why was he performing alone? The family was now a hive of nerves, afraid their London player-poet would offend. And indeed Katharine wondered at the current complexion of their French friends. Most of the duke's men did not understand English, but they understood the word *Agincourt*, and perhaps they could interpret the intensity of Will's performance. Were they imagining the knights and noblemen, their relatives, bloodied and slain on the fields that day?

Will paused. The family and their guests waited, expecting perhaps another actor or two would join him. But he remained alone when he commenced his speech. "If we are mark'd to die . . ." His voice took on a kingly timbre—commanding, earnest, humble and brave. The eyes and voice that beckoned to Katharine alone in the library or under the apple tree now gathered up everyone in the great hall, harvested them. Even the smallest serving boy stopped his business and looked.

Will was not a minute into his rallying call, when he started to walk around the hall and speak to one person after another, even the women, as though they were dressed and armed for battle. To Matilda, he proffered, "If it be a sin to covet honor, I am the most offending soul alive."

Stopping before Richard, he continued, "That he which hath no stomach to this fight, let him depart." Will seemed to grow taller when he faced Lord Strange and said, "He that shall live this day, and see old age, will yearly on the vigil feast his neighbors. Then will he strip his sleeve and show his scars, and say, 'These wounds I had on Crispin's day.'"

Those listening to Will's speech began as his subjects but were soon his soldiers, too. When Will came to Katharine with the words, "This story shall the good man teach his son," he lingered in front of her for a moment, and she held her breath. Then he moved on to Harold: "But we in it shall be remembered. We few, we happy few, we band of brothers." He passed by Ursula, who fanned herself. "And gentlemen in England now-a-bed . . ." He walked a few more paces, finally stopping in front of the duke, who had laughed with him at the banquet. Will's voice rang through the hall: "Shall think themselves accurs'd they were not here, and hold their manhoods cheap whiles any speaks that fought with us upon Saint Crispin's day!"

The duke stood and shouted something, and like an arrow, fear launched through the air. Katharine worried that the duke's party, many of whom had fought by his side and seen their brothers slain at Ivry last year, would rise up and start a brawl.

The duke swung his arm at Will. A few of the ladies gasped. But at the instant of impact, instead of assault the duke clasped Will on the shoulders, not with violence but with affection, as though they were brothers; he was, evidently, taken with Will's words, not angered by them. He said something about honor in French, and then all his men chimed in and lifted their tankards, while Will bowed low before the duke. The duke's men surrounded Will as if he were one of theirs. The duke, his arm still around the poet-player, called for a servant to bring Will wine and shouted, *"Salut!"* before drinking his own down in one gulp.

Katharine had never witnessed anything like this before. The family now gathered round Will, thanking him. Katharine was not familiar with the play and wondered from what talented playwright he had borrowed his speech. Will had been daring, both in the role he chose and that he performed alone, for all eyes had been on him only, no other players to distract or to defuse. The whereabouts of the traveling troupe still remained a mystery.

Katharine, who was not in awe of many, had always been in awe of Lord and Lady Strange. Ferdinando was considered a genius; Katharine had been a bit in love with him and used to dream that Ferdinando fell in love with her, despite her meager dowry, and asked her to marry him. But Ferdinando had made a sensible and smart choice in Alice, who, though contained, if not aloof, was genuine and certainly seemed like she had a good heart, and it was clear that Ferdinando and Alice were very much in love.

Lord and Lady Strange glided into their surroundings and remained close to each other throughout their stay. Katharine studied Alice on the rare occasions they were in the same room: she was petite with bone-white skin and large eyes that combined vulnerability with intelligence. Alice, just past the age of thirty, had naturally blond hair, gently arched eyebrows and delicate features that were gracefully aligned. Katharine marveled at the pair's easy elegance—there was nothing forced about their carriage or their countenance; they simply had the good fortune to be of highborn blood.

So it was with interest that Katharine watched how Will spoke to Lord Ferdinando, but kept his back to Lady Alice, in a stance that bespoke uncouth manners. Lord Ferdinando and Lady Alice had changed from their afternoon attire into garments of richer cloth and tighter fit for the evening's entertainment. Alice's lace ruff fanned out like flower petals, framing her lovely face, neck and chest. She wore rubies and gold around her neck, a longer chain of pearls knotted above her bodice. Ferdinando's full head of hair stopped above his forehead with a curl. He wore no ruff tonight, but a lace collar intricately stitched with pearls.

There was something of a taunt in the way Will ignored Alice. She glittered in a way that was impossible to miss, but Will's broad shoulders squarely blocked any contact. If Katharine were Alice, she would be perplexed and annoyed and intrigued all at the same time. Katharine had heretofore been impressed by Alice's splendor, but now she found herself a bit jealous of Alice's tiny white wrists and pale blue eyes.

Katharine approached Alice, and though they had seen each other that afternoon, they exchanged greetings again. Will's back was to Katharine now, too, and he was still conversing with the lord, though Alice clearly hoped to make his acquaintance. Finally Katharine tapped Will on the shoulder. He pivoted on his heel, his eyes sweeping past Katharine and landing directly on Alice's sweet face, as though he had known she was there all along but had been waiting for the right moment to make his entrance.

"Lady Alice Strange," Katharine said, "this is William Shakespeare."

Will gazed at Alice for a beat longer, then took her hand and kissed it.

"We so enjoyed your Henry and thought it a wonderful and courageous tribute to Saint Crispin," Alice said.

"Gramercy, my lady," he said, now glancing at Katharine and smiling. There was method to Will's attention, ambition to it.

"This Henry is by whose pen?" asked Lady Alice.

"My own, my lady, something I wrote a year ago and unearthed for this occasion."

"Your Henry felt alive, a person, not a deity, and that is good. You are a poet?"

"Yes, and I've been in London working as a player."

"And you pen plays?" she continued.

"I have pieces but nothing whole yet," he said.

Will had never spoken to Katharine of his plays, only of his poetry.

"What are you writing now?" asked Lady Alice.

"Sonnets and a longer poem. And there are my scraps for the theater that I will soon, God willing, stitch together into scenes, and then stitch those scenes into acts, and then stitch those acts into . . . plays."

"You have much needlework in your future," Alice said.

Lord Strange, who had been talking to Harold, now returned to them. "We have a talent here," he said.

"Gramercy, my lord." Will smiled and bowed. The music started. "Pardon, I must remove this rusty mail. It must weigh fifty stone."

"We trust you will join in the dancing," said Alice.

"They must teach dancing at those London theaters," said Ferdinando.

"I've learned a few steps," Will replied, smiling. "I'll change out of Henry and come back William." He bowed once more and took his leave.

"They say he's up from Warwickshire," said Ferdinando when Will was gone.

"His family is from Stratford," said Katharine. "And he's been in London."

"What the devil is he doing out here?" said Ferdinando.

"He was hired to help with the schooling of the boys."

"Not sure I would trade London for Lancashire if I were a lad in the theater."

"He is writing poetry," Katharine said.

"Is he a poet or a playwright?" asked Alice.

"He's one of those that does both, my dear," said Ferdinando.

"Have you heard of him?" she asked her husband.

Lord Strange shook his head. "No, but there are so many of these types in London now. And half of them have never been to university. How things change. Katharine, how are you, my dear?"

"I am well, thank you, my lord."

"You look more than well. You put the sun and the moon to shame," he said.

Alice nodded in agreement, adding, "I always wanted dimples, they enhance a smile so. And you are rich with them."

"You make me blush. 'Tis my legacy. My father had the same, as did his father, and his before him."

"I used to sit hours with my fingers pressing on my chin, hoping I could sculpt my flesh into a cleft, but as you see, to no avail."

Ferdinando held his wife's chin in his hand and then leaned down and kissed it. "You have a beautiful chin, my dear." Then he looked up at Katharine. "Can we not find you a husband, Katharine?"

"Ferdinando . . ." said Alice.

"Lady Alice, this question neither angers me nor wearies me," said Katharine.

"You are the virgin queen of Lancaster," said Ferdinando.

"I have been married, my lord, and I am no queen."

"Our queen has been married many a time, methinks, though no wedding band rings her finger. We must find a man suitable for you."

"Many have tried, my lord, to find me such a thing."

"Are we 'things,' then, we husbands?"

Katharine laughed. "I suppose not, for 'to husband' is an action . . . men husband the land . . ."

"You talk, you walk, you fight in wars, but there are worlds you can never enter," said Alice.

"I enter yours every once in a while."

"Ferdinando!" Alice smiled at him.

"I wonder why 'to wife' is not in use," said Katharine.

"Because 'to wife' would mean to take, to steal, not to cultivate or to carry out," said Lord Strange.

"Oh, dear, Adam and Eve again," said Katharine.

"I agree with Katharine," added Alice. "You things mention that rib at every opportunity. How we tire of it."

"I'll lose it, then," said Ferdinando.

"You lost it thousands of years past," said Alice.

Ferdinando smiled at his wife. Their eyes met, and Katharine marveled at their playful understanding.

"Are you reading, Katharine?" Ferdinando asked.

"I always read," she answered.

"Well, before the night is through you must oblige me a list of new books, those by Master Shakespeare's peers. Perhaps we'll read something of his someday. Ah, they have started to dance. Alice, the Duc de Malois has already asked to partner with you for the first pavane. Katharine, will you join me?"

"It would be a pleasure, my lord."

The musicians assembled with recorder, cittern, lute and tabor in the balcony at the end of the great hall. The stately sound of a pavane—a dance named after the strut of a peacock—encouraged couples to form a procession; the ladies' right hand lightly resting on the gentlemen's left, their eyes looking straight ahead, they circled the center of the hall—step, pause, step, pause, step, step, step, pause—in time to the music. The couples split from the group, spun round, then formed a circle again.

Katharine and Lord Ferdinando tilted their heads toward each other but kept their gazes forward as they spoke of Spenser and Sidney, and Katharine promised to send the lord her copy of Sidney's sonnets. They moved in a large circle, and as they were coming back to where they had started, Katharine noticed Will. He stood off to the side, watching, an amused glint in his eye. He was clad in a tight doublet of black with orange-gold silk showing through so many small slashes that the fabric shone like the scales of a carp. He wore no ruff, but, like Lord Ferdinando, sported a large collar, with an undercollar of the same orange-gold silk.

When Katharine passed Will, she saw he was watching her. She shot her eyes directly forward and continued on.

Katharine didn't realize she had flinched until Lord Ferdinando asked, "Are you all right, my dear?"

"Oh, yes," she murmured. She had stepped out of the beat. "I beg your pardon."

"Our player is well plumed tonight." Lord Ferdinando nodded toward Will as they passed. "Methinks he gets ahead of himself, as king and now as prince." He chuckled.

The pavane came to an end, and the young French nobleman with whom Katharine sat at the banquet asked her for the next dance. She nodded and smiled, and he bowed, took her hand and led her to the center of the great hall, just as the first lively notes of a galliard played. He was a good dancer, and when they were apart and it was his turn to step, he leapt in the air with a delightful verve. Katharine laughed. He had the same mirth with his movements that he had when he spoke to her in his scraggly English. His humor made her smile, and her own steps became spirited, as they hopped, skipped and twirled to the music.

"You dance intelligent," he said when they were together.

"Gramercy," she replied as she danced around him.

"You dance with much clever," he said.

She laughed. "You are very kind. And you dance with much wit."

"*Merci*. You dance with beauty," he said, then stepped back and spun around and kicked his left foot high in the air and then his right; his friends hooted and called to him and soon the whole room was watching them. Katharine was having fun, so she did not care. She had always loved to dance. She could lose herself. The next dance was Ursula's much-anticipated courante. The duke had taken Ursula's hand, so she had her wish. Lord and Lady Strange were together. Katharine's Frenchman bowed to her, and was reaching for her hand, when Will stepped in front of him and took it. Will turned and smiled at the Frenchman, who bowed again and withdrew.

Courante meant "running" in French, but the dance, by the time it arrived at the English court, was slow and subdued. Katharine's heart was beating fast from the energetic galliard. Will held her hand and they moved forward. He had not even asked her to dance—perhaps he was afraid she would say no. She supposed she was the only woman in the room, besides Sophie the duke's mistress, who would partner with a glover's son.

"How did I do?" he asked. "My little speech?" he said as they stepped back.

"'Twas well said. All those who watched were . . ." She paused.

"Were?"

"Convinced," she said as they dropped their hands and faced each other.

"You look beautiful," he said.

She said nothing.

"'I noot were she be woman or goddess, / But Venus is it smoothly, as I gesse.'"

"Chaucer," she said.

"'Tis the anniversary of his death today," he said.

"You succeeded with your audience tonight. No need for you to try to succeed with me."

"Thou art rose-cheeked," he persisted.

"Like Adonis?" Katharine said, turning. "I found marks upon the margins of Sir Edward's *Faerie Queene*. 'Twas not your book to ruin!" she said.

"A thousand pardons for my careless tracks. Thou art rose-cheeked just the same."

"I have been dancing," she said.

"So I have seen."

They glided forward and then backward.

"How was it that you performed without the company of players?" she asked.

"Never made it to the hall, waylaid a half day's ride from here, something with a horse or a cart."

"More likely you paid them to stay away so you could shine."

He chuckled. "I saw what you thought of my 'Venus and Adonis.' I could scarce read my words for all your circles, X's and lines."

"I marked when I saw fit."

"God-a-mercy. I have heeded all your marks and will send you what I've done," he said.

"You look a different man than when you were Henry," she said. "More borrowed flaunts?"

"No. A friend in London sent me to his tailor, a bonus for work I did."

"A good friend, to assume such a generous reckoning."

"Yes, yes, he is."

Lord and Lady Strange passed by. Will nodded and smiled at them but then brought his gaze back to Katharine.

"Will you dance the next dance with me?" he asked.

"Aye," she said.

There was scarce a pause before the quick pulse of the volta started: the notes themselves seemed to run and to leap in the air. This dance demanded that partners lock eyes, no matter if they were stepping or twirling or jumping. Katharine fixed her gaze on the pattern of black silk stitching along the edges of Will's orange silk collar, but Will reached over and lifted her chin with his finger so their eyes met.

They began with a few steps of a galliard, but then with the cadenza Will stood so close to Katharine that their hips were touching. He put his right hand on her waist and pulled her even closer. The sweet smell of herbs rose from his skin. He placed a hand firmly below her bosom on the stiff busk of her bodice, as was the custom. There were some parts of England where, in spite of the fact that Queen Elizabeth herself had danced it with Robert Dudley, the Earl of Leicester, the volta was forbidden. The Puritans did not approve of the close embrace.

Will slid his knee under her so that she was almost sitting on his thigh; then, with one swift movement, while she held his shoulder with one hand and her skirts with the other, he launched her into the air. He was stronger than she had imagined, and at the same time his limbs were surprisingly graceful. Where had the glover's son picked up the cadence that on him appeared so natural but with others took years of instruction by a dancing master and even then often looked awkward?

Instead of bringing Katharine down quickly, he lost pace with the music and held her close to him for a beat longer than seemed proper. The rules of the dance were that after the leap in the air, the woman was let down with a bounce, and the couple sprang apart, but Will slid Katharine down on his chest slowly so that at one point, before her feet hit the floor, their lips were touching. Then he set her gently on the floor and smiled.

Katharine did not smile. She was stunned—as much by his presumption as by how thrilled it made her feel. As they stepped and hopped and turned, she continued to look at him without smiling and he continued to smile. Was this a game for him? Shuttlecock or Barley Break? The next time he positioned his body to propel her into the air, his fingers grazed her skin above her busk before he placed his hand there.

"Thou art my sonnet tonight," he said as he brought her down after the leap. He lingered again, but this time pulled his head back, so their lips did not touch.

II

hen Katharine awoke the next morning, she recalled strange and vivid dreams. In one, several of her teeth were loose. In another, she was riding a wild horse. Then she was being chased: by whom or what, she did not know. Molly had rekindled the fire by the time Katharine rose from her bed. She was still in her emerald velvet dressing gown when Molly brought her a package.

"From?" Katharine asked.

"Him, mistress."

"Him?"

"Will Shakespeare."

"Ah, gramercy, Molly." When Katharine took the package she realized it was wrapped in pages of the sonnets they had worked on, with his writing and then hers.

Molly pulled back the sand-colored curtains and the sun came streaming in. "Miss Ursula was in her new gown, and they say she did dance with the duke," Molly said. "And she looked beautiful, her waist tiny and her yellow hair all glittery. I helped put the stones in her hair."

"Ursula looked splendid," Katharine agreed.

"And Master Shakespeare," continued Molly as she poured water from the ewer into the bowl. She dipped a cloth in the water and handed it to Katharine for her face. "No one expected he'd play King Henry. They say he played him so good that they didna see Master Shakespeare there at all, but saw a king. He had writ what he spoke. They say the words were so fine, miss, and his stature so proud, and the telling to his soldiers that to catch a wound in battle would be an honor, and to die in the field an honor, too, and that men who werena there would be in shame." Molly eyed the package on Katharine's lap. "They're off to a hunt today."

"I heard the horns in my sleep," said Katharine. Perhaps it was a wild boar that had chased her in her dream—his large sharp curved tusks going for her heart.

"Word's already come back they've killed a stag," Molly said, "and the duke slit the belly himself."

"I'm sure he did, Molly." Katharine wondered anew what business brought the duke to the hall, for a man of that magnitude would never come purely for pleasure.

"Can't hear the dogs na'more, so they must be far. They say the duke won't rest till he's got a boar."

"Did any ladies of the house go?"

"No, my lady, since it's boar they're after, the men thought it too wide with danger. He's gone, my lady."

"Who?"

"Master Shakespeare."

"On the hunt?"

"No. He took off on a horse before the hunt went out, before the light tipped the treetops."

"Oh." Katharine felt her heart shrink.

"He sits a horse passing fine. I heard he's a passing fine dancer, too."

"He is a good dancer," Katharine said. "Thank you, Molly. You can go."

While Molly hung Katharine's petticoat next to the fire, she asked, "Some broth from the kitchens, my lady?"

"No, gramercy. I have a question to ask you before you go. Would you like to learn how to read and to write, so you can read Master Shakespeare's verse before you deliver it to me?"

"I'd love to read a lot o' things, and that, too."

"Well then, I will teach you. We'll start tomorrow. And best not let your tongue wag till you've mastered the words. Then when you have, you can surprise everyone and say you taught yourself."

"Aye, my lady. I can't imagine what it's like."

"A whole new world, Molly. Many worlds. It will change you."

"I'm ready to be changed."

"I know you are. You go along your way and do your chores quickly tomorrow, for after dinner, we start."

Molly curtsied. "Gramercy."

Katharine smiled and nodded. After Molly left, Katharine picked up the package and felt it: soft at one end, stiff at the other. She untied the string and found within the creases of Will's pages the most beautiful gloves she had ever seen. They were made of white doeskin, the fingers long and slim and pointed at the tips. Folded inside each glove were new pages. Katharine slid the gloves on her hands. The soft leather flared at the wrists. The wide gauntlet was embroidered with silk and metal thread, and edged with silver-gilt lace, shiny flecks of metal and tiny pearls that trembled when she moved. The glove-maker had rendered the gauntlet a piece of art; a male peacock was emblazoned in the foreground of each glove, with a sweeping tail of purple, blue, green and gray thread.

Katharine carefully took off the gloves and unfolded Will's new pages. He had revised the beginning of his poem. He had followed Katharine's advice and steered the sentiment further, moved away from Ovid and Spenser, made discord where there had only been tension. Now Adonis loved to hunt but scorned love, while lovesick Venus was set on wooing him. Katharine took the black quill Will had given to her, dipped it into the inkhorn, crossed out two lines and wrote: *Let Venus be the huntress, but not for stag or doe or boar. Let kisses be her prey. You say here that Adonis is "more lovely than a man," describe how that is so. If he is "rose-cheek'd," is he then like a flower?*

She read on. The poem was better, certainly, and now began with a boldness that drew the eyes from one stanza to the next. The day passed with Katharine in her dressing gown at her table marking Will's pages. She put down her quill as the sun dropped behind the trees, and the clamor of horses and hounds returning from the hunt clattered upon the stones.

The dance called the volta was named after the Italian term for "the turn" or "turning." The turn at the end of a sonnet, which signified the jump or shift in the direction of the emotions or thought, was also called the volta, and that was just what had happened to Katharine when Will set her down after her last leap in the air. Something had shifted. The volta had vanquished boundaries, and as surprising as Will's lips on her hand at the banquet, he had opened his body to her at the dance and brought her to him, his lips on her lips. She'd let him take her hand after the last chord and lead her. As they walked from the center of the room Katharine had turned toward him, and without saying a word he had drawn her to him again, right there in the crowd, and held on to her, his lips light on her neck. Perchance no one saw it. When she had left him at the door, left the room with all the music, the torches and the people, her body had felt an instrument, with strings so taut that each step was a pluck, a vibration, a sound.

But now he had left, Molly said, before the sun rose, before the hunting party had gathered in the mist. He had gone. But where? And why hadn't he spoken to her of his leaving? Katharine sat, still in her dressing gown, her candle lit now. The sounds rose from below of tired revelers drinking after their hunt. She was unable to move, yet filled to her brim.

Will was like a gem, sparkling and bright, but on someone else's finger. It was not that he was married, because he rarely spoke of his wife or his children. He had, until last night, held part of himself away, aloft, and now she worried that when she saw him again, he would return to that island. He was never remote with his words, but his body told a different story, one that confused and intrigued her. She wondered if his wife felt that, too, if that was why she didn't mind that he had spent the last years away from Stratford, in London, working in a theater, and now up here in Lancashire, at Lufanwal. Perhaps even when he was at home, part of him was in exile.

Will had written to her at the bottom edge of his last page: *Gentle Kate, I am off to weather business in London. I will miss you. Will.*

The "I will miss you" pushed at her heart. She read over those four words and remembered how his hands felt when he pulled her to him after the dance. For that brief moment when he'd embraced her, he'd been her glove. Their bodies had fit together perfectly. He was so quick, so sure, so deliberate, his lips grazing her neck in the middle of the crowded floor. Katharine had thought: This is the beginning. She sat back in her chair by the fire and gazed into the inner light of the flames. The image of Will's slender fingers wrapped around a black quill came to her—the fine hairs on the back of his hand, his fingernails clipped and clean. She would miss him, too.

She had not eaten all day. The smell of braised meat from the hunt rose from the kitchens. The duke was to leave before All Souls' Day. The house would return to its normal rhythms, though in truth the rhythms had not been normal since Sir Edward had left. Katharine supposed she should show herself for the meal below. It would be improper not to say good-bye to the lively band of Frenchmen.

She wore her old green gown down to supper. The noise in the great hall was loud and raucous, an unwelcome change to her day, which had been delicious in its solitude. She sat with the younger folk, for she had grown tired of the duke and his party. Their presence seemed one long performance, though she was unsure who was the audience and who the players.

Katharine learned from her tablemates that the hunt was a success— they had caught two stags and a boar—but they had sidestepped disaster. The dogs were running crazy as the hunting party cornered a boar. The boar, startled by the dogs' frenzy, had charged at the duke, who lost his footing and fell. Henry had stepped in front of the duke and run his sword through the boar's neck.

"But the duke was swift and back on his feet in no time," said Henry, "and he dealt the beast the final blow."

"They say Henry was like a soldier in battle," Isabel chimed in. "They say he was so calm and brave."

"Oh, our dear Henry, how you've grown," exclaimed Katharine.

"'Twas nothing," Henry said.

"Henry, you saved the duke's life!" cried Isabel.

"And he thanked me for it," added Henry.

"And thank goodness the duke was able to kill off the beast. At least he kept his honor even if he lost his footing," Katharine said.

Isabel leaned toward Katharine. "Did you enjoy your dance last night?"

"Which dance?" Katharine said.

"The dance with the king!"

"The king?"

"The man who played the king? The player who played King Henry." Isabel looked at Kate. "That king married a Kate, and she was his queen."

"She was French. And this king has a wife."

"I've heard things."

"What sort of things?"

"Talk from the scullery . . ."

"Ah, there's a deep well of gossip."

"But you were only having fun, weren't you, Kate?"

Katharine forced a smile.

"He is handsome," Isabel continued. "Though, in sooth, there's something shiny about Master Shakespeare's eyes and his words—a glint like a shilling that on the ground attracts."

Katharine wanted to say: *You do not know him the way I know him. He is a man of substance, for how could a poet write such words without feeling them?* But she kept her mouth shut.

Henry stood up from the table. He seemed to have sprouted an inch since he'd sat down to supper. His mother, Mary, came to his side, put her hands on his shoulders—she was shorter than he was now and had to reach—and said, "You have made me very proud, my son. The duke has spoken highly of your actions today, and we may rejoice with God and thank Him for your safety and for the duke's. That which we call fortune is nothing but the hand of God, working by and for causes we know not. By God's grace my hands are upon your sturdy shoulders."

"It was you who made them sturdy, Mother," said Henry.

Out of any other mouth this sentence would have sounded like idle flattery, but Henry meant what he said. He looked down at his mother with a sweet smile. She pulled him to her and he dutifully held on to her in an awkward embrace. Henry had grown into a strong young man, but he hadn't arrived at the knowledge of what to do with women—of any age, even his mother.

"Go to your new French friends," said Mary. "And let them bathe you in well-deserved glory."

Amidst the flickering candles, in a field of glittery silks and plush velvets, Mary stood out in her somber navy wool gown, with a short white ruff and a white cap pinned over her graying hair. Tonight, Katharine wondered if perhaps Mary had actually converted to the Protestant cause. Something about her words echoed the tongue of a preacher, a new directness to the way she invoked God.

"I have news," Mary said, settling herself next to Katharine and Isabel. "We are to have visitors."

"More French?" said Isabel.

Mary shook her head. "We are to house three witches."

"Witches?" Katharine was aghast. "Oh, what would Sir Edward say?"

"We have not asked for this charge. We have been ordered to keep these women. They are guarded and chained and en route to Lancaster Castle, where they will be tried at the winter assizes."

"'Tis only too perfect for All Hallows' Eve," said Isabel.

"They arrive in a fortnight. All Hallows' Eve will have passed," said Mary.

Katharine and Isabel both crossed themselves at the same time.

"For how long?" asked Katharine.

"Only one night."

"And where will they sleep?" asked Isabel.

"The caves in the cellar where the mead and the roots are kept. Quib will have the men outfit three with bars and stakes, for they cannot be housed in the same cave. They have to be separated."

"And the children?" Katharine asked. "How will we keep them safe?"

"They will certainly be kept away. No one must look these wretches in the eyes."

"How did this come to pass?" asked Katharine.

"Richard and Harold could not decline," said Mary.

"And Matilda?" asked Katharine.

"The family could not decline. We are hoping this curries favor with the court."

"Since when has the favor of the court been a goal here? Our hall now a jail for witches? What next?" Katharine said.

"My dear, Sir Edward's sidestepping has gotten him where? In exile, in fear for his life and the lives of his family, of which by God's will you are considered a part. Edward's leaving was an act of leverage, my dear. The safety of everyone who eats at this table and sleeps under this roof was bought by his exit. You know that."

"Should we talk thus in front of Isabel?"

"I'm old enough," Isabel said.

"She's no child, Katharine."

Katharine was glad that Mary had finally used her name. The harsh way she said "my dear" made Katharine feel she was anything but her dear. And the words "his family, of which by God's will you are considered a part" stung. No one, in the history of Katharine's time at Lufanwal, had ever said anything like this to her. The arrival of the witches now seemed slight compared to Mary's evil words.

Katharine rose. "Well, the witches are welcome to my chamber, if they don't find comfort in their beds of rock."

Isabel smiled, but Mary frowned, saying, "Katharine, this is no matter for jests."

Katharine could not think of a quick or nimble response. "Good night, kind Mary. Good night, sweet Isabel. I will bid farewell to the duke, and then find solace in my bed."

Kind Mary, indeed.

Though Katharine had grown weary of the French while they were visiting, by the end of the week she began to miss them—or at least miss the entertainment. They had left in the midst of Hallowtide, when the soul cakes were still rising in the ovens. Before King Henry VIII abolished such practices, a continuous vigil was held from All Hallows' Eve to All Hallows' Night, and church bells rang all day and night to maintain a constant connection to the martyrs and the saints. On All Souls' Day, folk lit small fires and prayed for the souls of the faithful departed still suffering in Purgatory.

The queen's injunctions and liturgy in 1559, the same year of Katharine's birth, tried to put an end to official ceremonies for the dead, but in Lancashire tindles were still lit; oat soul cakes were still baked, set in high heaps on household tables and given to the poor; beggars still went from door to door "souling" for money to rescue souls; and the couplet "God have your soul, bones and all" was still called out by those who took the cakes and the alms.

With the third month of Edward's absence just begun, Will gone, Ned not yet arrived and the hours of daylight shrinking, Katharine felt all of her suns had set early. She was in her chamber before supper, the candle already lit, when Molly knocked on her door.

"Mistress," she called.

"Come in, Molly."

"I have . . ."

"Molly, you are out of breath."

"I have . . ."

"Yes?"

"Tidings for you." Molly presented Katharine with a letter.

They both knew the writing. Katharine wanted to tear open the seal. She was eager to read what he had written to her, but she was also afraid. What if he had sent his apologies? What if he had reconsidered his time here, thought his actions wrong, his heart too attached? What if he had decided to flee?

"Molly, tell me the letters here," Katharine said, remembering how his lips felt on her neck.

"'Tis one letter."

"No, from what I taught you last week, when I put the quill in your hands."

"I know your name, and I know his writing."

"How do you know 'tis my name? Tell me."

"That's a *K*, there," Molly said, pointing. "And the rest."

"Molly, tell me the rest."

Molly sighed and sat down on the stool next to Katharine. "'Tis an *e*."

"Yes, at the end of my name," said Katharine.

Will had called her "gentle Kate," said he would miss her, but what if, while away, he had decided it was time to return to his family for good?

"People sometimes mix the old English script with the new Italian script," Katharine said. "Ned used to write his letters in the old way and only sign them in the Italian way, but now he writes mostly in the Italian manner. Master Shakespeare is mixing the two types of writing here. Read the letters of my name and point them out while you read them to me."

Molly did as she was told.

"And I want you to tell me how those letters sound from what we did last time."

Molly sounded out the letters.

"And now put them together without pausing."

"Katharine."

"'Tis me, Molly! Now be off and let me read, and soon you will be reading his poems to me while I lie supine and stare at the clouds!"

"Yes, my lady." Molly curtsied and left.

Katharine broke the seal and unfolded the letter.

> *Dear Kate,*
>   *I am in Stratford and within the day will make my way to London. The house is very full. My wife is endless with her*

*invitations and the friends and relatives pour forth with alarming
haste. The guests are constant. The meals are constant. The
chatter is constant. I am not so constant, and this household
shatters my constancy. My wife likes to entertain. She is most at
peace, methinks, when her world wants for peace. I miss the quiet
of my lodging at Lufanwal, and the peace of my time with you.
It is good to see my children. They are bigger and brighter, and
my moments with them fill my heart. I wish I had verses to send
to you, but there is no air here to write, and no bright-eyed lady
with whom to share my meters and my rhymes. I wish you were
here, or I were there. I long to be with you. It will feel good to get
on my horse and ride again. London beckons with a different sort
of breath. I will exhale, finally, when I am back with you.*

*Adieu,
Will.*

Katharine felt with this letter Will hold her aloft and then draw her
down to him, the volta again. These words were his lips. She was buoy-
ant. She was sanguine. She had worried over Isabel's silly remark about
Will, and Mary's cruel comment about her place in the family. The report of the witches passing through the hall had only added to her ag-
gravation. But now she pulled on Will's gift of gloves and moved her
hands through the air in a dance. The peacock shimmered in the afternoon light.

There was a knock at her door. It was Molly again.

"Mr. Quib wanted me to tell you the men are bringing the virginals
from the gallery to the library as you instructed."

"Thank you, Molly."

Katharine pulled off the gloves one finger at a time and carefully laid
them on her table. By the time she got to the library, the men had set the

virginals on the table. She shut the door behind her then walked over to her old instrument, wiped off the dust with the edge of her shawl, walked around the table once and sat. She sifted through a stack of folios by the composer William Byrd. Each sheet contained four six-line staves with large diamond-shaped notes. Over the years, Byrd had frequented Lufanwal and was one of Sir Edward's favorites. He moved in the company of Lord Paget and other known Catholics yet had managed to skirt serious danger. He had not visited the hall since Sir Edward's exile.

A chill wind came in through the leaded glass. Katharine rose and walked to the fire. She stood with her hands open so the flames warmed her fingers. She walked back to the virginals and unlocked the lid. Then she thought of how Will said he longed to be with her. Setting Byrd's sprightly "Will Yow Walke the Woods Soe Wylde" in front of her, she exhaled, set her fingers on the ivory keys and pressed. With one note, then another, then a stumbling, then a chord, she began to play.

12

uring the following week, there was more talk of the witches—two old women and a daughter. The witches hailed from Pendle, and the charges against them were wide-ranging: from a goose that stopped laying eggs, to cream that curdled but did not come to butter, to a child going deaf, to an old man found with his throat cut. The house was abuzz with talk of the hags' impending stay. Sir Edward, Katharine was convinced, would never have allowed this: he would have thwarted the orders; he would have found a way to protect his family.

Lady de L'Isle, Isabel, Joan and Katharine went into town on market day. Over the centuries the town had grown from a settlement, with a few hundred people serving the land and the lord, to a large market town with better roads and a growing port to the west. Trade thrived now with skinners, tanners, saddlers, glovers, cordwainers, weavers, tailors, collar-makers, milliners, chandlers, soap-makers, ironmongers, pewterers, drapers, carpenters, painters, butchers, bakers, brewers and grocers. On this chilly morning, butter, cheese, poultry, yam and fruit sellers set up stalls by the cross in High Street. And down a ways the butchers were hawking their flesh, hides and tallow, with saltwains stationed nearby, offering salt for the meats purchased from the butchers.

Katharine bought gold threads for the unicorn bedcover she was embroidering. When Lady de L'Isle and her maid went off to the apothecary, Katharine and the girls crossed the street to the milliner. The little shop was crowded with head dressing of all types—simple white linen coifs, hoods edged in gilt lace and pearls, spangled net cauls, velvet, taffeta and wool hats decorated with gold or silver thread, lace, glass gems, buckles and feathers.

The girls rarely bought anything, but they went through hat after hat, hood after hood, a ritual where they turned, nodded and preened while Katharine smiled and laughed and told them the hats she thought worthy of their sweet young heads. Isabel always chose the flamboyant ones, while Joan liked a simple elegance.

Usually Katharine sat while the girls tried on hats, but today she stood in front of the looking glass, first pinning a gold mesh caul to her hair, then fitting her head with a sage-green velvet hat that bore the lines of a tall riding hat but looked more for show than for trotting. Its arched brim swooped down low in front, with silver thread along the rim: a glittery stone-encrusted buckle and a colorful peacock plume confectioned the satin band.

The two young women stared at her. The old stoop-shouldered milliner stared at her.

"You must buy this, dear coz," said Isabel.

Katharine looked at herself in the glass, saw the peacock feather, and thought of the fine gloves Will had given to her, realizing how they would match the hat.

"You must," echoed Joan.

"A jewel of a hat for a gem of a lady," said the milliner. He adjusted the angle of the hat, tilting the brim so it almost covered Katharine's left eye.

"Where would I wear a hat like this?" Katharine asked. "When?"

"There will be an occasion," said Isabel.

"Yes. There will be," chimed in Joan.

"A hat such as this will make an occasion," said the milliner.

With the glorious hat perched on her head, and the two girls and the milliner gazing at her, waiting, Katharine was overtaken with the narrowness of her life. Over the years, she had mapped the terrain at the hall. She knew her place, distinguished the open fields from the enclosures. She had contented herself with her lot and had poured her passion into the rich and varied world of words.

Katharine took off the hat. "Monsieur, your hat is *magnifique*!" she said, handing it to him. Her voice was weak, and she thought she might cry.

"I do not believe you have ever tried a hat on in this shop, my lady," said the milliner. "You deserve this hat. You are a beauty and the hat is a beauty and the two of you belong together . . . are betrothed, if you will. We can talk of the cost."

"Monsieur, you are an artist. You deserve to be paid well for this hat. I am happy to have had it on my head, if only for a little while. Gramercy."

Katharine nodded at him, then walked out of the shop. In truth she had no money for an extravagant hat, or almost any hat, for that matter. Sir Edward had been generous, and since she'd moved back to the hall a widow eleven years earlier, he had given her coins regularly. But either he had forgotten to tell Richard of this arrangement or Richard had failed to remember, because there had been no such allowance since Edward's departure.

The girls followed her out of the shop and the three of them strolled through the morning throng. The streets were overcrowded with folk, the stench of dung and rotten food rising from the ground, and the pungent odor of yeast and malt from the breweries clouded the air. The water mills along the river were voracious, forever grinding grain into flour, pounding wool with wooden hammers; the constant cacophony of their wheels and stone often made it difficult to hear one's own speech. Katharine wondered how the streets in London compared to this village. More people, she imagined, more smells, more of everything. She wondered if Will had left London yet; she worried that, once there, he would grow accustomed to his old haunts, and never return to Lancashire.

The weather had turned bitter in the last days. A damp wind blew in from the Irish Sea and Katharine pulled her cloak tightly around her neck. As they neared the river they got caught up in a procession. At the center of this boisterous group was a woman locked onto a cucking stool—a wooden chair constructed to look like the chamber pot it was named after. The poor hag was stripped down to her smock: neats' tongues hung round her neck; her head and feet were bare; iron staples restrained her arms and legs. The stool was attached to two long beams on wheels. They were bringing her to the water.

This shrew's face was pockmarked and red, and she was screaming at her captors at the top of her lungs. Dogs barked and children ran alongside the rig, poking her with sticks.

"What hath she done?" Isabel asked one of the revelers, a tall, skinny man with no front teeth.

"She didna heed her husband and did persist in shoutin' foul at him. Let that be a lesson to ye. The old scold's gettin' three dips." He laughed. "That'll cure her scurvy tongue!" he shouted as he ambled on.

After the first dunking, they brought the woman up from the cold current, and she was sobbing, no longer screaming, while water ran from her nose.

Katharine said, "We must go. Lady de L'Isle will wonder what's become of us."

The girls did not move, their eyes staring at the woman on the chair as it was lowered once again into the water.

"Isabel, Joan, we are not going to stand here and watch this. We must go!" Katharine took each one by the arm, turned them and marched away from the scene.

"What do you think that woman in the chair said to her husband?" asked Joan, when they were far enough away from the crowd to hear themselves talk.

"Most likely she hollered, *Could ye clean your sack breath before you kiss me!* or *Get your paws off me skin and leave me in peace!*" said Isabel with a laugh.

"Isabel!" Katharine said, suppressing a smile. "What would your mother say if she heard these words?"

"Ah, there's Mother now," said Isabel.

Matilda had visited several shops and stalls; her maid was laden with goods like a workhorse. Cries and cheers of the third dipping rang through the air. Katharine wondered at the plight of women, how their tongues were ripped from their throats or they were dunked in icy rivers more often for what they said than for what they did. Since most of her fair sex could neither read nor write, their voices were all they had.

The driver was piling their boxes and packages into the cart when Katharine caught sight of Mr. Smythson with his son. She didn't want more encounters; she wanted to get in the cart and start for the hall. She hoped Mr. Smythson hadn't noticed them, but he had, and walked over to their group. He and John bowed to the ladies. It was the first time Katharine had seen him without dust or dirt all over him.

"Mr. Smythson, what have you bought on market day?" asked Isabel.

"Nothing yet. We've just got here," he said, running his fingers through his dark curls.

"Are you from these parts, Mr. Smythson?" Katharine asked.

"No." He shook his head.

Katharine waited for him to say where he was from but he didn't continue.

"Better hurry," said Joan. "The stalls will be closing."

"Yes, we best get along," said his son John.

They took their leave. As the cart with the ladies rolled along the street, Katharine watched Mr. Smythson and his son. They were talking. Mr. Smythson put his hand on his son's shoulder and leaned in to listen to what his son was saying. Then he threw his head back, laughing. She'd never even seen him smile before, let alone laugh. The cart passed them and she craned her neck to watch, wondering what he could possibly be laughing about. Father and son seemed unaware of the bustling commerce around them, and she worried they might not have time to buy anything before the market closed.

Will sent a note telling Katharine he would make haste to her; he had no new verse but was certain that she would, as she always did, inspire him. Katharine prepared for his return with delight. She arranged for the wooden tub to be hauled to her room and water lugged up from the well. It was almost a day's work. While the water heated in a kettle on the fire, she instructed Molly to fetch rose petals and lavender stems. When the fragrant steam was rising from the tub, Katharine removed her smock, unbound her hair and stepped in.

"This feels lovely," she said. "Molly, you must use the tub yourself when I'm done."

"Thank you, mistress," said Molly.

Katharine sank into the water. Long strands of her thick hair floated on the surface. She dipped her head in fully, and Molly spooned a mixture of rosewater, rosemary and lye into her hair. Then she scrubbed Katharine's back and arms with a paste of honey, almonds and oats.

"Molly, fetch my clean smocks and hose from the laundress, please," said Katharine. "But stoke the fire before you go."

Molly did as she was told and was out the door. Katharine slid deeper into the water. His letters these past weeks had an eager heat in them. He had left his wife, his family and London, and he was coming back to her. She shut her eyes and saw his eyes, his ripe lips, his beautiful hands. She ran her hand from her thighs to her stomach, then over her breasts.

After her soak, she dried her hair by the fire and rubbed her skin with oils of clove, cinnamon and jasmine. She dressed carefully. She usually wore a partlet of lace or linen that stretched from the top of her bodice to her neck, but today she did without, revealing the path between her breasts, blocked only by the tight line of her bodice. The gown dipped down low in the back, and surely if her shawl were to slip her scars would show. He will have to take me scars and all, Katharine thought gaily as Molly threaded the bodice and pulled it fast.

"The old green gown always looks so comely with your hair, mistress," said Molly. "I'm glad you keep your hair natural and not paint it with that potion that makes it dull as buckram. Each strand of your hair has a million hues."

"A million, Molly?"

"A million, mistress," Molly said.

Minutes later, Katharine saw light in the library and threw the door open. Will had sent word through Molly he would be there.

"Good even." The sound was deep and masculine, but it was not Will. A tall man with a head of unruly hair was bending over the table.

"Beg pardon," Katharine said. "I thought someone else was here."

The man who raised his head was Mr. Smythson.

He bowed and Katharine smiled, and they said hello. Large drawings were spread on the table in front of him, and he wore a wool cape around his shoulders.

She moved closer. "What is this?" she asked.

"Lufanwal," he said. "'Tis plans for its change."

She had never seen such renderings of a house. The shape was fine, as though an artist had sketched the form. Mr. Smythson dipped a quill in the inkhorn and wrote something on the parchment. His writing was as neat and precise as the lines of the drawing.

"I am creating a hall along the side of the house here, so in the future you will not have to travel from room to room."

She rested her hands on the table and bent her head down to see.

"This is where the new chambers will be," he said.

"How well they fit with the line of the house," she said.

"One hopes."

They were quiet for a moment.

"Is it difficult to add to such an old and reworked dwelling?" she asked.

"Has its difficulties. Everything shifts. I try to maintain the symmetry or re-create it, if it's been lost over the centuries. 'Tis a bit of a puzzle, always."

"What's this?" she asked, pointing to part of the parchment.

He leaned over her to see. "Oh, those are windows, a line of windows——" he began, but was interrupted. Someone had entered the room. Mr. Smythson straightened.

Katharine looked up and saw Will. "How now, my good sir," she said, smiling. The sight of him instantly warmed her and spread from her flesh to her sinews and her heart.

Will stood in the doorway. He wasn't smiling. "I do not wish to disturb."

"Oh, you are not," said Katharine. "Mr. Smythson was here and has shown me his plans. You remember Mr. Smythson?"

"No, I think not."

"You met him in the garden. He is the builder, adding to the hall."

Will was oddly cold. Katharine remembered how he had talked to Mr. Smythson as though they were colleagues, and now he acted as though he had never laid eyes on him. Will turned to go.

"Don't . . ." Katharine began, flustered.

"I must go," Mr. Smythson said, rolling up the large sheets of skin.

"Your drawings are . . . beautiful," Katharine said.

"Many thanks. Let us pray they can make the leap from flat to full, for lines on a page are not stones in a wall. Farewell." He looked at her and he looked at Will.

"They will leap," Katharine said. "I am sure of it."

Mr. Smythson bowed and left them standing there. Will said nothing. Katharine wondered at his rudeness. The fire in the room crackled, but there was no other sound. She had mapped a different reunion, and a feeling of terror took hold of her. Had she lost him?

"I did so miss you," she said, echoing his recent letter. But the words hung stranded in the air.

He turned his back to her and looked at the books on the shelves. She sat by the fire. It was then she noticed his shoes. They were of fine leather, pigskin perhaps, or something more supple, vellum, with a soft tongue that hugged his slender ankle and side lachets that fastened over his instep with a black satin bow. She could not take her eyes from them. They were delicate, almost feminine but not pantofles, the slipper shoes made of velvet or silk that could only really be worn indoors. Will's shoes could be worn outside, she supposed, but only if it were dry; the slightest bit of rain or mud or any extended walking, would clearly ruin them. And they were red.

Between the shoes and the silk points that tied his hose like garters below his knees, Will sported fine black stockings that emphasized the bright color of his new shoes. The stockings looked to be of crewel silk and they had a seam down his muscular calf with a diamond pattern knit into the fabric around the ankle. It was as if he'd walked onstage and a lamp lit his shoes from below. The leather must have been treated with grease to make it shine so.

Will turned his gaze from the books to his shoes. "You like them?" he asked. "I got them in London at a cordwainer who makes shoes for Lord Essex. Not sheepskin, I assure you."

"They look very fine indeed." She wondered how he could have possibly afforded this shoe.

"I have a patron now, the Earl of Southampton," he said, squaring his broad shoulders and glancing in the large looking glass hung in an elaborately carved frame that reached from the high ceiling down to the wood floor.

Katharine had heard of the Earl of Southampton. Henry Wriothesley came from a long Catholic dynasty, his father having died under mysterious circumstances after helping the doomed priest Edmund Campion.

"I met a man once who had a pair of shoes I've never forgotten," said Will. "He was a lord. He's dead now. But he told me of this shop, and that's where I went. Made to fit my feet like a glove. On the wall was a letter from Essex, in his own hand, thanking the man for being such a craftsman. I believe, actually, he used the word *artist*."

"And now you've got them." She looked from his red shoes to his green eyes, but he was not looking at her. He was looking down at his new shoes. She wondered about his family back in Stratford and how they got by. She supposed his wife's family helped, because she had heard Will talk of his own father's debts, so she imagined not much help came from him.

"They're very fine, indeed," she repeated.

Will strutted around the library, pulling books off the shelves and then putting them back. "Latin, Latin, Latin," he said. "Italian, French, Greek, Latin. Where are the books in our native tongue?"

"Sir Edward has been buying them these last years." She had never seen Will thus. He had lost his joy. She wondered what she had done wrong.

"Perhaps I will hire that fellow Smythson when I buy Sir Clopton's fine house on Chapel Street in Stratford," he said.

"Yes," she said.

"New Place," he said.

"'Tis new, then?"

"No, 'tis old, but 'tis named New Place."

"Ah." She smiled.

He still did not smile. "Sir Clopton's house has ten fireplaces."

"Ten!" she said. She waited. She felt he wanted her to respond differently, with more enthusiasm perhaps, but she knew not this Sir Clopton, nor his fine house.

He was walking back and forth, his movements sharp, his body all edge. He had a book in hand when he stopped behind her; she felt his hand on her back. This is it, she thought. This is it. He dragged his fingers from the nape of her neck down to the rim of her bodice. Her shawl had slipped and he had followed the line of her scar. She held her breath. She waited, not turning. He did not say anything but left her and walked back to the wall of books.

"How was London?" she said finally. It took all the effort she could muster not to swoon.

"London was jolly." His voice was ice.

"Spenser calls it 'Merry London, my most kindly nurse,'" she said, trying to fan him.

"I was invited to a banquet. My patron brought me as his guest. The hostess was my sort of beauty, a goddess, long-limbed and lusty, with almond-shaped eyes, ample bosom, honey hair. And she was with child. She stood in the doorway of her lord's mansion, and she gazed at me and I gazed at her."

"How lovely," Katharine said, her eyes beginning to smart.

"She comes from much wealth, speaks many languages and has a most elegant chamber full of books. I believe her collection surpasses your noble Edward's. She was a delightful woman of great wisdom and learning. We talked the evening through. She was a heavenly creature, who disposed me to mirth. I was her captive knight, her bondslave, taken by the force of her beauty and her wit."

Katharine was silent, yet Will continued. "She found me pleasing, and told me so, and said that when I return to London, I must come see her straightaway." He paused, looking at Katharine. "What?"

Katharine had said nothing.

"'Tis not as though this lady and I are bedfellows . . ."

Katharine waited for Will to finish the sentence, to say *yet*. But he did not. He left the sentence cut off midway. She rose from her chair by the fire. She turned her head away from Will. Her eyes were full of tears. All she could bring herself to say was, "Fare thee well," as she walked out the door.

13

atharine could not sleep. She was in bed but did not snuff her candle. She lay motionless on her side, with her eyes wide open, staring at the flame. Through the night, she watched the wax turn soft and slide down the sides. By morning, when the light was lifting over the trees and the cocks began to crow, there was a puddle of wax where the wick had been. The scent of bath oils was still on her skin. Her night without sleep had drained her: anger adjusted to sorrow. Katharine rose with the sun, stirred the coals, then dipped the black quill he'd given her into the inkhorn.

> *Dear Will,*
>
> *I pray you have rested from your travels, your pupils are happy to see you and you have returned to your verse. I believe it best if we cease our conferences. The winter is nigh, the days have shortened and my duties to the family have increased. The time has come for me to step back. It pleases me to think that my participation, these last weeks, has been worthwhile and spurred you onward. The great and good thing is you are launched. You*

have finished sonnets and set the stage for 'Venus and Adonis.'
You have the conceit, the argument, the characters and their
destiny—'tis all there and 'tis wondrous. Your Venus is not the
goddess in Ovid or Spenser; your Venus is unto herself. We need
not meet in the future. It has been a pleasure, a pleasure, indeed,
and I treasure the time we have spent together. I think 'tis natural
for such relationships to shift and to settle, much like the earth
does over time.

    Fare thee well,
    Kate.

She folded the paper, melted wax, stamped the seal, and handed it to Molly. "I'll not be down today, Molly. Prithee, carry this to Master Shakespeare."

"Thou art tallow-faced, my lady. Mayn't I bring a bit of ale and bread?"

"I am dulled," said Katharine.

"Broth?" offered Molly.

"I have no stomach for it."

Molly peered at Katharine's face.

"Molly, I beseech you. Do not measure me."

"Your humors are off, miss."

"Yes, I suppose they are."

"Your spirit has gone out."

"I had a night without sleep." Katharine's voice was quavering; she tried to keep it level but was afraid if Molly stayed one more minute she would fling herself into her maid's arms and cry. "I will stay in my chamber and rest awhile," she said.

"Rest, then," Molly said.

When Molly was out the door, Katharine lay on her bed, placed her head under her pillows and burst into tears. She had not sobbed this heavily since she could remember. She did not understand why he ran hot one moment and cold the next. She had misread the situation. His talk of the gazing and the pleasing and the lady in London had been purposeful, instruction—he was tutoring her as to her place in his world, lest his attentions make her think otherwise.

She was still gasping when there was a knock.

"My lady—"

"Molly, you can leave the food by the door."

"He wanted me to convey these words to you."

Katharine sat up. She was not expecting to hear from him with such haste. With her note, she had let him off gently. She assumed he would go away, his dalliance with her done. She wiped her eyes and pulled her covers up to her chin. "Come in," she said.

Molly rushed in. "He broke the seal on your letter when I was scarce out the door. I was down the path when he beckoned me back. He looked very black. Mistress, your eyes are red."

"Did he send a note?"

"No, he stomped around a bit, and I waited. Then he said, 'Tell your mistress that I want to see her.'"

"Verily?"

"Aye. Then I said you were taken with a spot of illness."

"Gramercy, Molly."

"And he said he would come to your chamber himself, then. Fetch you himself."

"He dare not."

"He dare."

"Tell him I will see him in the library when the sun has set."

As soon as Molly left, Katharine regretted weakening. She would avoid him. Lufanwal was large, and she would take the back stairs and stay locked in her chamber all winter if necessary. She had written the letter as a stonemason, to build a wall. Why did Will desire to see her? She tried to imagine him stomping around as Molly had described; he seemed a man too much in check, not the stomping sort. And now she had agreed to meet him.

The first thing that caught her eye was an earring in his left ear. She had not noticed it in the firelight the night before, but now with sunlight streaming through the leaded windows the gold ring glinted. She was sure when he had departed for Stratford there was no hole in his ear. How strange, she thought. She had heard adventurers like Raleigh and Drake wore earrings, the gold brought back from foreign lands, but a player, a poet, a tutor? Will did, indeed, look the rake today rather than the dandy. His flat linen collar was open at the neck and he wore no doublet. His fine red shoes had been replaced with rough leather boots. Though it was she who had not slept the night before, it was Will's complexion that was pallid: his hair askew, his beard neglected, his sleeve untied, his polish off.

He was sitting in Katharine's favorite chair in the library gazing out the window when she walked through the door. She examined his profile: nose prominent like the Romans, rounded at the tip; brow a presence, shiny; hair gone at the temples, long in back; and now the earring, glinting, gold, new.

He turned when he heard her step, and she stopped her advance. She had never seen his face so serious. His eyes, she was shocked to see, held tears.

"I must speak with you," he said.

"Why? Methinks you spoke enough last night!" Katharine burst out. "If you were trying to sharpen a point, you have succeeded. We need not continue here."

"You have been too hasty in your decision," he said. "Kate, I——"

"I have brought the pages you enclosed with the gift." She had marked his "Venus and Adonis" verse that day when all seemed so hopeful, a future brimming. She walked to where he sat and held the verse and the gloves to him. "These gloves are a thing of beauty, but I cannot take them."

"*You* are a thing of beauty, Kate." His voice had none of the steel of the previous night; it was soft and slightly broken.

"I am a thing of beauty now? Where is the lady from London whose beauty so bewitched you? How could the statue you carved so fully and so real last night vanish so quickly? Or perhaps your golden goddess is not flesh and blood at all, for in truth she holds a strange likeness to Dante's *donna gentile*!"

The tears, no longer lodged in Will's eyes, now dwelt in hers. She turned from him and wandered the room, finally sitting in front of the virginals, her back to him. The spark that had prompted her to play them had been snuffed out. He came to her and sat down on the bench next to her. She could feel the warmth of his body.

"Give me your hand," he said.

She glared at him without speaking, her hands still on her lap.

Will had said that when a man sees his maid with another man he assumes they have couched together. She had thought the comment silly. Yet had he turned the brief unplanned moment she'd shared with Mr. Smythson into a sharing of a different sort? How utterly odd. And his anger. Was that because she had praised Mr. Smythson's drawing? Was Will the only male allowed to circle in the orbit of art? The peacock again. The stallion.

"Kate, your hand," he demanded.

She looked away but held out her right hand. He pushed his fingers between hers to spread them apart, as though the two hands were part of the same body and had come together in a clasp. He kept his hand thus entwined with hers, and at this moment she felt utterly naked; every tip of her tingled. He withdrew his hand.

"Be still," he said. He held one of the soft white gloves and gently, using both hands, pulled the glove onto Katharine's fingers, as though he were dressing her, then urged the soft doeskin up over her hand. The spangles glittered, the peacock on the gauntlet shone.

"Give me your other hand."

She took a deep breath and gave him her left hand. She still did not dare face him, for he was too close.

"There," he said. "My father made these gloves."

She put her gloved hands back on her lap.

"Your letter put us at an end," he said, "whilst methinks it marks a beginning. Kate, look at me."

She turned to him.

"I may be married but that will not prevent us from joining together."

Katharine nearly fell off the bench. She was not expecting these words.

"What we have is rare, precious, a pearl. I cannot deny it. You cannot deny it," he added.

"And your wife?" she asked. "Is your bond with her a rare and precious pearl as well?" As far as Katharine knew, Will was married to a woman he rarely saw. She pictured his wife, stoop-shouldered and coarse, with ruddy cheeks and rough hands, a survivor of her sex, with an absent husband whose dreams of art had bewitched him. Could Will's wife read his words? If she could, Katharine reckoned, wouldn't he have stayed in Stratford and at this very moment wouldn't he be dashing to meet her, showing her his verse?

"More a common stone," he replied.

Katharine waited, but Will offered no more.

"How is it," she pressed on, "that you did not finish a sonnet or a poem before you came to Lufanwal?"

"As you saw, I had a dozen starts, but I . . . I . . ." He paused. "I have never confided this to anyone, not even to my wife, Anne, but I was afraid if I seriously embarked on writing I would leave my family," he blurted.

"Oh," she said. "Yet now you have."

"I suppose I have," he said slowly, his countenance grave. "But I have found you."

She reddened, for she had no real family left on this earth and his words filled her heart.

"Let us meet in the schoolroom in the future," he said, "after the children have gone. The privacy will benefit our work. I feel anyone could wander in here at any moment. And let us meet more often. Will that serve you?"

"Yes," Katharine said faintly. In truth, she knew tongues would wag.

"Excellent," he said. The way he stared at her, she half expected him to lean over and kiss her. Instead, he shifted his gaze, placed his pages on the lid of the virginals and started to read what she had written.

"I agree, though Adonis is a huntsman, Venus is the hunter here, the huntress, the predator. Wonderful idea," he said, "I, too, have been pill'd."

I, too, have been pill'd. What did he mean by that? Who was his pillager? His wife who was eight years his elder?

Will looked up at her; his eyes, their usual brightness, lingered. "Beautiful. Brilliant," he said.

Was he referring to the words scribbled on the margin, or to the woman sitting an inch from him?

"You say here that I have not yet got fully at Venus's passion," he continued. "I have aimed at it, certainly."

"Yes, aimed, but the arrow has missed its mark."

"How then do I pierce the heart?"

Katharine pulled off the glittering gloves, snatched the pages from his hand and leaned into the light.

"Kate, methinks you are the huntress. I best be glad my fingers are still intact."

She glanced up. He was smiling at her.

"The sun is shining again," he said. "Our cloud has surely passed."

She wondered at his need to narrate.

"Two lovers after a quarrel," he said playfully.

"Lovers?" She narrowed her eyes at him, then returned to the page and tried to focus on the words there. *"Inopem me copia fecit,"* she said.

"Inopem . . . abundance . . ." He jumped from his seat and began to translate.

"Abundance makes me want, makes me poor," she said. "From your friend Ovid's 'Narcissus.' A tree laden with fruit breaks her own boughs."

"'Tis good," he said.

"Desire creates hunger, which it cannot satiate," she continued.

"Venus . . ."

"Venus to Adonis. She tells him that her kisses will not satisfy him but rather make him famished for more." She handed his pages back to him. His gold earring caught her eye again, and she turned away.

"You are always beautiful, Kate," he said. He was leaning against the virginals looking at her. "But today you are more beautiful than usual, your cheeks bone-white."

"Perhaps my illness has made me thus," she said, referring to Molly's earlier lie. "I have not dusted my skin with any powder, I assure you. I have earned my pallor quite naturally."

"My sweet Kate, methinks you are not much accustomed to compliments," he said. "What next?"

"What next?" she repeated.

"What next does our Venus say to the lovely-limbed boy?"

"Enough of her chatter, I suppose," Katharine said. She felt if she were another woman, Ursula perhaps, she would seize this moment, rise from her seat, place her hands on his shoulders, lean in and kiss him. But she did not move.

"So, if she does not speak more to him, what does she do?" he asked. His voice was tender, his words slow, as if he were talking to a child, but not a child, for there was something else in them, too, a wanton tone.

She still could not move.

"What does she do?" he repeated quietly.

"She snatches his hand," she said.

"Like you just snatched the page from my hand?"

"She seizes his hand," she said.

"His palm," he said.

"'Tis moist."

"A sweating palm, there is desire there, then, on his part, too. He is no innocent," he said.

She waited. He gazed at her.

"Kate, you and I are from the same skin," he said.

"We are?" she asked.

"We like being alone. I to write and you to read," he continued. "They are solitary acts. My wife loathes being alone."

Katharine stood and went to the fire. "But your wife is alone," she said, turning to face him, "for you are not with her."

"While I am not at home she keeps herself crowded at all times. While I am at home she crowds me. My wife does bridle me."

"Has it always been thus?"

"I was a lad when we wed, and after I did once or twice or thrice or maybe more find myself in a dark wood or grassy mead, reeking of mead, with other maids. In truth, the mead and the maids became my sport for a time."

"How long have you lived away from your children?"

"For much of five years."

"You return oft?"

"Once or twice a year, a' times thrice."

"Is that enough?"

"Nay. 'Tis my sacrifice."

"And theirs, too."

"Yes."

"How came you to leave?"

"My wife was carrying a child when we wed. After Susannah was born, I was . . . how can I relate it? . . . I was in a cave. I didn't wish to live in Stratford. I didn't wish to follow my father into his trades or businesses, within the law or outside of it, nor copy his many gained and lost titles in our town. Brew-taster, alderman, bailiff, debtor? I had no appetite for such roles. I had not gone on to one of our great universities as my mother had intended. I wondered all the while how I did get myself into this cave, for in truth I was to marry another wench when Anne did tell me she was with child. My other lass, when she learned of the Hathaway maid from Shottery, did toss every book and every piece of clothing I owned out the window onto the busy street. The folk in Stratford still laugh over a pint at the day my britches flew through the air.

"I was two years into my wedded *bliss*, when my Anne, nearing thirty, was with child again, and I took to carousing with my friends or anyone in the alehouse who would join me. I spent much time out, would bed a wench now and again. Was a lout and oft stayed away from the crowded house on Henley Street till the cocks crowed. I'd given up. One day, 'twas after noon, I awoke to find my wife standing in the doorway. Her girth was great with twins, though we didn't know that yet, and she was gazing at me. 'Tis an image I will never forget. The lantern in her eyes was out. She'd given up also. My head ached. My lids stung. It came to me whilst I lay there, the throb of mead pulsing in my head; I must leave. For that life, my dear Kate, would have been the grave for me.

"As a boy I was taken with schooling," he continued. "Enamored with history, Latin, marched like a good soldier through much of Ovid's *Metamorphoses*, but it was the poetry of Golding's translation to which I lost my heart. I would steal myself away from the noisy house on Henley Street and lose myself in its pages. As with Pygmalion's ivory image, once touched by Ovid I was forever changed."

"Would take a passing hard heart not to soften under such a stroke," Katharine agreed.

"I was pulled from schooling by my father's plight and found myself at fourteen currying and cutting kid for fine gloves. Then at fifteen up hither in Lancashire at the De Hoghtons' for a time. Then I found myself back in Stratford, tied to the town like a man on a scaffold, and I awoke one morn with three children and no Ovid . . . No Ovid! I could not live a life bereft of Ovid. I screwed my courage and left."

"Hence to London?" asked Kate.

"To Durham first for a spell with a company of touring players. Then to London, where I had as many jobs in two years as my father had in ten. But the playhouses drew me and 'tis where I seemed to cling."

"Make you London now your home?"

"My home for present is here. With you."

Kate smiled.

He looked at the gloves he had given to her on the inlaid wood of the virginals. "Do you fancy these gloves?" he asked.

"They are beautiful."

"And you will keep them?"

"Aye."

"Good. They are my first gift to you."

"Gramercy," she said.

He came to where she stood. He seemed taller than usual, as though he towered over her, or maybe at this moment she felt unusually small. She looked up at him and he brought his face down to hers, but his lips did not touch her cheeks. He turned his head so that her lips softly grazed his cheek.

"Carry on with your day, Kate," he said gently. "I will sit here by the fire and write. Fare thee well."

She wanted to stay, but his head was already bent over his pages, and she didn't want to disturb him. She left him there, a statue in the flickering firelight. As she walked down to supper, she worried that she should have acted differently—held him or turned her head to kiss him—that she had missed an opportunity by waiting for him.

14

"I will not have them here!" Matilda hollered.

Katharine was lost in thoughts of her recent encounter with Will, when Matilda's voice thrust her from her thrilling reverie. The words were loud and shrill and silenced the usual clamor at the long table.

"I will not have them foul our home, make rank and gross our ancestors' land. I will not have them lodge here!"

Matilda's scolding sounded heavy and strained from a well deep with anguish. She had displaced the code of the great house by shouting about these matters at dinner and by shouting at her stepson. Sir Edward would not have acted thus, and that she was a woman worked doubly against her. Katharine was in awe at the strength of her fury.

Richard stammered a reply. "It . . . it . . . it . . ."

"How dare you put this house in danger! We have children living here, Richard, and some of them are yours."

A servant tripped and an ewer went crashing to the ground; the ale sloshed across the floor.

"It will be so," Richard finally said, and then stood and walked toward the door. The servant had not finished wiping up the ale, and Richard did not notice the floor was still slick. He skidded and slipped and fell on his backside.

Katharine saw the servants smile behind their hands. They would never have done that when Sir Edward was at the head of the table. But it was not just the servants' snickering that caught Katharine by surprise, it was the scene that followed: no one, not one of the servants, nor anyone sitting, not even Richard's wife, Ursula, went to help him. Katharine did not hold much affection for Richard. He rarely said hello when he saw her, but after years she had accepted his coldness, thinking perchance the loss of his mother when his brother Harold was born had unhinged his humors and corrupted his nature. She couldn't remember ever seeing him smile, and to think he had married the young giddy-headed Ursula before she in truth even knew what marriage meant.

Katharine watched Ursula glare at her sour-faced husband as he, with ruff aslant, got on his knees and then pushed himself off the floor, almost losing his balance and falling over again. When Richard finally managed to stand, Ursula glanced at Harold, who was staring at her. Katharine wasn't sure if it was the way the corners of Ursula's mouth twitched, or the way she cocked her head or put her finger to her lower lip, still looking at Harold while he gazed at her, but it was after the sequence of these little movements that Katharine, with Richard limping now from his tumble and rubbing his hip, wondered if something was afoot between Harold and Ursula.

She recalled the day in the garden when Ursula and Harold arrived with Mr. Smythson. Maybe Ursula's flirtatious manner with Will had been a game to make Harold jealous. What would this entanglement do to pious Mary? Had Mary sensed this unnatural bond between her husband and her sister-in-law? But Mary had her own secrets. The week before, on a chair in the gallery, Katharine had found a Protestant prayer book wrapped in Mary's shawl.

The following day Katharine sat in front of the fire in the schoolroom. The wood had burned to embers, and there was a chill in the room. She had a wool cloak, lined with rabbit fur, wrapped round her. She was waiting for Will. He had sent a revision, and he had added new lines. She had read them and taken a quill to them.

"I crave a thousand pardons," Will said as he burst in. He bowed. He wore no cloak or cape or ruff. His doublet was of earthen shades dotted with specks of color, his collar of linen and ribbed with fine lace. His beard looked freshly trimmed. He went to the fireplace, added logs to the fire, then stirred the coals with a poker. "I could not leave my writing of our lusty goddess and her tender boy. Are you cold?"

"I have been warmer," she said.

"Has my verse not warmed you?"

She smiled. "You have written well."

"'Tis all?"

"'Tis much improved," she added.

"Much improved?" He paced in front of her.

"'Tis very good," she said.

"You are still cold."

"'Tis wonderful."

"You are, methinks, warming."

"'Tis on its way to brilliance."

"On a path, but not brilliant yet?"

"'Twill be brilliant when 'tis finished," she said.

Will sat on a bench across from her. "I am a schoolboy yet, I suppose, and you are my . . ." He did not finish his thought but smiled at her.

"I am your . . . what?" she said.

"You are my Kate." He reached across the table and grabbed her hands. There was silence. "Why are you not wearing the gloves I gave you? Your hands are frozen." He pulled her hands toward him and blew on them, then blew on them again, as if waiting for a flame.

"They are far too pretty to wear just any day," she said.

"Then I must get you a less pretty pair to wear just any day. I may not have a full purse, but I am rich in gloves, that I can assure you! I can still hear my father: 'Will, take these to Master Such-and-Such and those to Mistress Whose-It-What's-It and that pair over there, the ones with the glittery stones, to Lady What's-Her-Name.'"

Katharine laughed. "You talk of your father, you mimic him well, but I never hear of your mother."

Will sighed deeply. "No player could play my mother—not Edward Alleyn, nor Richard Burbage, not even Will Kempe, could build that role. Though the very idea makes me laugh. My father is neither a saint nor a scholar, but he reached high in our humble town. He gambled in his way, and lost more than he won. My mother is clever but not learned. My brain is from her. She comes from people who had more than my father's folk, a fact she has never let any of us forget. She schooled me in the art of pretension. I please my mother always, but I never please her enough."

"A harsh road."

"The maternal stocks. My mother lost two children before I was born, and two months after I was born, a bout of pestilence broke out and many in our town perished. I did not die, and because of that feat my mother always thought I was special. She reared me like a prince. She could not read nor write, but while I was in grammar school she sat beside me every night while I toiled with my studies."

"A good mother."

"Depends . . ."

"On what?"

"She was miserly of me. It was difficult for her to let me out of her sight. Aye, she bridled me."

"You were the anointed one."

"When I grew, my mother scorned that I might want a woman. One time, I was upstairs, in our cottage, with a maid who lived next door. I was new to my manhood and doing nothing with this maid. In truth, the lass had a fever and no one was at her home, so I offered my bed. My mother thought otherwise. Her rage, I can still hear those words, and feel her hard fists upon my back. I have always been able to tell when she is displeased, by a look in her eye or a tone in her voice, by the slant of her shoulder . . ."

"Or the feel of those fists pounding upon your back." Katharine felt anointed now; with Will's talk of his mother he had let his drawbridge down.

"Methinks that was the first time I discovered I could make myself weep," he said.

"How so?"

"A shower of commanded tears. In sooth, my mother's fists were no harsher than a light rain, but after her attack, I made my eyes fill, and then she felt horrid." Will stood, went to the fire and kicked the logs to start the flame again. When he returned, his eyes were brimming with tears. Then he laughed. "Others need onions wrapped in napkins for such a shift, or they must poke their fingers in their eyes."

"A good weapon to wield upon a stage," she offered.

"A good weapon to wield in life," he said with a chuckle.

She recalled the times Will seemed close to weeping—they had to be genuine, for why would he stand before her today and demonstrate his sleight of tears if he had practiced his false art upon her?

"Methinks the words 'time-beguiling sport' are perfect to describe kisses," Katharine said, referring to Will's new verse.

"Kissing is time-beguiling, as are other things," he said. "'Ten kisses short as one, one long as twenty.' Did you like that line?"

She gazed at his lips.

"Kate, how I love seeing you," he said. "The thought of our meeting wakes me in the morning and pulls me through my day. I want, if it pleases you, to meet as much as possible. I could not write this without you. You know that, Kate."

"I do."

"You must never leave me, Kate," he added.

"Where would I go?" she asked. Will would be the one to leave, for he had his life in London and his family in Stratford. He would leave her: she knew that well enough.

"Some suitor, I imagine, will snatch you away," he continued.

"Time for that is past."

"You do not know your powers, my dear. That stonemason felt your draw."

"Mr. Smythson? You misread the moment." She did not want to linger here. "Let us talk of your Venus, who has just plucked her prince from his horse."

"Her desire hath made her strong, hath made her nimble."

"In Ovid, they are reclining in the shade. She tells him a story and intersperses her tale with kisses," Katharine said.

"She's red and hot as coals glowing in a fire . . ."

"Write that."

"And he's red but not from desire, from . . . shame."

"Why shame?"

"Her lust shames him."

"Does not make sense. He is not so young."

"You have not been a boy."

"No. But I have been a girl."

"Did you not feel shame at the thought of lust?"

She didn't answer.

"And now? Do you feel shame?"

"No," she said quickly. She felt her face redden.

"She pushes the youth backward," he said. "She has tethered his steed, studded the bridle on a ragged bough. She throws him down and lies beside him. She strokes his cheek. He starts to talk in protest but soon she stops his lips with kisses . . ."

Katharine dared not speak. She was afraid her voice would prove unstable.

"Does it please you thus far?" he asked.

She nodded and bit her bottom lip.

"Good," he said, gathering his pages.

She imagined taking off her cloak and spreading it on the cold stone hearth in front of the fire. She pictured pulling Will down and stopping his lips with kisses. Will was standing and coming round to where she sat and helping her up, but she wasn't plucking him from his horse like Venus or pushing him onto the ground, nor was she drawing him down to her furry cloak before the fire; she was walking with him to the door, and he was pulling the hood of her cloak up over her hair, leaning down and kissing the top of her head. Then they walked out the door: he to his lodging at the other side of the courtyard and she to her chamber up the narrow stairs in the back of the hall.

Matilda lost her battle. As a justice of the peace, Richard had been pressed into taking the witches for the night. The custody of the wretched women would be passed from one justice to the next throughout their journey to the Lancaster Assize. As the night of the witches' coming drew close, the servants hauled out barrels of turnips, parsnips and onions, and bottles of mead and sack from the cellars, and the blacksmith fit bars of iron across the openings—the pigs in the sty had more air and more light. Bouquets of herbs and berries were hung throughout the house to ward off the possibility of evil spells: vervain, dill and rowan.

Despite these efforts, an awful wind swept through Lufanwal in the hours before the witches' arrival. Though the sky was clear, it was as if the three cages, flanked by uniformed men and dragged through the countryside on their way to the court, were the start of a tempest. The feeling was foul and thick and troubled; behind closed doors, in front of fires, at the dinner table and on the frost-covered stones in the court-yard, the tension grew.

Katharine watched from her window as the strange caravan slowly made its way up the road. It was a cloud of discord and discontent wind-ing up the hill. Rough men sat atop the thorny jails, whipping and shout-ing at the thick-shanked horses. Snorts of steam shot through the icy air. Sir Edward would never have allowed such an invasion. Katharine sensed from the start it was an ill-advised notion, and now, as she leaned over the sill into the raw afternoon, she was sure no good would come from it. These women, if they were indeed witches, were practiced in black sorcery, a path no one should have to walk in or to follow. And now they'd come to stay the night.

Matilda had ordered the women chained outside. And at first they were, their wrists and ankles manacled to the iron stakes in the court-yard usually used for horses. The women and the children of the hall were told to stay in their rooms, for fear even a glance from one of these hags would cause enchantment.

Katharine did as she was bade and withdrew from her window before the poor women were led from their cages—not because she believed in the superstition that looking at them could cause harm, but because she could no longer bear to see how they were treated with such brutality. She pulled her canvas curtains across to muffle their cries. The witches, in their tethered state, were more beast than human, and the three of them screeched and hollered into the wind. Their fit did not end, and their distemper rose louder and louder, so that finally Richard and Har-old, against Matilda's wishes, had the wretches brought into the dun-geons that had been prepared for them in the basements below, hoping the thick stone slabs of the foundation would silence their frightful mew-ling. But strangely, even before they were moved indoors, they stopped their racket. It seemed the poor women had recovered out of their fits but were now struck dumb; none of them spoke or even issued a whimper by the time they were dragged through the cellar doors.

15

ne had eyes made of glass," said Ursula.

"Glass, in truth?" asked Joan.

"Light blue glass, the color of those Venetian beads round your neck. And her glass eyes glowed with a weird and unnatural light," said Ursula, who was sitting on her bed brushing her spaniel's long, drooping ears. She had tied a gold ribbon on a tuft of brown and white hair on the top of Guinny's flat little head.

Katharine put her hand on Joan's shoulder. "Joan, dear, they may have looked to Ursula like eyes of glass, but I can assure you they were not. Perhaps the hag had poor eyesight, perhaps she was blind. That can cause the eye to discolor."

Katharine, Isabel and Joan had gathered in Ursula's chamber for a morning of needlework, but scarcely a stitch had been sewn. Instead, Ursula had transformed the time into the sewing of tales, for she, it seemed, had not obeyed the orders of the house, but had left her chamber to witness the witches. Having managed to hide behind a door in the courtyard, she had spied them while they twisted and screeched from their chains on the horse posts, and then as they were dragged into the cellars through the doors in the ground usually used for crates of food and drink.

"The other had a face so pocked that it was hard to see where her eyes began and the pocks ended," continued Ursula. "One had no teeth. She reduces food to dust with a spell and breathes it in," said Ursula.

"Breathes it in?" repeated Isabel.

"The dust . . . through her nose." Ursula sniffed in demonstration.

"The jawbone works even without teeth, for goodness' sake," said Katharine. "Your grandmother Priscilla has no teeth and she does not sniff her food through her nose. She mashes it with her jaw."

"And the third one was younger than I and barely older than you two and the daughter of the woman with no teeth."

"Did she have no teeth as well?" asked Joan.

"No," said Ursula, "but she did not have an arm."

Both Joan and Isabel gasped.

"Richard told me their names," Ursula said.

"To think they were once born from a mother, like you and me, named and baptized before God, to think they were babies once. 'Tis horrid!" exclaimed Joan.

"Widow Chandler and Widow Percy, and Widow Percy's daughter Susan," said Ursula. "And there were plenty they did bewitch. Two little girls, two sisters, were so with the spell on them that they fell into swoonings and fits and could not use their limbs and were at times struck dumb and could not speak and would cough deep and violent with much phlegm, and with the phlegm vomited crooked pins and nails. The little one spit up a twopenny nail with a very broad head!"

"A twopenny nail!" repeated Joan.

"And sometimes as much as forty nails at a time!" said Ursula. "Their father does swear. His own sister didn't believe him, but the girls were sent to live with her, hoping the spell would pass, and she saw them vomit pins and nails as well. Richard says they have the pins and the twopenny nails to be shown at the court!"

"How vile!" cried Joan.

"A mother and a daughter both witches," said Isabel, shaking her head.

"And it was when the daughter, Susan Percy, the one with no arm, stared at me that I felt pins prick my eyes," Ursula proclaimed.

"I am surprised you are not blind," said Katharine, pushing the needle of golden thread into the unicorn on the linen coverlet she was stitching.

Where was Ned? Katharine wondered. They needed Ned. Matilda needed Ned. It was time for him to return. The spectacle of the witches seemed only another sign that the humors of this great house were off. Things were not as they had been, nor as they should have been.

On the moonless night the witches were locked in the cellars, a strong wind had come up and raged howling and whistling through the great house. Molly had stayed on a pallet in Katharine's chamber that night, but neither really slept, listening to every sound. At certain moments, Katharine heard bells, objects falling from the roof, doors closing, strange clanging, high-pitched laughter. When the sky lit up red at dawn, the mood at the hall was still dark and disturbed. Katharine stayed in her chamber but watched from above as the women were dragged out of the cellars and into the cages. The men whipped them like cattle to get them to move.

Ursula had not dressed for the day but was sitting on her large bed without corset or farthingale in her white smock and petticoat. Every piece of fabric in Ursula's room was blue and white—bedcover, canopy, chair seats and curtains—like the Delft pottery she had grown up with in the Low Countries. Her blond hair was down, and the pale color framing her face gave her a rather witchlike appearance. She had always been small, but her face and arms had thinned of late. And today Katharine noticed the bones below Ursula's neck protruded in a sharp and alarming manner.

Ursula's spaniel Guinny stole the ball of gold thread out of the basket at Katharine's feet. The little dog ran under the women's dresses with her prize and broke Ursula's spell. Joan and Isabel chased Guinny around and finally wrested the wad of thread from her teeth. Then she scampered out the door, and the women, except for Ursula, bent their heads over their work.

"I am done," Katharine announced, tying the last knot of gold thread.

Isabel and Joan hopped up from their seats to look.

"Let's spread it out," Isabel said.

The girls took the corners and pulled the linen taut.

"Oh, Katharine, 'tis beautiful," said Isabel.

"Every stitch so even and so fine," said Joan.

"The likeness is so real," said Isabel. "Methinks the lovely animal is alive and will jump with cloven hooves from its garden of flowers and birds into Ursula's chamber this very second. The golden mane seems to move. You have sewn spangles in it! How brilliant!" she cried.

At the sound of a woman's scream, everyone looked up. Katharine tried to figure out from where the hysterical noise was coming. It was getting closer. Footsteps . . . running. Ursula's maid Audrey burst into the room carrying Guinny. Mary, dressed in somber gray with a simple white collar, came through the door behind her. Bright yellow pus bubbled from the dog's mouth and the pup howled and panted.

Ursula shrieked, jumped from her bed, rushed over and grabbed Guinny; the little dog spewed yellow ooze over her white petticoat. Moments before, Guinny had run through the room with gold thread streaming from her mouth; now she shuddered and shook, the sad little body a tempest of limbs. Ursula was still shrieking when Matilda entered, followed by Molly, who dashed in with a servant from the stable. Blood dripped from Guinny's mouth. The pup looked like she was on a rack—her body twisting and tortured. The howling changed from whimpering to gurgling. Then the little dog went limp—her eyes wide with terror.

Ursula stopped screeching. The women stared at the still body. The turn of events was so strange that everyone in the chamber, including Harold, who had just walked in, was utterly silent—until Ursula started breathing very quickly. She let go of the little body and it fell to the floor with a thud, its eyes wide open, its paws now sticking straight out. Ursula started wiping the blood and yellow vomit from her white smock, her hands brushing the stains over and over and over again.

Mary went to Ursula. "There, there, my dear," she said, putting her arms around her. "Come to my chamber while they take poor Guinny away." Mary's hair was pulled tight in a black caul. She seemed, in her new faith, to have lost any softness she once had; even her "There, there, my dear," sounded sharp rather than soothing, more tooth than tongue.

Ursula bent down, picked up her dead dog and started moaning and crying and kissing it. Harold strode over to her and with his good arm grabbed the thing by the throat. Ursula started hitting him on the head and on the back as he turned away.

"No!" she said, following him. "No! No! No!" Her fingernail somehow snagged the skin of his cheek, for a red line appeared with drops of blood.

In one swift movement, Harold dropped the dead dog into the arms of the stableman, turned around and slapped Ursula in the face, twice. The dog's violent demise was the first shock to those standing in Ursula's Delft chamber, and Harold's slapping her face the second. He stalked out of the room.

Mary's face was composed. She began petting Ursula's blond unbound tresses with swift little strokes, as though Ursula herself were a dog.

"'Tis the witch who did it!" screamed Ursula, a red welt rising on her cheek. "The witch! She bewitched Guinny!"

"The witches have gone, dear," said Mary.

"But she looked at me! And my eyes, they felt a thousand stabs."

"Were you not in your chamber when they were brought in?" asked Matilda, concern creasing her brow.

"I went down. I wanted to see them." Ursula was sobbing now.

Matilda crossed herself and murmured a prayer. Mary led the gasping Ursula to her bed and dismissed the servants as well as Katharine, Isabel, Joan and Matilda. Matilda did not put up a fight. With her ancient bloodlines, Matilda had a regal bearing, but there was a new frailty to her bones and a resignation in her gait Katharine had never seen before. Her shoulders had lost their meat over the last year and were slightly stooped.

When Richard returned from hawking he found his wife weeping with several servants around her. At supper Katharine heard that, after the lifeless dog was taken from Ursula and she was put to bed, they had brought trays of food from the kitchens, and cider, sack, wine, then mead, but she would have none. She had, it was said, cried less when her infant had died several years ago. Ursula did not pay particular attention to her living children. Nurses brought the three younger children to her once in the morning and once before bed. But her dog was a different story. She was rarely without Guinny. While Sir Edward presided, Ursula was forbidden to keep the dog on her lap while dining—hounds were allowed to eat scraps in the room but not at the table—but the day Edward left, Ursula made a point of feeding the dog from her lap during dinner and had done so ever since. And now Guinny, named after Guinevere, King Arthur's wife, was in the cold earth, and Ursula was inconsolable. Katharine did not want to believe the strange death had anything to do with magic, but what had befallen the poor dog was most puzzling.

The creaking convoy of cages making its way down the hill was not the last they saw of the witches, for in spite of the chains and the bars made of brambles, somehow the youngest one, the armless Susan, had broken free that day when the horses stopped for water. When a messenger arrived with the news, the house went into an uproar, with doors barred and the men sent onto the grounds to keep watch. A day later, the woman was found cowering in the hawk mews, naked. No one wanted to touch her, for fear of spells and enchantments, so they bolted the doors from the outside and waited for men from the jail to come get her. She was still alive when they took her out in a falcon cage, her body doubled over and her head pushed next to her feet.

Molly was bent over a wooden tablet with the alphabet, the numbers from zero to nine and the Lord's Prayer covered by a thin plate of horn. Katharine had borrowed the hornbook from the schoolroom. They were working through "*A* per se *A*, *B* per se *B*, *C* per se *C* . . ." Katharine stood by the fire and looked out the window. The November light had dimmed, the day cut short by the coming winter.

"'Tis your saint's day," said Molly as she carefully formed the letter *H*.

"'Tis," said Katharine.

"'Tis perfect for you. Saint Katharine was as learned as any lad, mayhap more learned."

"She knew her Greek."

"She refused to wed," said Molly.

Katharine remained gazing out the window.

"Ursula thinks the witch did make a hex on her and her dog," said Molly. "But I heard the men at the stables talking, and they said 'twern't a witch's curse that caused Guinny's death."

"Not 'twern't, Molly, best to say, *They said it was not a witch's curse*."

"They said it was not a witch's curse that caused Guinny to quiver and quake and puke up all her guts," said Molly. "They said it was poison plain as can be."

"Poison?"

"A strong'un."

"A strong one. Try to separate your words. Perhaps Guinny got into the poison somehow, thinking it was food."

"Or maybe someone poisoned the pup," said Molly.

"Who would poison a pup?" asked Katharine, but she was only half listening. Will wanted to meet with Katharine in the old chapel-cum-schoolroom.

"A mean type would," said Molly. "'Twould take a stone for a heart, that'd be cruel to a poor defenseless pup."

"You don't think Guinny was bewitched, then?"

"Methinks most oft the old shrews tagged as witches are the same as that poor pup. They tried to chain my grandma's sister for a witch, and the family that pointed at her was crazier than she! They were wretched folk, soiled and cheap and ugly as boils."

"But she was innocent?"

"Aye, she was. All she done was be so poor that she was starvin' and had to beg a bit of bread and ale. They turned her away and she then done curse at them, and the next day one did fall into a peat pit and die, and then they said she'd put a spell on them, but she was blessed 'cause she died before they could drag her to trial."

"Perhaps it was a broken heart that caused her death," said Katharine.

Molly looked up from her quill and stared at Katharine. "A broken heart? No. She was just old. Nothin' had broken her heart. Everythin' all right, my lady?"

Katharine sighed. "I must go out, Molly. Stir the fire and stay here, if you can, and try to finish your letters."

When Katharine pushed open the schoolroom door, she was surprised to find Will already seated. Usually he was late and she had to wait for him. She wondered if his need to make an entrance had something to do with his vocation as a player. The stage. The torches. The audience. Ned had told her of going to a large playhouse in London on the Bankside in Southwark—a real cannon was shot off during the play, and the roar of the crowd from a nearby bear-baiting pit drowned out the words of the players.

The fire was stacked full of wood, the flames reaching high into the chimney. The room was warm. Perhaps Will had tutored the boys in the morning and then never left. He was dressed all in black—doublet, breeches and hose. The lack of color in his attire made him look serious and severe.

"Kate," he said.

His voice was tender; she felt it on her skin.

"Your costume bespeaks a change of church," she said.

"I have witnessed too many changes of church for one lifetime. Every day, it seems," he said, coming to where she stood at the door. He took the cloak from her shoulders.

"The Puritans favor grim hues," she said. "Black suits you. Peacock plumes compete with your colorful intelligence."

He bowed. The black did make his face more striking than usual.

"Let us look at your 'Venus and Adonis.' I have questions and ideas." She sat down on the bench.

"A woman of business," he said, sitting next to her.

She looked at him and smiled. "Comparing Venus's hunger for Adonis to bugs feasting on the flesh of a deer sucks the beauty from the moment."

"I spent a whole morning on those lines." He jumped up and started pacing.

"Venus may have a strong appetite, but we must still love her."

"I like a lady with a strong appetite . . ."

"Instead of bugs, maybe Venus can be like a bird."

"A buzzard?"

"No." Katharine burst out laughing.

"I like a lady with a strong laugh. Oh, Kate, I should just take you here and now."

"I beg your pardon?" she said. Perhaps she'd heard him wrong. She took a deep breath.

"Why not a buzzard?" he asked.

"A buzzard would paint the same horrid picture as bugs. Why not an eagle?"

He walked to the fire, then to the side of the table where she sat, and sat next to her on the bench again. She was acutely aware of how close their bodies were, but not an arm, nor an elbow, touched.

"A hungry eagle . . ." he said.

"Much better," she said.

"You are right, though I loathe to part with my munching maggots."

"Why does Adonis stay with Venus yet turn his head?" she asked. "What keeps him by her side if he thinks her kisses, as you wrote, murderous? Instead of welcoming a woman robust in her attentions, fearless in her actions, Adonis thinks Venus immodest, her behavior amiss. He could easily push the fair goddess away. He is not tethered to her. He is free to go. Why does he not leave?"

"Conflict."

"Between the two?"

"Within him."

"The pair's connection is complex," she offered.

"I like complex connections," he said. His face was not a hand's length from hers.

Minutes before, their dialogue had felt like a lure; now it was a trap. She pointed to the next page. "'Tis very good."

"I get a 'very good' today. What happened to ''tis brilliant'?"

"Bear-baiting, bull-baiting, flattery-baiting, cockfighting. The sporting world of men does make me cringe. I've suggested changes," she said.

He took the paper from her hands. "Your words are better in most cases, perhaps in all," he said.

He began to read aloud. She stared down at the lines on the paper as he spoke, words he had wrought and she had rendered. As he read, her words became his words, and his words became her inward voice.

"'Look how a bird lies tangled in a net . . .'"

Will sat so near that she could feel his breath on her skin.

"'So fasten'd in her arms Adonis lies . . .'"

For a second Katharine turned her head to watch him, but then she looked back down at the page. By the time he reached the words "she cannot choose but love" she felt her whole being well up. She stared at the verse, but under the table she dug the fingernails of her left hand into the palm of her right hand.

"'Till he take truce with her contending tears,'" he read, "'which long have rain'd, making her cheeks all wet . . .'"

She breathed evenly and kept stabbing with her nails, not caring if she drew blood, because anything was better than tears at this moment.

He finished with: "'And one sweet kiss shall pay this comptless debt.'"

Katharine did not look at him. While in her chamber, she had read the stanzas, indeed she had reordered lines and pruned words, but she had not been overtaken by them then as she was now.

"You have used the word *shame* four times in fourteen stanzas. It repeats and repeats. Can you not think of another word?" Her face was hot, her voice trembled. She grabbed her cloak and hurried to the door. He sprang off the bench and followed her. She turned to him, her eyes wide.

"Fare thee well?" he said, a question.

She did not answer him, nor did she put her cloak on, but pushed out into the early evening, and raced down the path to the hall, eyes brimming. Once in her chamber, she flung herself on her bed, the rain of tears making her cheeks all wet.

Soon there was a knocking at the door. "Mistress, I have a note for you," called Molly.

Katharine wiped her face with her shawl, but she could not stanch her tears. She let Molly in.

"He wants to know your state. He insists on knowing. A hound on a hunt, he is." Molly handed her the letter.

"Did he ask you that?"

"No, he done wrote it."

"I won't be down for supper, Molly," Katharine said, then realized what Molly had said. "You read his words!"

"I guess I have. Beg mercy."

"All your hard work and you are reading now. Pray don't tell him anything."

"Yes, my lady. I'll keep me mouth mum. He is no friend."

"Why do you say that? He is a friend."

"A friend wouldna make you weep and such. Can I bring you some broth?"

"No broth, thank you. I need to be alone is all."

Molly left, but scarce a half hour had passed when she was again knocking at the door.

"Molly, I need to rest. Please do not worry," she called.

"Katharine." The voice on the other side of the wood was not Molly's. "Katharine."

She wiped her eyes one more time and then opened the door. Matilda, whose eyes looked as red and watered as Katharine's, walked in. She was dressed in her smock and a worn black velvet dressing gown. Her hair was down and uncovered. Katharine could count on one hand how many times over the years Matilda had come to her chamber.

"You have heard," Matilda said. Her voice was edged with anger.

"Heard what?" said Katharine.

"You have been weeping." It sounded like an attack.

"Yes. But I have heard nothing."

"Edward, my Edward, my dear Edward, is dead."

16

atharine slept briefly that night, a sleep that seemed more a single breath, a gasp really, than true slumber. Outside her window, in the gray light of dawn, the first snow had fallen, and the hills and fields were now hidden under white. Where were the noises of the day? Had Edward's death quieted even the birds? Silence, sad and still, rang through his house and his land. *For death has come up into our windows*, was writ in the Bible, in Jeremiah. And indeed it had.

Her grief was twofold. She had lost sight of where she and Will ended and where Venus and Adonis began. She felt as if she were living within Venus and that, in a way she could not quite—or rather did not want— to grasp, Will was encouraging this metamorphosis, *I should just take you here and now*. At the dawn of such a dreadful day, she was shocked to find herself thinking of Will when she should have been praying for dear Edward, but she was having difficulty distinguishing between her loss of Edward and her longing for Will. How odd. How horrid. She was a ship, foundering; she had to find a way to buoy herself. With such sharp and unforeseen shifts in the current of the family, now was no time to drown.

Katharine sat by her small window. With the sun behind the snow clouds, much of the land and the sky looked almost blue. What was out there, beyond the beyond? Endless white? Infinite loss? Eternal grace? Edward was one of God's flock: he had been pious, he had been faithful, he had believed in life everlasting. If, at the evening of life, one was judged on one's love, then Edward was now resting in peace. The Bible, in Hebrews, said: *And as it is appointed unto men once to die, and after this the judgment.* Katharine would pray for Edward, she would pray for his soul, but she had no fears for his final destiny—he was heaven-bound.

A prior had posted a letter with the sad news an hour after Sir Edward's passing. As Sir Edward was failing, with a fever that could not be quenched and his breathing loud and labored, he had asked for a cot at the nearby monastery, saying if he could not be at home surrounded by his loved ones, he would die surrounded by those who had dedicated their lives to God and His love. In the days preceding his death, Sir Edward had thrashed about and cried out, but on the final evening, the prior wrote, his body was calm, and with several brethren kneeling next to his cot he had prayed for many hours, his words slow, even and true— until his voice was spent. He had been alert but unable to speak when the priest anointed him with the sign of the cross upon his brow, gave him the Eucharist and performed the last rites. His eyes had been open and soft and full of peace. During the night's watch, the priest at his bedside understood that Sir Edward had departed out of the miseries of this life into the joys of paradise. For his repose, the sacrifice of salvation was to be offered, and at a signal from the bell, the brethren entered his room, prostrated themselves in prayer and began to say masses and to offer earnest petitions in commemoration of the blessed Edward.

"Whether we live or die, we are the Lord's," Edward had oft quoted from the Bible. He had been the Lord's in life, and now he was the Lord's in death.

Katharine had expected Edward to return to Lufanwal within a year, that the tension with the queen would settle, that other battles would replace her Roman paranoia. In the months since Edward's leaving, Katharine had thought him away but not gone, for Ned had been away much longer than Edward. She had not received one letter from Edward, but she supposed his duty in writing was to Matilda and their children. Katharine had not written to him, thinking it proper to wait for a letter from him and then to reply.

In Edward's library was a German book called *Totentanz*, Dance of Death. When Katharine was a child she pored over the macabre wood-cuts. The whole of society from the Pope down to the common laborer was represented in this work; grave subjects led captive by grotesque and mocking Death. Sir Edward, ever steadfast in his faith, had been preparing for death his whole life. From the prior's account, it seemed that in Edward's final hours he was not among the reluctant followers of the jig-maker Le Mort. Noble Edward, kind Edward, was at the end accepting and in harmony with God.

With Advent scarce begun, there would be no need to force a fast this season, for sorrow and lamentation would kill off all appetite. Katharine planned to spend the morning praying in the secret chapel. Surely no priest from a neighboring estate would venture forth; the last time one did, he was slaughtered and his head stuck on a pike.

Molly was at the door early, with kind words of sympathy and also with a note from Will. He again asked how Katharine fared, but now the news of Sir Edward's death was upon his page. Katharine could feel Will's urgency, yet she advised Molly to make no response. For her heart was overflowing with chaos.

Katharine sent Molly off with a note to Isabel, asking if she would meet her in the hidden chapel to pray. Then she sat down to write a letter to Will. She usually wrote letters easily, but today she wrote, crossed out, rewrote, then tore up the paper. She started with a description of how she was taking on the inmost life of Venus; then she changed the beginning to how her grief over Sir Edward's death, combined with the peculiar nature in which she felt she inhabited Venus, or Venus inhabited her, made continuing with Will impossible. If there was any bewitching going on at Lufanwal, she wrote, it was his poem that was casting spells, not the poor hags who'd spent the night. She tried to write without emotion, without passion, from the outside of her heart, not from within. She tried to sound like a man.

> *You are an exceptionally talented and clever writer, a diamond of brilliant cut, and you must write, you must write forever, for eternity. You are beyond nimble in word and thought, and now is the time for the poets of our land to be as brave and daring as Drake, Raleigh, Hawkins and Gilbert sailing the waters of the globe. Our poets have embarked on a wondrous expedition—to fare forth in our own language that which has heretofore been the terrain of other cultures. Our dearly departed Sir Edward once told me that the library at one of our great universities holds thousands of books but only thirty of them are in English! You have a grand future of exploring worlds and charting tales in our native tongue.*
>
> *Minutes before the end of our last time together I came undone, and I am still trying to comprehend it. To be more precise, I felt I had turned into one of those porcelain figures traded from the East, and that I might, given the lightest tap, shatter into a thousand pieces. I wept for hours and this weeping came upon me before I heard the sad news of our dear Edward's passing. As you go deep into your writing of 'Venus and Adonis,' I seem to be diving deep into another tale, the tale of us. Must I, I ask myself, take on the feelings that live within the walls of your story? Do you know the Latin word* vulnerabilis, *from* vulnerare, *"to wound," and* vulnus, *"wound"? As you become*

> *more* vulnerabilis *in your writing, more open, more able to*
> *penetrate your characters, I seem to become more* vulnerabilis
> *in my attachment to you . . .*

In the final draft of her letter, she did not call for a termination of their meetings—for she had already done that once and capitulated quickly. This time she simply told him of her twisting spirit, and then sealed the paper with wax for Molly to deliver.

Katharine dressed in a simple dark bodice and skirt and pulled her hair into a black caul. After Molly went off clutching the letter, Katharine sat back down on her bed. She wondered if the family's faltering faith had failed Edward. The snow had stopped falling, but winds stirred the crystals into a white swirl. Then, out of nowhere, a large flock of blackbirds fell from the sky. A blizzard of birds. Crows or starlings, she could not tell. But it was not the rooks returning. The air was thick with black flapping wings. The flock grew and grew until hundreds, maybe thousands, of black birds started to settle on the fresh snow—trimming the white-lined branches with black and carpeting the white meadow in darkness. They made a roar. What mythic gusts had brought these strange guests to this stopping place? Were they messengers? *Be ready for you do not know at which hour the Lord will come*, the Bible said in Matthew. *Be ready.*

In the old days, if one's kin died, the head of the house would have ordered the ringing of the bells before the funeral. Katharine waited for the chimes, for the message to be rung from their hill to every hill and valley in the region, but that clarion call never sounded. Lufanwal seemed enveloped in the strange silence of forgetting. After Sir Edward left, the secret chapel was rarely used. Katharine herself did not frequent the inner chamber, for the cramped windowless space felt more a coffin for the dead than a sanctuary for sacraments.

Built between the great hall and a stairway, the chapel was indeed well hidden. What seemed the back of a grand fireplace was in truth a large movable stone that led to a short passage and a door, then a second door inches behind the first. The doors were Katharine's height; only the taller members of the house had to stoop to pass through. She expected to meet other family members going into the chapel or already in there on their knees in prayer. Had the scant months of Edward's absence truly extinguished the family faith? Was it so flimsy it could float away so swiftly—paper rather than stone?

Katharine pulled the second door open. The candles were lit and incense sweetened the air, but the scene before her was not what she had expected. Ursula, her blond hair down, her bodice open, her smock undone or maybe torn, her breasts bare, was on her knees holding on to Harold's legs, sobbing and crying out to him. Harold was dragging the tiny Ursula with him as he moved toward the door.

"You cannot cast me away," she pleaded. "I love you, Harold dearest, I love you and you love me, you love me, Harold! You told me again and again and again how you loved me. I am your little La. I am your pet. I will be good, I promise. I will be perfect. You are my king. Pray, my love, say you will not leave me. I cannot live within this house without you. It will be a prison without you. I will perish . . ."

When Harold noticed Katharine, he shoved Ursula with all his might and strode toward the door. "I came to pray for our dearly departed Edward and she has preyed upon me. She is stricken. Quite possibly mad," he said. "She has always been fragile, as everyone in this house knows. These spells are coming upon her with haste and frequency. My brother would do well to keep her confined to her room."

"'Twas the witches have cast a spell on you, Harold! Curse the day I gazed upon their foul faces. First Guinny, then Sir Edward and now your love! All dead, dead, dead."

Harold was out the door before she finished repeating the last "dead."

Ursula, half naked, was trying to stand and go after him. "Harold," she yelled. "Harold!"

Ursula looked bloodless and pale, her chest sunken, her cheeks pinched. Katharine rushed to her and wrapped her own silk shawl around Ursula's bony shoulders. Ursula was silent, tears sliding down her face. She lifted her gaze to Katharine.

"I have come unmoored," Ursula said evenly, her usual singsong voice gone. "I have come unmoored," she repeated, her eyes wide with fear.

"You've had a scare," said Katharine.

Ursula allowed Katharine to pull her to her feet. "I am a whore," she said.

"We have all been staggered by the news of Sir Edward. Let me take you to your chamber."

"The news of Edward did not stagger me," Ursula responded quite frankly. "The man thought me a fool, and he was right."

"Do tie your smock and hook your bodice," said Katharine.

"I am a fool and I am a whore," said Ursula. And those were the last words she spoke to Katharine that night. She would not fasten her clothes, so Katharine adjusted the shawl around her. Ursula was silent, her eyes dry, as Katharine led her slowly up the stairs.

Molly found Katharine as she was leaving Ursula's chamber and handed her a note without saying anything. She didn't have to; the slant of the lettering announced the author.

"Gramercy, Molly. Have Matilda or Isabel been down?"

"No, my lady. Isabel is with her mother, but they have not come down."

Katharine could not return to the hidden chapel, she had no stomach for it. She called for a servant to light a fire in the library. When she reached the room the air was chilly, the wood just lit. Edward's old tattered robe still hung on the wall, as if he were indeed returning any minute, as if he were entering the room, putting it on and settling with book in hand by the fire. Katharine had witnessed him thus hundreds of times, and as the years passed, the gold and red brocade had worn smooth in patches, loose threads dangling from the hem, and there he sat—his hair gone white, his cheeks the color of apple skin, his eyes minerals carved from ancient rocks. Katharine took the old robe off the hook and pulled it on. After all these months it still smelled of Edward, of earth and moss, of drying leaves. She went to her favorite chair by the window and sat, wrapped deep within his cloth.

The blackbirds of the morning had departed. The sun was now burning through the clouds, melting the newly fallen snow. Katharine listened to the dripping from the gutters and the eaves. Mourning would displace merrymaking this coming Christmastide: melancholy would displace mirth. The snows had arrived early, before the first of December. Sir Edward had breathed his last breath on November 17, Accession Day, the holiday that commemorated the queen's succession to the throne. Edward always said that part of him had died the day Elizabeth took the scepter, for there was no doubt of her plans to advance her father's church, not the religion from Rome of her half-sister Mary Tudor or her cousin Mary Stuart.

Katharine opened Will's note: *How fares my noble lady?* he demanded.

> *Tell me. If I were not the lowly sometime tutor sometime player*
> *of this great house, I would rush the doors, much as a knight in*
> *battle, find you, sweep you up and ride off with you. Your note*
> *resounds in my ears, your line "the tale of us" still fresh upon my*
> *lips, for I have oft repeated it since my eyes first landed upon it. I*
> *have stayed separate this morn, aloof, for I know you are behind*

that stone and timber, embedded within walls of grief. How I
wish I could come to comfort you, Kate. I am, on this still and
saddled morn, at my table, quill in hand, with Venus and
Adonis, limbs linked, stretched upon the grassy mead before
me. I am but a dry cloth, yet with your clever comments, I mop
and shine, and try my best to bring out the luster of my frail
and humble verse. You, Kate, give me the strength to
continue with my poesy, make my bones feel sturdy when
they do falter and creak. You must use that might now to
support what is surely crumbling, a noble family made old
and weak by such young sorrow . . .

Her heart, burdened by the news of Edward, was at the same time brimming. She was thrilled by Will's words. Here finally was proof of his feelings for her. Was this not love? She closed her eyes and rested her head on the back of the chair, continuing the story he had begun, of his sweeping her up and riding off with her. Where did they go? To a cottage deep within the wood, where the snowdrifts reached past the windows, the smoke from the chimney curled endlessly into the sky and their footprints scratched a trail, like ink on paper, through the snow. After all the tilting of touch these last months—they finally set their lances aside and, as when he embraced her after the dance, he embraced her again in the snowcapped cottage in front of the fire, and this time there was no haste to part.

Will was, Katharine imagined, as precise and powerful in his movements with her as he was with his words. She had no qualms about giving herself to him. She was surprised but not troubled by her lack of guilt. Her feelings for him transcended her beliefs. Giving her body to him was neither lewd nor a sin: the only sin she could foresee was *not* to give themselves to each other. With the same hands she had watched countless times dip a quill and dash a line of words across a page, he did finally unlock her: take the cloak from her shoulders, unhook her bodice, untie the silk string of her smock. Will's fingers lightly circled her, his lips on her skin, his tongue on her skin. His warm hand reached under her skirt, under her petticoat. Was her back against the door? A wall? Or were they lying down now in front of the fire? She had these years been forgetful of her body, but now she felt lush, her juices ready.

She felt his fingers meet her moistness, and she gave a little cry, but he did not stop until he hit the mark again, and this time she groaned. Then he pulled off his doublet and his breeches, or maybe she pulled them off, and he pushed into her, invaded her, for now every muscle, every limb, every inch of her skin, felt him inside her, rocking and thrusting, and she loved the invasion, the occupation; she loved his army, all of it . . . .

She opened her eyes quickly as the door swung open, and she sank farther into the chair, hoping whomever had entered would be blind to her.

"I beg pardon. I thought the room empty at this hour." Mr. Smythson bowed. "On this sad day," he added. He stayed close to the door, a leather bag full of rolled parchments slung over his shoulder. He still wore his riding cape; his breeches and boots were wet with mud and melting snow. His dark curls were longer than before, but they were as untamed as ever. There was nothing coiffed about this man, but he was not exactly careless in his form, either.

Katharine could think of nothing to say. She stayed in her chair, wrapped in Edward's robe. She imagined she appeared slumped in a swoon from grief.

"I was sorry to hear the news upon my arrival, very sorry," Mr. Smythson said. "I lost my father a year back and I still recall his voice every day. I understand." He had not moved from his spot by the door. He pulled his bag off, then changed his mind and threw the strap over his shoulder again.

Katharine was surprised by Mr. Smythson's candor. She felt oddly mute and tried her best to pull herself from her imagined scene with Will into the present moment.

"I lost my wife fifteen years back when John was born, and she comes to me, even now, not when I try to conjure her but in the midst of the small details of the day. I might be sipping a mug of ale or stamping a seal or measuring stone or . . . I know not . . . walking across a courtyard, and there she is."

Katharine's eyes filled with tears—for the first time that day. She had not yet wept for Edward.

"Pray pardon, I did not mean to—" Mr. Smythson broke off mid-sentence and walked toward her. As he walked by the table, his bag caught the little box with the crystal ball that young Henry had tossed in the air that afternoon months ago and now, with the swipe of Mr. Smythson's leather satchel, the box and ball flew off the table. The ball landed on the hearthstone and shattered. "Fie! I am a clod," he said. He knelt down and started to pick up the pieces.

Katharine rose, still swathed in Edward's robe. "Leave it be, Mr. Smythson. You'll cut yourself. I'll call for the steward."

Mr. Smythson continued until he picked up all the shards. Then he stood, his large hand holding the jagged but beautiful bits he had gathered—an offering. There was nothing dainty about his hands. His knuckles were big, his fingers rough with calluses, his nails torn and lined with dirt. As Katharine came to him, she took a sheet of paper from the table. "Prithee, place them here," she said.

He emptied his hand onto the paper.

"You see," she said. "You have cut yourself."

There was blood on a finger of his left hand.

"No matter," he said, "my hands are my tools and get battered about. They are not, I'm afraid, the hands of a gentleman." He grinned and popped the finger into his mouth and sucked on it, while running his other hand through his dark curls.

His smile took Katharine aback. There was about him a serious air, and now the smile suddenly broke through it.

He held his finger to her. "The blood is gone," he said, and then opened his hand to her. "I will take that. No use you cutting your hand now."

She handed the paper with the shattered pieces to him. He folded the paper into a packet and placed it in his leather bag.

"I will find another," he said.

"No need," she said.

"I will. Sir Edward was of a fine and rare character. This room was his . . ."

"He loved to sit by the fire, there," she said. "He loved to sit and read. He was a scholar. He loved the written word and he loved his family and he loved his faith, and it was his faith that drove him away," said Katharine. "Where do you come from, Mr. Smythson? You are not from Lancashire, but from your accent I suspect you hail from farther north."

"Penrith by birth."

"The lands of ancient Cumbria. The shuttlecock of the Scottish chieftains."

"Aye, 'twas their riches. No recent raids, thank the good Lord. 'Tis now but a road to the south, not a bounty."

"The valley, I have heard, is beautiful."

"'Tis." He nodded.

"And do you make your home there still?"

"Have made my home in Nottinghamshire for many years, Wollaton, though my work takes me away from that village much of the year."

"And your children, do they travel with you?"

"I have but the one son, John. He does travel with me now. He's just out of grammar school, before he lived with my sister Elizabeth, while my houses took me away. He has cousins who are as brothers and sisters to him, as I trust you understand. He's a young man now, but my heart still breaks when he is not beside me."

Katharine nodded, wondering if when he said, *I trust you understand*, he was referring to her orphaned childhood, and if so, how he knew. "Take off your cape, Mr. Smythson, and set it by the fire. I am afraid our house is but fresh with mourning, and we are inconstant hosts. I will tell the kitchens to bring you some food and ale, for you must be hungry."

"Many thanks. I will be off soon. This is no time to discuss plans to alter the hall, when all is altered enough by grief."

"The day is unfortunate," said Katharine. "I am sorry you had to come all this way for naught."

"I am at work with my men on a new building not five leagues thither—Sir Christopher de Ashton's house. The snow stopped our hammering for a spell. I will ride back this afternoon."

"Farewell, Mr. Smythson," Katharine said, and held out her hand.

"Fare you well, my good lady." When he took her small hand in his, he looked as though he did not know what to do with it, whether to kiss it or to shake it as if she were a man. He did not lift his eyes to Katharine's but kept his lion head, with its mane of curls, bent. He seemed to study her hand with wonder—as if it were a new tool for shaving stones or cutting timber. Still holding her hand, he turned it so the palm faced upward. She knew not why, but she let him continue his examination.

"You *have* cut yourself," he said.

Katharine looked down at her palm. A red scab sliced across her pink skin where her nails had bit into her flesh when she last sat next to Will.

She pulled her hand from his grasp. "'Tis nothing. 'Tis an old wound," she said, rubbing her hands together and then pulling Edward's robe tightly around her. "Godspeed, Mr. Smythson."

He stared at her, his dark eyes quizzical. "Gramercy, my lady. Farewell," he said, and bowed.

Finally, she thought as she closed the door behind her. What did the stonemason think? That she was a saint with markings of the Savior's suffering on her hand? Nay, her wound was no miracle but self-inflicted—a sad testament to her own confused passion.

She would tell the kitchens to send Mr. Smythson a trencher of bread and cheese and some ale, and then she would find the other members of the house. Where was everyone? An unwelcome silence persisted within the walls. If Sir Edward were still here, *if Sir Edward were still here*, he would have called for a meeting.

Katharine was on her way down to the kitchens when she saw Matilda at the bottom of the stairs. She stepped down to embrace Matilda, but her aunt recoiled, frowning.

"Why are you wearing Edward's robe?" she snapped.

"I . . ."

"You have no right, Katharine, to wear his robe!"

"I . . . I put it on in the library because I was cold . . . I forgot . . ." She heard herself stammering like a child.

"Take it off now!" Matilda shouted. "Did you hear me? Why are you standing there like a fool? Remove Edward's robe now!"

As Katharine tried to pull her arm from the robe, Matilda grabbed the sleeve and yanked so hard the frayed material ripped. Matilda did not let go and tore the sleeve asunder.

"Look what you have done!" Matilda screamed, shaking the tattered sleeve in Katharine's face. "You, Katharine, have never known your place!"

Katharine stepped out of what was left of the old red and gold garment and let it drop to the floor. She was speechless, stunned. Rather than try to defend herself, she turned and walked evenly away. She had never, in her history at Lufanwal, been the target of such venom. Rounding the corner, she backed her body to the wall, shut her eyes and tried to breathe.

———

The day was without end. The melting snow seemed sand in an hour-glass, and everywhere Katharine went, in every room and every corridor, she heard the herald of time. She had no husband, no children. She had not planned on such a life. As she walked from the kitchens, where she had ordered the victuals for Mr. Smythson, through the great hall, where the servants were setting supper, she realized that her error was she simply had not planned. How could one plan after the unplanned death of her family scraped away every shred of hope? She had glossed over her desires, buried her dreams, allowed the day-to-day to become the month-to-month and then the year-to-year. Here was Will, mapping his course: patrons and poetry; a player with plans to own part of a theatrical company and to buy the biggest house in his town, the house with ten fireplaces. Ten fireplaces. The world in which he walked was all cunning, all stratagem, all future, while hers, she was beginning to comprehend, was all past.

She returned to her room and shut the door behind her. She went to the looking glass. She had never covered her head properly in the sun and now her face was crowded with freckles. When she was younger her dimples appeared only when she smiled, but they had with age become permanent creases on her cheeks. There were lines in her brow and strands of silver in her hair. She had said no to the various men Sir Edward had brought to her after her husband had died. She had said no because none of those suitors suited her. But she realized now another woman—a woman more like Will, with his visions of fine red shoes and ten fireplaces—would have said yes to one of those men. Katharine was amazed, not at what she saw mirrored in glass before her, but at what she saw mirrored inside of her. She was not poetry printed on a page—she was a word or two scribbled in the margins.

Katharine tried to make excuses for Matilda's outburst. The poor woman had lost her beloved husband. But her lashing echoed what Mary had said at dinner that evening weeks ago: that Katharine had never been considered part of the text of the family.

Katharine lay down on her bed. She shut her eyes and willed the cottage in the wood to come back to her. This time, the play in her head was different than before. There was still snow reaching up to the windows and the smoke curling from the chimney, but it was night, not day. And she had gone to bed, while he had stayed at the table, lamp lit, ink wet, quill bounding across the page. She was soundly asleep in her smock when he came to her; she was not against the door or a wall. After hours with his poem, he removed his breeches and snuffed the candle he had brought to bed. The moon was so round and so luminous that even with the candle out the little cottage was ablaze with light. She had her back to him and he kissed her neck and grazed her buttocks with his fingers, glided by her hips, her waist, her stomach, his hand soft and gentle yet assuredly a bird of prey. In partial slumber she opened to him, was quickly wet, and shuddered—which did not, as he'd suggested that day in the library, feel like a sneeze, but lasted longer and was richer, more an ancient fire, a sacrifice, a tingling that reached all the way to her womb. By the second time, he stirred hard against her, kissed her deeply, then climbed atop her, looked into her eyes, as if to conquer, and conquer her he did.

17

ou are raw-nerved," said Isabel.

Katharine had not realized that her left hand was tapping the table. "I am sad, as you are, gentle Isabel."

Isabel nodded and sighed. "I have wept. I have wept an ocean."

Katharine pulled Isabel to her and gave her a motherly hug. "You were well loved by your father, and part of him will live on in you."

"But my dear father will never know my children. He will never lay eyes on them."

"Oh, he will see them," said Katharine. "He sees you now, from his perch up high." She gently wiped the tears from Isabel's cheeks with her table napkin. "Come, eat. Yesterday was all famine for grief. Today you need fuel."

In truth, Katharine was having a difficult time sitting at the table. She waved to the servant girl to bring more wine. Will had sent more stanzas. The folded sheets of paper Molly brought were inches thick. Had he slept?

In Sir Edward's time, the dinner hour on Sunday was lively, always a banquet after mass with whomever was in residence or nearby—guests, family, neighbors. Even at Advent, when Edward observed the ancient abstinences, he still opened his hearth and home with whatever simple meals were allowed. But this Sunday, though Edward's russet-limned chair still presided at the head of the grand table, Matilda was not present, nor was Ursula, Richard, or Matilda's mother, Priscilla, who was gravely ill and could not rise from her bed.

Richard, who was making his way back from the witches' trial at the Lancaster Assize, would be shocked by the news of his father and by the change in his wife, for Richard had departed for Lancaster soon after Ursula had taken to her bed in grief over Guinny's demise. Katharine guessed Harold had caused Ursula's unmending and prayed that time would heal her broken spirit.

"You have lectured Isabel to eat, Cousin Kate, but you have not touched a morsel," said Joan.

Poor Joan was not yet fifteen but looked today as if she were past thirty, her mother Ursula's age. Joan had gained a stone since the summer and thickened around her middle, neck and chin. Her eyes bespoke an anxiety beyond her years. Katharine pictured Ursula's gaunt and bony form and imagined how Joan—nurse but never daughter—must have, these past few weeks, tried to convince her mother to eat.

"True, my dear." Katharine dipped a corner of bread into her goblet of wine. "Tell me news of Ned," she said to Isabel.

"Since my dear brother was soon leaving to return to us, when he received word Father's condition had worsened he made haste from Italy to France. Ned rode through the night but failed to reach Father in time. If only God had willed it, Kate. I so wish someone from our family had been by his side when the angels did take him." Isabel started to weep again.

"My dear," said Katharine, "your noble father was surrounded by those who loved him. He was and is at peace."

"Ned prayed at the priory the night and day through and then paid them well for taking such blessed care of Father," said Isabel.

"And now?" asked Katharine.

"He is bound home with Father's few possessions," said Isabel.

"Godspeed our dear Ned," said Katharine. "His arrival will be a beam of light in this darkening hall. And your sister?"

"She is at this moment with Sir Hugh on her way. All will bring comfort to Mother. But Ned the most, because he has been gone the longest and his absence has torn at Mother's heart for many years."

Ned had been in his own exile. First living in the city from which Dante had been banished, then moving to Rome. Early on, he had bought a villa in Florence, along the River Arno, with gold his father had released when he completed his studies. He claimed that poetry, sculpture and painting were the bread and ale of the people of Florence: beauty, he once said, was their nourishment. In his letters, he described cities bathed in golden light, where cathedrals and churches, bridges, piazzas and palaces were akin to jewels. Katharine did not know how Ned passed his time, but the months and then the years drifted by.

Katharine lit her lamp and sat in front of the fire with a thick pile of Will's poetry on her lap. He had written more than he had heretofore, fourteen stanzas since she'd last sat with him—the moon had risen twice. From the first line, Will's new stanzas anchored her. They were his best yet. He was on fire. Will had found the pulse of the poem finally and was writing out of it. The lines boasted a new solidity, a new confidence. When she'd started her work with him, his images at times lacked harmony: the two characters had at moments seemed wobbly, their intentions unclear. The lovers were riveting now, and the stanzas sharp in image and action. What a thing of gentle beauty did Will render Adonis. And how perfectly he painted Venus's lust for this landlocked lad.

Though Katharine knew the tale's end from Ovid and from Spenser, as she read Will's new lines she found herself wondering, What will happen in this battle of desire? Who will prevail? Venus entreated and implored Adonis to love her. The repetition of the word *lips* did, like seeds upon the fertile ground, make the passion grow. "'Touch but my fair lips with those fair lips of thine . . . The kiss shall be thine own as well as mine . . . Look in mine eye-balls, there thy beauty lies . . . Then why not lips on lips, since eyes in eyes?'"

Katharine sent a note with Molly that she would meet Will. An hour later, hooded, cloaked, gloved and booted, she took the stairs two steps at a time, chose not the course through the house to the old chapel, but pushed the oak door open and ventured across the icy courtyard.

Richard was coming through the gate on horseback. Katharine scurried down the path so he would not see her. Will had told Molly he would be there, but the schoolroom was empty. Katharine lit one lamp and then another, poked at the logs in the fireplace and sat on a bench. The fire awakened, the shadows shifting along the whitewashed walls. She sat and started to read his verse again. She dipped a quill into an inkhorn, adding to her notes: *fine* and *lovely* and *perhaps a different word*. Dipping the quill once more, she began to write lines of verse along the margin of a page. Engrossed in her writing, she did not hear Will enter. She had never written poetry before, and she had not even known when she put the quill to the page that a stanza would spill out of her. Indeed, when she looked up at Will she stared at him, trying to place him.

"Hast thou seen a ghost?" he said, coming toward her.

He was beautiful in the shifting lamplight.

"It seems we have been apart for ages," he said.

"'Tis been but a few days," she replied.

He shed his cloak and sat across from her, a schoolboy.

"How sits your sorrow now, Kate? Does grief still guide your day?"

"'Tis too sad to believe that Sir Edward has left this mortal earth."

"Your loss is heaven's gain. Look to your family this day, dearest Kate, not to me," said Will.

"Sir Edward's eldest daughter is coming down from the north, and dear Ned, the youngest son, is returning home from across the sea."

"The prodigal son," said Will.

"Ned will provide succor," Katharine continued. "'Tis hard not to feel a feast when he is around, even in the midst of famine. Our bond is blood, yes, but 'tis something of magic, too . . . 'tis hard to explain."

Her hands were clasped and resting on the table. Will reached across the table and covered them with his.

"I have made some marks," she said finally. "I was much impressed by the quantity."

"I hope the quality impressed as well," he said.

"'Tis your best work yet," she said. "It seemed to pour from your pen."

"I hope it read as though it poured from my heart."

"Thou art, now, master of your art," she said.

"Ahhhhh!" he exclaimed, rising and walking to the fire. He bent down and warmed his hands, then stood. "Kate . . ." he said, turning to her.

She was part thrilled, part terrified. "Yes," she said.

"I crave your pardon for making you wait here in the cold. I took my horse, fine Bess, yonder into the hills and the forest where the drifts are still deep. We jumped a fallen tree, a frozen creek, a pile of snow-covered stones. Bess is swift and sure of hoof. I took the whip to her and urged her on and on, faster and faster. Then I let her go, let her discover the pleasure of the speed. She met no resistance from the reins. She did not falter. She did not slip. Bess finally stopped on her own accord, then headed back to the barn. I was surprised when the sun started to drop, for I had not realized we had been out so long."

"Is she so named after our queen?"

He bowed his head in acknowledgment. "She is my queen."

"How fortunate for you to have a Bess you can subject, whilst being the subject of a Bess," said Katharine.

"Both are beasts, methinks," he said with a chuckle. "In sooth, you think this work my best?"

"In sooth, you let go the reins of your rhymes and found pleasure in the speed, for you wrote these many words with such alacrity. My quill did mark a word here and there, but I did not drench your pages with circled words or whole lines cut or questioned."

"Thou art no longer the surveyor perched upon a rock?" Will stood before her.

"I have not, quite yet, relinquished my mapmaker's quill."

"My sweet Kate, I would still be on the first line, perhaps the first word, of this humble poem if it were not for you." He was down on one knee. "I am, like Mars to Venus, your servant. You have mastered me."

He was a suitor looking up at her from below. "I will write a sonnet for you," he said, jumping up. "Verse will be my next gift to thee."

Katharine smiled.

"Let us look at what you found," Will said, pulling open the pages. He sat next to her on the bench. He leaned over her arm, looking at his verse. "What's this?" He pulled the page with the stanza she had written in front of him. "'Tis verse, Katharine." He called her by her given name. He read it aloud:

> *"Is thine own heart to thine own face affected?*
> *Can thy right hand seize love upon thy left?*
> *Then woo thyself, be of thyself rejected;*
> *Steal thine own freedom, and complain on theft.*
> *Narcissus so himself himself forsook,*
> *And died to kiss his shadow in the brook."*

He looked at her, puzzled.

"'Tis only a thought I had for Venus, that she touches on Ovid's Narcissus, in her quest for Adonis's . . ." She stopped.

"Adonis's what?"

"Lips," she said.

"'Tis well done, Kate." He had lost his smile. "'Tis most well done."
His tone was stiff.

She wanted to make him supple again. "You may have it," she said.

They were silent.

"Will," Katharine began, "I have never waded in such waters before."
Her words sounded solemn. She wanted to reprise them in a lighter tone,
but it was too late. She could not look him in the eyes, but focused on a
dark burl in the table.

"The waters of verse-writing?" he asked.

"No," she said. "Of us."

"Oh," he said. "'The tale of us.'"

"I have never waded in such waters before," she repeated. "I have had
a husband. I have had suitors. But I have never had this. My mind is most
confused. I know not what to do. I beseech your help in navigating
this . . . this . . ." She worried she would lose him further by her admis-
sions but forced herself to continue. "I know not how to say this . . ."

"Say it."

"I desire you."

"And I, you," he followed.

She felt her heart unfasten. Will was sitting but an arm's length from
her. He did not rise, but she saw his whole body sigh, as if he had been
waiting for these words, as if they were a release for him, too. When she
saw his smile, her eyes filled with tears.

"Kate," he said. His most gentle yet. "Such attraction is in our blood,
'tis our nature."

"I am but a novice in these arts," she said.

"Kate, I've had wenches of one sort or another since I was a lad, but
those days are past. And I have a wife. But what we have is most different." He paused. "You know me better than anyone else."

He rose from the bench and came round the table to her. When he held out his hands, she took them, and in one agile movement he pulled her to her feet. Then he drew her in close so she could feel his heart beating. She felt ease in the embrace and was surprised, after all the weeks of skimming his skin, she had found home. He lifted her chin so she looked him in the eyes, and then he gently placed his hands on her neck, slid them back into her hair and removed the ivory pins one by one. At the pull of each pin, she felt as though his fingers were on her bodice, and he was undoing one lace after another with tender care.

Her hair fell to her shoulders. His gaze never left her eyes. He leaned into her, hovered for a moment without contact and then kissed her on the lips. The kiss was slow and deliberate. *Lips on lips.* She had never felt such a passion before, and gave herself to him utterly in the kissing, until they both heard something outside the old chapel. Katharine pulled herself from him, turned and saw a shadow at the window. The colored glass made it impossible to see clearly. They separated. The specter could have been a child, a servant or a spy.

Will helped Katharine on with her cloak and was at her side when she opened the door. They heard a strange sound—a song, a sad song that hung in the air like mist. Katharine thought of the three witches. How had such hallowed ground become so haunted? They followed the melancholy tune until they came to its source. Ursula. Ursula, wearing only a white smock, was on her knees under a tree with her parrot in her hands. The bird's bright plumage was barely visible in the dim light. Katharine took her own cloak off and wrapped it round Ursula.

"She's dead," Ursula said. "I've come to bury her."

The earth was frozen and still covered with patches of snow.

"'Tis no time to dig a grave, Ursula. You'd best wait till the morrow and have one of the servants tend to it," said Katharine. She felt as if she were talking to a child.

Will went to Ursula and stood over her. "Hand me your bird, my lady. We will find it a home."

"'Tis not a home she wants, 'tis a grave."

"We will dig her a grave, then," he said.

Ursula's hair was unbound and unkempt, and it framed her face like a wild halo. She relinquished the bird to Will.

"Come with me, Ursula," said Katharine, and with unusual meekness, Ursula acquiesced. When Katharine helped her to stand, she saw Ursula wore no shoes, that her feet were bare.

Ursula stared at the bird in Will's hand, funneling all her concentration toward it, as if her focus would breathe life into its flesh and resurrect it. "I prithee place a stone atop the grave, so I will know where 'tis," she said.

"I will, my lady." Will bowed.

Katharine was impressed by Will's gentleness, by his ability to read the thought-sick Ursula.

"Gramercy," Ursula said. She moved her gaze from the dead bird to Will's face. "Thou art a sugar'd lad. Dost thou think me fair?"

"Thou art fair, my lady."

"Dost thou think me wanton?"

"If wanton means a lively creature, then aye, thou art a wanton."

"Dost thou think me tainted?"

"If tainted be a condition of thy heart, not thy soul, then anyone who hath ere been in love is tainted, so aye, thou art tainted, for I have never yet met a man or woman ov'r the age of twenty who hath a pure, unspotted heart."

Ursula burst out in high-pitched laughter.

"Let us go in, Ursula. The cold wind will o'erpower your skin," said Katharine.

"My pure, unspotted heart was doomed from the first second I crossed the threshold of this ill-erected hall!" said Ursula, then she laughed again.

Katharine looked at Will. He nodded his head slightly. Then she took Ursula's arm and steered her toward the hall. Ursula seemed even thinner than before: there was neither meat nor muscle the length of the poor dear's arms. Ursula sang while they walked.

> "Ah poor bird
> Why art thou
> Singing in the shadows
> At this late hour?
>
> "Ah poor bird
> Take thy flight
> High above the shadows
> Of this sad night."

She sang the same two verses over and over again and was still singing them when she entered the house. As they climbed the stairs to her chamber, she asked, "Do you think my voice good?"

"Aye," said Katharine.

"I have always wanted to sing for the family, but Richard says my voice has too much breath and that I wobble in and out of tune. Dost thou think I wobble or warble like a thrush?"

"I must hear more to make a proper diagnosis," answered Katharine.

"You are a doctor now?"

Katharine laughed. "I suppose I am."

"Doctor, might you play the virginals while I sing to the family?"

"I will," Katharine said.

"I know my voice is beautiful," said Ursula, standing at her door.

Katharine squeezed her arm in affection. "Get to bed, Ursula, for your limbs are quaking from the cold. I will send your maid up with something hot to drink."

"Your cloak?" said Ursula.

"You wear it until you are tucked in. I'll send Molly round to fetch it."

Ursula placed her hand on Katharine's arm and leaned very close to her. "Beware of his words," she said. "Beware."

Katharine tried to smile but suddenly she felt as cold as Ursula appeared. "Good night, Ursula," she said, and turned away.

Ursula's warning seemed to carry such caution, as though words were poison and could kill a person. Actions could kill, that Katharine knew, actions drew blood, but words? Nay, she said to herself, nay. She realized with her hair down from her moment with Will that she likely looked as unkempt as Ursula. As Katharine hurriedly made her way to her chamber, she couldn't get Ursula's silly ditty out of her head.

18

our eyes, dear Kate, are far away," said Joan. "But not from grief." Joan was a keen watcher of moods, having grown up with a mother whose humors changed by the hour.

A fresh square of linen lay on Katharine's lap, but the cloth remained without the first stitch: she was staring at a bare branch outside the window. Ever since meeting with Will the day before, she was ashamed she felt so light, so airy, when the whole great house was deep in mourning for the beloved head of the household.

"There are rumors, dear Kate," Isabel added.

"Rumors?" Katharine turned her gaze to the girls.

"You must know," continued Isabel. "You meet a fair fellow almost daily, whose tales precede him. Tongues wag in this warren. Walls have eyes, as do windows."

"Tales?" Katharine repeated. *The tale of us.* She wanted to remember forever how welcome it felt when he held her in his arms. If this was how it felt when they were fully clothed, well—she sighed—how wonderful skin on skin would feel.

"He's a lewd lad, they say," said Isabel.

"'The fictions of idle tongues,'" Katharine quoted Ovid. "Master Shakespeare is married! Her name is Anne."

"He's a lewd lad that one, all the same," countered Isabel.

"The blush of damask is upon your cheeks," said Joan.

"You can be sure our tongues are still," said Isabel. "But come, give us a little sugar, for our day is most bitter."

"I know not what to say, nor how to say it," said Katharine.

"Kate, you always know what to say and how to say it," said Isabel. "He hath struck you dumb. What do you do with him in that chilly old chapel?"

"'Tis now a schoolhouse," corrected Katharine.

"What do you teach the tutor, then?" said Isabel. "Or what does he teach you?"

"What love scenes do you play, for they say he's been in London, a player at the new playhouses," said Joan.

"The players upon those stages are all men, so his love scenes would have to be with boys," said Katharine. She wished she felt like laughing, but the topic of Will seemed to offer neither comedy nor satire.

"You *are* bereft of speech," said Isabel. "Come, dear Kate, we are only trying to make mirth on this dismal day, to speak of something other than our loss. I have been hoping you would use the wondrous wit God hath bestowed upon you to cheer our tearful countenance."

"I am in love," Katharine said, wondering how the words sprang from her lips before she could trap them. Where was her dignity?

"Oh, Kate," the two girls chimed in unison. They left their perches and, like bright-eyed sparrows, gathered round her.

"'Tis serious," chirped Isabel.

"'Tis wondrous," sang Joan.

"He is a player, Kate," said Isabel. "A poet perchance. A tutor when necessary. 'Tis not the right match. He is married. He has, they say, children, several. His father is a glover. He is years your junior. And this 'Will,' as you call him, is too . . . too glossy, for he is used to wooing spectators with his words and wit. He wooed my dear father before he left. This man you say you love has never been to university and my father hired him! Never, in the history of this house, has such an unqualified, unschooled man taught the children. He is no match for you, dear Kate. I would not trust my weight in what this Master Shakespeare says. Has he spoken of his love?"

"You sound as though you are my sister, Isabel, my elder sister, and in truth you are not yet twenty," replied Katharine. "I hold no interest in matches."

"You have never held any interest in matches, Kate! They used to flock around you and you hardly noted them. You dismissed them!"

"I did nothing of the sort."

"'Tis what Father said."

Katharine recalled the years after her husband died, when she was a young widow with no children and no dowry. "Perhaps I did dismiss them," she said. "None of them had true intelligence. Some had wealth. Some had age. Some had property. But none had brilliance."

"So this Will, this Shakespeare, has that?"

"He is the most brilliant man. He has pieced together a good education in an independent way. He has taught himself much . . ." Katharine paused and then tried a new tack. "There are certain human beings who are born with minds so quick and so curious they create kingdoms in whatever sphere they tread. The ancients, the philosophers, the poets we now read—"

"He does not seem on the road to kingdom come, I daresay," Isabel interrupted. "'Tis said the playhouses in London are worse than the bear-baiting pits! Where are his riches, Kate? Where is his gold? Where is his property? Where are his books, his plays, his poetry? He is six and twenty, Kate. He has a wife, for whom, from what the tongues say, he cares little; he has children he has abandoned. And you believe, my dear Kate, that he loves you? He may love himself, but you? You? Who in truth deserves so much. Does he love you, Kate? Hath he said so?"

Isabel was no serpent, but her words had such strength that Katharine, old enough to be her mother, was close to tears. Perhaps it was Isabel's father's death that moved the girl to such force.

Isabel did not stop. "Perchance the brilliance you see is *on* him, not *in* him," she continued. "Perchance, like a shilling, it is his shininess that attracts. He does know how to put on the polish. He was most buffed up after his performance on Saint Crispin's Day. You had left the dance floor when he applied himself to Lord and Lady Strange. To watch your Will court them, well, one would think he believed Ferdinando and Alice were alchemists who could change his silver to gold! I love you, Kate. And so does Joan, and we do not want to see you pained. Perhaps you are still blind to men who love you or could love you. You are not out of wooing range yet. The queen still woos."

"The queen," said Katharine, "is the queen! She truly has the kingdom from which to woo. Do I? I think not! You two girls will marry with wagons of gold—that is why our dear Edward fled! To save all these riches, these beautiful hills, forests of timber, bountiful fields, mineral mines, for all of you! But I have few true connections and no true claim. When we hear dear Edward's will, I will be but a pebble at the most, a grain of sand at the least, while the rest of you will be boulders!"

Katharine had stood during her speech and was horrified to find she had shouted the last lines. She had never wanted to blurt such things to these sweet young women. Why had she routinely dismissed her opportunities? She had fed on words and ideas and enjoyed her bookish company with Edward, and, with no children and no gold of her own, she was minutes away, seconds perhaps, from the poor scorned hags dragged through the cold currents or from those poor wretches dragged into cages and burned at the stake.

And, now, for the crown: she had fallen in love with someone whose goal was to hawk verses the way his father had hawked gloves.

"I am so sorry," Katharine said.

Isabel and Joan stared at her, their eyes soft with concern. Katharine had never seen such a display of pity directed toward her. She had brought this illness upon herself.

"Forget what I have said, I beg of you. I am overcome with grief for Edward's passing, and have lost counsel with myself. Forgive me, my dears." She placed a hand on each of their cheeks and held them for a moment, then snatched her bare linen and hurried out the door.

Katharine was out of breath by the time she reached her chamber. Young Isabel, dear, gentle, loving Isabel, Katharine reasoned, did not know the true nature of her friendship with Will. She and Will were forging a special bond without the customary boundaries or rules.

Molly handed a sheaf of folded papers tied with a blue silk cord to Katharine. "Suppose everyone does want you to read their verse now, mistress," Molly said.

It was not Will's paper, nor his handwriting.

"Mr. Smythson brought it for you."

"Mr. Smythson was here? Did he ask to see me?"

"No, on account of the house being in mourning for Sir Edward, but he bade me hand these to you and said he hoped you enjoyed them and he wished you well."

"Marry, Molly, does everyone think they're a poet?"

"Suppose they do," Molly said, brushing Katharine's hair.

"Are you a poet, Molly? Do you have a stack of rhymes ready for me to read?"

"I cannot write ev'n two score words yet. Methinks I might learn a few more before I 'tempt a thing like that!"

Katharine laughed and placed the packet of papers, unopened, on her table. "And Ursula? What news?"

"The doctor leeched her and gave her a draught and said she must rest, for she'd worked her nerves to a boil."

"That she had."

The following afternoon, the library door burst open just as Katharine was to enter. Richard was the first out the door, followed by Mary and Harold, arm in arm. Katharine could not recall them ever touching; their linked arms were a strange sight. The last time she had seen Harold was in the hidden chapel when he was dragging the pleading Ursula, whose frail arms were hugging his legs. Mary did not have a full smirk on her face, but her self-satisfied armor was cause for alarm. Katharine had noticed a newfound power in her gait and wondered what had energized her thus.

Sir Hugh, Grace's husband, next exited the library.

"How fares my dear Katharine?" said Hugh, trying to bow.

"I've been better, my dear Hugh," she said. "We all have."

Katharine looked past Hugh into the library, where Matilda sat flanked by her daughters, Grace and Isabel. Ursula was absent. Ned was the courier for Edward's last wishes, so the family group could not have been listening to the will—and Katharine assumed she would be invited to that gathering—but Matilda, sitting in Edward's old chair by the fire, was visibly distressed. Her two daughters were trying to soothe her by patting her back, petting her arm and cooing at her.

"His bones should be here, in this earth, in his earth," Matilda cried.

"But Mother dear, the body must stay in the ground for a long while yet," said Grace. "Then they will come."

"We must wait at least a year, Mama, until the bones can be moved," added Isabel.

"Will there ever be an end to this bloodshed and chaos?" Matilda wailed. "The monasteries around us are slighted and in ruins. The bones of men cut down in their prime are scattered across the country. To serve what? The evil whims of Her Majesty and her greedy ministers?"

"Mother, soften your voice," cautioned Grace.

"I have been mute too long. Eight years ago I saw my husband dragged from his home as if a criminal and imprisoned for a year. I have seen our turf appropriated and divided among them. They are rife with avarice. They are as conquerors with battle spoils and do with our manors, our halls and our farms what Elizabeth's father did with the friaries and abbeys. My own dowry, Lefford Hall with its thousand acres, was thus stolen from me two years past, when it was supposed to go to Isabel for her dowry. The Lord Chamberlain has increased his domain tenfold by robbing good and noble Catholics of their lands. Why this blight? Why this constant punishment? Why are we the ones who are made to suffer? If Edward had been in his house, if I had been able to care for him, to wife my husband, then he would not have perished. He forbade me to go with him, felt his banishment was but a short breath, but I should have gone after him, to be with him. It was my duty. Forsooth, I have lost all."

Katharine had not heard Matilda's voice so full of vigor since Edward had departed. Perhaps in her grief, in her loss, she had found strength.

"'Tis true, dear Mother, that much has been taken and much has been lost in fines to the Crown for our beliefs, but we have not lost each other," soothed Grace. "Think of many of our best families in Lancashire, their fathers jailed and tortured for much longer than a year, their sons gone off to the Continent, only to return newly ordained in our faith, their fate in God's hands."

"In truth, too many are hunted down and executed like murderers," added Isabel.

"Worse than murderers," said Matilda. "For the minute they step again upon the soil of their birth, the minute their ships let them down upon the sand, they are, in Elizabeth's eyes, traitors. And we have borne sad witness to her gruesome executions. Oh, poor Cuthbert Mayne, poor Edmund Campion, poor Robert Southwell. So many, many lads, their skin still soft, so true and so bright and so brave that risk not their souls but their blood . . ."

"We have lost no sons," said Grace.

"We have lost a father, who was a son once," said Matilda.

"Father died joyful, I am sure of it," said Isabel. "Joyful in being able to retain, till the very end, a conscience void of offense."

"Father died an upright, loyal English gentleman who at the end had liberty to worship God according to the dictates his conscience granted him. He was ready at all times to serve his country faithfully and honestly," added Grace.

"The crack in this land rends all honesty asunder, for now to be a Catholic means a man is no longer a natural Englishman," said Matilda. "The air I breathe reeks and suffocates and poisons."

Katharine entered the library at this point and shut the door behind her, for Matilda was on a rant, and she agreed with Grace that talk when loud and without counsel could seep into walls and floorboards.

"I was passing and thought it best to pull the door fast," said Katharine. It was the first time she had seen Matilda since their unfortunate encounter on the stairwell after the news of Sir Edward's death.

Grace greeted Katharine with warmth.

"Mother wants dear Father's bones to lie here," said Isabel.

Katharine nodded. "And they will in time. Yet his good soul will rest in heaven and for that we can thank the Lord."

"Mother, it will bide us a year to build his monument," said Grace. "And when his bones return we shall have a mass for his saintly relics."

"His monument is long ago built and resides in the lot of the man who carved the stone. Methinks my Edward designed it when he was ne'er past twenty," said Matilda.

"Our Ned is returning," said Grace. "We can rejoice in God granting us this gift."

"Godspeed dear Ned," said Katharine.

"Why did I allow Edward to leave without me?" moaned Matilda. "Why was I not at his side when he breathed his last breath?"

At that moment they heard horses and men shouting. The women stopped speaking and listened, for there was no amity in the tones rising from the courtyard. Quib's voice was adamant. "The master, Sir Edward, is dead," hollered the steward. "Get ye hence and leave his poor family in peace."

"What skirmish is this? The insult of another raid when I have so freshly lost a husband." Matilda's face was hard. "Do they not remember, they murdered our priest and the priest who came to give our murdered priest mass? Do they now seek blood from a stone? Let us open our doors to them. For once we have nothing to hide. The stain of their actions will be all theirs." She rose, pulled her dark widow's veil over her face, and with the bearing of a queen walked from the library; her daughters and Katharine followed her like ladies-in-waiting.

As Matilda descended the staircase, she ordered one of the gathering servants to open the great oak door. "Have you no shame?" she bellowed at the group of some twenty men. "This house is mourning our dearly departed master." The steward hobbled toward her, blood dripping from his forehead.

The leader of the men pushed past Matilda and ordered the men to "search every corner, try every floorboard, drown every fire and peer up every chimney as if it were a maid's skirt." The men fanned out across the house while the family and their servants were herded into the great hall.

"We have no priest here!" shouted Matilda.

"Who said 'tis a priest we're looking for?" said the leader, who identified himself as Hull, the new high sheriff.

Hull was unusually tall, with a large ruff and small head. He looked exactly like the priest who had given mass for Father Daulton and was murdered on his way back to the Molyneux estate. He had the same long fingers and long arms, the same pale skin with a hint of blue underneath, the same frail body yet large frame. Instead of a black chasuble, he was wearing a black doublet and a black cloak. The two, the murdered priest and the justice, were twins. Identical. How odd, Katharine thought, for twins to be on the opposite ends of the spectrum: one the hunter and the other his prey.

The last time Lufanwal was raided, the pursuivants took two days to search every nook and cranny, slighting furniture and any object, be it lantern or painting or looking glass, that stood in their way. The women and children were locked away in their chambers, the men rounded up in the courtyard, the Catholic servants segregated in different parts of the building and the non-Catholic servants made to stand watch. They did not find young Father Daulton, who was crouching in the ingenious hide in the wall above the well. The three hides at Lufanwal had concealed priests since the start of Elizabeth's reign—one high up in the well house outside the kitchens, another within the unused fireplace in the North Hall, and the third behind the tapestry and wainscot in the library.

Perhaps the ravaging would have happened again, if Richard had not walked into the fray, just returned from a morning hunt, his hawking gauntlet still fast upon his right hand.

"Hull, what goes here?" Richard called, recognizing the high sheriff, possibly from his duties as a justice.

But as soon as Hull saw Richard, he started shouting commands, and several men surrounded Richard, pinning his arms behind him and binding him with ropes. Then Hull pulled out a parchment and read the official order, calling for Richard's arrest for the treasonous charge of conspiring against the queen, describing a plot against her life that supposedly Richard along with the Duc de Malois had conceived.

Shock spread across Richard's face. "I am no traitor! I made no plot against the queen! Unhand me! There has been a grave mistake. I served as justice at the assize. I am no traitor! I serve our queen as do you!"

"We have evidence!" Hull shouted, and commanded his men to continue the search, for if they brought in a bloody seminarian as well, he said, "That would be sugar on the custard!"

A maid must have alerted Ursula to the plight of her husband, for just as they were dragging him out of the great hall, she ran up to the door from the corridor and tried to grab Richard. She looked like a ghost, her blond hair flying in all directions, her body thin. The men swatted her away, but she kept at them, clawing with her fingernails.

"You brutes! He is no traitor! He does not have that much steel in him!"

Katharine was stunned by the inaction of the rest of the household. All stood by and watched the scene with Ursula unfold. Hull had gotten hold of Ursula by the time Katharine was at her side. He had one arm around Ursula's neck and the other locking her arm behind her.

"Sir, she is not well. Prithee, let her go. I will take her," said Katharine.

"She looks like one of the hags brought round here last month!" Hull laughed.

Ursula uttered a strange howl, the type of sound a hurt dog might make. Then she sank her teeth into Hull's hand.

"Fie, you vile snake!" he screamed, and tossed her at Katharine, who picked Ursula up in her arms and started to carry her away, for she was afraid that Hull might attack them or, worse, might haul them off to jail.

"Foul wench, if thou art a witch and hath poisoned me, thou wilt be tied to a stake and burned!" he shouted. Ursula had bitten Hull so hard that his hand was bleeding. "Take the traitor out and hoist him up on a horse!"

"Noooooooooooo!" Ursula wailed.

Hull started to lunge at Ursula, when he was called by one of his men. They had brought Will in. He was not bound and they were not holding him, but he was flanked by three men. His doublet had been ripped open—no doubt they'd searched for the sacred Agnus Deis around his neck.

"We found a man who says he's a tutor but methinks he's a priest," shouted one of the men, whose cheeks were so ruddy, his eyes so bloodshot and his walk so wobbly that it would take a blind man not to notice he had been soaking up sack in the hours before the raid.

"Where hid the fiend?" barked Hull.

"Wasn't hid exact, he was in a room near the stone wall o'er there in the back. He was writing something. Says he's a player, like the boys who come to town last summer. If he's a player—'tis a priest playing a schoolmaster!"

"Did you find a Latin Bible or papal bull among his pages?" asked Hull. Possession of a papal bull was also punishable by death.

"Not exact," said the man. "He didna have no bull in his chamber. Nor any other animals neither."

"Papal bull, fool! 'Tis a document with a seal from the Pope," scoffed Hull.

"Still wouldna know if I saw one, 'cause I don't read words. Here, we seized these papers right outta his hand—the ink no' ev'n dry." He pushed the pages at Hull. "And he's quiet like a priest. And has a certain priestly dignity. I can smell a priest, I can. And look at his hands, pale as the moon . . . with long fingers, like priest hands, and his room was full of paper with words written in every which direction, priestly words, methinks, prayers for secret masses—"

"Enough, Pearson! Enough. Bring me a candle, and the rest of ye keep your pace. 'Tis yet another treasonous brother we come here for."

Mary had entered the great hall, clasping what Katharine assumed was a Protestant prayer book. Mary had changed in the past year, emerged hard and distinct, like a statue from a block of marble. "My lord is not here," she said.

"And where might he be, my lady?" said Hull.

"I have no idea. He left on horse this morning and did not say where he was off to," Mary said, and promptly held *The Book of Common Prayer* aloft so Hull could see the cover. She opened the book and started to read.

Ursula had gone still in Katharine's arms. Her eyes were open, but she had quit the moment. Katharine held her, yet she could feel in Ursula's body that she was elsewhere; there was no weight to her, as if magic had made her feather, not flesh and bone.

Will stood in front of Hull and waited. Katharine noticed where Will's doublet was torn his skin was smooth—not the bristly lawn of her long-dead husband. He held his tongue, did not even utter a syllable, while a servant brought a candle and Hull looked at his pages. As Will stared soberly at Hull, the rest of his features, too, betrayed nothing.

Hull started to read out loud: "Sometime she shakes her head, and then his hand, now gazeth she on him, now on the ground. Sometime her arms infold him like a band: she would, he will not in her arms be bound. And when from thence he struggles to be gone, she locks her lily fingers one in one. 'Fondling,' she saith, 'since I have hemm'd thee here within the circuit of this ivory pale, I'll be a park, and thou shalt be my deer: feed where thou wilt, on mountain or in dale; graze on my lips, and if those hills be dry, stray lower, where the pleasant fountains lie . . .'"

Katharine thought Hull would stop reading—for Will was at his most lecherous yet. Perchance the high sheriff did not understand Will's direction. Whatever Hull thought, he continued to read aloud: "'Within this limit is relief enough, sweet bottom grass and high delightful plain, round rising hillocks, brakes obscure and rough, to shelter thee from tempest and from rain: then be my deer, since I am such a park, no dog shall rouse thee, though a thousand bark . . .'"

The man standing next to Pearson had been biting a grin, and with this last stanza he could contain himself no longer and started to giggle.

Pearson, too, the sack he'd drunk making him weak, began snorting and guffawing.

"This is no papist mass!" screamed Hull as he flung the pages into the air.

Pearson and his fellow pursuivant quickly dropped their smiles and pressed their lips.

"This . . . this . . . these . . . these . . ." Hull stuttered, "are but carnal rhymes with harlot words . . . unfit for ladies or for gentlemen! You, sirrah," he said, pointing his bitten and bloodied hand at Will, "lack any sort of decency . . . are lewd-quilled and should not be the teacher of children! This lout is no priest, Pearson! He is a poet!" Hull spat out, then marched out the door to the courtyard, where Richard was now rigged atop a horse.

From his ungainly perch, Richard could be heard shouting, "I am no traitor!"

"Tie a rag about his mouth," ordered Hull, and he stalked off to find the men he had sent to the barns.

Hull and his marauding men looked for priest holes in all the wrong places, for the hides and the secret chapel were so expertly hidden in the main house that the men—as in the last raid—passed right over them. They had sniffed and tapped and rattled and thumped, but in the end they galloped off, with only poor Richard as their prize.

19

fter the sound of the hooves receded, the servants and the family cleaned up what had been shattered or destroyed. The charges against Richard, the family believed, were utterly false, and they needed to find a way to prove this and to secure his release from jail before he was carried off to London, for once he was there any true contact would cease and the chance for any legal maneuvering would diminish. Mary had known her husband was off to Lancaster but had not wanted to tell the high sheriff. Harold was still not back the next day. The family worried the men had snared him along the road while he was returning home.

When Katharine thought of the meeting in the library to which she had not been invited, she realized that Sir Edward's kindness had shielded her from the fact that she had never been fully accepted by the rest of the family. In truth, the years spent trying to appease and to please those to whom she was related by blood or by marriage caused her much strain. If only she could, by some miracle, leave Lufanwal. But how, when she had no riches, no estates of her own?

With help from Molly, Katharine removed her simple charcoal-gray mourning gown, replacing it with a silk partlet and matching sleeves, embroidered with gold fleurs-de-lis and couched with gold cord that Isabel had given to her the previous New Year's. She wore a black velvet bodice with gold silk stripes Ned sent from Italy and a black satin skirt open in front so the lace of the petticoat peeked through.

Katharine knew she was wildly overdressed for meeting Will; she wanted to glide into the cold, varnished old chapel as though she were a lady of wealth and nobility. She sprinkled rosewater liberally on her petticoats. She rubbed distilled lilac on the inside of her wrists and on her neck. She even let Molly dust her cheeks with cinnamon powder.

"'Tis so much gold in your bodice and blouse I would leave go your hair, for you have natural strands that match the golden threads of your cloth," offered Molly.

"I seem with the years to have grown a mine of silver strands as well. If all the silver and gold in my hair were coins in a purse, well then I'd be rich, wouldn't I! Put a few more pins in my hair, dear Molly, and then wrap me in my cloak and I will go down."

The house, with all the recent calamities, would think her mad, glittering from head to toe. She could quite possibly cause a riot if they caught her swathed in gold, but Katharine wanted to look lavish; she wanted to glow. She had expected after his last flood of verse Will would have sent her more, but nothing had come, so Katharine arrived at the old chapel empty-handed.

The sun was strong, even though winter had descended; a cascade of colors spilled through the stained glass. The fire was lit, and Will's papers were strewn across the table. Katharine removed her cloak. She knew she looked ready for Lord and Lady Strange's banquet table, not for sitting midday on an old oak bench with the children's tutor. She picked up one of Will's pages—the ink was not yet dry. She placed it back on the table. She stood next to the fire, walked into a beam of gem-like light from the windows, then walked over to the table again and peered at one of the boys' hornbooks.

Will burst through the door and she looked up. After their long kiss the last time they'd met, she felt they were almost lovers. She blushed. "Did you not take fright?" she asked. "When the men hauled you hence?"

Will pitched wood into the fireplace and fanned the coals. He gazed into the flames as he spoke. "My father was taken away after Campion was caught, scores of men were. I was living up here, in the employ of the De Hoghtons. My mother called me home, for fear I was in danger. After a short while, they let my father go. My mother's kin Edward Arden was not as fortunate. He was taken to the Tower, tormented on the rack and hanged at Tyburn in front of the morning crowd; his head was set upon a pole at London Bridge. He died protesting his innocence at every charge, declaring his only crime was the profession of the Catholic religion. The wife and daughter were released but the son-in-law was hanged and piked on the bridge along with Arden."

"And where do you stand?" Katharine asked.

"Why, next to you, my lady."

"What side do you take in this war?"

"I decided in my youth to step away from that game. The religion of our nation changed three times in twenty years. I quite like my head and see no reason to lose it." He paused. "Thou surely art the sun, Kate," he said, bowing low. He walked around her, appraising. "The prettiest Kate in Christendom."

She smiled and nodded as if she were the queen and he Lord Essex.

"Come," he said, sitting on the bench and looking up at her.

She sat next to him. They were close but not touching.

"I have brought something for you," he said.

She thought perhaps it was the sonnet he had promised, but he dropped a kidskin pouch, not folded paper, on the table.

"Open it," he said, pointing to the pouch.

She untied the silk string and turned the soft brown pouch upside down. A blue-green stone set in silver and strung on a black silk cord fell into the palm of her hand. She had never seen a stone of such a brilliant hue; it was opaque, not clear. The shape was not perfectly round, nor perfectly oval.

"'Tis beautiful," she said. "Many thanks."

"You are most welcome. 'Tis for your lovely neck."

"What is it?"

"Turquoise, mined in the Americas. I found it in a stall in London when last there."

"I have never seen anything like it. The color is so bright, so rich, 'tis almost unnatural."

Katharine put the stone round her neck and tried to tie the ends of the silk cord but could not. She blushed. "Prithee, kind sir, might ye help me," she said, mocking the accent of a wench. She turned her back and handed the ends of the cord to him. He touched the nape of her neck lightly as he tied them. There was such intimacy in the moment—she thought he might kiss her neck, or the scars that ran down her back.

"Let me gaze," he said.

She turned to face him. She felt a courtesan and she liked it. She did not want a match; she did not want to marry; she wanted to be his mistress.

"'Tis wondrous with your eyes," Will said, "that's why I chose it." He sprang from the bench and started walking round the room. "My poem is with me always now—a second skin. I sleep with it at night and wake clutching it like a pillow. It started, Kate, as such a lonely seed, but with your watering, with your sunlight, it has grown sturdy and strong. I am eternally in your debt." When Will stopped beneath a stained-glass window, the tinted light seemed to anoint him. He ran his fingers along one of the walls and leaned in close, examining the surface. "What lurks beneath the white?"

"The wall wore pictures of Saint George and such but was painted over when we closed the chapel," said Katharine.

"Before I was born, my father was elected chamberlain of the borough of Stratford," Will said. "My parents came from papist stock, and the daily edicts against the faith into which many were born and baptized caused much stress and strain. The town council decreed the paintings on the walls of the Guild Chapel be plastered and the storied stained glass smashed and replaced with clear. My mother was with child at the time—me—and my poor father was much conflicted over having to deface what he thought sacred. One of the murals was a portrait of Saint George killing the dragon. I was born on Saint George's Day—the same day the mural was smothered in white. A strange coincidence. The townsfolk tried to storm the church, and my father had to stand guard at the door and protect the poor men who were plastering.

"Years later my mother, who never plastered over her own papist beliefs, blamed that day on my father's blighted ambitions—though verily his star brightened for a time before it dimmed. My mother also maintained that her kin paid for the original paintings, so it was not only blasphemy and sacrilege against her church but against her family as well, and in our house my mother's family was as much esteemed as the Pope!"

Katharine could listen to Will talk all day and through the night.

"How art thou, my dear Kate? How weighs your grief now?" he asked, sitting next to her again.

"For months I have expected to walk through the library door and to find Sir Edward in his chair in front of the fire with a book in his hand. I still oft imagine him thus. But never again."

"'Twas the same when I lost my sister Anne," he said. His eyes filled with tears.

"I am so sorry," said Katharine, recalling how Will had shown her his skill at making himself cry. But she dismissed such an idea, for who would feign lamentation at losing one's own sister?

"She was a bright thing—grasped subjects like a boy—sitting next to me laughing one minute and then dead and buried the next. I will never forget the moment what we had feared became truth. One always prays . . ."

"Yes, one does, always," she said.

"What thought you of the lines read by that pebble-headed scut?" asked Will. "Forsooth, I never expected such an audience. What thought you of my portrait of Venus's forestry?"

"Venus's venery, more like. I thought it lewd and churlish."

He laughed. "Good. I sat this morn and wrote. I lost track of sun and time. I thought I might read to you, and you might gloss upon what words sound feeble and where the portrait I have drawn lacks strong lines."

"I am sure," said Katharine, "that every syllable is perfection."

"The day you tell me that, is the day I have no more use for you!" Will laughed and stood.

Her blood, so warmed, ran cold. *Is the day I have no more use for you!* This was what she feared most. She was on the verge of asking him what he meant, when—with one foot on the bench and his arm resting on his thigh—he launched into reading his freshly inked pages. Then he stood in front of Katharine. "Bestow upon me one word, my goddess of wit, or I shall faint right away at thy pretty little feet."

"Brilliant," she said, captive once again.

"Marry!" he said. "'Tis what I prayed for! My mad black quill did dash across the page this morn. It would not let me stand or take refreshment, but bade me sit upon this bench without a break." He smiled. "God-a-mercy. I never know."

"You must have a sense."

"Sometimes I do, when 'tis horrid, but that is not the work you see. That is never shown to you. There are words I've cherished, loved, and then I bring them to you, and you . . ."

"What?"

He sat down next to her. "You wince."

She laughed. "I wince?"

"It's as if I've inflicted some sort of pain on you . . ."

"A wound?"

"Yes," said Will, still beaming, so relieved she liked what he'd written.

"You have writ: 'For men will kiss even by their own direction,'" she said, touching the bright blue stone around her neck.

"Words that show how male desire is by nature unyoked and inherent," he said.

"Where is the instinct then from which you write?" She was baiting him. "You display it, my love, in words but not in deeds."

He smiled, his eyes on hers.

She waited for his action. She craved his lips, his hands, his skin. She felt the beautiful blue stone on her neck. *Then why not lips on lips*, and skin on skin?

There was a thud outside, then one scream followed by another and another, until it became waves of women wailing. Katharine dashed out the door. By the time she reached the cobblestones in front of the scullery, Joan was on her knees cradling her mother in her arms. An image of Ursula on her knees pleading with Harold flashed in front of Katharine. The servants crowded round, as did the family. Joan was not weeping, nor was she wailing, but her mouth was turned down at the edges and her eyes were wide with sorrow. Her face was ancient, and she seemed, in the winter-gray light, older than Katharine, older than Matilda, even. Joan did not look down at her mother, but stared straight ahead while the bright red blood flowed through Ursula's blond hair, over her white skin, into the dark folds of her white smock and onto the icy stones beneath.

20

hen Harold returned from Lancaster, he found Richard hauled off to jail and Ursula dead. The servants were washing and straightening the poor woman's broken body as best they could. Ursula would be interred as quickly as possible. By flinging herself from the parapet she had committed the most profound of sins, though there was a chance her madness would soften the charge. A priest would have refused her burial in consecrated ground, but Katharine hoped that, without a priest to give the mass, Ursula would be placed near the old chapel in the earth that was consecrated long ago by Father de La Bruyère.

Katharine, Isabel and Grace sat with Joan late into the night and tried to console her. Katharine reassured all that she was ready to assume a stronger role in Ursula's younger children's lives. And there was, of course, the tutor, who would keep the boys, at least, occupied in the mornings. All eyes, when Will was mentioned, turned to Katharine.

Katharine expected Molly would be asleep when she finally returned to her chamber. But the poor girl's eyes were wide.

"Might there be a letter for me?" asked Katharine.

"No, my mistress, nothing from him," answered Molly. Her lip was quivering, and she was wringing her skirt.

"Molly, dear, what ails you?"

"'Tis what ails this house, should be more the question! The rest of them in the scullery and the stables and such are talking now that 'tis verily bewitched, this house. First the leaving of the rooks. 'Tis an ill omen. Foretells the downfall of a family. Then the hags put a spell on the hall the night they were chained in the cellars. 'Tis topsy-turvy, with all the family dying or being dragged off as traitors!"

All did indeed seem topsy-turvy. "'Tis more the time, Molly, than witchery," Katharine said finally. "'Tis our burden, our lot, the path of suffering God has set for us."

Molly nodded, but her eyes were filled to the brim, and she did not seem the least convinced. Katharine, in truth, was not at all sure she was convinced herself. She took Molly by the shoulders and hugged her.

"You are right to weep, Molly." Katharine started to cry as well. "This house is filled with sorrow. But we shall get Richard back, and it was Ursula's time to go, we just did not know it yet. She had been disappearing before our very eyes and we were blind to it. She wished to vanish."

"They say she didna eat more than a bite or two a day for months," added Molly, wiping her eyes with her skirt.

"She was stricken," said Katharine.

"I never heard of such a thing. Stepping off a roof."

"'Tis, we must assume, God's work," said Katharine.

"Or the work of the devil," said Molly.

"Not that, I do not believe that."

"And now my lord Harold has taken ill," added Molly.

"He was riding for days and perchance the cold has taken hold of him," said Katharine.

"'Tis not an illness of the throat or lungs, they say, but deeper down. The pains shoot through his stomach."

They were quiet for a while.

"If there is a letter," Katharine said, "even if 'tis very late this night, prithee would you slip it under my door?"

"Yes'm."

Molly helped Katharine out of her bodice and her skirt. When Katharine was sitting in her smock, Molly began to brush her hair. "Might I be so bold as to ask you something?"

"Yes, Molly."

"'Tis not my business, nor my place . . ."

"Charge ahead. I am captive beneath your brush."

"Have you lost your heart to him?"

Katharine sighed and was quiet. "I have," she said finally.

Katharine expected Molly to be thrilled by the mention of love, for she was a young girl, her head probably full of such thoughts, but she was not.

"I worried you might've," Molly said gravely. She was braiding Katharine's long tresses now.

"Molly, do not worry about me, and pray do not worry about the house. Ned will be here. Ned will make this house strong again, bring this house right."

Katharine was not certain of this, but she wanted to say something to comfort Molly. Ned had, in the past, been more inclined toward merrymaking than management of his own affairs. Perhaps his years in Italy had reined him in, brought wisdom where there had been frivolity.

After Molly left, Katharine checked twice before she snuffed her candle to see if a letter from Will was under the door, but the wooden floor was bare. She got into bed feeling bereft. She remembered the day when Ursula was on her back in the grass staring at the sky. She had said she wanted to be free, and now perhaps she was. Ursula might have, with time, become sane again. Yet, she was gone now. And Richard. Was Richard involved in a plot against the queen? That prospect seemed as unlikely as Katharine herself being involved in such a scheme. The house had lost its rhythm. She couldn't remember the last time she had read to the children. When the women had gathered around Joan that night, they spoke of Harold going into exile now, too. Katharine had grown up immersed in the ancients and now felt she was living in their world: Ovid exiled; Seneca exiled, too, and then forced to take his own life for a supposed conspiracy; Lucretius, driven mad by a love potion, had also committed self-murder.

Ursula's burial was unadorned, without the pomps and vanities she had come to display while upon this earth. Harold was not present because Harold was in bed writhing in pain. His stomach had worsened. The pains that attacked him after supper had sharpened, becoming deep and frequent. In another time, when their religion was not against the laws of the land, a priest would have been called to Harold's bed to perform unction with *oleum infirmorum*, the oil for the sick that had been blessed by the bishop. But there were no oils and no unctions. Harold refused to eat. Mary was stuck to his side, they said, silent, unmoving, a fly gummed in pine resin.

Ursula's grave was dug. The family gathered and prayed. Her three young children stood like little soldiers, straight and silent. Katharine planned to read to the children in the library the afternoon after the burial. She would do her best to bring them away from their hour of woe with a tale or two of brave knights and strong women. A few minutes before she was set to go, Molly brought a letter. Will wanted to see her, and he had sent more of his poem. All of a sudden Katharine's body hummed again. It was unseemly at such a time of tragedy, but she could not resist him. She sent word to change the time for the children, and then she stood in front of the looking glass in her room and stared at herself: she was dressed plainly and darkly. Her chestnut hair was bound in a black caul; the blue turquoise Will had given her was round her neck.

She waited on the same bench on which she had sat with him the day before and many days before that. As a girl of ten, she had sat one night in the chapel lit with the wavering flames of tapers, listening to Father de La Bruyère lecture her on grief: she was not to carry on about her family, for tears and wailing and other such laments, he said, would show the world that she did not believe the souls of her loved ones would land in heaven. She should pray, not cry. She should pray, not weep. She should pray. And that was what she did.

Katharine unfolded Will's pages and started to read. In his fresh verse, Adonis's escape was impeded by the flight of his steed, which upon the sight of a lusty breeding jennet "young and proud" did break his rein and rush after her.

"Ah," Will said.

Katharine looked up from the paper. She hadn't heard him enter. He was light and easy in his step. His beard was neat and newly trimmed. Her face turned hot; her cheeks flamed as if with fever.

"What competition your eyes do give that stone about your neck," he said.

She flushed anew and reached with her fingers for the turquoise hanging from the black silk cord. He sat opposite her. She was thankful the table stood between them; a moat perhaps would have been even better.

"You have covered much ground," she said.

"The sad tidings made sleep impossible. I burned one candle and then another. How fares the family?" he asked.

"One wonders if they can welcome any more grief."

"The children?"

"A blow. They will learn to live with their history," she said.

"As you did."

"Yes." Katharine was wrung tight, like the skirt in Molly's hands the previous night. Katharine was not prepared for the rush of tears, but they came, spilling down her hot cheeks. Will handed her a cloth the children used to wipe their hornbooks. "Sweet Kate, your time is precious, and I am not worthy of it." He stood.

"No, prithee, sit, sir. There is nothing to be done this moment," she said, wiping her eyes.

"Read to me," he said.

She looked at him and cocked her head.

"Where you left off when I did enter. Read to me. Let me hear my verse from your soft lips."

"As you please." Katharine squared her shoulders, straightened the paper and read out loud Will's keen and delicious detail of Adonis's errant charger. Katharine stopped reading and looked across the table at Will. He was smiling. He had written much the same words he had spoken to her when they first met, in the very place they were sitting now.

"That first night here, you described *me* thus!" she said. "A horse trader! You have no shame!" She laughed. She had no shame, having fun while the rest of the house was in pain.

"My humble words turn proud when 'tis your voice that speaks them," he said.

She looked across at him. He stunned and beguiled her. She was helpless to it.

"I will away for Christmas, Kate." He saw her look. "Come, come. 'Tis no eternity but little more than a fortnight. I will, while there, write you a sonnet, my New Year's gift to you, for writing of you, my constant Kate, will bring me solace."

Katharine wished to ask him why he returned to the family in Stratford from which he seemed askance. She felt like a loom, the different threads running in and out of her, the shuttle pushing the loose threads taut. While Will was now writing from his core—the words spilling from his pen—she was confused right down to her very core. He was across from her, the table now as wide as the sea, and she would have to swim a thousand leagues to stand and walk over to him. What if he, like Adonis, turned away from her advances? She shuddered at the shame of it, and then, out of desperation, she tried a different tack.

"I have fallen in love with you," she said simply.

His eyes glinted.

"And we will love each other and continue on," he returned.

Her heart trilling, she wondered: What next? Perhaps he had needed to hear those words, before he could truly love her back. Perchance this was where Venus had gone wrong. She had crowded Adonis with lust, but left little room for love.

He stood. She stood. What next?

"We will speak of this anon," he said, gathering his papers, gazing at her, his eyes full of thought.

"When go you hence?" she said, her voice weak, displaced, uneven.

"Now, dearest Katharine . . ."

He had called her by her full name. There was love in that, she was sure of it.

"I leave tomorrow," he said. "I will return by Candlemas."

'Tis too long, she thought. She was afraid after his departure she might never see him again: she would die. He had breathed life into her. The poem, his presence, had awakened her. She remembered when Harold had dragged Ursula across the floor of the hidden chapel. Her eyes filled with tears.

"'Tis harder for you than 'tis for me," he said.

She nodded. His voice was soft, his eyes loving. His words puzzled her.

"I am here, Kate, look at me. I am standing here next to you. I may go off, to Stratford or to London, but I will return. I am, in truth, not going anywhere. You were, at a tender age, unmothered and unfathered. I will not abandon thee. What we have is special."

She nodded.

"Let me hear it from your tongue."

She wiped the tears from her eyes and slowly repeated his line. "What we have is special," she said. She felt as if he had asked her to undress in front of him. She added, "You will not live here always, that I know."

He did not move to her but looked intently at her. "We have the rest of our lives, Kate, you and I. Ten, twenty, thirty, forty years, God willing. You must not leave me. I will buckle at the knees and fall if you do. You must remain by my side."

"But you will leave," she said. "It takes no soothsayer for such a prediction."

"Well, if I do, you will come with me."

"How . . . can . . . that be?"

"If I make my perch in London again, well, dear Kate, you will come with me."

"Verily?" She sat back down on the bench, for she could not trust her legs to hold her.

"Yes. How can I write without you? For writing is living now. I will cease to write when I cease to breathe. You urge me on, you command me. Night after night, as I sit in that damp chamber scratching my quill across the page, I write for you. I have been mapping plays for the playhouses in London whilst here at Lufanwal. When the time is right, I will show you all I have."

Katharine was filled with the promise of what was to come. She let herself peer into the future: a life, somehow, with Will in it. After weeks of his calling her brilliant and beautiful, she had begun to feel brilliant around him, and beautiful, too.

Will helped her on with her cloak. They parted with a tender embrace. *What might be*—those words coursed through her body. She could step away from the misfortune that circled round her. They might live in London in a house with a small garden, not too far from the playhouses. They would, their heads bent over his pages, stay up late, burn one wick after the other, until the dawn itself would light their work. She imagined Will's first book, their book, the leather the color of wine, gilt leaves sprouting up the spine. *Venus and Adonis* by William Shakespeare—her name written on a page in thanks and dedication and love. She saw stacks of his burgundy books sold by a bookseller in St. Paul's churchyard in London. On future books, she would fix rhyme and meter, deliver one image when another did not fit, tame his errant spelling, make constant the marks he used between words and clauses. The sheets of paper with writing scattered across tables and chairs would be their children. She had lived a life of reading books—now she would live a life of helping to create them.

She was hurrying down the path, her head dizzy with such thoughts, when she bumped into someone.

"I crave your pardon," he said, bowing low.

"Oh, Mr. Smythson," she said.

"Madam," he said. His dark breeches and doublet were covered in white dust.

"I was saddened to hear what happened and hastened here to tell you—" he said.

"You hastened here to tell me? Why me?" she asked, but then was sorry she had said it. She saw the confusion on his face and quickly came to his aid. "I am grateful to you, Mr. Smythson. These are, indeed, trying times for us all. *Gementes et flentes in hac lacrimarum valle.*" She was eager to be alone, dreaming of a life with Will.

He nodded gravely. "Would you care to walk a bit before the sun has left us? These December days, like too many lives, are cut short by winter. You have no gloves. Are you warm enough?"

"Yes," she said.

He smiled. "Good."

He turned and waited for her. She realized he had misunderstood her "Yes," thinking that she had agreed to walk with him, when she had responded merely that she was warm enough.

"Wear these," he said, pulling a worn pair of gloves from the leather satchel slung over his shoulder.

"No, Mr. Smythson. I'll tuck my hands in my cloak. Thank you."

Not knowing what else to do, she started to walk with him.

"The sun baked away much of the snow," he said.

They stayed on the stone path that split the orchard. Not a piece of fruit or shred of leaf remained. The branches of the cherry and peach trees on one side reached out like an old woman's fingers: the apple and pear trees on the other looked as crooked and wizened as an old man's elbows and arms.

"How is your hand, Mr. Smythson?" she asked.

"My hand?"

"The crystal ball that shattered in the library."

"Ah, yes, of course." He opened his large hand and examined his finger, as if he had not done so since they had last met. Then he showed it to her. "Healed. That mark has now taken its place amongst the scars that map my skin."

Katharine thought of the other meaning of *scar*, a rocky cliff, and how the craggy nature of Mr. Smythson's face was interesting and even quite beautiful: it reminded her of the steep limestone scars she had seen years ago at the Yorkshire Dales up north when visiting Grace.

They stopped at the crest of the orchard before descending the stone steps to the outer garden. They stood, without speaking, in the quiet of the evening. Mr. Smythson was a curious fellow. She recalled his son and thought how fortunate this lad was to have a father who knew stillness, for with stillness came an inward peace. Her own father, or what she remembered of him, was always in motion, and the house that she was raised in was always in motion, too. He had never felt comfortable in his own skin, had to talk or to move or to drink. But her years at Lufanwal had taught her differently, had made her understand solitary life and learn from it.

To the west, between the hills, the sun was setting the sky on fire. Indeed, the clouds were ablaze with the spectrum of a flame, yet other colors, too: garden tints, those found in rose petals and fields of violets. The sky was so extraordinary that Katharine sighed deeply.

"We must not forget nature," said Mr. Smythson. "It replenishes the soul."

She nodded. They stood a few minutes longer, not speaking, and then they turned and started to stroll back to the hall.

"I brought you some verse. Did your maid deliver it to you?" he said. "I heard you read much," he added.

"I do. But I have not yet read what you kindly gave to me." She had been so caught up with Will's poem that she had completely forgotten about the packet from Mr. Smythson, yet she thought it sweet that he had acted upon what he had heard about her. "Do you write, Mr. Symthson? Are you a poet?"

"No," he said. He laughed—the sound deep and rich.

What was he, this man beside her? Perhaps the primeval rock with which he worked had influenced his matter.

"I met a young woman, and she has taken to writing and gave me pages of her verse, and I quite admire it and thought you might, too. She has nothing whole yet, she told me, but bits and pieces of poems and prose. She is with Lord Hunsdon, is his . . ."

"Daughter?" Katharine offered.

"No." Mr. Smythson laughed again. "His . . . concubine." He continued, "Henry Carey is a very old man, for her. She is just twenty-one. He is forty-five years her senior. She is the daughter of a court musician originally from Venice."

"Verily!" Katharine was surprised Mr. Smythson spoke so forthrightly. *Concubine* seemed an awkward word. "Is not Lord Hunsdon the Lord Chamberlain?"

"Yes, the queen's bastard half-brother and her cousin, too. 'Tis a fraught heritage, but he is a sympathetic soul, and treats this young woman very well."

"And she writes?"

"She does, and is a lively lady whose parents died early. She lived at the house of the Dowager Countess of Kent, was given lessons along with the countess's daughters and later became attached to the household of the Countess of Cumberland. She has been much at court and has a most musical mind. I thought it might interest you. She is a woman, and she writes poetry."

Again, she was startled by his manner. She was not used to such directness.

"Zounds!" she exclaimed.

"I crave your pardon. If I said something . . ."

"No, Mr. Smythson. 'Tis nothing you said. In truth, I have completely forgotten the children!"

"The children?"

"I gave my word I would read to the children this afternoon, and now the sun is all but down and I have missed the hour. Oh, how could I have been so blind as to the time at a moment when their earth does quake? Mr. Smythson, I must take my leave. Perchance the children are still in the library. I will read this lady's verses with interest. Fare thee well."

"Fare thee well, my lady." He bowed.

This time she did not give him her hand. She nodded to him, and before they had even passed through the orchard, she dashed toward the house. She realized, as she raced down the path with her petticoats hiked up above her ankles, that the picture she was leaving with Mr. Smythson was far from ladylike, but there was a quality about the mason, a tolerance perhaps, that made her feel her behavior wouldn't offend him.

21

ill left the next day. Katharine watched him go. He sat a horse well: his back straight, his movement graceful. Katharine was intrigued that Will was so richly attired for his return home. A blue brocade arm with silver slashes peeked through his short riding cloak. She had checked the map pinned in the library; Stratford lay on the Roman road northwest of London and before Colchester and was roughly two days' ride from Lufanwal. Maybe Will was making a stop on his way to Stratford.

What did the townsfolk in Warwickshire think of Will, the boy who had worn a smock in his father's rank shop, returning as a dandy from places they would never see? Did his three children miss him during his long absences? Did Anne? How could his family not yearn for him, as Katharine did, the minute he was out of sight?

She picked up the packet of verse Mr. Smythson had given to her, untied the dark blue silk cord and unfolded the papers. The handwriting was tiny and elegant and not unlike her own. The name on the pages was Aemilia Bassano. Katharine wondered why this Aemilia had given her writing to Mr. Smythson, and how he had happened to meet her. Perchance he had worked on a house where she resided. 'Twas fascinating this young woman was the paramour of such a powerful person and that everyone seemed privy to the affair—along with, Katharine assumed, Lord Hunsdon's wife.

There were fragments of a poem on the Passion of Christ, which argued in iambic pentameter how men—not women—were responsible for the crucifixion of Christ. Bassano first contended that "Adam cannot be excus'd," from his part in the fall. Eve's fault was only "too much love," which made her give the apple to her dear. As for men's sinfulness in the crucifixion: the author pointed to the guilt of Pilate, who had failed to follow his wife's sage counsel. Bassano then proposed that since men's fault in Christ's death was "greater" than women's, women should have "Libertie againe" and be equals, "free from tyranny." Katharine admired the boldness of this lady's ideas.

The next page was a farewell letter to an estate in Cookham where Aemilia had lived, describing its peace and tranquillity, and how the gardens and grounds encouraged meditation and withdrawal from earthly things. Katharine put the pages down. Lufanwal had been her cloister, yes, but it had been her foundation, too, her education, yet perhaps, as with Aemilia and Cookham, it was time for Katharine to bid farewell. *You will come with me*, Will had said. The idea of leaving the hall was both exhilarating and frightening. Aemilia, like Katharine, was an orphan with no dowry. This poetess was clearly clever, with a most educated mind. Only one and twenty years of age, she was maintained by a rich and powerful lord, and perhaps therein lay a certain freedom, the *Libertie* of which she wrote, for Lord Hunsdon had a wife and, Katharine recalled, a huge family of twelve children or more.

An hour later, Katharine emerged from her chamber dressed in an old skirt, boots, cloak and hood. She bade the boy at the stables to saddle one of the smaller mares. When she was younger and rode with Ned, Edward had given her horses of her own, but her riding in recent years had waned. As a pastime, a sport, it did not interest Isabel or Joan, and Katharine was too old to ride with the boys—though she had heard the queen had maintained her love of horses and much to the dismay of her counselors she spurred her Spanish steeds with vigor and still rode long distances at great speeds.

The ground was hard this afternoon; patches of ice now replaced the snow. Katharine and the mare shot puffs of white breath into the cold air as they descended to the valley below. The river had never regained its volume after the drought, and once horse and rider reached the crusty stream they made it easily to the other side. They climbed through forest and wood. Katharine loosened her reins and let the horse traverse the incline, so it could gain momentum in ascending. As a girl she rode every day in the warm months, often alone as she was now. And until Matilda made her sit with her legs to the side, she had worn a pair of breeches under her skirt and ridden her horse astride like a man.

Katharine was pleased she was out in the fresh air, yet she felt out of time with the horse—her hands weak and her sinews soft and unused to the saddle. But she kept on, and once she reached level ground, she changed the gait to a gallop and let the horse run until both she and the mare were taxed and out of breath. Her hood had fallen to her shoulders; her hair was unpinned and streaming down her back. The silence calmed her, and the wind on her skin stung and invigorated. Mr. Smythson had been right when he spoke of how nature nourished the soul. God, indeed, was revealed in the harmony of nature, for God had created the world; it was His work.

The air began to fill with specks of snow. She pulled on her hood and turned the horse back to Lufanwal. After crossing the river, Katharine veered to the road because of the snow: the trodden path would make her return easier. Two storms, and Christmas not even come. The foul weather following the months of scant rain foretold a harsh winter. Through the squall, she saw three dark figures on horseback followed by several horse-drawn carts. She wondered if this caravan had come for Harold or if Richard had been released—though the presence of the carts worried her. Was Richard in one? Had he turned sick, been tortured? Was he dead?

Her heart froze as she neared one of the carts: it was draped in black and a chest the length of a man lay within. The men on horseback, their dark cloaks dusted with white, waved her on. She passed them, then leaned into the snow and set off in haste toward the great house. When she reached the courtyard, she dismounted on her own, called for a servant to take the horse, then sent word for Matilda. Once in the door, she tore off her wet cloak and, without changing her attire, dashed up the stairs. When she burst through the door of Matilda's sitting room, Isabel, Joan and Matilda looked up from their stitching. Grace had returned to Yorkshire with her family.

"Dear Katharine, where have you been?" cried Isabel.

"Riding in the hills."

"In the snow?" said Joan.

"'Twas not yet falling when I went out, but I am here to tell you there is a band of men on the road. And there are horses with carts . . . and in the cart—"

Before Katharine finished, the three of them heard clamor rising from below.

Matilda rose.

"Mother, we can go," said Isabel. "You stay."

"Hand me my shawl," was all Matilda said.

Joan wrapped the woolen shawl tenderly around Matilda.

"Come, girls," Matilda said, passing in front of Katharine.

Isabel and Joan followed her out the door. Katharine trailed the sad procession and wondered if one of the witches had indeed placed a curse on this house. They had not descended the stairs, not even passed through the gallery, when they saw a man striding toward them.

Matilda stopped abruptly. Isabel gave a cry. Joan gasped.

It was Ned. He was down on his knees in front of his mother. She put her hand on his head, and ruffled his dark curls the way a mother would a young boy rather than a grown man. Tears spilled down her cheeks.

Ned had brought his father's body back. It was no small feat. Katharine could only recall one other such journey in recent times—that of Sir Philip Sidney's body after he was felled at the Battle of Zutphen. Usually a nobleman who died across the sea was interred at the place of death and then the family could move the bones. In the olden days, the corpse was "boiled up" for the long journey home: the body disemboweled, dismembered and cooked, the flesh and entrails buried nearby and the bones taken to the burial site. Or the body was buried locally, while the heart made the crossing.

All had assumed Sir Edward would be buried at the monastery, but Ned had done the nigh impossible. Ned recounted how he had arrived at the monastery too late for his father's final breath. The brethren assured Ned that his father's passage to the great beyond had been gentle and pious, a good death. The prior told Ned that Sir Edward, with the pallor of death already upon him, had sat up in bed—while one of the brethren steadied the paper—and described his last wishes. He had wished his body returned to Lancashire for burial in the ground of his ancestors. Ned had worked miracles: his father's embalmed body was encased in lead and carried across the Channel from Calais to Dover in a ship rigged with black sails; the coffin was placed in the sterncastle of the ship, two candles burning around it. Upon the ship's docking, the coffin was loaded onto a cart and draped in black, as were the horses, traveling first to London and then on to Lufanwal.

The family would give him a proper burial, as proper as they could with no priest in the house. But he would be buried in his earth, with the bones of his people around him. Ned's presence at the dinner table was like a candle: his flame flickering and bright. He had grown into his body, no trace of the sapling remained. He was fully a man now. He had changed from his riding clothes into a velvet and satin doublet; plum and violet threads coursed through the fabric, highlighting his amethyst eyes. Katharine had seen the servants carrying trunks from the carts, trunks filled, no doubt, with riches from Italian tailors.

Two young squires, Englishmen who like Ned had been living abroad, had traveled with him and were to stay at Lufanwal for a time. They were both fair and close to Ned in age. One hailed from a town in Berkshire down south, and the other was raised in Warwickshire, a few towns from Stratford. The two gentlemen were vague about their travels. The squire from Berkshire had matriculated at Oxford but left to study in Rome. The young man from Warwickshire was shy and spoke little. Their speech and manners conveyed education and gentility.

That night Ned came knocking at Katharine's door.

"I so hoped you would come," she said. She was in her smock and her tattered emerald velvet dressing gown; her hair was brushed and down.

Ned clasped her hands, and they stood gazing at each other, both smiling, both moved to tears.

"Why are we weeping?" Katharine asked with a laugh.

Ned brought her hands to his lips and kissed them. "I have missed you, dear Kate."

"Oh, and I have missed you," she said. "How could you leave me for so many years? I should be furious with you, dear, sweet, gentle Ned, but 'tis impossible. The years do wear on me, yet you wear them with beauty."

They embraced and stayed together, as if the moment could erase the lost stretch of time.

"If I believed you were worn and weathered," Ned said, "I would not hesitate to tell you, but as I sat at the table tonight, I marveled how in my absence you have merely ripened."

They stood apart.

"How is it," Ned continued, "that a woman past thirty can look as lush and enchanting as a maid half her age?"

"'Tis nothing more than the trickery of candlelight." Katharine brandished a strand of hair. "'Tis silver."

"And thou art gold and as precious a metal as when I left, more precious, methinks."

"Come, enough flattery, sit by the fire," Katharine commanded. "I had forgotten how you fill my well with serenity, and serenity, my dear Ned, is what I long for."

Katharine sat. Ned added more wood to the fire, then stretched his long legs and slid comfortably into the chair next to her. The fire before them caught the shine of his black hair.

"Mother looks ravaged by time," he said.

"Time has been a cruel verse of late," said Katharine. "Every day brings a new line of tragedy. Poor Ursula."

"'Tis God showing us the way," said Ned, then added, "Jesus suffered for our sins."

Katharine remembered when Ned, as a boy, seemed to care little for the Bible. He had matured, she saw, in many ways.

"I am afraid to ask, but will you stay?" she said.

Ned looked into the flames and then turned to her.

"I have come home. Though I may not be in residence here at the hall at all times, I will not be abroad."

"You will commit to court and charm our Protestant queen?"

"I will not dally at court, nor will I pander to Her Royal Highness."

"Where will you be, Ned, if not here at Lufanwal, nor at court?"

"I have my work," he said.

"Your work?"

"My work will take me far and wide."

Ned's solemn tone surprised Katharine. As a lad he had been all gaiety and mirth.

"What work?"

Ned stared into the fire and did not answer.

"Ned? Are you an agent?" Katharine ventured.

He turned to her, still silent.

"For the queen?" Katharine pursued, for she had heard how the queen turned young Catholic men into agents to spy and plot against their own kind.

"Dear Kate," Ned said softly. "I am an agent of God."

Kate gasped.

"'Tis that bad? My vocation?" he said.

"Oh, Ned." Katharine leapt from her chair and knelt by him, taking hold of his hands in hers. "I did not expect this."

"Did you think my life these seven years was all folly and foppery?"

"Well . . . I . . ."

"You did."

"I might have thought it was aglitter."

"It was for me aglitter, but not from candles at court."

"But what of Florence?"

"'Tis a city that outshines all, but not a place to dedicate oneself to God. Too many delicious distractions."

"And all these years?"

"Spent in study."

"And these young men with you are seminarians, too?"

"We are priests and we are Jesuits and we are members of the English mission and will try to carry on that for which our martyrs have died."

"Did your father know?"

"Father and Mother were the only ones who knew. These times are harsh."

"Isabel?"

"We thought too young."

"Your older sister?"

"We thought she might tell her husband."

"Oh, Ned, and I thought you a—"

"Dissolute, drunken, dissipated, disreputable rogue?"

"Aye." Katharine laughed, then stood and started to pace. "How did I never guess your business, when you lived all these years in the land of the Pope? Sir Edward kept the secret well. He must have been so proud of you, Ned. But now the air is foul for such a calling. They'll string you up a traitor if they catch you."

"I desire to offer to God my blood and my flesh as He offered for me," Ned said.

His voice was calm, content even. Katharine marveled at his strength and his conviction.

"How did you pass from sea to land?" she asked.

"My two brethren and I said we were three brothers of plain and humble origins bringing our father's body back home for burial. We flanked Father's coffin on the ship and on the road."

"But how did you explain the cost of such transport?"

"We spoke of father and sons having prospered abroad, as cloth merchants in trade and export, and how it was our honor and duty to our father to comply with his last wishes—that part was true. We maintained an air of coarseness throughout the journey—laughed loudly when we could, spoke words rude and uncouth in nature. We played the parts of those whose coffers are newly brimming, spent money wildly and comported ourselves with utmost vulgarity."

"You had fun!" Katharine said, sitting sidesaddle on her bed.

"We did." Ned rose.

"Art thou weary?" she asked.

"I feel awake with an odd, restless vigor."

"'Tis your first night home in a house newly framed with sorrow."

Ned was quiet and looked as if he did not know what to do, which way to turn.

"Sit by me a few minutes more, dear Ned. You have heard many stories tonight of the fate of your family, but I have yet another story to tell."

Ned removed his boots and his doublet, and they lay side by side as they had when they were young, but now with age they seemed an old married couple. Ned sighed, a deep sigh.

"This is home. I might never move from your bed, Kate." He rolled onto his side and, resting his head on his hand, said, "Begin."

She told him of Will, how he had left his family in Stratford to go to London to the playhouses, then came to Lufanwal to tutor, rarely, and to write, much, and how she had in a manner started to tutor him, to help him first with sonnets, then guide him in the long poem he was writing. She told Ned of Will's smile, his rich voice, his skill with words, his swift intellect. "His mind does move like a bright goldfinch hopping from branch to branch," she said. Then she told him of the embrace at the dance, the unpinning of her tresses, the kiss when he lingered.

"There's more," she said.

"You are in love with this man," said Ned.

"I am."

"And what will come of it? A man like that may linger in a kiss or an embrace, but he will not linger here."

"He said he would take me with him."

"Where?" Ned's eyes opened wide.

"Well, to wherever he goes next. To London, methinks."

"And you think he will?"

"He has said it."

"He has said much to you, dear Kate, and in exchange for all he has said you are giving him much. He is wont to play with you in exchange for what you inspire in him. But is this a man who translates words into action? If the air is as fiery as your description, why has he not gone farther with you? You have, as you say, been quite alone with him. Most men, being naturally of a beastly nature, would have pressed on with their desires."

"Perhaps he is trying to protect my position," she said.

"You are unmarried and you have but meager goods and chattels. I am sure my father has marked you in his will, but that I assume will care for you while here, at Lufanwal, in the utmost comfort. I am not trying to be cruel; I am trying to help you see the reality. What position is he trying to protect?"

"Perchance he is trying to protect my virtue."

"Come, now, Kate. You are a widow of many years. Is there virtue lurking about you? Under those skirts? In this bed? I pray not!"

Katharine smiled. "You are a priest, Ned, you are not to speak with such lewdness!"

"I am a priest, yes, but I am your kinsman and your friend and I have loved you dearly for many years. I fell in love with a poet once."

"I remember."

"Words are sport for them. And they use words as instruments or tools, sometimes as weapons. What they say, dear Kate, or what they write might not necessarily issue from the heart. Your gentle soul, your open heart, are not accustomed to such dissemblance. And with this Will, thou art doubly in trouble, for he is a player as well. He has skills you might not dream of, knows how to employ his voice, his eyes, even the slant of his shoulders, to tug at the emotions of those who pay their pennies to watch him. I have witnessed those players—they are artful and quite able to confuse the stage with my lady's bedchamber—or my lord's."

"Do you ever think of your poet?" Kate asked. "Did he break your heart?"

"He practically broke my back, but he didn't break my heart. He was too much for me."

"Oh, Ned, you mustn't talk thus."

"You love it when I talk thus."

Katharine laughed again. "'Tis true. What happened to your back-breaking poet?"

"I used to hear reports of him. He, too, writes for the playhouses and has had success. He was crazy, but utterly entertaining. I was young. He was young but older than I. I was provincial and not Oxford-bound and his wit was savage and divine."

"Did you love again?"

"Florence is a city full of sumptuous men—fine and elegant even when they are not rich. And the light is always in their eyes. I must have fallen in . . . well, a lusty sort of love or a loving sort of lust, at least ten times that year."

"What happens with your heart now?"

"I have bequeathed my heart to God, I suppose. I have much to do on this island. I cannot let my heart or any other part of my anatomy get in the way of the mission here. We have to bring our dear country back to the Pope." Ned yawned and closed his eyes. "Lo, what look will be planted upon thy servant's face when she finds me aslumber in your bed, dearest Kate? The tongues will wag."

Katharine watched Ned sleep. After seven years, they had fallen right back into the roots of their affection. Ned was in truth more beautiful than Will; the source of Ned's beauty lay deep within. He had always been sweet and honest; his newfound conviction added a stunning depth to his features. By stepping on English soil, a Catholic priest was in Elizabeth's eyes a traitor and could be executed. Katharine leaned over and kissed Ned's forehead. She remembered the years when they were young and spent hours on her bed, laughing, eating, reading, writing, whole afternoons filled with idle talk. Ned would rest his head upon her lap, or they would lie on the bed, their limbs linked.

She knew, for he had told her, of his passion for men, but there were moments in the spring of their youth when their bodies were drawn to each other—more as softness and flesh and the tenderness of trusted love, than as man or woman. She remembered they would kiss on the mouth sometimes, but they would not linger there, and she wondered now if their reluctance to spend one more second lip to lip was because in spite of his preference they might travel from closed to open mouth and from there, well, they would untie, unbutton and unhook. Katharine looked down now at Ned's beautiful face; his countenance had lost its childish smoothness: the skin around his mouth had manly creases, mayhap from the Italian sun, mayhap from smiling. His dark wavy hair cascaded to his shoulders; his black beard was like night upon his pale face.

She gently took a strand of his hair and wrapped it around her finger, slid her finger from the coil and watched the curl fall on her pillow. God had granted Ned many gifts while on this earth, and now, humble and devout, with his future full of risk and danger, Ned was returning those gifts. Katharine placed her shawl over her cousin, snuffed the candle and climbed under her blankets.

22

e's in agony, he is," Molly told Katharine. "He claws at his stomach. The gashes bleed and the skin throbs and swells and erupts with pus!"

Harold's pain now issued from his flesh, where he dug at his own hide, as well as from within, where the torment in his guts worsened daily. Servants hurried from his chamber carrying cupping glasses filled with blood. The doctor ordered his hands bound to prevent Harold from scratching through fresh layers of skin, and Mary ordered his mouth stuffed with lamb's wool and tied with a cloth, so that his cries would not disturb the house.

On the morning of Sir Edward's burial, the doctor was called anew: Harold had started to vomit bile similar to Guinny's, Ursula's poor deceased pup. Mary told a servant girl, who then told Molly, that the venting of bile was good, for Harold had an excess of wrath, and the successive vomiting was a sign that he was finally ridding himself of his rage. The doctor was not convinced that Harold's spleen had anything to do with his current illness and was said to have asked several attendants and finally Mary if Harold had any enemies in the house.

"Enemies?" Mary asked blankly.

"People who might seek your husband's death," said the doctor.

Mary's face had gone pale. She collapsed by her husband's bedside and was carried off to her own chamber. The doctor was with Harold when Ned began the *missa defunctorum* for his father. *Requiem aeternam dona eis, Domine, et lux perpetua luceat eis.* Grant them eternal rest, Lord, and let perpetual light shine on them.

Ned held the requiem mass in the hidden chapel. Harold's cries for mercy could be heard faintly but relentlessly as Ned moved from the *Kyrie eleison*, through the mass to *Dies irae*, then to the absolution and the prayer for Sir Edward to escape the avenging judgment, *Non intres in judicium cum servo tuo*, and on to the *Pater noster*. Ned did not wear a chasuble or a black cope.

Matilda had regained some of her stature since Ned's return. She stood erect and proud while her son led the mass. *In media vita*, in the midst of life we are in death, and this was true for this house and this family. Seneca's line, "He will live badly who does not know how to die well," befitted Sir Edward. He had died well—pious, honest, in God's hands—and now he would be buried well. He had made plans for his burial years before. The simple monument had been carved in stone and was now fetched from the local sculptor. He would not have a magnificent tomb in the local parish church, for the local church was no longer of his faith, nor was the parish, nor was the entire country. He would not be interred in his own family chapel, for that had been stripped of its sanctity when the queen had continued the assault her father had begun. Sir Edward's bones would reside in his land, packed deep within the earth he loved. From the sculptor's chisel emerged the De L'Isle family coat of arms with its two unicorns and griffin's head, framed by a toad, a mouse and a serpent entwined with dandelions, holly and a thistle with a cicada on its thorn.

The men had been up most of the night warming the hard ground with torches and then hacking and scraping the earth as best they could. The air had turned bitter again, and Katharine stood with the small group of mourners as Sir Edward was lowered into his final resting place and dirt was cast upon his coffin. On this gray morning, Saint Lucy's Day, with the Christmas season fast approaching, the flame of this noble family had all but gone out: their figures cloaked and hooded, indeed shrouded in black. How, Katharine wondered, could the Protestants champion the idea that the fate of the soul was sealed at death and the actions of the living gave no influence on the dead? It was preposterous. How could the Protestants sleep at night with such uncertainty of the hereafter? Did they believe the virtuous soul went straight to heaven? Whither the Resurrection? Whither the Judgment? Katharine would continue her prayers for Sir Edward and Ursula and try her best to order her life for their salvation. *Requiescat in pace. Requiescat in pace.*

The gray soon turned dark, for the days were ruled by night this time of year. Katharine found Henry in the library, his chair pulled close to the fire, his eyes squinting at a book—Saint Augustine's *Confessions*.

"How can you see the words? You will ruin those beautiful blue beams." She lit several candles and lamps and then sat on a stool next to Henry.

"Today is the Feast of Saint Lucy," he said. "They gouged her eyes out."

"They did indeed. She often carries her eyes on a plate in paintings. Henry, what happened to the rakish pamphlets by the men Master Shakespeare calls his friends? These writers of riot no longer hold your interest?"

Henry smiled.

"Oh, Henry, it seems ages since I've sat and talked with you, and we live in the same house. Where have you been? Where have I been?" She knew where she had been: she had been swimming in a sea of Will. She had put her toes in first, waded, then slid her whole body in, and now she was afraid her head was under and she was drowning.

"I have been in my chamber reading."

"For months?"

"For months." His voice had deepened and was lower even than his father's.

"And are you learned now?"

"I am."

She laughed. His beard had grown in, fine and blond. He'd cropped it short and close to his chin.

"Do you know the ancients?" she asked.

"Intimately."

"You will teach me, then."

"You are, Cousin Kate, still leagues ahead of me."

"I am not so confident," she said.

She noticed another change in Henry more disturbing than the depth of his voice or the length of his beard: a sadness in his eyes. How could this young man, who as a child overflowed with joy, be shouldered with such sorrow? She guessed the answer. The ugly dance between his father and mother had taken its toll, as had the news that his stricken father was getting worse by the minute. Henry could not escape the pall that hung over Lufanwal: no one could. Katharine hoped and prayed that Ned would save them all somehow.

"I have decided to go abroad to study," Henry said. He closed the *Confessions*. The book lay heavy on his lap. He opened his strong hands wide and laid them, the fingers splayed like a fan, on the leather cover.

Katharine had imagined those hands in the future rough with sport, from jousting pageants, archery and hunts. But 'twas not to be. She knew the path before he even explained it to her. He would follow his cousin Ned to the English College in Rome, and she knew that he, too, would become a priest and that if the tides did not change for their religion, he, too, would be a condemned man if he ever set foot back on English soil.

"Oh, my dear boy," she said, springing to her feet, her eyes full of tears. She clasped Henry tightly to her. She never wanted to release him. In a different time, a different hour, a different minute, it would have been a battle she was sending him off to—his life just as dear and endangered. She would lose him now to study and to vocation.

"I want to go," Henry said, still holding on to her.

She nodded, the tears spilling down her cheeks.

"Sweet coz, I am not going to the gallows . . . yet. I have mountains of study in front of me, and who knows what the state of England will be . . . in five years, even in a year, or tomorrow?"

"Oh, Henry, I am so sorry. It all came over me in a rush," she said, sniffling. "I've just about flooded your shirt and your Saint Augustine. You are right to go, and I will miss you and pray for you."

"Ned is arranging my passage, and I will settle through his contacts there."

"When do you depart?"

"After Candlemas."

"You are brave and you are wonderful, Henry, and I've loved watching you grow into such a strong and noble man."

At the door, he leaned down and kissed the top of Katharine's head.

Saint Clement and Saint Barbara, Saint Nicholas, the Conception of Mary, Saint Lucy, Saint Thomas the Apostle, Saint Stephen, Saint John the Evangelist, Holy Innocents, Saint Thomas of Canterbury, Saint Sylvester the Bishop—for centuries these holy days had threaded through the dark Decembers from Advent to Christmastide, with masses and prayers and fasting or feasting. But with the shifts from Catholic to Protestant and back and forth again, some feasts were banned, revived, observed and then abandoned again. Customs like dressing a boy in vestments on Saint Nicholas's Night and parading the child bishop from house to house were suppressed, then brought back, only to be abolished for a second time.

Sir Edward had steered his own course through these choppy waters: the family was Catholic and would follow the Pope's calendar. This year, without a priest or Edward, the religious proceedings at the hall had halted; Richard and Harold seemed to lose interest in their faith as soon as Edward sailed away. In the days that followed Ned's return, he held masses in the hidden chapel, for his mother, sisters, Katharine and young Henry. It was a select group, sworn to secrecy, for Ned did not trust the rest of the house, the soup still at too much of a boil from recent events—he would wait until it simmered.

Usually on Christmas Eve the great hall was adorned with rosemary, bay, holly, ivy, laurel and mistletoe, and the house was abuzz with preparations for a banquet. Where were the candles in the windows this year? Where were the smells of roasting capons, hens, turkeys, geese and ducks? The sides of beef, the legs of mutton? The nuts, pies and cakes? The plums and spice? The sugar and honey? Lufanwal was still in mourning and awaiting news of Richard when, on Christmas Eve morning, the family was dealt another blow. Harold passed on.

Harold had been in torment: the convulsions, delirium and vomiting would not stop, and when all the juices in his stomach were gone, the very flesh of his insides, it seemed, were coming up. When the doctor confirmed that Harold had gasped his last gasp, Mary could be heard wailing, but it was not from her husband's death that her voice reached such a pitch, it was because the doctor had gone to town and inquired at the local apothecary's. Mary had bought a jug of arsenic at the beginning of December, telling the shop owner she was buying the powder for all the women at Lufanwal, for arsenic mixed with vinegar and chalk was known to whiten skin and prevent creases. The doctor grew suspicious when Harold's fingernails changed color. On the very morning of Harold's death, the doctor returned to the hall with the high sheriff, the same man who had arrested Richard, but now it was Mary's turn to be hauled away.

"I found him in my own bed with a serving wench!" she screamed as they dragged her out the door. "She left strands of her yellow hair on my pillow! It was long and blond—a Saxon whore! I have short, dark hair!" Mary pulled her dark coif off her head. "See? My hair no longer grows!" she screamed at the sheriff. "He didn't even use his bed! My bed! Mine! He promised to come back to me after Ursula, to me and me only! Do you understand? He deserved to die. I warned him I would murder him if I ever caught him at it again, and now I have."

Henry and his brother, Thomas, stood outside in the cold as their mother was carted away. Katharine went to the brothers and put her arms around them. Henry had appeared so grown-up the day he told her of his plans to go abroad to study, but today he looked a child again. "You two come in," she said, leading them toward the door. "The air is as raw as our hearts."

Ned and his two fellow priests emerged from hiding after the sheriff left. Harold's body would be bathed, kept cold and buried on Saint Stephen's Day, the day after Christmas. There was an old country saying that as long as the Yule log burned, evil spirits were kept at bay. The servants finally cut the log that afternoon, dragged it to the great hall and lit the fire, and while Katharine warmed her hands in front of the flames that evening, she wondered what protection the log could possibly afford the family now, for hadn't the evil spirits already stormed the gates?

Sir Edward, Ursula and Harold dead. Richard and Mary gone. In a time of pestilence many family members felled in such a short time would be commonplace, but the plague on this house was not from disease or battles or flames. The days of Christmas plodded on, with shock turning to sorrow and then back to shock again. No merrymaking this year. No mirth. Grief was now woven into the fabric of their lives. One had to eat. One had to sleep. Loss became routine. Ned and his fellow priests consoled the children and the adults, and brought them back to the sacraments and to prayer. What was left of the family and a few trusted servants squeezed into the windowless chapel on Christmas Day; Ned held three solemn masses, starting with Matins.

The three seminarians had orders from Father Henry Garnet, the Jesuit priest who ran the English mission; they planned to split up after Christmastide, journey east and south, with Henry acting as one of their squires until he made passage to Calais. Saint Stephen's Day came and went without the customary wren hunt or feast but with Harold's burial. On the following day, Saint John the Evangelist's Day, the three young men, disguised as dandies, ventured out for the first time to nearby Catholic estates to give mass and the sacraments. Ned was gallant in his fine Italian apparel and exceedingly well horsed. To the passerby, he would seem none other than who he was: the adored son of a noble Lancastrian family, finally come home from his sojourn on the Continent.

Whenever Katharine was alone, she shut her eyes and escaped into scenarios with Will—the same way she used to escape into her books. She tried to recall every feature of his face, the warmth of his voice, his tender touch.

A packet came from him.

He was writing, he said, even during the daily festivities of Yuletide. He was writing, he said, because Venus and Adonis kept him up at night and woke him in the morning. He was writing, he said, because he craved to set his humble verse in front of her: *How fares my dear Kate? I beseech you, tell me how thou art?* His patience was too thin, he said, and thus he was moved to ship to her what he had of recent inked: *The youth must dance and sing and the aged sit by the fire, but I am neither and do neither, for I sit at a plank with quill in hand and scratch my music upon the page.* His family did not know how to take him, for never before had he been so lacking in mirth and merriment and yet so completely contented.

> *Once Anne said I found no comfort in my own skin, and I have in the past proven that I wanted to jump right out of it, but the act of putting down word after word does, as if by magic, calm my sinews and my soul. No more need for mead nor maids. By sundown I am a tired farmer who has with ink on paper plowed many furrows and sown many seeds. By God's troth, I might even call myself serene. Whilst the rest of the house does eat and drink and make good cheer, I sit sequestered in the second floor, a weird hermit, and write. 'Tis in my blood and in my bones and verily I may not sleep until this poem is finished. What will this harvest bring? I miss you, dear Kate, sweet Kate, with all my heart. I will, at the end of these festivities, spur my steed on and in great haste be on my way to your door.*

He knew nothing of the recent tragedies. He'd finished the section with Adonis's horse. The palfrey and the mare ran off into the wood, leaving Adonis unsaddled and furious. When Venus reappeared, Katharine dipped her quill into the inkhorn: *Why not have both Venus and Adonis brimming with contradictions?* she wrote. *Adonis might peek at Venus from under a hat—coy like a woman—so that Venus cannot help but notice him. Make her skin with hues of white, then red, magnify her conflict.*

She plowed into the verse he'd sent line after line, marking when a beat was off or a word astray. This stitching of his words focused her, funneled all her concentration, and it gave her hope.

On New Year's Day, despite the sorrows of the holiday season, Isabel and Joan came to Katharine's chamber and presented her with the beautiful green plumed hat she had so loved that day in town.

"You should not have done this, you silly girls," said Katharine as she pulled the stunning hat out of its box. "And I thought no one was exchanging New Year's gifts this year."

"Dear Kate, we do not care," said Isabel.

"We bought the hat scarce a week after you visited the shop," added Joan.

"And you have kept it a secret all these weeks. I am sure I do not deserve such kindness. My hands are empty of gifts, but my heart is full of love," said Katharine. She pulled the girls to her and kissed them both.

When the girls left, Katharine resumed her work on Will's verse, for she wanted to be fully through it by the time he returned to Lufanwal.

Venus was no closer in her conquest.

Katharine copied lines of Ovid's tale of Salmacis and Hermaphroditus on Will's pages as a guide, how the water-nymph beseeches a kiss from the youth, while clasping him "about the Ivorie necke," how she is "so far beside hir selfe" by his naked beauty that she casts off her garments and dives into the pool and catches the lad up fast in her arms and the wrestling and struggling, the hugging and the grasping commence: "The members of them mingled were and fastned both togither."

Leaping from her seat, Katharine pulled on her cloak—though in truth the lines from Ovid had made her skin hot. She stepped out of her chamber and with a fast gait was down the stairs and out the door, striding through the inner courtyard. Even with snow still on the ground, she was determined to march around the perimeter of the grand house. She kept apace out in the cold dark air, wanted to feel her heart beating within her. When Katharine neared the scullery door, she saw a small figure crouching in the snow. As she got closer, she saw it was the milkmaid Mercy on her knees without a cloak. She was vomiting.

"Mercy, can I help you? Are you ill?" Katharine asked, stooping down.

"Came on at supper," Mercy said. "The victuals' smell sent me out here retching. Dunno. Was fine but a few minutes ago." She wiped her mouth with snow.

As Katharine helped Mercy to stand, she noticed a stone on a black ribbon resting above the girl's white smock and generous bosom. Katharine leaned in close and saw in the small light of the silver moon that it was a turquoise.

"How old are you now, Mercy?" Katharine asked.

"By Shrovetide I'll be fifteen."

"Time shoots by. I remember when you were born."

"My mother worked the cows then."

"Aye. She carried you in a pouch on her chest when she did the milking," Katharine said. "Go in, Mercy, before the cold air gets into your bones."

"You, too, my lady, and gramercy."

"Yes, yes, Mercy. A good even to you."

"A good even to you, my lady."

When Katharine got to her chamber, she didn't wait for Molly but pulled her own cloak from her shoulders and undressed. She was sure there were many such blue-green stones in this world, mountains full of them in faraway lands. As she climbed into bed, she imagined market stalls in London and other cities overflowing with soft kidskin pouches of these bright, opaque stones.

23

efore the end of Christmastide, when Katharine and Isabel were returning one day from town, the groom took a different route on account of a tree felled along the regular road. They happened upon a stately new mansion lined with so many windows it seemed more glass than stone. Katharine realized they were passing Sir Christopher de Ashton's house, for it was on the spot Mr. Smythson had mentioned. There were men gathered round the grand house, still working in spite of the cold and the holiday season, putting on the finishing touches, Katharine supposed.

"I wonder if Mr. Smythson is in there," said Isabel, when Katharine told her this was the house he was building.

"I wonder," said Katharine.

"Let's stop and see!"

"I think it best we carry on, don't you, my dear? The darkness will soon be upon us," said Katharine, though in truth she was interested in how one built a house. She'd seen Mr. Smythson's careful drawings that day in the library, of the alterations he was going to make at Lufanwal.

"'Tis far from dark, and this house is the most beautiful house I've ever seen. Look at all the windows! The light must pour in all day. Not our old, dark, gloomy hall, where it's hard for a ray of the blazing midday sun to find its way into the chambers. Sir Christopher de Ashton must be a rich man, to afford all those thousands of panes of glass. And the lines of the windows and the roofs are so even."

"'Tis most symmetrical," agreed Katharine.

"Isn't that tall man there Mr. Smythson?"

"I suppose it is."

"We must stop and say hello," Isabel continued. "I've met him several times at the hall. He's a nice man. A bit serious but nice. Have you?"

"What?"

"Met him."

Katharine nodded. She didn't know why she was feeling so resistant to stopping, because Mr. Smythson had only shown her kindness, but in a strange way she felt his kindness diverted her from Will, and she did not want that distraction. She wanted to shut her eyes at any instant and think of Will, and only Will. But Isabel had her way, and their driver stopped the cart, and the ladies got out. Mr. Smythson was so busy with his builders that it took them a few minutes of standing there before he realized he had visitors and walked over to them. It looked as though he'd been crawling around on stone, for dust covered his black coat and breeches.

"I love your building!" exclaimed Isabel.

"Many thanks," said Mr. Smythson, bowing.

When he lifted his head he was smiling, which surprised Katharine because he seemed to smile so seldom. Isabel must have noticed it, too, for she burst out in a grin.

"Can we look inside?" she asked.

"Isabel, we mustn't disturb Mr. Smythson when he's in the middle of working—"

"I would be honored for you ladies to come inside. I can't guarantee your skirts won't get a bit of dirt on them. The place is finished on the inside but hasn't been cleaned yet, so there's a film on all the surfaces from cutting the stone and the wood. There's no furniture yet, but Sir Christopher says he's moving in before Twelfth Night. Somehow I don't think that will come to pass."

The ladies followed Mr. Smythson into the house, and he escorted them from room to beautiful room. If they thought the outside of the mansion was handsome, the interior was astounding, with elaborate columns, chimneypieces and friezes of carved stone and richly embellished plasterwork. They looked up at vaulted ceilings and walked on floors of intricately patterned stone. There were no curtains yet, so the light from the outside did, in truth, pour forth into every nook.

Katharine found herself drawn into conversation with Mr. Smythson: how could she not? The way he explained the designing and construction of the house intrigued her. The process seemed akin to writing a piece of music, there were so many elements to take into account. The house had taken him eight years to design and to build, and now, after all that time, the house would soon be inhabited.

"Even without people living in this house, what you've created is alive," said Katharine as he helped her into the cart. "Everywhere the eye looks, there's vitality."

"Gramercy, madam. You and Miss Isabel have made me very happy this afternoon. When Sir Christopher visits, I hear of all the things I've done wrong, so 'tis truly a pleasure to hear of all the things my men and I have done right."

"That was glorious," said Isabel on the way back to Lufanwal. "We had such an adventure, didn't we?"

"I do feel as if I've been away for months, not just an afternoon," Katharine admitted. "Oh, dear, I forgot to thank him for the verse he lent me."

"He lent you verse?"

"A woman poet. Most interesting."

"Mother said this Smythson was one of the men Grandfather hired all those years ago when he added the chambers and the priest hides."

"'Twas before I came to live at Lufanwal," said Katharine. "Mr. Smythson must have been not even twenty then."

"Mother said he agreed to work on the hall again, even though he's become such a sought-after builder, because he was familiar with it, having worked on it so many years ago," Isabel said. "But I think maybe he had other reasons."

Katharine said nothing. She was thinking of the priest holes Mr. Smythson had built at the risk of his own young life, and how those hiding places had, over the course of decades, served their purpose well and saved lives.

"I think," Isabel pressed, "Mr. Smythson fancies you."

"No," said Katharine.

"Yes," said Isabel. "He was perfectly gracious to me, but he was passing attentive to you. He was trying to show us the rooms, but he could hardly keep his eyes from you."

"My sweet Isabel, you have got that wrong. He was paying attention to me because I was asking him so many questions about the building process. I was a student, and he was acting the teacher, that is all. He was being polite."

Isabel smiled at Katharine, then leaned over and kissed her cheek. "Dearest coz, thou art a curious being."

"I am curious. The world is full of wonder. As in the case of how stone is cut and fitted and a wall goes up and doesn't fall down—I'm always desiring to know more."

"I didn't mean it that way. I meant curious as in odd, because you seem so clear-sighted in certain ways and so blind in others."

Katharine sighed. She wanted to talk of Will, not of Mr. Smythson, but her last conversation with Isabel about Will had ended badly, so Katharine kept quiet for the rest of the ride home.

The Christmastide entertainments at the Derby houses—Lathom, Knowlesly or New House—were a custom several centuries old. The revels continued daily during the twelve days from Christmas Eve to Epiphany: feasting, jousting, masquing, dancing, disguisings, cards and plays performed by traveling troupes—now most often by Lord Strange's own players. Lord Strange's father, Earl Henry, still maintained a household of one hundred and fifty people, and when the family opened their doors at Christmas, the number often swelled to over four hundred. "His house in plenty is ever maintained," they said of the generous earl, and this night, Katharine was sure there would be a surfeit of food and wassail, music and dance. The earl's guests were almost all local people, and every year the De L'Isle family was invited.

There had been much debate at Lufanwal as to who would go this year or whether anyone should go at all, since the house was still in mourning and the turmoil not yet ceased. But Matilda and Ned had decided for Isabel's sake a small group would venture forth to Lathom House for one night; Isabel was of marrying age and if the past year had not been interrupted by Edward's departure and the ensuing events, the planning for Isabel's future would have taken precedence. Sir Edward had spoken of a match with the De Hoghtons, one of the premier families in Lancashire—the family Will had served when his father's fortunes had first taken a turn—but the young man chosen for Isabel had fallen sick and died. It was time to consider Joan's future as well, but her mother's awful death and father's imprisonment were too fresh for her to consider partaking in any kind of revelry.

Lathom House, a castle-fortress on the scale of a royal palace, was just outside the village of Ormskirk. And it was to Lathom House that Katharine, Isabel, Ned, the two squire-priests and sundry servants went—the men on horseback and the women in carts—to celebrate the Twelfth Night of Christmas. The ascent to the ennobled and enduring seat of the Earl of Derby never failed to astonish Katharine; visible from a great distance, its towers rose up majestically toward the heavens. But today Katharine did not feel exhilarated by the sight, for it seemed to loom in the gray winter light, not to soar. Indeed, as the cart rattled over the icy road toward the outer gates, a mournful little melody played in Katharine's head: "Farewell bright gold, thou glory of the world . . ."

As they came through the ornate gate, the park stretched before them. Sir Edward had joined Earl Henry on many a deer hunt within the park's gates. And in the years Katharine was invited to ladies' hunts, she'd seen the richness of the land: moss fields, water mills and stone-paved fords along the River Tawd, natural springs deep with water. A wide moat encircled the outer wall, which encircled the castle and its courtyards. When the cold travelers were ushered through the imposing oak-and-iron door by a flock of handsome youths crisply outfitted in the ancestral Stanley livery of orange tawny and green, it was as if those from Lufanwal had been delivered from a dark cave into the sun, for the castle was so grand, so ablaze with riches and elegance, they almost had to shade their eyes from its noble shine.

This was the final night of twelve days of feasting. For hundreds of years, the Stanleys had displayed their power, wealth and glory by dispensing copious food to crowds coming to the house, with equal profusion left over for the poor at the gate. This Yuletide was no different. The Stanley steward had prepared chambers for the men and the women, so they could change and rest during the afternoon and evening, with servants at the ready to attend to their needs. Katharine always felt royal when she visited the Stanley houses, for they treated their guests as such.

In previous years the De L'Isle family would have stayed for several days, but this year they would ride back in morning. There was dinner, then Lord Strange's players would perform, after which supper would be laid and later dancing, disguises and more feasting. The common theme of this eve of Epiphany was that the normal order of things was topsy-turvy, the world turned upside down, which indeed seemed apt for their life this past year at Lufanwal.

Katharine had no inclination for reverse-dressing this year—though in the past she had enjoyed the fun. One year she had been a page, another year a milkmaid like Mercy in a gray smock and wooden shoes. Katharine's only disguise this year was in a leather carton on her lap: the glittering peacock gloves Will had given to her and the beautiful green hat Isabel and Joan had presented to her on New Year's Day. Molly had fixed a black silk veil to the hat, to hide Katharine's face and hair. She would change from her green gown into the new gold and silver threaded bodice and skirt Ned had brought from Rome.

At such a holiday as this, the number of guests was so vast, with knights, gentry, clergy, their attendants, officials, tenants and servants, folk from town and from the country, the family used the ancient great hall for the feasting, music, dancing and entertainments. The high table at one end of the hall was where the special guests sat with the Stanley family; the long tables below were crowded with everyone else. Katharine was grateful to the good Stanley family for placing the De L'Isle family at the high table again this year, for with the splendor and hospitality all around her, Katharine was able to push aside her woes.

Earl Henry was getting on in years and frailer in girth, but his eyes and wit were as sharp as ever. He was still very much in the fore of all festivities at the Stanley houses. Earl Henry was no ordinary nobleman; he was in many ways more like a king, who ruled over Lancashire, Cheshire and the Isle of Man. His court was considered second in size and splendor only to the queen's. He was a descendant of King Edward I; his ancestor Thomas Stanley, the first Earl of Derby, was stepfather to King Henry VII; and his wife, Margaret Clifford, was the great-granddaughter of Henry VII.

Katharine was seated between Lord Strange and his father the earl. She did not know what she had done to deserve such an honor, but it soothed her like a salve, and she chatted and quipped and ate and drank and felt better than she had in a long time. The earl and his son were both brilliant men, and they talked to her as their equal, which always surprised and pleased her. Earl Henry said that if he were not so very, very old he would like to take Katharine for his wife. His son Ferdinando reminded him that his mother, the earl's wife, Lady Margaret, was still very much alive—though this was said in jest, for it was widely known that Earl Henry and his wife had been estranged for many years, and that he in fact had four children with his mistress Jane Halsall, who sat flanked by their two daughters at the other end of the table. Earl Henry chuckled and said in his dotage it seemed his memory was now failing.

The earl's second son by his wife, Margaret, was also at the table, and though William would have been a wonderful catch for Isabel, his father had other plans for him. Two possible matches for Isabel, a Hesketh and a Barlow, from prominent Lancastrian families, were by the gracious design of the Stanleys sitting on either side of Isabel.

The clamor rising from the long tables below made it impossible to hear the musicians in the balcony and nigh impossible to hear what Earl Henry was saying, so Katharine leaned in close to him as he spoke, and when she threw her head back to laugh, she thought she saw Will staring up at her, across the great hall, from the steward's board. Her pulse quickened. Her heart pounded in her ribs. Perhaps the light from the torches and candles was playing tricks on her. She squinted. Now she couldn't see him. I am conjuring him, she said to herself. He is in Stratford, ensconced on the second floor, writing his poem: he is not here. Katharine continued the pleasant persiflage with the earl and Ferdinando, yet her eyes searched the tables below for Will among the rows of merrymakers.

Not finding him, she soon broke off her hunt and gave her full attention to her hosts.

Ned was but three people to Katharine's left, and at one point in the lavish feast she caught his glance and they both smiled. To have Ned back was a blessing. Sir Edward had been the kindly park where she could roam with books and ideas, but Ned was hearth. Perhaps it was their blood ties, or perhaps it was a miracle of nature, but he stood as a fortress for her, and his return from Italy and the immediate and mutual manner in which they opened their gates made Katharine realize how unusual their bond was—truly a treasure, a generous gift from God.

When the feasting came to an end, the high table was dismantled and the elevated end of the hall was transformed into a stage for the players. The Stanleys were legendary patrons. Lord Strange had started his own company, Lord Strange's Men, when he was just past twenty, and his players as well as the Queen's Players stayed at either Lathom House or Knowlesly several times a year. It was impressive—that the Stanleys paid for such frequent entertainments, but also on the part of the touring company, for the road to Lancashire was known for its difficult terrain.

Katharine and Isabel shared a chamber with several other ladies from Lancashire's grand houses, with gentlewomen in attendance to wait on them. There was but half an hour to touch up hair and dab vermillion on lips. Molly had woven threads of gold and silver into Katharine's hair, and when Katharine moved to a long looking glass to tuck the errant ends back into her upswept locks, she overheard one of the De Hoghton ladies talking to Isabel.

"He's a wanton lad. My uncle did employ him for a time. He was but barely with a beard then. Mayhap he's changed. Mayhap he's not. He borrowed my cousin's books and in secret read to her, and sat with her, and we all thought she had lost her heart to a glover's son—and she had . . . for a month. He didn't stay long, and after he went back to Warwickshire we discovered that he had been busy plowing through the serving wenches while making honey to my sweet coz. I was only six, but I remember how my sisters and cousins made up rhymes mocking his name after he left. A player is the right path for such a lewd lad. He has it in his blood—for he convinced every one of those poor maids he was in love. I heard he was at your house now. Someone told me, it escapes me who, that he'd gone and married a wench in Stratford old enough to be his mother when she was with child, and then after they had a few babes she pitched him out."

Isabel looked into the mirror at Katharine, who had stopped fixing her hair.

"I am all right," Katharine said, turning to Isabel, answering a question not asked.

Katharine wanted to tell this young lady from Hoghton Tower that perhaps Will used to behave like that but did not now. She wanted to say: *He may have been false, in his youth, with a maid or two, but he is a man with a wife now and children, and he is a wonderful poet with important friends in London, in the theaters and bookstalls, and he has a life in front of him, a real life, not the brittle pomp of ladies primping in front of glass. Will would go far,* she wanted to lecture, *and there was no reason for him—at this point on his path to success—no need, verily, for him to dissemble or to deceive.*

Isabel started to say something once the young lady moved away, but Katharine put her finger to Isabel's lips to silence her.

"Ancient news," said Katharine, shaking her head. "Let us not speak of it further."

As Ned, Katharine and Isabel took their places in the great hall behind the Stanley family, Katharine noticed Robert Smythson was also taking a seat to watch the play. She had not seen him at dinner, but quite possibly he had been lost to her sight by the dazzle of the banquet. Katharine nodded her head to him, but he seemed oblivious to her and to the multitudes of people laughing and drinking and now gathering to watch the play. Mr. Smythson's mind was so definitely not of this place. He was gazing up at the arches in the ceiling, indeed all of his concentration seemed focused there. Katharine realized she had never written him a note of thanks for the poetry by that interesting young Bassano woman.

The clapping began as a sign to quiet the crowd, and the musicians started a song. Soon a man dressed in the Stanleys' livery announced the evening's play, *A Pleasant Commodie of faire Em the Millers daughter of Manchester: With the love of William the Conqueror.* The author, said the man, was anonymous. He listed the characters and then with no more than an "*Actus primus. Scaena prima,*" he was off the stage, and six players climbed on.

Before the first word was uttered, Katharine recognized Will. So he was not in Stratford. He was not with his family. He was in Lancashire, at Lathom House, in the company of Lord Strange's Men playing one of the lords in William the Conqueror's entourage. Will. Why had he not mentioned this to her? A little piece, a shred, of her heart came loose. Had he not written in his letter that he would make haste to her door? Why had he not said, *I will be at Lathom House?*

Katharine tried to listen to the play, but the thoughts in her head were ten times louder than the words on the makeshift stage. The other two lords spoke, but Will, as Lord Manville, said nothing in this first scene. Katharine's eyes were stuck on Will. He was in full ruff and slashed purple doublet, attire befitting a young fop at present, not 1066. William the Conqueror had taken a fancy to a portrait of the daughter of the king of the Danes. The language was stilted, the humor contrived. William the Conqueror, who in life was no doubt a tremendous warrior and leader, seemed bloated with vanity, yet strangely flat as well. Calling attention to his own epithet, he referred to himself as Conqueror at Arms.

Oh, weary, weary, weary, thought Katharine. William the Conqueror exited the stage Denmark-bound, disguised as Sir Robert, a knight who was ready to win Princess Blanch for his wife. In the next scene, the story of Em emerged, the comely daughter of a knight, now a miller, who had sunk to the life of a peasant by the "sad invasions of the Conqueror."

A character named Trotter brought a sip of mirth to the play, because the player made every move and word a thing of jest, so the scene was sharp, rather than dull. By Scene Three, the fickle William—an odd conceit for a conqueror—decided at first sight that Blanch was not for him, but that he desired another princess, Mariana, who was the love of his friend the Marqués of Lubek. Katharine closed her eyes and listened to the dialogue between Lubek and William/Sir Robert. "That is my love. Sir Robert, you do wrong me," said Lubek. Then the conqueror proceeded to tell his friend that he had just as much right to love Mariana as Lubek did.

Katharine opened her eyes when she heard Will's voice in the next scene, for the character of Lord Manville emerged from behind a screen with his heart brimming for Em, though acknowledging that a lowly born miller's daughter should not be loved by a gentleman. Katharine was not enjoying the play. There was nothing poetic about the lines, nothing poignant about the feelings and nothing jolly about the jests. Trotter was back trying hard to be the fool. The three men who played women wore gowns and ruffs at the Danish court. Em's attire was crude, whereas the others' were fine, but all three had faces in white and lips in red, with wigs upon their heads and bodices so tight that Katharine wondered how they could breathe.

When Manville, played by Will, ranted jealously of two other lords, Valingford and Mountney, and called poor Em, who loved Manville, "cunning and defraudful," Katharine saw, for the first time since Will's Saint Crispin performance, how he shone onstage. But it was Em and Manville's next exchange that echoed in Katharine's ears: "May not a maid look upon a man without suspicious judgment of the world?"

asked Em. And Manville replied, "If sight do move offence, it is the better not to see. But thou didst more unconstant as thou art, for with them thou hadst talk and conference." Then Em: "May not a maid talk with a man without mistrust?" Then Manville: "Not with such men suspected amorous."

Will had said months ago that when a man sees his maid with another man, he always suspects betrayal. Katharine wondered if Will had penned this "anonymous" play himself. Well, she thought, if Will had indeed authored this play, he certainly needed her help with it—perchance he had another woman who labored over his plays by candlelight as Katharine did his poetry. Katharine weathered the rest of the performance as best she could. Manville, after having seduced poor Em with his words, forsakes her. At the end, with all the characters gathered on the stage, William the Conqueror settles for Blanch. The actor who played Trotter then trotted upon the stage, did a jig, sang a song and made a speech about Twelfth Night, where "nothing that is so is so."

Katharine wondered if Will would come to her. Earl Henry and his son Ferdinando spoke graciously with the players while the great room streamed with servants. The actors, still in their costumes, were given tankards of ale, goblets of sack and cups of wassail. Katharine watched Will talking with the Stanleys. He was saying something and they were all laughing. Earl Henry even placed his elegant hand on Will's shoulder. Now he was working his magic on the Stanley clan.

The Stanley father and son continued to move through the crowd and speak with guests. They stopped and chatted with Katharine, Ned and Isabel, and Katharine promised to dance with both the elder earl and the younger lord only if she recognized them through their disguises. Will was talking to his fellow players and to others who came up to him. When he finally caught Katharine's eye and smiled, she forgave him for not telling her of his part in Strange's Men and chided herself for thinking he might not come to her. She was so happy he was in this grand hall with her, so in love, so hopeful for what this evening and the future could bring.

Will was apart now from any group in the crowd and not too far from where Katharine stood with her cousins, and he was staring. But it was not Katharine who held his gaze. It was Ned. Will's intense green eyes were locked on Ned. His stare was so full of force and need that Katharine almost dropped to her knees. She watched Will watch Ned. Katharine recalled the first time Will had stared at her that way, long and hard at the banquet for the Duc de Malois. She had sensed his gaze even before she looked up at him. She remembered what stirred in her then, when she felt his eyes on her. Now, this moment, this horrid moment, seemed a double show on Will's part: for Ned to see Will admiring him, and for Katharine to see it, too. Will was well aware that Katharine was watching. A whole life span seemed to pass while Will fixed his eyes on Ned.

Will walked to where they were standing. Isabel grabbed Katharine's hand and squeezed it. Will stood in front of Ned, waiting to be presented, as if they were at court and Ned was a famous duke. Katharine was silent. She felt utterly shut out of this realm. Will did not even glance at her, but he stood, waiting for the introduction—he must have known the man standing next to her was Ned.

Finally, she said, "William Shakespeare." Her voice was unsteady. "Edmund de L'Isle, just returned from Rome."

Will bowed and then immediately embarked on talk of Rome, as if he knew it, as if he, too, had been there: the fabled Colosseum, the Pantheon, the ancient Egyptian obelisk uncovered at the Circus Maximus and newly resurrected on the Piazza del Popolo. Now Ned and Will, both of similar stature, faced each other, only inches apart. Ned, being Ned, polite and yet also a man who loved men, loved, Katharine saw, how this handsome player was sticking to him like honey. Ned laughed. Will laughed. Ned's eyes fluttered in a feminine, almost flirtatious way. Will had not looked at her.

She was watching a castle crumble before her very eyes.

She withdrew from the two of them with Isabel trailing her. By the time she was at the side table with a goblet of wine, Isabel had put her hand around her waist. Katharine drank the wine in one gulp and poured another. She drank that down, too.

"That man, my dear, sweet cousin Kate, that man is no friend of yours," whispered Isabel.

"Did you see?" Katharine said, her eyes filling with tears. "Am I mistaken?"

"He knows how you feel?" asked Isabel.

"About him? Yes. And he knows what Ned means to me. I invoke Ned often, because of how magnificent Ned is and how much I love him and how I have missed him all these years. I brought Ned into conversations with Will because Ned has always been my light and I wanted to share that light. I have cherished Ned since I was a child . . ."

"And he has cherished you," said Isabel.

"What we witnessed was not just man-to-man. There was something of the conqueror in the way Master Shakespeare wielded his eyes, as if they were . . . a weapon! There was something . . ." Katharine did not finish her sentence. There was something of lust in the way Will had swooped down upon Ned. Katharine had her back to them now. She could not bear to look. Friends and acquaintances came up to her, and she nodded her head and spoke to them and forced a smile, yet all the while she was feeling as though Will had brandished a sword, and that the sword was now lodged mortally in her heart.

She spotted Will one last time before she left the hall to ready for the dancing. He was no longer with Ned, for Ned was talking with William

Stanley, the earl's second son, but Will stood gleaming—slashed purple velvet doublet puffed out like a bird—still gazing at Ned. Katharine thought of Will's poem, the lusty breeding jennet and the strong-necked steed. There was a touch of animal in the way Will was tracking Ned. Every once in a while Ned glanced up and saw Will staring at him— clearly, his priestly vow of chastity had not banished such attractions.

Katharine tried. She tried to continue with the evening. She put on her hat with the veil. She changed into her new Italian-stitched attire. A servant helped her with her peacock gloves. Isabel had donned breeches, a cap, and carried an archer's bow on her back. Katharine wished for arrows with sharp and deadly points, so she could use her skill with Isabel's bow and target Will's darting heart.

"You have not spoken a word," said Isabel as they entered the great hall once again.

"I am stricken beyond speech," said Katharine.

"'Tis this night, my dear," said Isabel. "'Tis Twelfth Night. Nothing is what it seems. Everything, dearest, is turned inside out."

"I wish this night were the cause, but I fear what has happened could happen any night," said Katharine. "I am undone."

They found Ned. Ned, like Katharine, was not flashing a grand disguise. He had pulled a vizard of gold leaf and a gold and black velvet doublet from one of his Roman trunks. His two squire-priests wore masks and aprons from the scullery.

Katharine leaned into Ned. "Did you see the way he stared at you?" she said. She could not contain herself.

"Who?"

"Master Shakespeare."

"Aye, the player. Do you know him?" Ned asked.

"He's my poet, Ned! My poet! The new tutor at Lufanwal!" she exclaimed.

"Oh, my dear, sweet coz. I didn't know. I thought he was just some player with Strange's company." Ned pulled Katharine to him, and they held on to each other for a minute. "I saw," Ned said finally.

The music had begun and the couples were lining up.

Katharine knew Will would recognize her because she was wearing the peacock gloves, but he did not come to her. She did not search the crowd to try to discover his disguise. She played her role. She started dancing. She moved to the music but did not hear it. She recognized the earl, who carried a golden staff and wore the same glaring and bearded mask of Zeus every year, and she danced with him as promised. The floor was awash with silk, velvet, satin, damask and taffeta, and also cambric, buckram and fustian, for the range was high to low, from finery to rags, from voluminous to scanty, from tasteful to gaudy, from colorful to plain. Guests had sported elaborate masks and headdresses, beards and wigs.

Katharine spied a reveler dressed as a poet, wearing a gown and a laurel wreath and carrying a scroll, but it was not Will. Another roisterer was framed in a farmer's long coat, another paraded past with her hair pinned under a cap, a miller's wand in her hand and grain dropping from her smock. Katharine recognized the high sheriff who had carted Richard and then Mary away. He had a sword in one hand and a buckler in the other like a ruffian. A flock of sheepskin-covered folk ambled by her on all fours, their shepherd with his staff and a jug following them.

In years past, the wild range of lush and unusual weeds had delighted Katharine, but tonight it was all too much. Rich, grand and gilded—the air was afire with unnerving excess. Katharine danced with Ferdinando, who was easy to spot because his only change in garb was the addition of a jewel-encrusted vizard from the Orient. While Katharine was switching partners in the first almain, she took the hand of a small elegant figure dressed as a male peacock in the most extraordinary display of real peacock feathers, a headdress that dazzled and peacock gloves that were almost exactly like those Will had given to Katharine and which she had on her very hands this very minute.

"'Tis me, Alice," said the peacock, who Katharine now saw was Lady Strange. "We have the same gloves!"

"Yes, yes," said Katharine.

"Mine were a gift," said Alice gaily. "This New Year's Day."

And before Katharine could ask who the gift-giver was, Alice had moved on to another partner.

24

atharine did not sleep that night at Lathom House, but stared into the darkness. Jealousy was not something she had much experience with, and certainly to be jealous of her beloved Ned seemed a sin, but here she was filled with a searing, unstoppable, wild jealousy. In one of Will's sonnets, he had called jealousy as "cruel as the grave" and compared it to "fiery coals," and indeed those coals burned within Katharine now. He was finishing his poem, and now perhaps he thought it was time to finish her off—his words came rushing back, *The day you tell me that, is the day I have no more use for you!*—but that he had embroiled Ned in his game was perhaps the most malicious thing of all. He had sensed her deep connection with Ned, and then he had used it on her—not to wound her with a dagger but to put her to the sword.

The little group returned to Lufanwal the next day. Katharine tried to seem lighthearted during the ride, but her heart was in such torment she said little. Once back at the hall, she kept to her turret. She was on her bed, curled in a ball, her knees almost touching her chin, when she realized she had not seen Mr. Smythson after the play. She had not even thought of him. Perhaps he had been there with a clever costume on, and she had not recognized him—though in truth he did not seem the sort to wear a disguise.

She replayed the strange scene with Will and Ned in her head. It was a tyranny. If Isabel and Ned had not supported her vision, she would have thought her eyes wrong. This was her question: Did Will act thus toward Ned to wound her or because he could not help himself? She felt in some strange way he was jealous she was seated at the high table, that it was envy that made him retaliate, the same way jealousy of Mr. Smythson had made him retaliate that day he returned from London. He'd been asked to perform with Lord Strange's Men and perhaps didn't understand that the Stanley and the De L'Isle friendship went back many generations, and the De L'Isles would be invited as they always were to the earl's Twelfth Night revels. Or perhaps he had not thought of Katharine or the De L'Isle family at all.

Katharine could not settle on the reason for Will's behavior, but he had discarded her, in truth dispatched her, with his unbridled focus on Ned and his disappearance at the dance. Will and Ned were both dazzling—and perhaps, in that instant of introduction, when eyes met, emerald to amethyst, beauty to beauty, Will and Ned had fallen in love. Perhaps Will's inclination for men was the same as Ned's, and Katharine had never known it. Perhaps that was why he had never bedded her. Perhaps right at this very minute, while she lay with a blanket of wretchedness wrapped round her, Will had returned and was laughing and talking with Ned, her Ned. Perhaps her Ned had become his Ned. She tried to push back the images of their nakedness entwined, but Ovid's words of Salmacis and Hermaphroditus flared up, "the bodies of twaine were mixt . . . the members of them mingled," the wrestling and the struggling to and fro, the hugging and the grasping of the other.

Was this what Will did in front of his wife? With maids and lads? Was this why, as the young woman from Hoghton Tower had said, his wife, Anne, tossed him out of their house?

It was a whole new vision of Will: that Anne made him leave. Perhaps Anne realized if he were to stay, all of her attention, focus, mothering, nurturing would go to him: to flattery to make him feel that he was the only one, the special one, the brilliant one, the one with the ideas, and to vigilance—that she was a sentry of sorts—to make sure he was not in a meadow or a bower kissing another. Perhaps Anne understood that if Will stayed, he would suck the lifeblood out of her, that her bond would be with him and him only because that was what he required, and their three sweet children would go unmothered because her minding would go to her husband, and unfathered because all Will's minding would go to himself. So now, in Katharine's eyes, Anne was intelligent, heroic even, in that she chose her children over Will.

Katharine's belief in men, good men, came from Sir Edward and from Ned. Was Will a good man or a bad man? At first she'd thought him good, a gem, but now it seemed the cut and carat came with a steep price. Katharine was helping Will navigate the human heart in his verse: love, yearning, passion, desire and loss. He clearly understood these feelings. But did he embody them? Or had he shut the door on them? If he had, when? Why? Maybe he was born that way. Maybe God, in creating Will, had gotten something wrong; the humors were off. It was a mystery—the curious, brilliant alchemy of his mind. And if she hadn't fallen in love with him, she would have been able to admire his mind for all its strange gaps and incongruities.

Perhaps this imbalance could be blamed on his craft, the theater, portraying one character while living his true self beneath. She recalled once when he demonstrated every manner of talk the islands of Britain had to offer: from Ireland to Scotland to Wales to the whole compass of England, the strange swallowed sounds of the south to the almost perverse lilt of the nobles at court, a lisp that seemed false and only for effect. He had shown her how he could cry at will. And he had an amazing memory—he could repeat verbatim poems, pages of plays, passages from poets living and dead.

But with this hall of mirrors, with the mimicry and the memory, there was the gnawing question of what Will in truth was feeling. Reflections were only surface. No one could hold a looking glass to the soul. And it wasn't, Katharine decided finally, that his skill as a player was to blame. She had met other players over the years: one who had tried to drown himself in the river because of a broken heart, another who had proclaimed he was in love with Katharine and sang under her window one night. They were passionate, a bit silly perhaps, but without the words of others on their tongues, they were who they were, regular folk. Yet Will oft seemed he was playing a role, even when he was not. He seemed to control his image at every breath. Katharine wondered if he mapped out their meetings before they met, as if they were both characters in a play, with their speeches, their actions, their entrances, their exits already writ.

She sat in front of the fire. Reading was impossible. Dressing was impossible. She stared into the blaze. How had she let herself be seduced by this glover's son from Stratford? How had she, Katharine de L'Isle, who'd believed she'd gained some wisdom after one and thirty years and come to some understanding of life, let a man mine her emotions and then extract what he needed like ore?

Molly came with a letter from Will. He had returned to Lufanwal. So he was on the grounds—in his chamber, in the schoolroom, riding in the hills, laughing with Ned perhaps. Katharine took the letter and threw it into the fire unread. An hour later Molly came with another letter, and Katharine threw that in the fire, too. Why had he not tried to find her at the dance? She had been wearing the gloves he had given her—he would have recognized her. Her mind was a wheel now, running round in circles. Perhaps he'd thought she was Alice. Perhaps Alice was wearing gloves he had given her also.

After Katharine tossed the third note from Will into the fire, she grabbed a quill and, dipping it deep into the dark ink, started to write through her wrath. She felt as worn as a pebble on the shore. She had no idea what was in his heart, or even if he had a heart at all. She wrote and wrote and then threw each page into the fire and watched the flames consume her fury.

She pulled a new sheet of paper in front of her and without intention found herself writing verse. She wrote and rewrote long into the night, going over each line, changing words for rhyme and rhythm. Perhaps it was all these months of working with Will that made the poetry flow from her veins. She warmed her hands by the coals and went back to her words, and by dawn the following morning, without an hour of sleep, she had finished a sonnet:

> *O call not me to justify the wrong*
> *That thy unkindness lays upon my heart:*
> *Wound me not with thine eye but with thy tongue,*
> *Use power with power, and slay me not by art.*
> *Tell me thou lov'st elsewhere; but in my sight,*
> *Dear heart, forbear to glance thine eye aside.*
> *What need'st thou wound with cunning when thy might*
> *Is more than my o'erpressed defence can bide?*
> *Let me excuse thee: "Ah, my love knows*
> *His pretty looks have been mine enemies,*
> *And therefore from my face he turns my foes,*
> *That they elsewhere might dart their injuries."*
> > *Yet do not so, but since I am near slain,*
> > *Kill me outright with looks, and rid my pain.*

With the hills still cloaked in shades of blue and purple and the light just rising from the east, Katharine told Molly to deliver the sonnet to Will and tell him she would meet with him today. Face-to-face, not paper-to-paper, Katharine would tell Will that she would not sit with him again, not read his lines, not pore over his words. Was he more a trickster than an honest man, who used his trickery for people's hearts, not their gold?

Even without tragedy, the dark days of January were always a descent after the heightened pitch of Christmas. The hall resounded with the recent deaths and jailings. Katharine tried to pray and not to dwell on Will staring at Ned, but to no avail. She imagined that Will might take the opportunity of her shutting him out to welcome and to cultivate Ned—though in truth Ned had other business to attend to, for he now spent days traveling to the grand houses of Lancashire and York to re-kindle, amidst secrecy and danger, the flame of their religion.

Katharine dressed with care—she could not help it—and donned her black and white bodice with the scallops of black and white lace. Why, she asked herself, as she patted cinnamon powder on her cheeks, could she not free herself from the desire to pull Will in, even after that vile Twelfth Night? And why did she send him her sonnet? She had never written a sonnet before. Did she think that pretty attire and witty verse would make Will love her? He was as coy and tempting as his Adonis, and now she, Katharine, was as entrenched with lust as his Venus. And what of all Will had promised her? The move to London? *Thy unkindness lays upon my heart*, she herself had writ, but here she was, hair done up in pearls and scallops of lace framing her breasts.

She was at the door of her chamber, Will's pages posted during Yuletide in her hand, when Molly came to her. She supposed Molly had another letter from Will.

"He is waiting for you in the great chamber," said Molly.

"I thought he was in the schoolroom," said Katharine.

"Mr. Smythson, my lady," said Molly. "He begs a word with you."

"Oh, Molly, 'tis of Master Shakespeare I thought you were speaking . . ."

"And Master Shakespeare has changed the place of meeting to his lodging."

"Pray, what can Mr. Smythson want?" Katharine asked. In sooth, she was thinking: Pray, what can Master Shakespeare want? His lodging? She was surprised by Will's boldness.

When Katharine found Mr. Smythson, he was standing in front of the fire. He looked up when she entered, then bowed. Will would have said something flattering about her apparel or her eyes, but Mr. Smythson seemed not to focus on her details. He smiled at her.

"Good day, my lady," he said.

"I saw you at Lathom House," said Katharine, "but missed you after the play. I have wanted to say how much I enjoyed the poetry you gave to me. I have no recollection of a woman putting quill to paper in such a manner. It inspires."

"She has much skill." He paused, as though he were trying to gather his thoughts. "I left before the dancing. I had spent much of the week walking through Lathom House. They want to alter the house and have asked for my services. My son and I were eager to return to our cottage on the sea west of here, so I left before the festivities ended."

"I thought you hailed now from Nottinghamshire?"

"My wife's family is from land near Poulton. The house passed to my son. We spend time there when we are not in Wollaton."

"Must be bitter cold at the cottage this time of year, with the winds off the sea."

"'Tis raw, but the house is in truth not large, and we keep the fires going and a family lives there year-round to help. The snow is less there than here on account of the shore. 'Tis beautiful any time of year, for you can see the water from many windows and the waves even in a tempest sound like music. Perchance you will see it someday."

His last sentence hung in the air, and she was silent, then she began.

"Mr. Smythson, I am not young . . ."

"You are younger than I."

They were in front of the fire facing each other.

"I feel much past the years when I might wed . . ."

"Our own queen has many years on you, and they still try to marry her."

"She is our queen," said Katharine.

"You are scarce past thirty. I have built houses for the Countess of Shrewsbury, who married for a fourth time when she was seven and forty years of age. But I have not asked you to marry me."

"No," she said. "I crave your pardon . . . I . . ."

"But you are not wrong in your interpretation of my attentions," he said, running his hand through his curls.

"Prithee sit, Mr. Smythson," Katharine said.

"You were going out," he said, noticing her cloak.

"I will stay a moment," she said.

When he sat down in one of the chairs in front of the fire, his shoulders immediately went slack—how different from Will, who was so conscious of his bearing, an actor upon a stage.

"Mr. Smythson . . ." Katharine sat down opposite him. She still had Will's pages in her hand.

"Prithee, call me Robert."

"And you may call me Katharine. Robert, I do not know you well, but from the scant time we have spent together I feel I can speak to you honestly."

Mr. Smythson was not looking at Katharine but at the large rough hands clasped in front of him. "Do," he said.

"At eighteen, I was married to a man thrice my age. When I was twenty he died."

Mr. Smythson looked up at her. His profile was sharp, and yet his face was not unpleasant, for there was something lovely and open about his large brown eyes. He waited for her to continue.

"After the death of my husband, I moved back to Lufanwal and have been here ever since. Over the years, suitors came and suitors went, and I . . . I . . ."

"Never found the right fit."

Katharine thought of when Will pulled her to him, how it felt like a glove, but she continued, "I was a boulder that would not budge. You work with stone. You must have certain stones that do not conform to a wall, whether it be outside a house or in the very house itself."

Mr. Smythson leaned his large frame toward her. "Miss Katharine, I am a stonemason. I cut stones, shape them to fit, that is my trade. Most stones do not conform to the contour of a wall or a stairwell or a floor naturally but need the hands of men to help them. But I would never presume to shape you—you are not stone but flesh and blood. I do not know you well but find I think of you often, perhaps too often, and that I wish to see you. I have kept myself back many a time, not let myself jump on my horse with some excuse to come to a house where I am not even at this time working. I am a busy man with a business that is, thank heavens, flourishing. I have a son with whom I spend as much time as is possible—while we are deep in the building of a house and also when we finish work for the day.

"But I know this: I know that I am in love with you. I do not know how it came to pass or why, but it is the simple truth. 'Tis no secret your people are from a much higher breed than mine. I come from generations of men who worked with their hands, first with iron, then stone. I expect my low birth bothers you and I understand that, and I do not expect you to love me or to think of me when I am out of the room, but I wanted you to know that if you ever need me or it comes to pass that you might want to spend time with me, I am here . . . or rather there . . . or wherever I am, and I can come to you. The tragedies this house has endured are profound and very sad, and perhaps 'twas improper for me to come to you at this time with such words, but I felt I must."

He stood. She remained sitting.

"Mr. Smythson . . ."

"Robert."

"Robert, I thank you for your honest words. I wish I could return the sentiment but I cannot."

"I did not expect you could. I only wanted to offer my support if ever you might need it."

She rose and walked to the fire. "This has nothing to do with your standing," Katharine said. She felt a rush of tears and she knew not why.

"I crave your pardon. I have upset you," he said.

"No," she said, wiping her eyes with the edge of her cloak. "It is just that . . ." She did not finish, but what had caught her and upset her was that no man had ever said in all her years the words, "I am in love with you," and now Mr. Smythson had.

He pulled a cloth from his pocket and handed it to Katharine, and she again wiped her eyes. She was ashamed her dam had broken. Will had never said he was *in love* with her. He had said, "And we will love each other and continue on," which she now understood as: *You will love me and we will continue on, with you loving me.*

Katharine grabbed Mr. Smythson's strong hands and held them in her small ones. "Gramercy, for all you have said. You are a brave man."

He smiled and gently pulled his hands from hers; then he put his hand on her head and let it rest on her hair for a moment. "I must be off," he said, lifting his hand and looking down at her. "Fare thee well."

"Fare thee well," she said.

He bowed, took his worn leather satchel from the floor, pulled it over his shoulder and walked out the door. Katharine did not follow him. Will was waiting, but she sat down in front of the fire again. Her throat was tight. She felt choked and weepy. She could barely swallow. Mr. Smythson had been so kind just when she needed kindness, and he had been so warm just when she needed warmth, and he had been so loving just when she needed love. Mr. Smythson had left the door ajar, and now she studied the doorway, half hoping he would turn around and walk back through it, but he was walking away. She listened to the sound of his footsteps receding.

Will had proposed his quarters. At first she thought it mad, and improper, for the house was already a gossip bowl, and the sight of her ducking in and out of Will's lair would surely make it spill over with talk. But, nevertheless, layered in wools and covered with a hood, she walked through the January chill to Will's door. She would make this their final meeting. She would sever their strange rope. She would let him go. She thought of Mr. Smythson's kind words and of the artless manner with which he placed his warm hand on the top of her head.

Will's lodgings were near the old chapel in what had been the priest's quarters until the hunts began. Katharine sat on an oak chair next to the fire, her cloak wrapped around her. Will sat on a joint stool. He wore no doublet. His cambric shirt was open at the neck. His beard was neatly trimmed. His belongings were tidy: books in stacks, shoes and boots in a row, papers in a pile, black quills lined like soldiers on the table; his clothes, she assumed, were neatly folded in the trunk. It was as if he had invited her into his home in Stratford, when his wife and children were out, and had brought her into his bedchamber. She did not know where to look. There was something inappropriate but utterly compelling about finding herself sitting in this small space with him.

"How fares my dear Kate?" he asked.

The way he said her name made her heart go soft. She wanted to fling herself in his arms, bury her head in his shoulder. She now wondered what he had written in the letters she had thrown into the fire.

As if guessing her thoughts, he said, "All my letters to you have gone unanswered."

"'Tis all a shock," Katharine said, avoiding his eyes.

"The dreadful news thrusts the sorrows of this house to the zenith. My deepest sympathies. I've spoken with the two older sons, Henry and Thomas—they seem as deer cornered in a hunt." Will took a package wrapped in gray paper from his table and handed it to Katharine. "For the New Year's Day past," he said. "Not gloves." He smiled.

An image of Lady Strange's peacock gloves glittering across the dance floor flashed in front of Katharine. She opened the package and found two books. The first book was of buttery kidskin; embossed gold vined up its spine. Inside was a page with: the title, *The Countesse of Pembroke's Arcadia*; the author, "written by Sir Philippe Sidnei"; the family crest; and "London, printed for William Ponsonbie—*Anno Domini*, 1590." In a long and loving inscription to his sister Mary, the Countess of Pembroke of the title, the poet wrote:

> *I could well find in my harte, to cast out in some desert of forget-*
> *fulnes this child, which I am loath to father. But you desired me to*
> *doo it, and your desire, to my hart is an absolute commandement.*
> *Now, it is done onelie for you, onelie to you: if you keepe it to your*
> *selfe, or to such friendes . . .*

She read on. A line resonated toward the end of his dedication: "You will continue to love the writer, who doth exceedinglie love you . . ." Was Will, by giving this to her, trying to convey what perhaps he could not say himself?

"Your beloved Sir Philip," said Will, "fresh from the London book-stalls."

"Gramercy," said Kate, opening the second book, entitled *The Arte of English Poesie* by George Puttenham.

"I gave my mother a New Year's gift, a hat of velvet, silk and feathers bought at the milliner's in the village here, a hat of elegance and taste."

Kate wondered why Will was telling her this.

"She did not fancy it at all," he said.

"Did she say so?"

"No. She did not utter a word, but her eyes were icy and the manner in which she pursed her lips spoke of her distaste. I went out directly and bought her a shawl."

"Did she fancy that?"

"Her eyes were warmer. It gives me great pleasure to give gifts, but my mother is particular. I feared you'd taken ill when you didn't respond to my letters yesterday, but then your sonnet arrived," he said. "I thought your sonnet quite good."

Katharine placed the two books on the table in front of her and waited for Will to continue, for him to comment if not on the whole sonnet, at least on some of her lines.

"Read what Puttenham has to say about our English language," was all he said, tapping the book with his finger.

Katharine nodded. In truth, she cared little about her sonnet at this moment. Writing served her—from last night until this morn—as a raft onto which she clung so she would not drown. She did not want to ask Will about her poetry; she wanted to ask him why he did not try to find her at the Stanleys' during the dancing. Why? Where was he that night? And what about his circling of Ned as a hawk does its prey? What was that? She wanted to ask him all these things, but the words were strangled and did not issue from her mouth.

"My pace has been slow with the poem." He corralled her with his eyes. "I have in truth not written a word these last weeks."

He cannot write without me, Katharine thought.

She was aware of his bed, of how close their bodies were in the small chamber.

"'Tis a pity," she said. "You were marking such fine speed. You were on fire."

"The festivities at the Stanleys' stalled what heretofore was in motion," he said.

How long had Will lodged at Lathom House? While Katharine had pictured him steady at his verse in Warwickshire with his family swarming around him, he'd been but several leagues from her, partaking of the Stanleys' abundant hospitality.

"You seemed to have found your stride when writing at your home at Christmastide, even with a house in merriment," she said. "Here, where solitude reigns, you should be able to advance your stanzas—unless you are off again with Lord Strange's Men. I've brought the sheets you sent from Stratford. I've marked them."

He took his verse from her. "I filled in at Lathom, one of their regulars had taken ill. Did you enjoy *Faire Em*? Was my skill what you expected?" he asked.

She waited for him to say something, anything, about Ned. "You are well skilled, an excellent player," she said finally.

The fire crackled while he read what she had written.

"A brilliant suggestion—to use Ovid's tale of Salmacis and Hermaphroditus as a guide." He put the pages down and added wood to the fire. Katharine waited—for what, she was not certain. He leaned against the table, gazing at her. Minutes passed. Then he said, "Full gently now she takes him by the hand. A lily prison'd in a jail of snow . . ."

"Our Venus might beseech him once again." Katharine did not want to involve herself in his lines, yet she couldn't stop herself.

"Once more the engine of her thoughts begins," he said, smiling.

The words were on the tip of Katharine's lips: she knew she could without hesitation become Venus's tongue. She pretended she had to think, that it took time. "Would thou wert as I am, and I a man, my heart all whole as thine, thy heart my wound . . ." Katharine offered slowly. "For one sweet look thy help I would assure thee, though nothing but my body's baine would cure thee."

What am I doing? Katharine asked herself.

"She wants something out of him, that he can't give her," Will continued. "He wants his horse back and he wants her to let go of his hand and he wants her to leave him alone . . ."

"Then she challenges him to act more like his steed, to take advantage when presented with joy, to learn to love," said Katharine.

"Yes, yes," said Will, pacing. "And then our fair Adonis launches into scorn. 'I know not love,' he says, 'nor will not know it, unless it be a boar, and then I chase it.'"

Katharine nodded.

Will bowed. "'Tis like the old times, Kate!" he said. He leaned down to her, cupped her burning cheeks in his hands, and continued: "'Tis much to borrow, and I will not owe it: my love to love is love but to disgrace it, for I have heard, it is a life in death, that laughs and weeps, and all but with a breath." He let go of her cheeks, walked back to his table, dipped his quill and, still standing, started writing.

Katharine had been so resolute, but now her moat had dried up and her wall had fallen. She stood. There was an old legend that witches could enchant furniture, and now Katharine wondered if the joint stool in front of her, still warm from Will, had indeed cast a spell.

"I must go," she said.

He turned to her. "I will write all through the night and send you pages and——"

She was quickly out the door. When she reached her chamber, Molly was there.

"Dowager Lady de L'Isle asks for you to come to her," said Molly, helping Katharine out of her boots.

"Did she mention why, Molly?"

"No, mistress."

"I know why," Katharine said. "She will reprimand me for my visit to Master Shakespeare's chamber. I am no child! How this vexes me!"

A few minutes later, Katharine was standing in Matilda's antechamber.

"Come sit, Katharine," said Matilda. She still wore her widow's veil in public, but in her chamber her face and head were bare. She was swaddled in a shawl, kid gloves on her hands. "I cannot seem to rid myself of a chill," she said. "I suppose I should move around, but my bones want strength. Come sit by the fire, Katharine."

Katharine did as she was bade. Matilda seemed in the last year to have shrunk to the size of a child.

"Katharine, Robert Smythson came to speak with me."

Katharine's face flushed red.

"He said he had spoken to you."

"He has," was all Katharine said.

"And that you heard him graciously but spoke honestly that you could not return his affections."

"Yes."

"So if he were to make an offer in marriage, you would decline?"

"Yes."

"Katharine, do you know that he is a master stonemason and that in the last years he has designed and built some of the most important houses in England?"

"I suspected."

"And do you know his business is thriving and that he is a man with considerable means?"

"I never thought of that."

"Of course you didn't. I am speaking frankly to you, as frankly as I have spoken to my daughter Isabel, who has today accepted young Barlow's offer of marriage."

"How wonderful," said Katharine, who in truth had never heard Isabel utter one word of him. "Isabel must be very happy."

"Isabel is sensible. She is happy in knowing that her husband's family hails from good and noble stock, and was first knighted, as ours was, by King William when he conquered these lands."

This was just the sort of speeching that made Katharine glad she had entered into adulthood without a mother or a father.

"Katharine, I would hope, after our talk today, that you would reconsider Mr. Smythson's offer."

"But he in truth did not offer . . ."

"I realize that, but he knows you well, it seems, and did not press on with his offer, for fear you would shut him out completely."

"I will not shut him out. I am fond of him."

"Perhaps, then, over time, you could learn to love him."

Katharine rose. Her eyes were filling with tears. It was Will she loved, and it was with Will she wanted to be. She wanted to fling that in Matilda's face. She was sure now she had misinterpreted Will's staring at Ned. Katharine wanted to say to Matilda: *Will Shakespeare loves me. Will Shakespeare desires me. Will Shakespeare said I am brilliant and beautiful and clever. Will Shakespeare pulled my body to his and kissed me after we danced the volta. He undressed my hair. He said I know him better than anyone else. He said we would know each other for forty years, that this year was just the start of our bond. Will Shakespeare has asked me to move to London with him.*

"Would you consider what I have said to you, Katharine? I don't have to say, but I will, that the air has changed at Lufanwal. My dear Edward's exile was the beginning of the end of a way of life here. Richard is still in jail. Ned has become a priest and thus forfeits his legacy. Young Henry is soon off to Rome, and it remains to be seen if he, too, will follow his cousin into the priesthood. The future of this house is, indeed, uncertain. I am old. My end will come soon."

"No, my lady, no. Do not speak thus," said Katharine.

The Matilda of Katharine's childhood was strong and proud. The small woman sitting in front of Katharine seemed a parody of the towering woman who had presided over Lufanwal for so many years.

"'Tis true," Matilda continued. "Death is no secret. 'Tis God's will. I have this small chest for you, Katharine. Do not open it until you have returned to your chamber. I have been a jailer of a branch of Edward's spirit. 'Twas not gracious nor kind that I kept these, and that is something I must live with and ask for God's forgiveness and for your forgiveness until my eyes close forever on this life. I have tried to love you, but in truth my envy has most often clouded my affections. I coveted the way in which you were a rich soil for him; he could speak and write to you in ways he could not to me. He never taught me to read or to write, but showered all his learning onto you. I'll never know why he chose you, but he did. He chose you. I thought that by holding on to these maybe I could hold on to a part of him that I was never able to grasp, but that you seemed to seize easily and naturally." Matilda handed Katharine a wooden box with ivory inlay. "Go," she said, "and take this with you. I am tired and cold. Think on all I have said."

When Katharine returned to her chamber, she sat on her bed and opened the box. Inside was a bundle of letters addressed to her from Edward—his seal broken. The sudden sight of his handwriting, the thick, stolid letters, brought tears to her eyes. It was as if he had entered the room and was sitting there with her. As she read, beginning with a letter that dated as far back as his journey, he came back to her in a rush of flesh and voice. Her tears dropped upon his pages. How she missed him. She had wondered why he had not written but had thought it not her place to ask if any letters had come for her. She drank his words, his descriptions of people and places. He was, she read, making the best of his plight. He greeted each new day without regret or woe but with energy and curiosity. He had never been on a ship, never traveled out of his beloved England, and the strange customs and languages entertained and compelled him.

"Oh, Edward," she said out loud. "I can hear you." She wiped the tears from her face with her hands and dried her wet palms on her skirt. "Dear, dear Edward." He must have thought her cold and unkind, for she had—thinking he had not written to her—not written to him. Katharine spent the afternoon and evening reading every word Edward had written to her. Nothing secretive or inappropriate hovered in his tone: he would have welcomed Matilda's reading them. Katharine hoped someone had read them to Matilda. There was something about the warmth and honesty in the letters that made Katharine think of Robert Smythson. She'd never thought of it before, but there was a similarity to the timbre of their voices and the deep, clear tone with which they spoke.

25

ou have heard my news," said Isabel. Katharine and Isabel were sitting in Isabel's chamber. They had their shawls around them, and their stools pulled close to the fire.

"Your mother told me, dearest." Katharine put down her stitching and gazed at Isabel. "I recall sitting next to him at dinner on Saint Crispin's Day. Are you pleased?"

"I am pleased that Mother is pleased," she said.

"Is there goodness in this Nicholas Barlow? I could not bear to have you married off to a man without goodness."

"Time, I suppose, will teach me if he has goodness. 'Tis good in the match, even if there is no goodness in him."

They were quiet.

"I cannot imagine you not here," Katharine said.

"I cannot imagine me not here," Isabel said. "I will not be far away. Three hours by horse."

"Well, I'll drop by several times a day!"

"Mother told me of Mr. Smythson's offer."

"Yes, we women are like goods and chattels. Or perhaps slaves is more apt."

"Kate, he was not offering to buy you."

"No?"

"No. He may not be exactly of our . . . well . . . he is not . . ."

"Of our kind?"

"Well, no, but he has a business that is surely growing, Kate. That he designs those beautiful houses as well as builds them—is remarkable. He has the hands of a sculptor."

"And the face of a rock," added Katharine.

"Kate, have you not had your fill of smooth faces and smooth voices?"

"And smooth verses?"

"Yes."

"I do not mean to poke fun at Mr. Smythson," said Katharine. "He may have the face of a rock, but he has a very warm heart. He is a nice man, and in truth the mansions he builds are breathtaking."

"And you turned him down."

"Tell me more of Nicholas Barlow."

"You will meet him again, for Mother is giving a small banquet in our honor."

"And I will have a chance then to quiz this Nicholas Barlow on his goodness," said Katharine, kissing Isabel's cheek.

Back in her own chamber, Katharine sat in her high-backed oak chair with her cloak still on and stared out the open window. The air outside was frigid, but she sat there, letting the cold seep into her skin and questioning if heaven was indeed beyond the clouds. Maybe God was finally granting her His love in the form of this love with Will, a love that only felt mutual sometimes—and it was therein that the confusion, the canker, lay. She could not eat tonight. She could not concentrate. She was not able to keep anyone's company. She felt weak, almost ill. Finally, she shut the window and lay down on her bed, fully clothed, with her cloak still on. She rested her head on her pillow, stared up at the ceiling and watched the shadows of her candle flame dancing on the wood. Mayhap he thought her too old, not fair enough, not rich enough, too clever. Tears filled her eyes and slid slowly down her cheeks.

She had Molly fetch Ned—he, his fellow Jesuits and Henry were to depart from Lufanwal after Candlemas.

"My dear," Ned said when she opened the door. "My dear, you are ill, return to your bed with haste."

"I am not ill, Ned, but 'tis true I am stricken. I have to know, Ned. I must know. You have to, if you love me, pray be honest. I will not fault you. I will understand, because he is so . . . he is so charming, so cunning. I will not fault you. I must know. Please, I beg of you . . ." Katharine, in her smock with her hair down, pulled Ned to sit next to her on the bed. She was holding him by his collar. "I beg of you . . ."

"What, my dearest? What?" he said, gently taking her hands from his collar and holding them.

"Did you . . . did he . . ." The tears were streaming down her face. "Are you with him? Have you been with him? In secret? Has he seduced you, too?"

"Who?"

"Will?"

"Will Shakespeare?"

"Yes, he."

"No," Ned said simply. "I barely met the man but a few days ago at the Stanleys'.

Katharine threw her arms around Ned's neck and clung to him.

"Dearest Kate, you're most distraught."

"Since our return, have you been meeting with him and hiding it from me? Dear, sweet cousin, pray tell me the truth."

"No. I swear upon the Holy Roman Bible I have not."

There. Ned had said it. Ned had said it, but why could Katharine not believe him? What work of the devil was this: to make her doubt her cousin who had always been her solace, her peace and her home?

"'Tis better you stay apart from him," said Ned. "You have the look of a wolf about you, my dearest, a hungry wolf. I have seen that haunted look on others, but never on you."

"Why did he say those things to me? Why did he act thus? Why did he make me Venus to his Adonis?"

"Some men do such dalliance for sport. Some men need to play the god. Some men need others to worship them, and they will do anything and say anything for that to come to pass. 'Tis a sickness. 'Tis debauchery. They ruin lives."

"Oh, Ned, do not leave me," she said.

"You will survive."

"But will you survive, dearest Ned? There are gallows everywhere."

"'Tis for God to know. I have His work to carry out."

"I will die if anything happens to you."

"Kate, you will not die. You're made of strong and sturdy stuff."

"You are a wonder, my sweet Ned. I crave your pardon for my ill-versed questions."

She held out her hand and he took it and kissed it. Then she reached for his cheek and tenderly touched it.

Six days, and Katharine did not see Will, nor did he send any pages. He did ask to meet with her, and she sent word through Molly that she could not at this time, for her duties at the hall crowded her. The fever of Will was beginning to lift. She could, perhaps with time, become immune to him.

On the seventh day, Molly brought her a letter from him.

Dear Kate,

Gramercy and gratitude for the enormous amount of brilliant attention you bestowed upon the verse I sent at Christmastide. Your ideas did much improve my lines. Kate, I never take you for granted, but I thought you should know that I am wholly grateful and thankful for all you have done. 'Twas a bit hard to endure some of your words writ upon my page, not because you are wrong but because you are right and it reminds me of how far I have yet to travel as a poet. I will try to toil and to continue on, as you recommend. I shall brook no excuse for not moving ahead. I have read through what I have got, and I must say it sits well, which is much for me to say. Verily, I must advance, though I'm now stuck as to what follows. I cannot seem to set my quill upon the page with any ease. I hope you are well.

Adieu,
Will.

Will was playing the humble and appreciative student. Katharine threw the letter in the fire and burst into tears.

On Candlemas, Ned said mass in the hidden chapel, for it was a day of hope, purification and renewal. Katharine tried to listen, tried to take it in, believe it, but hope seemed far away, purification unattainable and renewal utterly impossible. Then Ned and his squires left for a Jesuit mission. Young Henry went with them, to journey as far as the coast, where he would book passage on a ship to the Continent. Parting with Ned and Henry was a sad and serious blow, for Katharine simply did not know if she would ever lay eyes on either of them again.

The following day, Isabel and Katharine were in Isabel's chamber, trying to warm themselves like cats in the only patch of sunlight.

"'Tis one thing to be young and naïve," Katharine said.

"And you are neither," Isabel finished.

"I am as a teller of a tale. I see what goes, I see what he doth do, but at the same time I am a character, too, and am strangely tethered to him and his poetry. I stay in the story as it unfolds. I've tried, Isabel, I've tried to break away." Katharine put her face in her hands.

"Perhaps he loves you," said Isabel.

"How I have hoped for that, dreamed of it, but I am not at all sure he knows how to love. And what of his family? His wife? His children? He rarely speaks of them. What about passion? He seems to have it for his writing and the stage, but nowhere does he seem to have it for people, or a person. I thought in the beginning he had a passion for me, but I was wrong, for if he did, I would not be sitting in front of you wringing my hands. What of chaos? What of messiness and tangled lives? He can write a poem that snares this, but he stays at the remove, while others play it for him."

"But was it not his ambition and the chaos in your heart that did excite you at first, my dear?" Isabel asked.

Katharine did not answer Isabel, for it was true. But now that very bedlam he created did threaten to bleed her dry. "Perhaps he loves Ned," said Katharine.

"Loves Ned? I think not," said Isabel. "Your bones are showing."

"Food holds no interest for me." Katharine gulped a cup of wine like it was water. "Why this shaky cosmos, Isabel? Why the fire and then the freezing and then the thaw? I had such hopes for something special, grand in truth, because I felt we were two ends of a ribbon, not a ball and chain. He made me say it once."

"What?"

"He made me repeat after him. Say it, Kate, he said, say, 'What we have is special.' And I said it. I repeated it. He said, 'We have the rest of our lives, Kate, you and I. Ten, twenty, thirty, forty years, God willing. You must not leave me. I will buckle at the knees and fall if you do. You must remain by my side.' He said those things. I remember every word he ever spoke to me. Today, this minute, I feel there's been yet another death in my life. That a vision of a future with him, some sort of life, has sustained me all these months and now 'tis finished." Tears rolled down her face. "He has not mentioned London. He has not reprised his offer." Katharine continued, "What am I left with? He's kept it all so contained, while I have let it invade every breath I take. Now I see it. 'Tis winding down for him. His poem will be finished soon. And he has made his mark with the Stanleys. He has done, I suppose, what he came to Lufanwal to do. He has crafted his future, and he will leave. And he will not think of me after he leaves, whereas I will hold on to this year with him. I will hear it and see it and feel it forever. I cannot bear that this has never amounted to anything more than a kiss at the dance or the pulling of pins from my hair. Did I tell you he leaned in and kissed me on the mouth and I opened my lips once? Did I tell you that?"

"Yes, you told me," said Isabel, hugging her weeping friend. "You seem tired of this man."

"I am. I feel slightly ill always now. I have been fighting a war that was at first battle exhilarating, but now the constant mutilation makes me weary."

"Dearest, sweetest Kate, I have never seen you thus."

"I am on Ursula's trail."

"You are not and must not talk thus. You must not see him. What started as a tonic has turned toxic."

"And when I am with him I feel as if in a dream, because I am lost to him, because I cannot *not* meet with him."

"Yes, you can. Pray, be strong. Do not see him. You are stricken," said Isabel. "You need a priest."

"Yes, what a shame dear Ned has gone, for he must perform an exorcism here at Lufanwal," said Katharine.

That night at supper, she drank cup after cup of wine, and with each sip her anger grew. In her chamber, her head lurching, she dipped her quill in her inkhorn and let her words spill across the page:

> *Dear Will,*
>
> *Do you in truth desire to be a poet? I wonder. I am a champion to those who desire it. I wonder if in some way you do not. You are so gifted 'tis uncanny, yet not a word was writ the weeks we did not meet. What happened? Hast thou ever tried to bare thy soul? Much of the time, I have no idea from whence you come or indeed what you are feeling. I no longer care what you think of me or how I might fit into your life. You and I are as different as the sun and the moon, and after these many months perhaps that is, alas, crystal clear. Poetry is not a game. 'Tis not the muck of players, of changing fine flaunts for a role. 'Tis from a well far deeper. You could have written these weeks, as you did during Yuletide. Yet you have nary a line created, when you could have much. Your pouch overflows with talents of word and thought, of rhyme and meter. From your pen flows pure abundance. You know how you feel when you are writing from that place. Perhaps it makes you afraid, makes your world whirl with inward uproar and unruliness. If so, then you are right to cease. Leave your quill and paper, and as is your inclination, mouth the words of others upon a stage.*
>
> *Adieu,*
> *Kate.*

She stared into the darkness much of the night, tossing from side to side. She found no peace, no even keel. When she awoke, her head was heavy, her body in a sweat. Molly had replenished the fire and brought her bread and ale.

"Art thou ill, mistress?" Molly asked.

"Demons raided my sleep, is all," said Katharine, wiping her brow with her sleeve, pulling her damp hair from her neck. She swung her legs over the side of her bed and sat like a child, feet dangling, not quite touching the floor. "Molly, did you . . ."

"Yes, my lady, I slipped your note under his door."

"Ah," said Katharine, her mouth dry. She wished now she had thrown her missive into the fire.

Molly pulled open the curtains and poured a pitcher of water into the basin. Her red hair shimmered in the sun. Though light was streaming in, the day seemed not yet begun, for Katharine's mood was as black as night. She recalled what she had written to Will, the words like spears. *Do you in truth desire to be a poet? I wonder . . .*

"Is it late, Molly?"

"The sun is high," said Molly, leaning over Katharine and touching her forehead with her cool hand. "You mustn't read 'em no more," she said.

"What, Molly?"

"The papers he sends to you. 'Tis lewd, that lad . . . in person and in word . . . but 'tis not his lewdness that makes me warn you off his verse . . . 'tis what I see happening to you, mistress. Look at yourself." Molly brought a looking glass to Katharine.

Katharine stared. "So?" She handed it back to Molly.

"Don't you see?"

"See what, Molly?"

"How ye've changed."

"Verily?" said Katharine, taking the mirror back and looking again. In truth, she saw a change also.

"This man and his poetry are not fit for a lady. They say in the scullery—"

"I know what they say, Molly! I know. I know." Katharine's eyes filled with tears and when she moved to wipe them, the looking glass slipped from her fingers and fell with a crash to the floor.

"Oh!" It was Molly who let out the cry, for there was nothing good about a broken mirror.

Katharine was stunned and silent while Molly fetched the broom and swept up the shattered pieces.

When Katharine finally rose and bathed her face, her heart felt heavier than stone. She moved through the morning with a certain caving and cleaving and carving within. She stayed in her chamber—as stooped and slow as an old hag. She waited. In the late afternoon, Molly brought a message. He wanted to speak with Katharine now. This news did not thrill her, as it might have days or weeks or months before. She sank even lower. What had she done?

"I cannot see him," she said, "but I bid you, dear Molly, bring this letter to him."

Katharine dipped her quill in the inkhorn with such gravity, 'twas as if she were on her deathbed composing her will. *I've come undone. I am unmoored. I cannot find the light. I crave your pardon for the letter writ late last night.*

When Molly returned, the paper from Will was harsh and sealed with anger.

What did I do for you to deliver such cruelty? I did not write much these past weeks and now you fling my empty pages at me as though I have committed thievery. You judge. You slander. "If

so, then . . . cease," you hurl at me. If so, then cease? I am not
dressing in character, as you so archly scribe. I cannot not write.
These past months here have thickened my blood, made sauce
where broth did run. If so, then cease? Would you then cut off my
finger, dismember my every limb? I once more ask you: What
did I do for you to deliver such cruelty?

Katharine walked her floor, her hair down, her hands clasped behind
her back. What had she done? What had she wrought? Ned at the Stanleys', the almond-eyed lady in London, the serving wenches at the De
Hoghtons', all the sordid tales from the scullery and beyond . . . had she
blasted Will unfairly? Created a plot where there was none?

I crave your pardon, Katharine wrote on the back of the paper he had
sent her. *I am so very sorry. My thoughts are poison. My words are pikes. My*
shame is a heavy mantle. I believed you were in love with me, and now cannot
abide that you are not.

There. She had said it. She had bared her soul just as she had urged
Will to do.

She did not go to Will. She started to walk down the path that led out
of Lufanwal, through one courtyard, then another. The tiny flurries of
snow that fell from the sky did nothing to cool the hot misery she felt in
every joint and every limb. She had not touched the bread Molly had
brought, and now sorrow filled the spot where hunger should have been.
She had not been this unsettled since her family had perished, but she
had been so young and out of tune with her feelings then that she had
gone on to her new life at Lufanwal Hall without much change in her
complexion. Then her own babes had died, one born, the other not yet.
She had survived.

Katharine wished she were made of a different mettle now or, indeed,
it was metal she was made of, for she felt her flesh being peeled from her

very bones. She saw in Will strange and mismatched threads, but she had dispatched her heart to him. His need, so strong, so childlike, thwarted her from ending things. Perhaps, if she had children of her own, his craving would not woo her thus, or perhaps it would have. There was, after all, the specter of his wife and the gossip that she had cast him from their home. Again Katharine thought perhaps this Anne was strong rather than weak, who acted thus so she did not have to give ceaseless suck to the needy infant who had fathered her flock.

It occurred to Katharine that Will needed someone to sit beside him while he worked as his mother had done while he was home at night after grammar school. Katharine had always imagined poets such as Sidney and Spenser alone at a table, squinting into the candlelight, but perhaps she had been wrong. Perhaps Will's self-professed ability to be alone was not a true mirror. Will said his wife and children crowded him, yet he wanted Katharine to read his words and to meet with him every day. And crowding? Well, he had come north to a family that, though the house was grand and the grounds vast, was beginning to crowd itself.

As Katharine turned and circled back, passing the stables and then the barns, she heard cries and groans more human than animal, and in a move that was unlike her, she did not venture in. It was a woman in pain, but there were other women there, too, for she heard a voice saying over and over again, "Now, now, there, now, now"—a sort of cooing chant meant to soothe the poor soul in distress. Katharine stopped and listened. "Now, now, there, there, 'tis the will of God, Mercy. 'Tis the will of God . . ."

God. With Katharine's focus on Will, she had been neglecting God. She had put Will before God. She would make a confession of her sins when Ned returned. And she would pray for Will. There was nothing Will had done to her that could be judged in a court of law as overtly unjust—and certainly a man seducing a woman with words and embraces was nothing new—why, the character Will had played in that silly play at Lathom House had done just that to poor Em.

He sat erect, a statue. It was the next morning. They were again in his lodging—by now the whole house was assuredly full of foul and vulgar rumor. She sat on the stool across from him. Without changing from her smock before she left her chamber, she'd pulled on her worn velvet dressing gown, then her cloak and hood, and now in his lodging she kept her cloak wrapped tightly around her. Her hair was not up but braided by her own hand in a queue down her back like a servant girl's.

He slapped the pages on her lap. "Read," he commanded. "'Tis Adonis first." His profile was sharp, his jaw set and his look of such blackness that it nearly threw Katharine from her seat. She had never seen him thus.

She took the paper and leaned into the light and read. Adonis's lines stung her eyes: "'Remove your siege from my unyielding heart, / To love's alarms it will not ope the gate.'" While Venus's lament broke her heart: "'What, canst thou talk?' quoth she, 'hast thou a tongue? / O would thou hadst not, or I had no hearing!'"

"Is this the muck of players, Kate, of changing fine flaunts for a role?" Will nearly shouted as he recited:

> *"Say that the sense of feeling were bereft me,*
> *And that I could not see, nor hear, nor touch,*
> *And nothing but the very smell were left me,*
> *Yet would my love to thee be still as much;*
> *   For from the stillitory of thy face excelling*
> *   Comes breath perfum'd, that breedeth love by smelling—"*

"I—" she interrupted, but he continued:

> *"But oh what banquet were thou to the taste,*
> *Being nurse and feeder of the other four!*
> *Would they not wish the feast might ever last,*
> *And bid suspicion double-lock the door,*
> > *Lest jealousy, that sour unwelcome guest,*
> > *Should by his stealing in disturb the feast?"*

"I must hail from a shallow place, then!" He fairly spat the words at her. "And not from a well far deeper."

There was silence. She had never seen him so full of rancor, yet she felt oddly satisfied that she was able to move him thus—at least that, she thought, at least if not love, then anger.

"The words you wrote were heartless, beneath you," he said.

"Everything about this is beneath me," she said.

As quickly as he flashed his fury, he quelled it: with haste the merchant usurped the poet. "Let us forget this moment," he negotiated. "Let us not speak of these things. Let us continue on as we have."

This could have been the end—her final resolve. Katharine sat in his small room, surrounded by his black quills, his order, his paper stacked neatly like hay after the harvest. This could have been the end, but she nodded and leaned again into the light to read the rest of the stanzas he had thrust at her.

"There seems an even field where mountains and ravines should be," she offered. "There is little action here between Venus and Adonis. We've heard enough of idle chatter. Cannot Venus fall in a faint?"

"What makes her swoon?" he asked. He was sitting on his cot. His doublet and shirt were open. The skin of his chest that showed was smooth and without hair. "What makes her faint?" he demanded, there was nothing gentle in his tone.

"His look," Katharine said, shifting her eyes to his face.

"How so?"

"His look is so full of anger, so racked with fury, so verging on hate, that when she sees that, before he even speaks, she is struck down."

"And when she falls, Adonis comes to her," he said.

"Yes, he might. The silly boy believes she's dead," Katharine said, wishing she could feign a swoon.

"He claps her pale cheek," Will added.

"Till clapping makes it red," she continued. "For on the grass she lies as if she were slain."

Will darted to his table, dipped his quill, wrote, then spoke: "Till his breath breathest life in her again."

"To mend the hurt that his unkindness marred," Katharine offered. "He kisses her, and she does not rise, so he kisses her again. She opens her eyes."

Will was staring at Katharine. "Her two blue windows," he said.

He lingered in his look at her. She countered him, her eyes on his, unwavering. Perhaps all that had gone on was just stone upon stone—what they were building—and she would, after all, make a life with him and go to London as he had promised.

He dipped his quill and bent his head. "The night of sorrow now is turn'd to day," he said. "His kiss has roused her." He tapped the point of his quill on the paper, making a trail of little black dots. "And as the bright sun glorifies the sky, / So is her face illumin'd with her eye. / Whose beams upon his hairless face are fix'd . . ." He scratched the words across the page. "She opens her eyes, beholds him leaning over her," Will said. "Her eyes are caught in his eyes, and his in hers. She feels his hot breath upon her face."

"Her dream made real," said Katharine. The untied ribbons of his shirt caught her eye.

He stood.

She stood.

She kept thinking, This is it, now he will run his hands down my face and kiss me tenderly; after all this time of waiting, now comes the eternity of his mouth on mine. Or he will, in a passion, tear the clothes from my body and crush me with his kisses. But there was no such blessing, and no such kissing. He did not move from his spot. He did not come to her, so she went to him. Her cloak still on, she took the quill from his fingers, then put her hands, not on his shoulders, but on his waist. She felt her way under his shirt to his skin and pulled him to her, but he did not yield. She put her mouth on his. The Will who had kissed her after pulling the pins from her hair was gone. This Will was not insistent with his tongue, nor was he the hunter, indeed he didn't seem keen on her advances, and turned his face away, but she pressed on.

She took her hands from his waist and moved his ruby-colored mouth back to hers. Lips on lips. She was not soft; she was not gentle. She had imagined myriad stories of this moment, but what was actually happening matched none of them. She was driven to this harshness because anger had seeped in, appalling and uninvited, but there it was nonetheless. She would've given herself to him so many times in the last weeks, but now she had to take him. And that was how it played. She held his wrists to the wall, and she kissed and kissed him, as if her thirst could not be quenched. He had said a few weeks back, "I, too, have been pill'd," and now she was his pillager. She felt his smooth chest with her hands. She kept her mouth on his.

He finally gave in, and they moved to his cot. But after all these months of his maneuvering her with his eyes, now he would not look her in the eye. She undid his breeches and, without taking off her cloak, she pulled up her smock and pinned his hands above his head as she climbed on him. He stirred hard against her. At least, she thought as she moved on top of him and felt him inside of her, at least he is not resisting, yet after all that had occurred, after all the teasing, the tenderness, the flattery, the focus, after all the words, he did bed her but he did not welcome her.

She wanted him to hold her after it was done. She wanted him to kiss her, but he rose and so she did the same. He pulled a doublet on and buttoned it, sat down at his table and picked up his quill. She tried to convince herself that everything was fine, that what had happened was progress, that she'd written a cruel letter out of desperation and he'd gotten angry, but this was now a part of their history and finally they had given themselves to each other, and his lack of attention during their act of love was due to leftover fury from the letter she'd written or maybe because she'd been too aggressive with him. But didn't he want her to be Venus, the huntress? Katharine bent over Will at the table and carefully kissed him on the mouth. She would mend the final hurt of her unkindness—replace any drops of vinegar with honey.

"Write well," she said from the door.

He nodded but did not look at her.

26

hat night, Molly arrived with more pages from Will. He had continued from the moment when Venus awakened to find herself freshly kissed by Adonis. "'O where am I?' quoth she, 'in earth or heaven . . .'" Then Venus beseeched and demanded that Adonis keep kissing her. When Adonis replied, his tone was softer now, his tongue not laced with scorn. He addressed Venus as "fair queen," and begged her to measure his "strangeness" with his youth. "'Before I know myself, seek not to know me,'" he said.

Before I know myself, seek not to know me. Was this a message from Will? Katharine wondered. Was Will, though six and twenty, feeling yet half grown and hence not ready for her? Perhaps she had utterly misjudged him, thought him promiscuous when he was principled, deemed him philandering when he was pure. Katharine moved from her bed to the table, and in her haste to dip her quill into the inkhorn, she knocked over a mug of ale Molly had brought her. She was relieved the ale did not drench Will's page. Without waiting to find a cloth, she snatched her beloved silk shawl from the back of her chair and mopped the table with it. Then she circled his lines of verse and wrote: *Think of an image here of youth, of unripe years. A green plum sticks to its branch and when plucked early 'tis sour, while a ripe plum falls and is sweet with juice.* She barely recognized her own handwriting. There was something wild about the shape of her letters. She hoped he could read her writing, for she barely could.

Will had made Adonis, as dusk descended, a man of negotiations. "'Now let me say good night, and so say you; / If you will say so, you shall have a kiss.'" After Venus accepted the terms of Adonis's contract, like Ovid's Salmacis and Hermaphroditus, "Her arms do lend his neck a sweet embrace; / Incorporate then they seem, face grows to face." Will's next lines seemed a winged horse: with words like "breathless," "sweet coral mouth," and "Their lips together glued, fall to earth . . ." There was in his pace a panting of word and rhyme, meter and foot. A stanza with "And glutton-like she feeds, yet never filleth. / Her lips are conquerors, his lips obey . . ." ended when Venus indeed became a vulture. He'd used the image that weeks ago Katharine had thwarted; he then described that ravaging:

> *And having felt the sweetness of the spoil,*
> *With blindfold fury she begins to forage;*
> *Her face doth reek and smoke, her blood doth boil,*
> *And careless lust stirs up a desperate courage,*
> *Planting oblivion, beating reason back,*
> *Forgetting shame's pure blush and honor's wrack.*

Though Will had turned Venus into a monster these last stanzas, Katharine could not read his words fast enough. "Hot, faint and weary with her hard embracing" charged on to "He now obeys, and now no more resisteth, / While she takes all she can, not all she listeth." Next Will shot his arrow directly at Ovid's Pygmalion: "What wax so frozen but dissolves with temp'ring, / And yields at last to very light impression?" While she continued reading, she held the paper with one hand and pulled every pin out of her hair with the other. Then ran her fingers through her thick locks. His poem, these words coursing across the page, seemed to her a living, breathing thing that filled her head and penetrated her heart. "Were beauty under twenty locks kept fast," Will wrote, "Yet love breaks through, and pricks them all at last."

Then, "For pity now she can no more detain him . . ."

She had to go to him.

Will's chamber was bitter, the fire almost dead, and the sun long gone when he let Katharine in. She found it hard to believe that it was just that morning when she had been with him on his cot. He wore a green suede jerkin over a white blouse, hardly enough cover for the dank air. She wore a cloak over her skirts and bodice: her hair was a wild waterfall of tresses. She placed his pages on the table and remained standing. He looked at her in silence.

"Your verse," she said.

"My verse?" He cocked his head to one side and raised an eyebrow.

"Your verse," she began again. She did not know how to say it. She had already said she was in love with him, and she had given her body to him, or rather taken his, in love, but this feeling was something more, or in addition, perhaps, to love. His words were now a bounty, a harvest, a surfeit of richness and majesty.

He was but inches from her. He did not kiss her. His lips never touched hers. He pulled her to him and reached down her bodice and grabbed her breast—there was no softness to his touch. He raked his nails across her skin; the sting shocked her. Then he pushed her onto the bed, his action so abrupt, so brusque, so unexpected that she let out a cry. Within seconds he was on top of her and had yanked up her skirts and her petticoats. He was not smiling. He pinned one of her arms to the bed. The motion of him above her and the way he pinched her wrist made her fear a bone would break. This was perhaps retaliation for this morning. Will worked at it and worked at it. Each thrust burned; each thrust felt like a brand. She wanted it to end. But he rode on without heed to her discomfort, without heed to her. At the height of his incursion, he shouted, "I will win!" through gritted teeth, and then rolled off.

Mayhap the "I will win" applied to her, though she doubted it, for he seemed not to notice her. It was some strange battle he was fighting in his head. In this vainglorious instant, of some undetermined triumph, she could have been anyone or anything.

A man of abundant words, he said nothing after he rolled away. He left her on his cot. He did not look at her. He strode out the door and left her.

She picked herself up, pulled down her skirts, passed the table strewn with brimming pages, and when she walked outside, he was nowhere in sight.

Though the chair Katharine sat on was covered in gold velvet, she felt uncomfortable and sore. "I'll meet you outside," she said to the girls.

The last time Katharine had been in the hat shop, all had seemed so simple with Will then, so hopeful. Today, while Isabel was fitted for a pearl headpiece, Katharine was barely aware of the two girls chatting about the betrothal and the banquet. In the many scenes Katharine had concocted in her head of bedding Will, none matched what actually happened. He could have taken her at any moment in the preceding weeks. He knew that. Why had he waited, forced her to it? Perhaps the jousting with language finally failed them and the cot had become their tilt field.

After both encounters, Will had said nothing. The first time he seemed indifferent, the second time angry. Katharine recalled his sonnet, which conveyed the fury of the speaker after the physical union.

Maybe, she thought, Will embodied the shame he gave Adonis. She had been digging to find the real Will, and now perhaps she had.

Katharine stood in front of the shop. The month of March just starting, the air still felt raw. A tall young man caught her eye. She watched him for a moment, then decided to cross the street to greet him. John Smythson bowed.

"You've been shopping, I see," she said.

He held up his package. "Aye." He grinned. "A gift for my father."

"Lovely. What did you buy him?"

John opened the leather carton and pulled out a glass case with a large blue butterfly pinned inside.

"How extraordinary," Katharine said.

She looked from the opalescent wings to John's beaming face.

"He fancies things like this," said John. "Odd things. They fill his rooms."

"What sort of things?"

"Oh, shards of pottery from the Greeks and the Romans—a handle, the neck of a jug, part of a bowl. And old glass. Shells. Oh, my, the shells he picks up at our cottage on the shore. He arranges them and won't let the maid touch them. He dusts them off himself. He found a few feathers last week, wild turkey, I think, maybe pheasant, where they were molting. He was so pleased and showed me how each feather had a different design but were all from one bird."

"Will he make them into quills, then?"

"No. He'll stick them in a vase like flowers. Then he'll pull them out when he's designing a mantelpiece or some such, to follow the lines and the dots. He says 'tis uncanny how full of patterns nature is. I guess he's right." John carefully put the blue butterfly back in its leather box.

"Your father will love your gift, I'm sure," she said. For some reason her throat tightened.

"I think he will," said John. "I couldn't take my eyes off it when I saw it. Someone brought butterflies back on a ship from somewhere and put them under glass. There's a whole lot of them at that stall over there," he said, pointing. "I should get on with my business. Father sent me here with a list of items and I've gotten distracted."

"That's what happens on market day," said Katharine. "How is Mr. Smythson?" She didn't want John to go. He was as affable as his father, and she wanted to bask in his warmth for a minute longer.

"Oh, he's fine. He's up to his ears in work. We are."

They were silent for a moment, then she said, "Well, you best be off, then. Please send him my regards." She wondered if the father had shared his intentions about her with his son.

"I will," John said, bowing. "Farewell."

"Fare thee well, John," she said, and watched him until he disappeared into a maze of stalls.

The great hall was alive with candles. Dishes savory and steaming framed the tables. Matilda had invited other known Catholics from local estates, for the Barlows were as tied to the old religion as the De L'Isles. Katharine recognized some faces and not others. She snatched a goblet of wine and drank it without breathing. She welcomed the distraction of Matilda's small banquet for Isabel and Nicholas Barlow. She'd had Molly pile her hair high on her head. She'd dressed in her golden gown—too large now—and a blue velvet doublet borrowed from Isabel.

Isabel came to her. She was wearing a rose silk gown with a bodice of silver weave. A headpiece of gray pearls crowned her head.

"How beautiful you are, my dear," Katharine said. "Your cheeks hold the same blush as your dress."

"Here he is," said Isabel.

Katharine remembered Nicholas Barlow's intelligent eyes from when they had been introduced on Saint Crispin's Day and then at the Stanleys' revels, but she had been in such a state she hardly recalled more about him. The young man walking toward them now was no taller than Isabel, but the fit of his garments showed a good shape in leg and waist.

"I have heard much of you from your fair cousin," young Barlow said, bowing and taking Katharine's hand. "I am never one to bother with details, and have a terrible memory, cannot recall the names of any of my horses except for the one I'm riding at the moment, which is . . . I can't remember, but I have retained some important information pertaining to the agreement our esteemed parents have drawn up. There is a provision therein that specifically states Isabel have unlimited access to you," he said, smiling.

"How fortunate," Katharine said with a laugh, "that I am considered a part of dear Isabel's dowry."

"At the very least there is mirth in him, and that is good," whispered Katharine to Isabel. "My gut says there is goodness in him."

"You are most welcome whenever and always at Bridgeton Manor, Miss De L'Isle."

"A thousand thanks, good sir. Prithee, call me Katharine, for we are to be cousins now."

"And call me Nicholas," he said, bowing deeply. "Dear Isabel," he continued, "Lord Barlow and I have walked the grounds of Bridgeton Manor, and he is quite keen on making changes. No one has lived there for a long time, and Father is thrilled we are to have it. We had that man Smythson up to look at what he could do. He seems to have a hand in every house north of London and south of Edinburgh."

"We know him. He's been here!" Isabel exclaimed, looking at Katharine.

"He had but an hour to spend before he was off to his wedding, but in that short time he came up with impressive ideas."

"His wedding?" asked Isabel, her eyes wide.

Katharine's blood ran cold. "Mr. Smythson is to be married?" she asked.

Young Barlow nodded. "In London."

Katharine raised her eyes from Isabel to see Will entering the great room. He was standing talking to folk she did not recognize. There he was: his black doublet snugly fit, white collar pointed and starched, beard shaped and trim. Who had invited him? She had not seen him since their last encounter, nor had he sent her any words.

She waited for him to come to her; she would make the perfunctory introduction to Isabel's betrothed. She waited for Will, but he never came. In fact, Will acted as though she weren't even there. She charged out of the great hall and ran up to her chamber.

If Will had wanted a different type of bond with her, Katharine thought, pacing the floor, if he wanted love, he would have aimed his dart and landed his mark—the way he was aiming at everything else he wanted: sonnets, a long poem, a patron, a part with Lord Strange's Men, a coat of arms, the largest house in Stratford.

And what of the Smythson news? He, it now seemed, dissembled as easily as Will. A mere trifle of time after he'd told Katharine he was in love with her, he'd gone off and wed. He had moved on. A nunnery was heaven compared to this prison.

As the days passed, Katharine began to doubt God. Her life thus far had been built on faith, but she could not find that faith now. Even deep down there was nothing but emptiness and darkness. If there be God, she thought, please forgive me. She had such a deep longing for God, but she could not find Him. She had no faith left, no love, no zeal. She sought refuge in the ancients, made Molly bring her books from Edward's library. She reread Ovid's *Epistulae Heroidum* as if it were the gospel, immersing herself in all the mistreated, neglected and abandoned heroines from Greek and Roman mythology: Penelope, Phyllis, Briseis, Phaedra,

Oenone, Hypsipyle, Dido, Hermione, Deianira, Ariadne, Canace, Medea, Laodamia and Hypermestra.

"You should give him up for Lent, mistress," Molly said. She set bread, cheese and ale on the table and with a click of her tongue she handed Katharine several sheets of folded paper.

Katharine opened the papers and read: "'The boar,' quoth she: whereat a sudden pale . . ." Katharine felt as if Will had struck her. The boar—it was only a matter of stanzas until Adonis would leave to hunt the boar with his friends.

Venus, with her arms around Adonis's neck, "He on her belly falls, she on her back."

> *Now is she in the very lists of love,*
> *Her champion mounted for the hot encounter.*
> *All is imaginary she doth prove;*
> *He will not manage her, although he mount her:*

Katharine drank the ale in one gulp as she read on. "The warm effects which she in him finds missing / She seeks to kindle with continual kissing." He seemed to have plucked his words from the night she'd shared his cot.

> *But all in vain; good queen, it will not be.*
> *She hath assay'd as much as may be prov'd:*
> *Her pleading hath deserv'd a greater fee:*
> *She's love, she loves, and yet she is not lov'd . . .*

She jumped to her feet and threw the pages into the blaze. He'd done it again! He had mined her ore! Her jaw was set. Her eyes wide. *"She's love, she loves, and yet she is not lov'd!"* she shouted. How could he do this? What had she done but love him and help with his verse?

She stormed out of her chamber. *"She's love, she loves, and yet she is not lov'd,"* she chanted as she swept down stairs and through doorways. *But all in vain,* he wrote. *But all in vain . . .* Katharine wanted to kiss him and to crush him all at the same time. These past months, now seeming a whole life, could not, must not, would not be in vain, for if they were, what was there?

She pulled the hood over her head and flew through the house and out the door. She was a witch, for it was not her natural limbs that propelled her thus, but a sick wrath that boiled in her veins. She marched to Will's door, envisioning him, quill in hand, poised mid-thought, mid-rhyme perchance. At first she did not knock. She tried to pull the door open, but it was latched from the inside.

Later, she tried to recall if he had begun to open the door before she banged her fist on it, or if her banging had roused him and made him open it. She played the scene over and over again in her head. The door opening, but only a sliver.

"Who goes there?" he asked.

"'Tis Kate."

She waited, expecting him to open the door farther, expecting him to let her in.

"How now," he said.

How now.

How now was all he said, but he did not invite her in, nor did he open his door wider. He stood there behind the door. *How now.*

Her vessel cracked.

"You told me: 'I may be married but that will not prevent us from joining together!" Katharine hissed.

"I said that?"

"You do not recall?"

"No."

He could spew stanzas of Chaucer or lines of Ovid as if his mind held a mirror, but he could not summon up what he had said to her a few months past. The words had seemed fine gifts to her then, like pearls or gems or strands of golden chain. She had mulled and mused over those words, drawn them into her heart. Now he did not remember them. Now those same words seemed knots on a shroud or spikes in a coffin.

"When I said I could not continue, when I said my heart had become attached. You said we had forty years, a future together, London! Why? What was I to think? When a man says such to a woman."

"I must've been afraid you would leave me."

"I see," she said. She was not sure whether she should feel flattered or shattered by the words he now tossed at her.

"You have done this," she said. "You are like our queen with her courtiers—you need people to fall in love with you. You had to harness my heart and make me love you in order to write your poem. I know that now."

"I've done nothing of the sort."

"You have! You dangled words that kept me fastened to you!"

"I have not."

"You will say what it takes." Her voice was rising. "My love hasn't just nourished you, you've fed upon it! You're a child who drinks his mother's milk to thrive, and you're a beast who devours the flesh and bones of its prey to survive!"

"Stop this mewling, Kate!" he ordered.

"Did you make merry at the Stanleys' Twelfth Night?" she asked.

"Aye, verily," he said coldly.

"Did you make merry with Ned?"

"Who is Ned?"

"Ned, my cousin. Ned, the lastborn son of Sir Edward?"

"Oh, that Ned."

"'Oh, that Ned'?" she screeched. "Along with advance and retreat, you have added retaliation to your tactics!" she fairly spat at him. "Perhaps you should be a general—certainly the queen could use a man who commands his troops with such fearless strategies!"

"What is it you seek, Kate? 'Tis no surprise you have taken no second husband," he said.

She could not see his face completely, but she could fill in the flesh of his sneer.

"Or rather one has not taken you," he continued. "'Tis no surprise at all, for your behavior would thwart even the strongest of men. I am surely not fit for such a task. 'Tis a wonder they were able to marry you off to that old man who was your first, but 'tis no surprise he died so soon. Methinks perhaps you best lay off the mead, if that is what urges you to such tawdry business. You have caused me much offense, Kate. You have wounded me down to my very bones."

Will's malevolence fanned her fury. "What is this?" she bellowed, the words issuing from deep within. "I know not what we have. Friendship? Love? A poem? I am not your mother, wench, wife, whore, nor your Venus! What was that fit the other night on your cot? Not love, verily, nor lust, but more akin to the siege of Troy! 'I will win!'" she mocked. "I am no Helen, surely. What do we have here? What! What! What!" She was shouting, but she did not care. She was at this instant begot from her beloved Greeks, from Euripides, Aeschylus, Sophocles. She was Medea, Clytemnestra, Antigone. She continued, the bile rising. "Why did you say such false things to me? Why? Why did you say you missed me? Longed for me? Why did you kiss me? Pull the pins from my hair? Why did you give me gifts? I should have listened to the gossip: 'A bad lad, that one. A lewd lad. A wanton lad. A swain whose own wife sacked him, for he was caught in the sward too many a time with too many a lass.' I was deaf to such rumors. You are a man profligate with words, yet parsimonious with love, a man who flings words at people to conquer them. Desire, secrets, a special bond, forty years, London. Love. Fie on you!"

By the end of her speech she was shrieking. She still saw Will's face through the door, but behind him, on the bed, she saw something move in the candlelight, a body, skin.

She turned. It was as if the house of her childhood were burning all over again. She put her hands to her ears to block the screams as she fled. She remembered the terrible smell, a blazing timber crashing. She made it down the stairs before the wood gave way. She was running through the garden with her smock in flames, then rolling down the hill. And now she was running also. When she was partway down the path, she tripped and fell with such a fierce force that her hands could not stop her and her head hit the stone.

All was quiet. She did not move. Her bones felt at rest finally. Her cheek was stuck to the icy path. Her knees were raw and throbbing. She had not died in the fire, by some miracle, but she might die in the cold on this sable night. She would go deep, to sleep and then at some point, a tick only God knew, she would take her last exhale. Her flesh would go stiff; her body would freeze. She was calm. She accepted that she had loved Will. She could not change that history, just as she could not change the fate of her family.

She heard footsteps, a scampering, light and weightless, like a small animal, or an angel. Then she felt warm breath on her neck, and she smelled a sour scent. Perhaps this was it, then, death—though she was surprised at death's heat.

"My lady," a soft voice cooed in her ear. "My lady."

Katharine opened her eyes but did not move her head.

"You've had a nasty tumble." The small face moved in close to Katharine's. Katharine said nothing but tried to focus on the little upturned nose and the large blue eyes. "You've cut yeself. There's blood. Canst thou move, my lady? 'Tis Mercy here, 'tis Mercy. I will fetch someone."

"Gramercy, Mercy, but no need."

Katharine remained still, bathing in Mercy's blessed breath.

"I was come from the scullery in the big house, when I saw you running. You've banged yeself above the eye," said Mercy.

"I will get up, Mercy, though this hard stone feels like a feather bed, and if you were not here I suppose I would fall asleep upon it."

"'Tis too cold fer ye to do that," said Mercy. "Uncle drank a jug of sack and then lay down on the snow one winter night and died. 'Tis too cold. 'Tis not e'en Shrovetide yet. Your blood will ice. I'll bring you to me mum—she can fix your head and give you some hot milk with honey."

Katharine did not answer, but started to raise herself on her hands. Mercy helped her up, and they slowly walked toward the cow barns.

"How fares your winter?" Katharine said, after they'd walked a ways in silence. "You were sick when I saw you out in the snow. Have you your health back?"

"I was puking my guts out in the snow, but turns out I wasn't sick, my lady."

"No?"

"Turns out I was with child."

"Oh, Mercy."

"I done lost the babe, came too early, came too fast, and we buried the little thing out yonder. I feel better now."

"I am so sorry, Mercy. Methinks you have plenty of years ahead of you, plenty of time to have plenty of babes. You told me last that you were nigh fifteen."

"Just, my lady. Me, the babe—'twasn't meant to be. The lout who made me so did promise to be with me, take me to London e'en, then slammed the door on me face when I told him I was with child. He said he had too many brats already."

"To London, Mercy." The word *London* pricked Katharine's heart.

"To London, we were to make a life there, he said, and I would wear my hair up high with pearls in it and meet grand folk."

Though Katharine was walking slowly on account of her bruised knees, all of a sudden she had trouble catching her breath.

"Should we stop and rest, my lady?" asked Mercy.

"Were you with this lad a long time, Mercy?"

"No, 'twas a few months but felt like years. He started at me the minute he got here before the harvest. Oh, the words he did employ. He said I was special to him and said so soon I knew him in a way no one, not e'en his wife, did, like we had a special bond, like we was meant to be together. The gifts he give me—never seen such fine things—and we were together soon after. He was my first one."

"Did he give you gloves, Mercy?"

"Aye, he did. The likes I'd never seen before, with beads and skin that felt like silk upon me hands. He loved me hands. Methinks they are ugly, so red and chapped on account of the milking. He said they weren't the hands of a lady and he loved me for that. He would trace me stubby, rough hands with his fingers, as if me hands were somethin' fine. He had the lightest touch, then, sent shivers down me. That's how I fell for him—'twas the way he touched my hands, as light as a feather he was. Now I know better. He's a trickster, he is, a trickster and braggart and a bawd, who apes his betters in dress and manners but is no true gentleman. His heart is filled with lechery."

"He isn't fit to tutor, is he, Mercy?"

"Nay. How did ye know it was he?"

Katharine stopped. "I'm feeling as if to faint, Mercy," she said.

"Must be the cows. I don't e'en smell 'em anymore 'cause I was born amongst them. Hither. We lodge in the back of the barns, me mum and me sisters and me. Come. We'll attend to thee."

27

n the ides of March, Molly came to Katharine's chamber and, though Molly was busying herself with the fire, Katharine could tell something was wrong. Katharine had not seen Will since the night of her fall on the icy path.

"Prithee, Molly, your face is an open book. Tell me your worries."

"'Tis *him*," said Molly.

"What of him?" said Katharine.

"'Tis confusing."

"What is, Molly?"

"He pulled me aside the other day . . ."

"Yes?" Katharine thought perhaps he had finally inquired after her.

"And he said he was furthering his poem and asked me to read it."

"Asked *you* to read it? How does he know you read, Molly?"

"I told him once or twice I thought him good with the words and the rhymes, and he asked me how I knew, and I said you had taught me to read and a' times when he was passing his verse to you I would take a peek at it now and again."

"I see."

"And he said I wasn't to tell you that he had asked me or that I was reading it—'twas to be our secret. His voice changed when he said that, and he leaned into me in a way that is, well, was almost . . ."

"Uncouth."

"Yes, that. And said he wanted to know what I thought of what he had written, and he started saying how clever I was, how he could tell by how I spoke that I had a good mind and that I was in luck because my face was good, too, and not every wench had the two combined. I blushed from head to toe when he said those things and methought how this might bring you pain."

"Did he give you his poem?" Katharine asked. She imagined his table, the quills, the sheets of paper overflowing with words. Where was Venus now? she wondered. Had Adonis gone off to hunt the boar? Was he dead? Katharine kept her jaw set, in an effort not to weep.

"He did give it me. Do you want me to bring it to you?"

"No, Molly. No. And Molly?"

"Yes."

"Please never mention him to me again. Would you do that for me?"

"Yes'm. I crave your pardon."

"And Molly, you do have a good head and a fair face and you also have a good heart."

"Gramercy," Molly said, and curtsied low.

What amazed Katharine about Molly's tale was that Will would seek to murder her anew. Did he do such things out of cruelty, or was he thinking only of himself and his needs rather than of retaliation? Katharine had thought he needed her for his words, but she now realized what he'd needed her for was her worship, and when that stopped, he no longer had any use for her.

Not only was the Ides of March the day Caesar met his fate, but it was the ancient Roman holiday honoring the goddess Anna Perenna as well. Ovid had written of the goddess and of her sister Dido, the lovesick queen of Carthage, who fell in love with shipwrecked Aeneas and then killed herself when he deserted her. She'd taken Aeneas's sword atop her funeral pyre and plunged it into her flesh. Katharine reckoned she didn't need Aeneas's sword, for if she'd survived the death of her family when she was ten, then she could at one and thirty survive Will Shakespeare.

As a player, Will could mimic accents and manners, and as a poet, he could imitate the terrain of the heart without ever truly visiting it. That, Katharine supposed, was his genius—or part of it—that he could project himself into a great variety of people and situations, allowing in his words on a page or his actions upon the stage a humanity that he, in truth, failed to possess. She'd always trusted words, and now she no longer found shelter in them, indeed she felt betrayed by them, for Will had shown her that words were not truths: they could be used as bait; dressed up and trotted out; spun like the gossamer threads of a spider's web.

A month later, in April, with the sun lingering in the sky and the summer birds returning, Lord and Lady Strange were due to attend a banquet at Lufanwal in honor of Richard's release from prison. Were it not for Isabel's pestering, Katharine would have stayed up in her self-made convent. She had begun to wonder if perhaps she had erred, for as the days became longer, and with Ned still in the north, she found she missed Mr. Smythson. She'd seen a tall man in a black coat one day in town, and she'd run up to him, almost tripped, only to discover the man wasn't Mr. Smythson at all. Katharine imagined his wife as all sorts of people, some of whom she approved of and others of whom she did not. She found some comfort in thinking that maybe he'd married the poetess Aemilia Bassano, whose bold verse still echoed in Katharine's head. Such a cunning and bright woman would make a good wife for him.

Tonight Katharine was amongst most of her kin, her folk, and she was alive, and for that she was thankful. Others were not. The casualties this past year had been great and wide. Sir Edward, Ursula, Harold, and they had received notice that Mary, whose case was to be tried in the summer assize, had died in jail. Before Mary died, she had made a confession, more a tirade, though she was too ill to stand, and what she had shouted was a scandal to all: her husband, Harold, she said, had Father Daulton killed, for he wanted Sir Edward to think the queen was coming after him. It was Harold who had Lord Molyneux's priest murdered after the funeral. And it was Harold who had suggested exile and convinced Sir Edward of its urgency. Mary said that Richard's arrest was of Harold's doing also. First he was going to try to pin the poor priests' murders on Richard, but then thought the plotting against the queen a better device, for Harold had wanted all the estates for himself.

Katharine had not seen Will. She had refrained from asking if he still resided at Lufanwal, so it did not occur to her that he might be at the banquet, but there he was, rushing into the great room as if it were his. Will, being Will, had flattered someone into an invitation. Perhaps it was Lord and Lady Strange themselves who had requested his presence. However he got there, get there he did, and Katharine, upon seeing him, turned her back in his direction. He was across the great room where, she hoped, he would stay. But he did not. Her back still to him, she was aware at one point that he was but five people to her left. He was with Lord Strange—fawning, she supposed, toadying his way into the lord's rarefied sphere. Katharine recalled how Will had invoked Lord Essex when he returned from London with those absurd red shoes. She remembered how pleased Will was that he used the same cordwainer as Lord Essex. Katharine imagined how Will would act if he ever met Lord Essex: she winced at the thought of the blandishments Will would spew to buff that lord's luster.

Would that her back were a wall, thick as stone, or better yet a mountain peak, but alas she was mere flesh and blood, and all she could do was turn herself on her own strings like a puppet, so as not to face Will. Katharine was talking with Nicholas Barlow, when she felt someone slam into her hip and slide his buttocks across her backside. The impact was so strong, she jumped and let out a yelp, and when she turned, she saw Will scurry away, disappearing into the crowd. What an odd and vulgar thing. Was this how the lads in Warwickshire treated the lasses? With a bump and a slam as rude and loutish as a stall boy?

Katharine turned her back again. She would not react to his stable game. She resumed talking with Nicholas, who had seen enough of Will's strange performance, and how the skin on her face was now drained of blood, to ask, "Everything all right, madam?"

Before she had a chance to answer, she felt a tap on her shoulder, and she turned around.

"Will Shakespeare," he said, bowing with a flourish.

He was wearing the most astonishing array of gold, his doublet and breeches the color of ivory, with shimmering gold silk that oozed from oversized slashes as though they were indeed gashes with gold blood pouring forth. His hose, too, glimmered with gold thread, as did his white ruff. Was this peculiar costume culled from his player's trunk or from the patronage of some rich earl? And his hair. What had he done to it? It was longer, combed back and glistening as though he had poured a jug of oil onto it. Katharine was as taken aback by his appearance as she was by his bizarre courting of her.

She crossed her arms, trying to keep from slapping him.

"How art thou?" he asked, smiling, as though he had just seen her that morning, as though what had gone on between them were a game at court, and everything was fine.

She thought him utterly mad. Was this some sort of a taunt?

"'How art thou?'" she said, stepping toward him. "'How art thou?'" she repeated, so loudly and distinctly and with such edge that several people in the great room stopped talking and looked at her.

She grew at that moment, felt herself growing, now a giant towering over him, reeking of scorn instead of worship, stinking of disdain instead of love. Perchance it was her giantness that scared him off, for he turned on his heels and ran out of the great hall. Gone. Katharine felt triumphant, as if she were an army and he the enemy and she had forced a retreat.

The last time she saw him was a week later. She'd spent the morning with the tailor charting Isabel's wedding dress, and there was more cause for celebration, for Matilda had announced Joan was betrothed to William Hesketh. Katharine decided on this beautiful spring day to bury the Agnus Deis she had pulled from Mercy's neck. In the afternoon Katharine walked through the woods picking flowers. She stepped on stones across a full stream: with the spring rains came hope the drought would not return this year. She found the stand of trees where Father Daulton had breathed his final breath, and, kneeling on the ground, she dug at the earth, first with a sharp rock and then with a stick. She interred the Agnus Deis and set the flowers atop the fresh mound of dirt.

With the thud of a horse's hooves, Katharine looked up. The rider was tall, the horse big. She stood rooted in the spot where she had placed the flowers. Mr. Smythson reined in his horse and trotted toward her. What surprised her was that he looked at her with the same kind expression he'd worn in their previous encounters, and she felt that was wrong, since he had launched into marriage so recently and so quickly and should only in truth look that way at someone he loved. Was every man a Shakespeare, then?

"Good day, Miss Katharine," he said. He dismounted.

"Mr. Smythson, I must offer you my congratulations," she said, not bothering to return his greeting. His forehead was more furrowed than she remembered. What had Isabel said that day she was trying to persuade her to reconsider Smythson's offer: *Have you not had your fill of smooth faces and smooth voices?*

"Thank you." He bowed.

"I'm sure you will be very happy." She tried to keep her voice steady.

"Happy? Well, I don't know about that, but it will surely be a lot of work."

She nodded, thinking this was an odd way to speak of marriage, but perhaps an honest one.

"And my coffers will surely be fuller," he added.

Katharine was taken aback by Mr. Smythson's brazen take on his wife's dowry.

"I brought something for you," he said. He pulled a wooden box from a sack on his saddle and handed it to Katharine.

"Mr. Smthyson, many thanks, but I cannot accept this—whatever it is." She tried to give it back to him.

"Why not?"

"Because you shouldn't go around giving gifts to women when you are already married."

"Married?" The creases on his brow deepened. "Married?" he repeated. "What gives you the idea I am married?"

"I heard all about it."

"You, Miss Katharine, know more about my marriage than I do."

"Didn't you?"

"What?"

"Wed?"

"No. From whence did you hear this ill-gotten news?"

"From a Mr. Barlow, whose house you visited."

"Bridgeton Manor? Lord Barlow?"

"His son, Nicholas, who is to marry Isabel. Nicholas said you were off to your wedding." And just as Katharine said this, she recalled how Nicholas Barlow said he had no head for details.

"Ah," said Mr. Smythson. He smiled. Then he laughed. "My brother's wedding. My brother in London." He dipped his head close to her face and looked into her eyes, which were brimming. Then he pulled a cloth from his pocket and handed it to her.

"What were you talking of, then, with all the work and all the money?" she asked, wiping her eyes.

"My new commission. Lady Shrewsbury has chosen me to build her a new hall on her Hardwick estates in Derbyshire. I have been drawing up the first plans. It will be a mansion of symmetry and light. She is a very smart woman with a very good eye for all things, and since her husband has passed on—they were verily on terrible terms—she has enough money to make something stunning. I cannot sleep, I am so thrilled with what we will be able to create."

"Congratulations." Katharine tried to smile but felt like weeping.

He bowed again. "You were distressed at the thought of my marriage," he said.

"Yes."

"Why?"

He waited.

"Because I realized I made a dreadful mistake," she said finally. "I found myself thinking of you, heard in my head different things you had said. You stayed with me in a way I cannot quite articulate. And I saw with your son—"

"John?"

"Yes." She paused. "That you indeed know how to love. And I thought maybe I'd missed a great opportunity"—she wiped her eyes again with the cloth he had given to her—"to learn from you."

"Open the box," he said gently.

She did. Inside was a crystal ball, a shewstone, like the one he had broken that day in the library.

"Gramercy, Mr. Smythson."

"Robert."

"Robert, am I to be like Dr. Dee and use this to peer into the future?" she said in a mocking tone.

He stooped down next to her to look into the orb. Then he took it from her hands, held it up to the light and examined it. "I see Mrs. Smythson in there."

"Your late wife? 'Tis a strange shewstone that lets one look into the past."

"No. 'Tis the future. 'Tis you, the future Mrs. Smythson," he said, handing it back to her. "Take a look."

"I am not the stuff good wives are made of, Robert," Katharine replied, handing the stone back to him without peering into it. "My own father said I would never be tamed, and it has come to pass he was right."

"I know," said Robert.

"I am not landed, have no riches, no grand houses, no leas of wheat."

"I know."

"I've had a horrid experience of late. And I am terribly afraid of . . . of love." She couldn't stop herself. She wanted to tell him.

"I know," he said.

"You know?"

"Would take a blind man not to notice."

They were silent for a moment.

"Is it over, then?" he asked finally.

"Aye," she said. "And I am surely past the age—"

"You are young. You will always be young, even when you are old. And need I repeat, Lady Shrewsbury wed at seven and forty, and my own aunt Peg had a child at two and forty, and you are a mere one and thirty—"

"Two and thirty in two weeks."

"A mere two and thirty in two weeks, then. You have a life in front of you," he said. "With me, if you accept."

And so she did.

That evening after Robert left, she went out into the orchard after the rain shower and strolled in the lilac breeze under the moonlight. He had described how she could spend summers at the cottage near Poulton and winters in Wollaton, while he was back and forth these next years from Hardwick Hall. She was so focused on her own thoughts that she practically bumped into Will before she noticed him. He was a short ways from her, the light of the moon so bright upon him that it was as if he were standing under a torch. He had his arms wrapped around a young maid no older than Mercy. Katharine thought for a moment she had conjured the image.

"Ho, Will," she said, hoping it was a trick of the moonlight and the couple would vanish.

Will and the lass looked up at Katharine as she walked by.

"Good-den," he said, as if she were a mere acquaintance.

"Good-den," she responded without breaking her stride.

She walked on, not stopping, not turning. She drifted back to the hall, opened the heavy oak door and passed through it, as if she were a spirit floating from one world to the next.

28

he grasses bowed with each gust of wind. The week before, an end-of-summer storm had stirred the bay into such a frenzy that Katharine laughed with delight as the waves leapt over the dunes. This room was so different— with its walls washed in white and floors the color of sand—from her turret high up the endless stairs at Lufanwal. She never needed a lamp during the day here; even when the sky turned gray the light poured through the windows and touched everything. How uncanny that *she* lived by the sea, not Father Daulton, when he was the poor soul who had envisioned such a life.

In the month since her marriage, she had not missed Lufanwal. She had asked Matilda for a hundred books from Sir Edward's library for her dowry. The books were now safely in shelves Robert had built at the house in Wollaton. Her wedding had been small and quiet and a month after Isabel's. Sir Christopher de Ashton had offered his stunning new house for the occasion. In his will, Sir Edward had kindly provided a sum for Katharine with no stipulation that she must marry. She'd taken her virginals and her unicorn coverlet from Lufanwal when she left. And she'd taken Molly.

There was a knocking. Molly was off to town. Robert and John were at work in Derbyshire. Katharine rose from her chair to see who'd come, but it was only the breeze, pushing the door against the large white stone that held it open. She shifted the stone with her foot to stop the rattle.

Will had gone to London with Lord Strange's Men before Isabel's wedding. He'd not come to Katharine before he left. He'd stayed away. Though he was too lowborn to be a courtier, he could play one and would figure how to get on in London, for certainly it was a place that favored such cunning, such desires, such brilliance. Katharine still thought of the poem every day. She had learned many of the lines by heart and recited them—sometimes to herself, other times out loud. She wondered if the poem would ever be published, if she'd see it in a bookstall, open the leather cover, see his name, read the words.

Across the bay stretched an island with beaches, fields and forests of ancient pedigree that had been given to Robert's first wife's family generations ago by the lord of the manor for some deed well done. There the island sat, untouched. For Katharine it was a beacon; she checked it daily. She would, she knew, never make it to the Continent, but next summer she would ask Robert to take her to that island, and eventually, maybe, they would build a house there.

AUTHOR'S NOTE

Katharine and the De L'Isle family at Lufanwal Hall in Lancashire are from my imagination, though my great-grandfather Wallace Torrey Chapin built a Norman-like castle on the Hudson River in New York State at the beginning of the last century and named it Lufanwal. I have, throughout my novel, interwoven historical figures with fictional characters and would like to provide some context for the two main real-life characters here.

It is not known when William Shakespeare arrived in London, but it is assumed that the "upstart crow" whom Robert Greene chastised in print in 1592 was the actor-turned-playwright from Stratford. Several of Shakespeare's early plays had already been staged, but not published— plays rarely appeared in print at that time. Records show that *Henry VI, Part I* was performed at the Rose Theatre by Lord Strange's acting company in the spring of 1592. That September the city council ordered the closing of all the theaters in London because of a severe outbreak of the plague. Nine months later, in June 1593, Shakespeare's narrative poem *Venus and Adonis* was published in an elegantly printed volume, dedicated to his wealthy and influential patron, the nineteen-year-old Henry

Wriothesley, Earl of Southampton and Baron of Titchfield. The book was an immediate and enormous success; it went through at least ten editions in Shakespeare's lifetime. His second narrative poem, *The Rape of Lucrece*, followed within a year and was even more popular.

Shakespeare had, by age thirty, achieved every Elizabethan poet's dream: acceptance into the rarefied sphere of the university-educated poets, praise by critics, a respectable and dedicated publisher, multiple printings of his books, and a wealthy patron whose deep pockets guaranteed a lifestyle far more glamorous than the rough-and-tumble world of the theater and the scant pounds a playwright earned when he sold a play. Shakespeare's two narrative poems had brought him far more literary fame at this point than his dabbling in texts for the theater. He was launched, on his way to the cushioned life of a court poet.

But he never wrote another long narrative poem, and he never offered his well-established publisher another manuscript. He let his prized relationship with the Earl of Southampton run fallow. He published the short poem "The Phoenix and Turtle," in a collection titled *Love's Martyr* in 1601. He is thought to have continued working on his sonnets but did not seem particularly interested in publishing them, and indeed, they were not printed for the public until 1609.

When the London theaters reopened in the spring of 1594, Shakespeare dove back into the very collaborative art of writing plays and acting in them—apparently shutting the door on the social and literary aspirations that must have so fiercely driven him when he started *Venus and Adonis*. It was unique, if not unheard of, for a young poet of his standing to abandon what had brought him great success and to dedicate his life to the theater—yet that's just what Shakespeare did. It was as a playwright that he learned to make his fellow actors the mediums through which he reached the emotions of the audience, and it was as a playwright that he developed his genius for creating rich and varied characters who defied the bounds of time.

The master mason Robert Smythson is considered one of the first architects in England; in the Elizabethan era, the concept of an architect, though known in France and Italy, was new. Smythson was an innovator who developed an English Renaissance style by fusing elements of Flemish and Italian architecture with English gothic design. The buildings designed and built by Smythson, his son, John, and later his grandson, Huntington—with their dramatic display of symmetry, their elegant façades and huge grids of windows—were the most remarkable and romantic structures of their time. While some examples of these magnificent houses have survived, such as the splendid Hardwick Hall, others have been demolished or unwisely renovated or have deteriorated beyond repair.

ACKNOWLEDGMENTS

I am deeply grateful to all who helped bring *The Tutor* to publication. I want to thank my stellar agent, Leigh Feldman, for her immediate and unswerving belief in this novel. Her conviction was a gift and gave me courage. I feel extremely fortunate that Megan Lynch at Riverhead Books was my editor; her complete understanding of my story and my characters made working with her a thrilling experience, and her brilliant editing pushed the book to a new level. I wish to thank my terrific UK editor, Venetia Butterfield at Viking, for her helpful and important edits. And I would like to express my appreciation for my new Riverhead editor, Sarah Stein, who did an excellent job of ushering this book into print.

Many thanks to Michael Frank, Jean Garnett, Mark Hage and Mercedes Ruehl, whose frankness and close readings made this a better book. Michael, an incredible reader and friend, sometimes said things I didn't want to hear, but in the end I did listen. And Mercedes' ability to translate her talents from the stage to thoughtful criticism was a blessing. I wish to thank Elizabeth Gaffney for her editorial insights, advice and lovely friendship during our parallel journeys on perpendicular streets. Huge appreciation goes to Maren Kugelberg, my Enthusiastic Reader, for reading every draft I wrote, for listening to me read countless sections out loud, for demanding to know if I was working on my novel and, if I wasn't, for herding me back to it.

James Shapiro's wonderful book *A Year in the Life of William Shakespeare: 1599* first gave me the idea of writing a fictional account of one of Shakespeare's "lost years." I am extremely grateful to Professor Shapiro for his enthusiasm and generosity; his suggestions for sources were immensely helpful, as was his reading and commenting on my manuscript. My profound gratitude goes to Sir Bernard de Hoghton, the fourteenth Baronet of Hoghton Tower, for meeting with me and recounting the fascinating stories of his ancestors and for sharing his boundless knowledge of Lancashire and Catholics during the Elizabethan era. And thanks to Jack Herney, who many years ago taught me to love history and research.

Special thanks to the early readers whose insights and comments were very important: Anne Cattaneo, Alexis Chapin-Downs, Jennifer Cobb, Julie Novacek Godsoe, Patty McCormick, Mark Millhone, Dr. Carmela Perri, Sally Wofford-Girand. And special appreciation to Marisa Bartolucci, Kate Crane, John Eastman, Louise Eastman, Anne Edelstein, Rachel Foster, Tom Hahn, Betsy Israel, May Katz, Jennifer McCarthy and the late Eileen Roaman for their help and encouragement. Much appreciation goes to Michael Keller and Jim Vandernoth. At Riverhead Books, thanks to Dave Cole for great catches and excellent queries and to Alexandra Cardia for cheerful assistance. I'm thankful also to The Writers Room in New York City, where I started working on this book, and to the Folger Shakespeare Library in Washington, D.C., for its fine collections and exhibits.

I am eternally grateful to my family—David, Brandon and Carden. I could not have written this novel without their belief in me. I am thankful for their love and for their continuing with daily life while I sat all day and often much of the night with my laptop open and my head in a trance.

He just wanted a decent book to read ...

Not too much to ask, is it? It was in 1935 when Allen Lane, Managing Director of Bodley Head Publishers, stood on a platform at Exeter railway station looking for something good to read on his journey back to London. His choice was limited to popular magazines and poor-quality paperbacks – the same choice faced every day by the vast majority of readers, few of whom could afford hardbacks. Lane's disappointment and subsequent anger at the range of books generally available led him to found a company – and change the world.

'We believed in the existence in this country of a vast reading public for intelligent books at a low price, and staked everything on it'
Sir Allen Lane, 1902–1970, founder of Penguin Books

The quality paperback had arrived – and not just in bookshops. Lane was adamant that his Penguins should appear in chain stores and tobacconists, and should cost no more than a packet of cigarettes.

Reading habits (and cigarette prices) have changed since 1935, but Penguin still believes in publishing the best books for everybody to enjoy. We still believe that good design costs no more than bad design, and we still believe that quality books published passionately and responsibly make the world a better place.

So wherever you see the little bird – whether it's on a piece of prize-winning literary fiction or a celebrity autobiography, political tour de force or historical masterpiece, a serial-killer thriller, reference book, world classic or a piece of pure escapism – you can bet that it represents the very best that the genre has to offer.

Whatever you like to read – trust Penguin.